The McClane Apocalypse
Book Three

Kate Morris
Ranger Publishing, Copyright 2014

Ranger Publishing

Copyright © 2014 by Ranger Publishing
First Ranger Publishing softcover edition, September 2014

Ranger Publishing and design thereof are registered trademarks of Ranger Publishing.

For information about special discounts for bulk purchases, please contact, Ranger Publishing @gmail.com.

Ranger Publishing can bring authors to your live event. For more information or to book an event, contact Ranger Publishing @gmail.com or contact the author directly through KateMorrisauthor.com or authorkatemorris@gmail.com

Cover design by Ebook Launch.com

Author photo provided by Julie Ann Wayble

Manufactured in the United States of America
Library of Congress Cataloging-in-Publication Data is on file
ISBN 13: 978-0692276280
ISBN 10: 0692276289

Acknowledgments

I'd like to send out a huge thank-you to the fans of the series. I love hearing from you, and your letters and emails have meant so much to me.

I would also like to thank my friends and family who have encouraged and supported me throughout this process. It's been quite the adventure with many ups and downs, but through it all your words of inspiration kept me going.

Chapter One
Reagan

"Wake up, Reagan."

John's voice startles her from a dreamless slumber, and she blinks confusedly. She automatically reaches for the pistol on her nightstand. His hand stays hers.

"Reagan, wake up, babe."

His face is inches from hers and very pinched with worry. His deep baritone is barely above a whisper so as not to awaken Jacob at her side. Their room is almost dark as pitch. A low-wattage nightlight in the closet allows just a small shaft of shadowy light partway into the large space.

"Come on, babe. We need you. Doc needs you."

"What's going on? What time is it?" she asks with delirium and clears her throat. What the hell? It's still dark outside, too, no light coming through the windows or French doors.

"It's almost five, but your grandpa needs you. He said to get you. The boy's not doing so good," he tells her softly.

She glances to her side where Jacob is fast asleep in her big bed with her.

"Don't worry about him. I'll take him to Sue. Come on. Get dressed."

John pulls her to a sitting position and hands her a shirt, bra and jeans. She swings her legs over the side and slips into the pants first, not caring that he's seeing her in just her panties and a cami top. If Grandpa is sending him up to her, then it's bad. John turns his back to her so that she can pull on the rest of her clothing and goes to the other side of the bed to gently scoop the sleeping baby into his arms. His rifle is slung over his shoulder. Night vision gear hangs from the heavy cord around his neck.

The "boy" is with the visitors' group, the group her damn worthless Great-uncle Peter brought to their farm two days ago. When he'd announced that he was traveling in those massive RV's, which had rambled and sputtered down their drive, with sick women and children, they all knew that turning them away wasn't going to be an option. Yesterday she'd worked tirelessly trying to come up with an answer to this sickness the two patients are carrying. She knows that her grandfather has been doing the same. They are the only doctors within a twenty mile radius, maybe further, and there is no other help coming to their rescue, no hospitals to transport them to, no clinics or FEMA centers from whom to seek aid. She and he are the clinic, the only help that these people will get. Nothing about their illness makes sense. But it hadn't stopped her from trying to diagnose it. This was one of the reasons she'd gone into medicine in the first place. She loves to solve complex problems. And solving this one could mean life or death and the life or death of some of her family members should they contract it, as well. However, when she'd wanted to follow in her father and grandfather's footsteps and go into medicine, she'd foolishly thought she'd have access to any modern medical equipment she'd ever need. She'd been very wrong. She hadn't accounted for a worldwide apocalypse destroying most of the hospitals, society as a whole and the humanity of many.

"How long have you been up? *Why* are you up?" Reagan asks him, her voice groggy and weak. This isn't his watch shift, and he'd not slept much the day before, either. John still hasn't caught up on his sleep from their city trip, and he definitely needs to unless he is doing some sort of new post-apocalyptic sleep deprivation study.

"Your shoes are here at the end of the bed," he gestures as he sways back and forth to keep Jacob asleep. "I just couldn't sleep well. Don't like our new visitors. I went down to hang with Kelly and Derek, and that's when Doc sent that young girl to the back door to get one of us to fetch you. Guess she's been in there acting as his nurse all night again."

The tight-lipped young girl had also been with Reagan all day, as well. Has she even slept at all? Why had she not gone back to her group of people and allowed one of them to relieve her? Reagan's mind is too fuzzy to focus on the finer details of it.

She snags a rubber band off of her desk for her hair and pulls it into a haphazard ponytail before she and John descend to the second floor where her sister Sue already waits. Her eyes are worried, but she takes Jacob without pause and retreats back into her room. John descends the stairs first as Reagan follows. They are practically running, and Kelly is waiting on the back porch with his rifle. He's holding a small flashlight so they don't have to turn on all of the house lights. The other Army Ranger's body language is tenser than normal.

"Reagan," he acknowledges her, his deep voice grave.

"Bad?" she asks Kelly.

"Yeah, real bad, I guess," he admits.

Kelly lowers his eyes to the ground. Reagan breezes past him in a sprint and beats John to the door of the med shed.

"Don't come in here," she warns him, and John stops in the threshold instead. The teen girl Sam is indeed in the shed with Grandpa, and he has given her scrubs and a mask and latex gloves to wear. Reagan dons the same type of gloves, a mask that she pins behind her ears and a surgical gown that she retrieves from the pile in a plastic bin near the door.

"I'm here, Grandpa. Is he coding?" she asks calmly. The boy is on a cot that Derek carried up from storage that would've been for guest overflow at the house someday when too many great-grandchildren came for a weekend, summertime visit.

"Not yet," Grandpa returns on a whisper, a frown marring his features. "He's declining quickly, though."

Their grandparents had always made grand plans for the farm to eventually be used in such capacities by the girls and their own families. That day is never going to come. Now the cots are being used to treat people with sickness likely spread by end-of-the-world diseases. The woman rests on a second cot against the back wall of the shed. Reagan notices a third, smaller cot in the other corner near the back, which also effectively blocks the door to the arsenal. Someone has been sleeping in it. Her Grandpa takes Reagan to a side area of the shed so they can speak privately.

"Is anyone else sick?" Reagan indicates toward the third cot.

"No, that's for Samantha. I insisted Derek bring it in here for her to rest from time to time. She seems reluctant to return to their camp," he explains to which Reagan frowns and nods.

"What's the situation with Garrett?" she presses about the boy.

"I'm afraid he's getting worse, honey. He's had three mild seizures. I had to pull the feeding tube because he kept choking on it involuntarily which led to more vomiting," he states his observations very quietly.

Reagan returns to the unconscious boy on the cot, removes one glove and feels the skin on his arm and forehead.

"He's freezing cold, clammy. Skin's pale. He was like this yesterday, just not this bad. He actually woke up a few minutes here and there until I sedated him again. Elimination yet?" she asks. Grandpa nods. The boy's body organs are failing. They were failing when he'd arrived two days ago. There just hasn't been an improvement.

"Yes, about twenty minutes ago," he tells her.

"Cheyne-Stokes breathing pattern present," Reagan observes.

"What does that mean, ma'am?" the girl with the funky black hair asks.

"Short breaths in and long, deep breaths out. Just the opposite of what it should be," Reagan's mind is a flurry. "Come on, damn it. Think!" Without knowing exactly what illness is destroying this boy's body, it is making it so difficult to properly treat him. The pregnant woman looks just as bad.

"His IV popped, Reagan. I couldn't get one back in. He's just eliminating everything anyways."

Her grandfather isn't ready to accept defeat with this kid, either. It's written all over his tired features with grim determination.

Grandpa says, "We have to get liquids into him again so that we can run another IV."

"John!" she shouts to the door without looking because she knows he'll be there. "Go get me some towels or a blanket, please. Stick them in the dryer to heat them first. We've got to get this kid warmed up. Hurry!"

"We have to get fluid in him, Reagan. He's beyond dehydrated. I don't think he'll make it if we don't," Grandpa says with anger in his tone as John sprints away.

4

"Let's do another IV," Reagan states impatiently.

"Reagan, his veins are done. They're like the desert, honey. I tried and couldn't get one in," Grandpa affirms once more.

They debate a while longer as Sam paces the tile floor in the med shed chewing her thumb nail. She's a ball of tiny nervous energy, and Reagan's pretty sure by her dark circles that Sam has not had much sleep. In the meantime, Reagan had caught up on some much needed sleep the two previous evenings from the city trip. She's finally feeling human again and able to better reason things out with the few extra hours of shut-eye. The stress of the city trip and being in constant danger for four days had lent its toll on her body. She's not sure how John is still functioning, however.

He comes back into the room twenty minutes later holding a small blanket. John, on the other hand, has apparently only slept a few hours before he was back up with the other men both nights. Derek told her yesterday that he'd only come back downstairs after she'd gone to sleep with the baby. John looks frosty, ready to take on the day with only those few short hours of sleep each day. Reagan's puzzled by him, which is nothing unusual. It has to be their military training.

"Thanks, but get back out now," Reagan tells him firmly and takes the cozy, warm blanket and covers the small child with it. John obeys without question and goes to the door. He is watching intently though.

"I want to run a jugular catheter," Reagan says firmly.

"Honey, those are so dangerous, though," Grandpa says as he removes his glasses.

"Yeah, I know. But he's not gonna make it if we can't get something into him and try some new meds. I was thinking about this last night before I went to bed. I want to try a different combination of meds in…" Reagan argues. Before she even finishes her sentence the boy makes a horrible retching sound and coughs sputum and blood that lands on his shirt and on the sheet. Then he jerks, twitches, gasps for breath and stops breathing at all.

"Goddammit," Reagan shouts and is on the kid in a second. She rips off her face mask and starts chest compressions. "Here, Grandpa."

Reagan wipes out Garrett's mouth as best as she can and blows deeply. Grandpa counts off another series of pumps, and she blows again.

"Come on, kid. Fuck!" she mutters angrily to no one.

This isn't happening again. Not to this kid and not on her watch. Losing their neighbor Mr. Reynolds had been devastating. Reagan still blames herself for his death, although that she knows in her mind that his wounds were fatal. It does not diminish her feelings of guilt. She blows again. She gets nothing.

"Again!" she says to Grandpa, though he is already on it. "Come on, damn it," she grinds through her teeth with anger and frustration. Grandpa pumps again and Reagan breathes, and by some miracle the boy coughs.

"Got him," Grandpa says.

Reagan looks at her grandfather. His bony fingers are at the boy's throat. His stethoscope is at his chest.

He declares, "It's faint, but it's there."

"I'm starting that line," Reagan says and goes to the side counter where everything is kept and already waiting in trays.

"This may be the only option we have left for helping him, honey. We'll go slowly with it," Grandpa says quietly as he joins her at the counter.

He's done these before because Reagan remembers him telling her that he did a few while at the E.R. in Boston. She also remembers him telling her how difficult they are.

"Ready?" Reagan asks as she sets the tray on the metal cart beside the bed and glances at Sam, who has tears running down her face. "You might not want to watch this if you're squeamish."

Strangely enough the girl shakes her head. Good, she'll make a fine nurse to her and Grandpa which is probably why he's allowed her to stay in the first place.

Reagan takes a second to glance at John who is stoically standing there in the entranceway with an uncharacteristically unreadable expression on his chiseled face. He gives her a quick nod of encouragement, though, and for some bizarre reason it actually gives Reagan the fortitude to do it. She's done this only twice before while alongside other doctors at the university's hospital. And now she is standing next to one of the best medical minds of the century in her opinion. Herb McClane's literally seen it all during his years of

6

practicing medicine, coupled with his voracious hunger for studying diseases.

After the first miss, Reagan gets the main artery and has the line in. Another small miracle because these are a bitch to run on someone so dehydrated.

"Hot damn, Reagan. You hit it," Grandpa whispers and breathes a long sigh of relief. "She hit it."

He calls this proclamation over to John.

"Didn't doubt her for a second, Doc," he calls back.

Reagan has to force herself to suppress a smile that threatens to escape. For some reason his belief in her, his unwavering belief in her makes her swell with pride as she attaches the bag of nutrient rich fluids to the new IV.

"I say we hit him with another steroid, but directly this time," Reagan says to her grandfather. "He vomited yesterday and probably brought up most of that oral dose. I mean, what the hell can it hurt at this point? I also want to try a different antibiotic. The other one is showing no positive effect yet. It should've done something by now."

"I agree, Reagan. I was waiting for you to come out for your shift because I wanted to discuss it with you first so that you'd know I changed it up. I was thinking the same thing. They've both been on the low dose antibody for over thirty-six hours with absolutely no results. We have to go at this more aggressively," her grandfather concludes.

He retrieves the correct vial of steroids with Samantha, explaining the name on the label so that she can get them for him and Reagan sometimes, too. Reagan also gets into the small refrigerator which is now stocked to the gills with medicines thanks to their trip to the city. She pulls out a tiny bottle and doses a different, stronger antibiotic into a syringe.

She can hear him showing Sam how to load a shot and how to read the syringe and the measurement. Grandpa is frustratingly slow sometimes. Reagan takes the time to do a pulse count and notates Garrett's chart which is basically a sheet of yellow legal paper attached to a clipboard. It's funny how her and Grandpa's handwriting is so similar which is not something she's ever noticed before. It makes her feel strangely assured of herself to be any small amount like him.

"Grandpa, can you do injections 101 some other time? I'm kind of waiting here," Reagan says impatiently while she rigs up an Albuterol treatment into a mask that will need to be held over the boy's face since he is not coherent enough to take the medicine on his own. If he gets to where he isn't breathing deeply enough, they can always inject him with Ventolin in place of the Albuterol. Reagan's hoping it doesn't come to that. She also injects his IV line with the new antibiotic which can be quite painful administered this way, but he's so out of it that he shouldn't notice the pain. Plus, she read Grandpa's notes, and he'd given him a dosage of fever reducer two hours ago that contains pain medicine, as well.

"In my day, little missy, this is what was called a teachable moment," he lectures. "This young lady here may need to help you tomorrow when I'm catching up on my sleep. Or today, I suppose. I've lost track of the time."

Reagan rolls her eyes and grins as he extends the wet cotton swab and the stick to her. Two swipes with alcohol on the boy's hip and she gets the injection of steroids into him. This one isn't coming back up.

Reagan rinses and sterilizes her mouth at the stainless steel sink with mouthwash and disgusting tasting, sterilizing, mouth solution. She tastes like a mixture of mint and a chlorine chemical factory, but on the bright side she no longer has morning breath.

"Samantha, keep an eye on the patients for a moment while I confer with Dr. McClane," Grandpa says lightly.

The young girl looks confused.

"But I thought that you were Dr. McClane, sir," Sam says.

"We're both Dr. McClane. She's just the young pup version, and I'm the older, more distinguished gentleman version," he tells her.

Grandpa shows her how to hold the breathing treatment mask on Garrett's small face. Then he follows Reagan outside with both clipboards.

The sun is just starting to rise as they both sit on the cement stoop outside of the shed. John stands behind them with his rifle in both hands.

"Look at these notes. I've been scratching my head all night over them. I sure wish I could get into a lab right now and look at all of this under scopes, grow a culture and get some chest x-rays done," Grandpa bemoans.

"I know. A CBC, liver enzyme check and some specimens would be great at this point. This sucks. This wasn't exactly how I thought I'd be spending my first year in medicine. I was about a second away from hitting that kid with adrenaline. This is like some Old Testament shit. Maybe we should sacrifice one of those damn goats and see what happens. Might work better," she complains, and John and Grandpa both chuckle softly. Their laughter is short-lived, though, as the situation is grim and downright depressing, and they all know it.

"Doc, should Reagan have given that kid mouth to mouth? I mean, couldn't she get that sickness from him?" John asks.

He's standing behind her, his voice etched with concern. John's turning into her constant protector, it seems, and it's not something she likes to dwell on. There are a lot of things between them lately that she doesn't want to dwell on.

"She sterilized afterwards, and she's been vaccinated for just about anything you can possibly catch. You probably have been, too, being in the Army. But this could be something we've never seen before," Grandpa says.

"How's that?" John asks.

Reagan cuts in on this one, "Because sickness can morph, change, become resistant to drugs and transform into what you could call biological warfare or super bugs capable of wiping out millions of people or animals. They can change into something that we can't cure because we can't research them and come up with drugs that will kill them. Not anymore. Unless someone knows how to get into the Center for Disease Control. Hell, that is if it's even still there," Reagan explains sarcastically and looks up at John.

He shrugs, but Grandpa puts in, "The C.D.C. is still there for now. Or at least it was six months ago when I last heard and could make outside contact. There isn't much they can do other than keep it locked down. The C.D.C. and W.H.O. centers have so many biological weapons-grade diseases stored for research and for use to make cures that there's no way they could completely close it. At least they can't unless they are going to destroy all of the samples first. But for all we know, the people there could've abandoned it."

9

"I'm sure they did. If they had families, too, then they probably left," Reagan agrees with a nod. "I couldn't go to sleep last night. It just kept bugging me. This presents like bronchitis or pneumonia, but the blood, the weakness, dehydration and liver damage points to something else."

There were other reasons she couldn't go to sleep last night, but they had nothing to do with sickness and disease. She'd been hypothesizing about the night she and John returned from the city and he'd kissed her in her closet before they went to bed. She'd written it off to being too exhausted, his irrational kissing of her. Had he actually wanted to? Doubtful. But sometimes when she actually makes eye contact with John, he looks at her that same way he had right before he'd kissed her two nights ago. He's staring at her like that now. So naturally Reagan turns quickly back to her grandfather.

"I agree. It's symptomatic of influenza, but the wet chest isn't. The erratic, faint heart rates, low bp, the liver. It's got me puzzled, too," Grandpa agrees and scratches his messy hair.

"At first I thought TB. Easy diagnosis, right? But it just doesn't add up and wouldn't matter anyways. We don't have any of the three or four drugs that are out there to treat TB. Unless, of course, someone wants to do that run to the C.D.C. or the W.H.O., which is probably a waste of time anyways. Their lymph nodes are swelled huge."

"Right, Reagan. This isn't an easy diagnosis for sure. Maybe we should get the goat…"

"Holy shit!" Reagan interrupts loudly and runs for the house. She can hear John and Grandpa discussing her. She sprints straight for Grandpa's study, nearly running Grams and Hannah down in the hall. Once she's in his office, she rummages and digs until she finds the book she's looking for and then races back out the kitchen door again, leaping from the porch and not bothering with the stairs.

"This is it!" she blurts and starts flipping through the journal with lightning fingers.

"What's it? What the heck are you doing?" John inquires uneasily.

"Don't be scared, John. This is just how her little brain works. She's done this ever since I've known her," Grandpa explains.

Reagan would like to tell them both to quit talking about her like she's not right in front of them, but she's almost found what she

10

is looking for. Grandpa casually pulls his pipe from his pants pocket and starts packing it full with tobacco. He still wears his cotton, button down shirts and khakis or navy, cotton slacks most days. The only thing that is missing from his old work uniform is a tie. He's just never going to fully retire from being the town doctor.

She jabs her finger at the page. "Look. Look. Right here!"

"What'd you find, honey?" Grandpa asks.

His tone is patient, just like he used to speak when she'd bring in an injured bird or want to look for the millionth time at something under his microscope at his office.

"All the symptoms fit. Remember when I was thirteen and I went through that phase where I wanted to study the plagues of the dark ages and how they can reoccur?"

"Yeah, because that's what most thirteen year old girls want to study," John remarks.

Grandpa smiles and nods over his shoulder at John. Reagan ignores them and continues.

"Whatever. Well, when we were talking about the goat sacrifice and the Old Testament reference, it came to me. This is a plague. That's why neither you nor I have ever actually seen this. It's 'cuz we *haven't* ever seen it. Understand? This is pneumonic plague," Reagan rushes so fast that some of her words blend. John's still staring at her like she's an alien life form.

"Depending on where these people hale from, your theory could prove true. It says here that the southern to southwestern states have had this problem in the past," Grandpa says more calmly. "How the hell did you even remember this?"

Reagan shrugs and shakes her head in response. John is giving her that weird look again. She returns it with a scowl.

"Parts of those states aren't even there anymore," John adds when he's done staring at her.

"That's true. But this could be an all new occurrence of the disease because of what's happened. Every single symptom fits," Reagan explains. John looks strangely at her again as she continues. "Sometimes diseases spread because of filth and sickness. Just like cholera outbreaks or typhoid fever. But I'd already ruled those out, of course."

"Of course," John says with a smirk.

Grandpa chuckles. What was that supposed to mean?

"Reagan, if they both have this pneumonic plague it says here that if it's not caught and treated within the first twenty-four to forty-eight hours, then the disease is fatal," Grandpa reads.

"I know," she answers quietly. "I already knew that part before I even went to find this book. So let's hope I'm wrong. It's also highly contagious." She scratches her scalp and paces a few feet.

"It also could be a variation of your pneumonic plague," Grandpa offers, trying to be hopeful.

"Those two in there look like they have the same symptoms as Jacob's mother, and I'd bet that it's the same thing," John says.

Reagan's already thought of this, too, and she nods up at him.

"Samantha, could you come out here, please?" Grandpa requests of the gangly teen girl.

Reagan has a chance in the morning light to get a better look at her. She's thin, not particularly tall, but taller than Reagan. Her face reminds Reagan of one of those Japanese anime cartoon characters. Her black hair looks like it was cut with very dull scissors into a chin length bob. The pieces and ends are a thousand different lengths. Her eyes are way too big for her small face and are startlingly blue against her black hair, and her mouth is tiny and bends up at the corners like a cupid's bow.

"Yes, sir?" she asks passively.

The young girl looks at her feet which are covered in short, black leather boots. She wears dirty jeans and a blue polo shirt with a logo for Damien Riding Stables over in Clarksville. Having just come from that crap city, Reagan can say for certain that Damien Riding Stables is likely under new management.

"Where did this woman come from? Is she from the Southwest?" Grandpa asks.

Sam looks away and then at the camp set up by her people and back to her feet. She doesn't answer.

"What about the boy?" John asks and gets the same response from her.

"Honey, we need your help," Grandpa says.

He's using his most soothing doctor voice that Reagan has heard many times over the years. He'd had to use this tone on her once when she'd been given the grade of a B in Home Economics class which she'd been forced to take at the age of eleven since she was nearly in high school at that point. She'd cried and threatened the teacher, but Grandpa had explained in his special voice about how knowing how to perform brain surgery was more important than sewing a pillow. Reagan had sewn hers inside out, thus the B.

"It's important that we get some information about the boy and the woman because it will help these doctors to help them," John assures her.

"I... I don't know, sir," Sam answers unsurely as her eyes flit to the camping area again.

Reagan doesn't miss the look of heightening anxiety over these new trespassers that passes between John and Grandpa.

"How long have they been sick?" Reagan demands. She has no time or patience for this. Her tone scares the girl.

"I don't know that, either, ma'am. Since I've been... with them they've both been sick," she finishes in a rush and looks at the camp once again.

"How long have you been with them?" John asks.

The girl is staring at the ground again and shaking her head. John's eyes meet Reagan's, and she knows he's getting angry but not at this waifish, innocent girl.

"Ok, it's fine. We'll figure this out without all the details. Thanks, Samantha. You can go back in and keep watch if you like or return to your group and get some rest," Grandpa says.

Sam frantically shakes her head. "No, sir. I'd like to stay and help."

Reagan notices that she answers rather expediently for a person with dark circles under their bright blue eyes. Reagan is always surprised by the genius of her grandfather's tactics with getting information from people and making them feel comfortable enough to give it. That one interaction between him and the girl has told them all they need to know. Sam wants nothing to do with those people at the camp and would rather tend to sick people who could pass their strange disease on to her than get some much-needed rest with her traveling companions. This is going to be a problem with the men in Reagan's family and especially her grandfather. Suddenly, John is tense, alert, standing taller.

"Where the fuck is my kid?" comes a male voice behind Reagan.

John snatches her behind him and puts himself and his rifle between her and the man. Grandpa steps forward. This is the man Reagan was so nervous about the other day. Even behind the tinted glasses, his eyes are cold and malevolent.

"I presume you are speaking of the boy?" Grandpa asks.

"Yeah, Garrett's his name. Are you guys fixin' him or what?" he asks rudely.

The man rubs at his scraggly beard. His yellowy tinted eyeglasses are creepy and keep his gaze partially concealed.

"Hey, pipe down. These two doctors are doing all they can for him. You can help them by answering some of their questions," John says.

He states this with enough force that the guy stops advancing toward them. Reagan definitely would've suggested the same move. She's seen what John can do when pushed. How does John flick the switch on this personality trait within him that turns him so instantaneously violent and hard? Reagan's not sure she really wants to know the answer.

"Yeah, whatever, man."

"What's your name, sir?" Grandpa asks, trying to calm him.

"Frank. My name's Frank, and Garrett's my boy. His twin brother's out at the RV. He's worried sick about his brother," Frank with the dirty beard explains.

He is about the same height as John but thinner, leaner and has a malevolent demeanor about him. For a father who is supposedly so worried for his son, he's taken over thirty-six hours to come and check on the kid. Reagan could have never left his side for even a moment if he belonged to her. Garrett is so small and frail that she would've been too scared he'd die if she left his side and wasn't with him every minute.

"Look, Frank, we're not going to lie to you. Your boy is very ill. Can you tell us how long he's been this way?" Grandpa asks and gets ready to notate it on the makeshift chart.

"Um, I don't know. Like three or four weeks or so," the man explains so clearly.

"Have you traveled from the West or Southwest regions of our country like Arizona or Colorado?" Grandpa inquires with more patience than Reagan knows he feels.

14

"What? No, man. We're from New Mexico. But when the shit got bad, we joined up with friends in Arizona and Ohio and headed this way. Peter's the one who said we should come here. I didn't want to come all the way out here to the damn boonies," Mr. Personality answers.

The last Reagan checked, New Mexico is a part of the Southwest, but she'll have to consult her map later. She's surprised at this man's negativity toward them. Shouldn't he be just the least bit appreciative that they've allowed them to stay temporarily on their farm and that they are treating his young son?

"Have any other members of your group come down with this sickness?" Reagan breaks into Frank's moving speech. Immediately she can tell that he doesn't want to answer because he plunks his hand on his hip and juts out his jaw. But he does look her up and down in a lewd, leering way which gives her chills. Instinctively she inches slightly closer to John.

"Answer the question, dude," John warns with his usual quiet, deadly intent.

John's hand slides behind him and flattens against her hip, staying her. Reagan doesn't step away from him or out of his grasp because Frank scares her. He's more than a little disturbing. She's had enough of dangerous men and their sinister stares and their heinous behavior.

"Yeah, a couple," Frank answers.

"How many?" John pushes.

"Four."

Reagan hears her grandpa utter "shit" under his breath. This situation is getting worse.

"And? What happened to them?" John pushes again.

His questions are just as good as what Reagan and Grandpa would've asked this man of questionable character who has now lit a cigarette. He inhales and blows directly toward Reagan, making two small rings of smoke.

"Answer," John grinds out.

"They died. What the fuck ya' think happened to them?" Frank reveals rudely, showing his love of manners again.

Reagan feels the tenseness in John and notices the way the veins stick out on his hand that grips his rifle. Grandpa turns to look at Reagan who is still standing slightly to John's left. This isn't good. They could all be wiped out by this disease.

"Were any medicines given to those who were sick? Were you able to get them any medical help at all?" Grandpa asks.

Kelly has joined the discussion, but Frank is completely unaware of the hulking presence behind him just ten feet away. His rifle is in front of him and not slung on his shoulder, and he's eating something. His manner is more casual and relaxed than John who looks like he would prefer to just shoot the visitors. And after their nightmarish trip to the city, Reagan's surprised that he hasn't already. She understands why his Army comrades would've given him the nickname of Doctor Death.

"Yeah, we took them to urgent care. No way, man. In case you haven't been off this farm, old man, shit's bad out there. There ain't no doctors left," Frank says.

John's hand tightens on the rifle. Reagan stills his hand by placing hers over his. She feels the tendons under her palm tense and flex.

"His name is Dr. McClane to you, dirtbag," John warns. "Call him 'old man' again and I'll turn your head into a Jell-O mold."

Though she knows it is not meant for her, John's threat sends a shiver down Reagan's spine.

"Make that two Jell-O molds," Kelly repeats nonchalantly.

He tosses his apple core to the ground and scares the crap out of Frank who spins to see him. Frank's stunned expression is almost comical.

"Look, sorry, man. I'm just stressed out, ok? You know, worried about the kid and all," the creep says complacently.

It's not a good excuse to disrespect her grandfather who has opened up his farm to them and is providing medical care to their sick.

Frank rambles on, "We ain't bathed or eaten good in a long time. Can we just get some water? We filled up our containers in a creek up the road, but the water's all gone."

"You may use the pump at the horse barn. Someone can show you to it," Grandpa offers more kindly than anyone else would have.

"Cool. I'll tell the others and get the jugs," Frank says and walks away quickly to find his friends.

16

He had not even asked to see his son, and this fact is not lost on any of them. Reagan even smirks.

She comments, "What a dick." Then Reagan removes her hand from John's, but not before he glances down at her with a look of possessiveness in his blue eyes.

"Jell-O mold?" Kelly asks with a grin. "Seriously, bro. We gotta work on your insults. It's ok to cuss sometimes."

John laughs loudly, and it helps to ease the tension.

"Yeah, son. That was kind of sad. But at least I think he got the point," Grandpa adds.

Reagan full-on grins.

"Yes, sir," John says with an embarrassed smile. "I'll work on it."

Derek has joined their group, as well, having come from one of the barns. John brings him up to speed while she talks again with her grandfather on the meds and the patients.

"All right, I guess I'll take these dipshits to get water," Kelly offers.

"Nah, I got it, Kelly," Derek counters.

Her brother-in-law jogs toward the visitors' campsite near the driveway, nearest the exit which they'll hopefully soon use to leave their farm.

"I'm going in to get a drink and ditch the night vision. Be back in a few," Kelly tells John who still stands watch over the shed, though the danger seems to have passed.

"I don't like this, Reagan," her grandfather says to her.

She readily agrees. "I know. This sucks even more now."

Grandpa sighs. "The fact that these two have had this for weeks and are still sick, not better at all isn't good," he adds and removes his eyeglasses again to wipe the lenses on his shirt.

"Yeah, no shit. Why didn't Peter tell us this? And four of them already died from it? Seriously? Why the hell did Peter even bring them here? He knows this is fatal," she vents angrily and scuffs her shoe at an errant pebble on the cement.

"Don't say that. There's always still hope," Grandpa is quick to disagree. "Don't ever give up hope, Reagan. It's our job to keep hope alive until the end. We're the only two people on this farm who might have any chance at all of saving those two in there. You must not give up on them. Do you understand?"

"Yeah, I understand. I get it, Grandpa," she tells him with a forlorn nod. He lays a weathered hand on her shoulder and gives it a gentle squeeze. She tries hard not to shirk his touch.

"That's my girl," he tells her.

His words discompose her in front of John.

"Um… Grandpa, you should go to bed now," she says in a fluster of hot cheeks. "I'll keep watch and send for you if I need you. I think we're just waiting for these two to show any signs for the better and from what that idiot just said, I don't think we can expect much. I'll start the new series of meds on the woman and see if I get anywhere with it." Grandpa nods in accord.

When her grandfather retreats to the house, Reagan turns to John.

"Thanks for sticking up for my grandfather," she says and looks him directly in the eye.

"I'm not letting anyone talk like that to any person on this farm. And your grandfather is too old to defend himself against a jerk like that," he explains and taps the tip of her nose.

Reagan studies him a moment, studies his blue eyes with keen interest. His gaze can change from cold and heartless to warm with desire and compassion like when he looks at her, like the way he is looking at her again. She blinks hard, and her mouth opens just slightly. Luckily, her recovery is just as fast.

"Yeah, if you guys weren't here, we'd kind of be screwed. I mean I could've shot most of them, but then Grams would've got pissed at me," she jokes and John smiles broadly at her. She hates it when he does this. It makes butterflies in her stomach.

"So you're glad I'm here, huh?" he queries and raises his eyebrows at her.

"Wanna' kiss?" she taunts because she knows that he is already freaked out about her mouth to mouth resuscitation of Garrett.

"Believe it or not, boss, I'd take that kiss about now," John teases in return and raises one eyebrow jauntily at her.

Damn! That had backfired on her.

"How about, instead, you can come in and help me with these patients?" she asks, working another angle and raises one

18

eyebrow in return. "Might catch a case of the plague or whatever shit they've got."

"Nice," he says dryly and frowns down at her.

That's another thing she hates about him. He can tower over her.

"Suit yourself," she says and pivots to go back into the med shed.

"Thanks, boss, but I'll wait right here," he answers and resumes his post.

Reagan answers with a short chuckle at his state of discomfort and germ-a-phobia.

She's not quite sure why he is standing guard outside the shed because this is not how the watch rotations are supposed to go. He should be going about his chores while Cory watches the shed from the porch. Perhaps the run-in with Frank has left him unsettled. It has left her more than unsettled and the memories of her night at the university threaten to creep up on her. She just needs to stay busy. It is the key to blocking out all unwanted memories, including the one of her and John kissing in her closet.

Chapter Two
Kelly

It's not quite six a.m. when Kelly gets downstairs to his bedroom where he can stow away his night vision gear and his jacket, neither of which will help him make hay or clean out the loafing pads in the cow barn as the sun gets higher. After he uses the bathroom attached to his bedroom, Kelly comes out and startles.

"Hannah!" he exclaims quietly so as not to awaken the children also on the lower level down the hall from him. "You scared the crap outta' me, baby."

She blushes, walks closer to him and reaches out.

"I'm sorry. I didn't want to knock and awaken everyone."

"What's wrong? Why are you up? You don't have to get up this early," he tells her with concern. She needs to rest. The last few weeks have been stressful, and she's been working her butt off finishing the canning with the women and taking care of the big house and also helping out with the kids. It is all too much for someone as delicate as Hannah. She shouldn't be working so hard.

Her hair is tousled slightly from sleep, and she wears a long, lightweight robe of the palest pink over a predictably white nightgown.

"I'm fine. I just thought I heard arguing outside my window that woke me and I got concerned."

"Oh, that. Yeah, that kid- the sick one- his dad came over to the shed and was being an ass, stirring up trouble and being insulting. It's all under control now, though," Kelly reassures her as he takes her frail hands into his own in front of him and then kisses them both. She has no idea how alluring she looks right now. He drops another kiss to her smooth forehead.

20

"That's so terrible. Perhaps he is just feeling very anxious with his child being so ill. Then again that kind of behavior isn't going to help anything, either," she tells him.

"Derek's taking some of them to get water at the barn. I don't know how much they have for rations, but they're out of water already," he informs her.

She frowns and adds, "Oh my. Do you think they have enough food?"

"Hannah, I don't know, but don't go spreading good will to them yet. We don't know anything about them, honey. They could be a threat for all we know. They had guns," he warns while trying to read her facial expressions.

She frustratingly answers in a way that upsets Kelly.

"We can't just turn our backs on people, Kelly. They have children with them. What do you suggest? Letting them starve to death?"

"No, but those decisions have to be made as a group. Your grandfather will have the final say on how we handle those people. Besides, that sickness out there could've spread to the others and they just aren't showing symptoms yet. You could get sick from them, Hannah."

"I've been praying for the sick boy and woman to get better," she tells him.

He doesn't tell her that the man, Frank, didn't go in to see his kid. This would be too much for someone as tender as Hannah.

"I know you have, Hannah, but they might not pull through. The vibe I got from Reagan and your grandpa wasn't too good," he tells her gently and pushes her hair away from her forehead.

"I feel so bad for Reagan and Grandpa. It's such a burden of responsibility for them to have to deal with this. Reagan especially is so critical of herself anyways. She didn't take the death of Mr. Reynolds very well at all and totally blamed herself for it," she confesses softly.

She is always concerned about someone other than herself, even their neighbors, the Reynolds.

"Don't worry about them, honey. They're both doctors. This is what they do. Reagan told me that she's done work at hospitals and E.R.'s, so she'll be fine. I just want *you* to take care of yourself and keep away from those people, ok? And keep away from the sick ones for sure," Kelly orders.

Her funny little frown almost makes him smile. The only reason he doesn't is because he believes that she is being impertinent.

"I'm fine, Kelly Alexander. You don't need to worry about me. I'll be just fine."

"I mean it, Hannah. Stay away from them. I don't trust them, especially those men out there. Some of them are kind of… shifty," he tries to explain without terrifying her.

"Ok, Kelly, I'll stay away from them, not just because of the sickness. Even though, I must say, it seems like they could use our help. I will listen and stay away, but only because you asked so nicely," she mocks with a smug grin.

He's just about to pull her to him for a stolen kiss when something dawns on him. "Hey, where's the grandparents? I don't think you should be in here. We don't want everyone to know about us yet."

"I heard Grandpa go to bed right before I came down here. And Grams isn't up yet. She's been sleeping later than usual. I think this is just all too much for her," Hannah frets.

"Grams is tough, Hannah. She's a lot like you. You're tougher than you look," he explains and tugs her closer so that he can wrap an arm around her slim waist.

"Yeah? You think I'm tough?" she asks with a certain amount of orneriness. "Maybe I can even take *you* on if I'm so tough!"

Kelly chuckles and plunks a kiss to her mouth, startling her.

"You better get a whole lot tougher, little woman. Besides, I don't want you to be too tough. I like taking care of you."

"I kind of like it, too," she tells him with a crooked grin.

This is something new for both of them. It's very new to Kelly. He's never had to look out for anyone in his life except for himself and now here he is with two siblings and Hannah to watch out for. Actually he and probably the other men on the farm pretty much feel responsible for every last member of the family's safety. He doesn't mind it, though. He'd much prefer taking care of Hannah than to have someone else do it. Kelly also doesn't feel that anyone else can do the job as well as he can. His fierce determination to keep her safe is what gets him up in the morning. He's also willing to do whatever it takes to keep her that way.

22

"Oh yeah?" he teases.

"I like some other things you do, too," she hints.

His woman perches on tiptoe and kisses the bottom of his bearded chin. Kelly has to suppress a groan of desire. This is also new for him. This wanting, longing for another person that is so all-consuming is like nothing he's ever dealt with before he met her. He's never felt anything like this for another person.

"Hannah, I need to get outside and help John with some chores so Derek can go to bed," he informs her, though he'd like nothing better than to do things to her, lots of things. Since he made love to her last week it's been all he's been able to think about. Plus she surprises him sometimes with how sensual she can be and how she sometimes makes highly erotic, highly sexual and inappropriate comments. When no one is listening, of course. Her right hand slips from his and trails down the front of him right to his crotch. Kelly snatches it back.

"I miss you, Kelly," she purrs and nuzzles her nose into his chest through his thin t-shirt.

"I miss you, too, baby," he declares. "But I gotta go out and work with John. I'll see you later today, though." She pouts so prettily that he almost gives in.

"Fine!" she says testily. "At least give me a kiss to think about you while you're being too busy for me!"

She's also quite the conniver when she wants to be. Kelly laughs heartily, snatches her into his arms, lifting her off the ground and plants a searing kiss to her mouth. He explores her at his leisure, taking his time, leaving them both short of breath and dazed and wanting more. When he finally sets her to the ground again, Hannah is clinging to him like he knew she would be, and he is fully aroused which he also knew he would be because of the way she has always ignited this fire within him.

"Are you sure you don't want to stay just a short while?" she whispers against his mouth.

"You do drive a very convincing bargain, ma'am," he teases and kisses her mouth, only at the corner this time lest he won't be able to leave her.

"I know. I know. You need to help John. Will you miss me?" she asks with a lovely smile.

Her smile takes his breath away every time.

Kelly places both of his hands on either side of her face and pulls her forehead to forehead with him. Of course, he's stooping quite a bit. "You have no idea how much I'll miss you."

Hannah sighs softly, tips her head sideways and presses a kiss to his palm. "I know."

Sometimes Hannah says things like this, but he knows she doesn't mean it to be arrogant. She's just so honest with her feelings and thoughts that she doesn't hold back what she needs to say.

"I love you," Kelly tells her so easily. It's always easy being around her, and the love he feels for her is also easy. It's just not the right time to deal with any of it.

"And I love you, Kelly," she confesses.

Her candor makes him smile down at her.

"Come," he commands. "I'll take you back upstairs."

Hannah nods and they leave his room together, going down the long hall. The door to the children's room opens and Em stumbles sleepily into the hallway.

"Good morning, Miss Emma," Hannah says to her quietly.

How the hell she knows it was Em and not Justin or Ari, he'll never know.

"Hi, Hannah," his kid sister returns. "Good morning, Kelly. What are you guys doing? Why are you down here, Hannah?" she asks on a wide, confused yawn.

"Um, we were just…" he tries at something but comes up with nothing.

"We are going up to start breakfast, or at least I am. Wanna' help?" Hannah jumps in to cover.

She's a sly little fox when the situation calls for it. She'd certainly managed to manipulate him into making love to her even though that wasn't his plan. His plan was to leave the farm that next day, but having made love with her, Kelly knew he couldn't leave her after that. Now she is just another responsibility that he'll bear. Not that he minds this extra duty. He's been in love with Hannah McClane from that first day he'd come to the farm. And he can't imagine leaving the responsibility of her well-being to anyone else.

Hannah doesn't unloop her hand from his arm, but she frequently walks around like this with different people on the farm so that she doesn't have to use her cane. It is not behavior that would alert anyone to their new, closer relationship since she relies on people to help her since she's blind. It had been difficult to get used to when he'd first come to the farm. Hannah, being Hannah, would simply latch on to whomever she was closest to and start walking. She doesn't have much of a sense of respecting people's personal space. But it just ended up being one more thing about her that makes her the unique woman that he's come to love so deeply. She'd even done this once outside with John which had made Kelly mad with jealousy. However, he knows that his friend's heart belongs elsewhere on this farm and that he only looks at Hannah like a sister.

"Sure, Hannah, I can help with breakfast," Em offers kindly and takes Hannah's hand, basically separating her from Kelly.

It doesn't bother him, though. Em has taken to Hannah, and Kelly's glad for it. His little sister needs to be around women and not just be stuck with him and Cory. Hannah only smiles knowingly over her shoulder at him as they all ascend the stairs.

When they get to the kitchen, Kelly departs, leaving his little sister and her messy, wavy hair in Hannah's capable hands. He and Hannah are trying not to let anyone know about them yet. Right now, just getting rid of the visitors is the number one priority for all of them. Nobody needs to be bothered with his and Hannah's love lives.

The sun has completely risen, and he catches up with Derek as he escorts different members of the new group to collect water from the barn and haul it back to their camp.

"How's it going?" he asks Derek quietly as they trail thirty or so feet behind two men and one woman lugging buckets.

"Ok so far. They're gonna have to do this every day until they leave, though," Derek answers, squinting against the bright sun. "That woman up ahead, the blonde, said they've been out of water for a few days. So if they don't get it from the farm here, then they don't have water now."

"You think that could be a problem?" Kelly asks directly as the blonde to which Derek had referred looks over her shoulder at them. Her tiny blue-jean shorts barely cover her ass cheeks and look to have been cut off this short on purpose.

"Could be," Derek tells him. "This farm is running on two different spring-fed wells. We're watering livestock and supplying water to the whole family and now a whole lot more people."

"Think they could run dry?" Kelly inquires.

"I don't know. I think we should talk to Herb about it. Seems to me like they could. I remember Sue told me once that her grandparents had a problem with the one well going dry a few years ago when there was a bad draught. If it happened before, it could happen again," he informs Kelly.

"Yeah, and that was when it probably would've just been Doc, Grams and Hannah here. There's a shit ton of people on the farm now. Not to mention the livestock," Kelly agrees readily as the blonde passes another flirtatious peek that carries a bit of suggestion behind it toward him and Derek. She's also sauntering her hips suggestively when she walks, and it's definitely not by accident. Derek looks at him and rolls his eyes. It reminds Kelly of Reagan which makes him laugh.

"We definitely gotta discuss this with Doc later," Derek adds.

They come to the visitors' campsite near the equipment shed. Kelly immediately notices that two of the men are missing from the group. There should be ten of them, not counting the two sick ones in the med shed.

"Where'd the other two go?" he barks point blank to the nearest person. It just so happens to be the large black man named Levon.

"What's it to you?" he asks snidely.

However, seeing Kelly's hand on his rifle, the man quickly amends his rudeness, but only slightly.

"Went into those woods over there to take a shit. Is that a problem, too?"

"Yeah, you guys put a lot of restrictions on us," the woman with the dark hair retorts with venom. "Don't go there, stay over here, don't do this. Whatever, man. We're just tryin' to survive like everyone else."

"That will be made easier for you, too, if you do what you're told while you're here on this farm," Derek informs her without raising his voice.

Grams's brother, Peter, descends from one of the RV's in a cloud of smoke. It has a sweet, yet pungent aroma. Kelly's pretty sure it's marijuana or some other type of drug able to be smoked. It's definitely not from a cigarette.

"Hey, man," he slurs.

Kelly's not sure which of them that he's addressing because his eyes are unfocused, the pupils dilated. Movement beyond the uncle proves to be the teen boy with black hair and Buzz, the bald, shifty dude who seems passive, but still on the squirrely side. Kelly knows enough about people to not trust that this man is passive and a non-threat. He's seen young people and women blow themselves to smithereens in crowded markets in the name of religion. Appearances can definitely be deceiving.

"Do you have enough water for now?" Derek asks with a touch of impatience.

Kelly can tell that he isn't in the mood to argue or renegotiate a new living arrangement already. They'd been given ground rules, only two days ago, and here they are bitching about them so soon.

"Sure, man, we've got plenty for a while," Rick answers.

He is the other black man and seems cool and collected, unlike some of his traveling companions.

Rick even adds, "Thanks. We appreciate you all letting us stay."

"Yeah, man, we're all good here," Peter says as he stumbles into a lawn chair before plopping down into it. "It's cool we got somewhere like this to drop anchor for a while. I knew it would all work out. My sister wouldn't kick us to the curb. We're glad we could stay, man."

He hacks twice and spits into the weeds. Nobody else in the group returns this sentiment, but he and Derek also don't give a shit. Derek doesn't answer but gives a curt nod before him and Kelly walk away.

"Think they're going to give us problems?" Derek asks him as they close in on the med shed.

"I sure as shit hope not, man. Grams is gonna be really upset if we have to kick them off the farm," he answers. "I just hope they stay the hell away from the women and the house."

Derek sighs audibly as they continue to walk.

"Yeah, I know," he finally concurs.

The dynamic of the farm has changed considerably. All of them are on constant high alert with this band of virtual strangers cohabitating it with them. Kelly still has a bad feeling about the situation, but he'll bide his time and adhere to the wishes of Doc for now.

Chapter Three
Hannah

The biscuits are baking in the oven, the sausage is on the griddle cooking on low and her kitchen has the familiar, lovely smells of home-cooking wafting about it. She and Em just about have breakfast prepared when Sue comes into the kitchen. She carries Isaac with her. A second, louder baby lets Hannah know that she's also carrying Jacob, the orphan John and Reagan have brought back from the city.

"Oh, Miss Sue, let me help," Em says in a rush and a flurry of movement.

Her sister chuckles and answers, "Oh my goodness! I guess that's what it would've been like if I'd ever had twins. It's a good thing Jacob is a little underweight or I might not have made it down the stairs with the both of them."

Hannah also laughs. Em is baby-talking to Jacob which makes him giggle. He seems to be adjusting well to the farm, and Reagan said that he sleeps through the night, which is fortunate since her sister has no experience with babies. Sue had volunteered yesterday to let him sleep in Isaac's crib with him and that she'd take care of him, but Reagan and John had both quickly shot down that idea. They must both feel a great deal of responsibility to this baby.

"Here, Sue, let me take Isaac for a while," Hannah offers her sister.

"Thanks, Hannie. My arms feel like rubber," she acknowledges with a smile in her voice.

"Can you do something for me while we get Jacob's bottle ready?" Hannah asks as she moves toward the refrigerator to take out a bottle of milk for Jacob. Sue will breastfeed Isaac on her own, so he'll have to wait.

"Sure, what's up?" Sue asks.

"I need to know how many people are in the med shed with Reagan so that I know how much food to make. Grams said yesterday that if Samantha is going to be working alongside Reagan and Grandpa, then we need to make sure she eats to keep up her strength," Hannah tells her.

"Right. We're not too sure how much food those people have. It only seems fair that if she's helping out our family in the shed, then we should be feeding her," Sue agrees before going out the screen door.

"Here's Jacob's bottle, Em. I have some hot water on the back burner. Just place it in there to warm it for him. Then he can eat some solid food with the rest of us at breakfast," she tells the young girl who is a great sous chef to Hannah. She's learning her way around the kitchen so quickly, and Hannah had taken time the other day to show her how to properly store the fresh herbs from the garden in the horse barn's grain room to properly dry. Em's also talking more with her, which is a very good sign that she's coming to trust everyone on the farm.

"Ok, Hannah. I got it," Em answers with her tiny mouse voice.

For a girl of twelve, she sure seems petite. But Sue has told her that Em is actually tall for her age. She just has a little munchkin voice. If she's going to take after Kelly and Cory, then she might just end up being a six foot tall Amazonian warrior woman. However, she has the sweetest disposition of any young girl ever in Hannah's opinion, so she doesn't see Em wielding a gun like Reagan.

A few moments later while Hannah stirs the pan full of grits on the stove, Em takes Jacob to the music room to feed him his bottle and mostly to keep him occupied while the women in the family pull the breakfast meal together. The back door opens and shuts loudly again.

"We've got a few extra guests, Hannah," Sue explains. "Ran into Derek and Kelly and they said that Sam is still out there. She told them that Garrett's twin wants to see him. He misses his brother something terrible, I guess."

30

"I can't even imagine," Hannah replies with a heavy sigh as she transfers Isaac back to his mother again.

"I know. It's so terrible. I feel so sorry for the little guy. They are both so cute and too damn young to be going through anything like this," her sister curses in agreement.

She'd better get that out of her system before Grams rises for the day.

"No children should have to go through what any of them have gone through, Sue. It's just heartbreaking," Hannah expresses sadly.

"I know. Hey, Hannie, you don't have to do so much of that by yourself," Sue tells her. "Wow, Grams must be beat if she's sleeping this late. Let me just get him fed and then I'll help you out."

It's hardly late. When she presses the button on the digital clock, it gives her an audible reading of 7:10 a.m. Grams should have been up by now for sure, but perhaps she's talking with Grandpa alone in their suite since Hannah had heard him go in there a while ago.

"You're fine. Just feed Isaac because you know the other two will be up soon, and until the men lift the ban on playing outside, the kids are stuck in here all day," she answers Sue, referring to her sister's other son and daughter.

Sue groans loudly, and a chair's legs at the island scrape roughly against the hardwood floor as she pulls one out to sit.

Sue says, "Oh boy. That's not going to make them happy. It was great of Em to help keep them entertained yesterday, but I can't imagine them not wanting to go outside again today."

"I just hope that Grandpa and Reagan can get the patients well enough to move their caravan on somewhere else soon. It feels odd having strangers here. It's like Reagan mentioned yesterday that they could always set up a more permanent camp on some other farm. Just look at the Johnson's farm. I never thought they'd move away and leave their farm and they did. Great-uncle Peter's group can just find somewhere like that to go," Hannah explains as gently as she can, though she's starting to wish Kelly had not allowed them to stay at all. Holding Isaac in her arms a few moments ago had made her realize how easily he could become sick. Life is so fragile, especially now.

"I agree, but I'm kind of hoping Peter will take the group much farther away than the Johnson's. Heck, I just hope he takes himself far away," Sue says with a laugh.

Sue, like Reagan, has never liked or had much tolerance for Peter. Hannah refrains from answering because it feels unkind to say such things about family, even if they are alcohol and drug dependent.

"We need to finish our canning, so the garden has to be picked," Hannah changes the direction of their conversation from something that is only bound to get more negative to something that is practical.

"Right, I agree. We got another hundred pounds of potatoes stowed, but the cabbage will be ready in a few days and so will the rest of the peppers," Sue updates her.

"Do you think Derek will let you go out and do some picking today so that we can get some of the canning done?" she asks of her brother-in-law.

"Good grief, I hope so!" her sisters says, miffed. "It's been an adjustment having him around so much. When he was deployed, I was left to my own devices. I'm not used to having to answer to Derek. Our marriage has definitely gone through a total overhaul having him here."

"Having him around can't be bad, though. Right?" Hannah asks with a smile.

Sue pats Isaac, probably on his back, before answering.

"Yeah, it's great. I just used to do whatever I wanted or needed to do when he was gone, so it's just kinda' surreal. But I like him being home."

"Good, because you two are great together. He's a very devoted dad, too," Hannah adds as she takes the fluffy breakfast biscuits out of the oven.

"Yeah, he is pretty great. How's it going with Kelly?" her sister asks, stunning Hannah.

A warm blush creeps onto her cheeks, and she refuses to look in the general direction of Sue.

"Um, he's fine," Hannah answers noncommittally. There is no way she can tell Sue or anyone else on the farm what has transpired between herself and Kelly.

32

"I didn't ask if he was fine, Hannie. What's going on between you? The last time we spoke, you told me you were sick of him being indifferent and constantly pushing you away," Sue reminds her.

Hannah remembers that conversation all too well. She doesn't need a reminder. It was one of the reasons that she'd decided to sneak into his room and seduce him until he could no longer withstand her. That plan had worked rather well.

"Nothing, nothing new to report. We're getting along just fine, though," Hannah evades as she takes the sausages from the griddle and places them in the oven to stay warm.

"Hm, okaaay," she answers sarcastically.

The back door opens and shuts again, letting Hannah off the hook for the time being by whomever is interrupting them.

"Hey, babe," Sue remarks with a smile in her voice.

It must be Derek for Sue to speak such an endearment.

He greets her with his own endearment, and they must kiss or embrace because it is silent a moment. That is, until the other two kids come dashing into the kitchen screaming, "Daddy!"

"Ok, ok, guys!" Sue scolds. "Grandpa's asleep and Daddy needs to get to bed. He's been up all night keeping an eye on the place while you rugrats were sleeping."

"They're ok," Derek corrects her. "Smells good, Hannie."

"Want some before you crash?" she offers. Of course, he says that he does. Sue makes him a plate, and Derek eats at the island as Grams descends on the kitchen calamity, as well.

"Oh hey, Derek," Sue interjects. "I need to pick today. We have to get the crops brought into the house so that us women can get them canned and put up, hon'," she tells her husband.

"Yeah, I know, Sue. I don't like you guys being out there around them, though," he argues around a mouthful of food.

"Well, if you don't want to just eat eggs all winter, then we have to can," Grams adds in.

She's joined Hannah near sink and is rinsing a basketful of crops that they'll use for dinner later.

Grams remarks to no one in particular, "These tomatoes will make a nice sauce for a stew maybe tomorrow."

"Hey, that reminds me, Grams," Sue adds. "I want to make something special for John for dinner tonight if you don't already have something planned."

Her sister moves around toward the fridge. Em has also returned from the music room with Jacob who is a bundle of squeals and giggles. Ari is doing something that is making him laugh.

"Oh?" Derek asks in jest. "Is there something I need to know?"

"No, silly!" Sue counters. "I want to make his favorite meal for him. I was just so shocked at how much different Reagan seems since they went to the city together. I think something could've happened there that bonded them because she's not so mean to him– or the rest of us!"

Hannah has also noticed over the last few days how Reagan seemed just slightly… softer.

"I think I can guess on that one," Derek jokes.

Hannah chortles. Derek must receive a slap from his wife because he quickly amends his bawdy joke.

"I'm just kidding. Sorry, Grams."

"No offense taken, Derek," Grams assures him. "I noticed, too, Sue. And so did your grandfather because he mentioned it yesterday. Perhaps it's the baby. Or perhaps it was something that happened. We'll probably never know because she won't admit to it, not to anyone."

Sue jumps in, "Yeah, if there's one thing for sure about Reagan, it's that she's bull-headed."

Her husband gets in a return dig, though. "Oh? And you aren't? I think that's a McClane woman thing."

"You, hush!" his wife scolds. "I just need to know what he likes so we can make it, mister."

"Hm, let me think," Derek pauses. "I remember he used to like meatloaf."

"Shocker. Meat," Grams says dryly and everyone laughs. "I think that's a man thing!"

When the laughter and the squealing of tiny children die down, Sue presses her case again, "We still need to work out the garden harvesting, Derek. It's gotta get done, babe."

"Fine," he sighs with defeat. "Just take Cory maybe, and tell the guys to keep an eye on the shed when he's going to be with you instead of keeping watch over it."

"That works for me," his wife eagerly agrees. "The sooner we can get done with all the canning, the sooner I can get the kids started on some sort of schooling around here."

Justin groans, but his parents both just laugh at his dramatic anguish.

"Grams, do you think we should just feed the kids at the island this morning? Seems like everyone is all over the place today. Grandpa's sleeping, Reagan's out in the shed, some of the men are going to bed, some are up on watch. Geesh! It's a madhouse right now," Hannah expresses. Derek and Sue verbally agree.

"I suppose that would be all right, Hannah dear," Grams answers.

Everyone knows how much it means to Grams for her family to gather around the dinner table for at least two meals a day, but with the visitors being on the farm and everyone's schedules being rearranged, that isn't bound to happen for a while.

"What about Reagan and Samantha and the two sick patients in the shed? Should we take them food?" Sue asks as Cory comes in the back door.

"Got the milk and cream, Miss Hannah," he blurts into their conversation.

"Great, Cory," Grams tells him. "Just put it all in the pantry, dear. And, Hannah, I'll take a tray of food to Reagan and her assistant. I don't know about those patients. The woman drank some chicken broth yesterday and ate a half a piece of toast, but that was it. And the boy isn't even taking broth. Maybe today will be better."

The screen door slams again.

"Hey, got the eggs for you," Kelly calls out to whomever, probably her. "Man, that smells great, ladies."

Hannah smiles widely at his praise. He's always praising her cooking, though she's hardly a five star chef. Army food must not have been very tasty.

"I didn't help her today, Kelly," Grams interrupts.

This interrupting of each other and people coming and going and the general chaos of the kitchen area is the norm on the farm.

For a blind person, it was sometimes difficult to have so many bodies in her kitchen. Thus she bumps into people in the kitchen on a regular basis.

Grams just continues on with her praise, "Hannah did it all by herself this morning. These old bones weren't moving too fast today."

"You probably just need some rest, Grams," Kelly tells her grandmother gently.

He sounds like he is standing right next to Grams. A slap, slap, slapping sound alerts Hannah that Grams has probably patted his hand or shoulder. His tender concern for her elderly grandparent is so touching and poignant that it brings tears to her eyes, and she has to turn back to her stove.

"Oh, I'm fine, Kelly. Don't you go worrying yourself over me. Give me the baby, Sue, so that you can make the children's breakfast plates," Grams tells her sister.

Kelly and Derek pair off in the hall with Cory in tow to discuss the women picking vegetables for canning and the adjusted security patrols. Their low, deep voices come down the hallway in the form of a jumbled murmur. A moment later, Cory is out the door again. Apparently, they've worked things out.

"Let me start getting this all on plates for the kids, honey," Sue tells her.

Her sister effectively snaps Hannah out of her daze about the men and their planning. Hannah mumbles an answer and moves surreptitiously closer to the hall where Derek and Kelly are still discussing plans.

"Em, let me hold Jacob while you eat, sweetie," Hannah tells the younger girl who is still babysitting the newest member of their clan. He greets Hannah with a handful of slobber against her neck.

"I'll make a plate and cut the food up small for you, Hannah, so that you can feed him," her sister calls above the noise.

Hannah just nods absent-mindedly. She is too engrossed in the tidbits of information she is hearing in the men's conversation.

"…no way are they squatting longer," Kelly is saying.

There is venom in his voice. This is not the soft, baritone voice he uses when he speaks with her.

"Right, to hell with that," Derek agrees.

His voice is also tight and strained with tension.

36

Derek continues, "When that one asked about staying on permanent, I told him hell no that it wasn't even an option. But they seemed pissed to hear it."

"Too damn bad. They aren't staying here after their sick get better. Not even good ole' Uncle Peter. Hell, I'll even help them pack when the time comes," Kelly jokes half-heartedly.

"No, I made it quite clear that staying isn't happening. That big dude, Lebron, Levon- whatever the hell his name is- was giving me some hard looks, but he didn't try anything," Derek informs him.

Kelly laughs once. "That was smart on his part. He tries anything when I'm around and I'll take care of it, bro."

All three Rangers seem to call each other this. And they all have each other's backs more so than anyone Hannah has ever known or even heard of.

"I know, Kel," Derek says earnestly.

Derek says something else that makes Kelly laugh again, but Jacob starts fussing too loudly to pick up any conversation but his raucous cries. Hannah decides to give up all pretenses at becoming a secret agent and just moves into the hall so that she can join in their conversation.

"Hey, Hannie," Derek says to her. "Hey, big guy."

Her brother-in-law takes Jacob's tiny hand in his own and shakes it around, making the baby giggle and bounce on her hip.

"I just wanted to get in on what you guys are talking about. It seems important," she confesses as Sue also comes to stand beside her. She has Isaac again as Grams must be doing something else in the kitchen now.

"We're just going over some of the issues we're dealing with concerning the visitors," Derek says, probably to his wife. "Here, babe, let me take him. I don't get to see him much with these idiots messing up my sleep schedule."

His complaint is heart-felt and genuine. Derek truly loves her sister and their children. And Hannah believes that he would do anything he had to do to protect them.

"Yesterday John followed one of them and he went in the hog barn," Derek informs herself and Sue.

Kelly had explained to her yesterday morning when they'd stolen ten seconds of alone time before the others had arisen that

Derek pulled rank on the rest of them and that they would adhere to his decisions. But he'd also added that Derek trusted them enough to make important decisions without him, too. After all, they'd all been Army Rangers for years. Not to mention the fact that they all have a lot to lose.

"Great," Kelly says angrily. "What the hell was he doing?"

"John said he was just lookin' around, but he was probably up to no good. He said the man seemed snoopy," Derek relays.

"Which one?"

"The Mexican dude. I think his name is Willy," Derek replies.

"What happened?"

"John followed him 'cuz he overheard the guy tell another one up at their camp that he needed to take a piss. John just figured he'd head into the woods, but he didn't. He sneaked around the back of the corn crib and the chicken coop. Willy didn't know John was near the chicken coop and within earshot. So John followed him, and the dude was wandering around in the hog barn picking up shit, checkin' out some of the equipment that's stored back there- you know, up to no good like I said. And John told him to get back to his camp."

"That ain't good, man," Kelly says with mounting stress in his voice.

"I can't believe any of them would do that. It's kind of scary that they'd be so bold," Sue expresses nervously.

"Hell, I know it. We told them not to do that, and here they are not listening already and we're only a few days into this shit."

Her lovely brother-in-law swears. It's somewhat understandable, but Hannah's also quite sure that Grams is nowhere near them to overhear it.

"Yeah, that woman with the dark hair was creepin' around the chicken coop this morning. I saw her when you were down at the horse barn getting water with some of the men," Kelly discloses.

"Shit," Derek swears again.

"I mean, maybe she was just curious. Or maybe she was hoping to get some eggs or something, but that chic looks like… trash," Sue says.

There is a certain amount of rudeness in this statement that is uncharacteristic of her sister.

"Hell yeah she does. Most of them do," Derek agrees. "I don't trust any of them, Kelly. They not only brought sickness here that could kill us, but they don't seem to take direction well, either."

"A couple of them don't seem so bad, but the ones who are wandering around and not listening to our rules are bad enough to make me want to throw them all out," Kelly adds.

"Just be diligent. I've already talked to John about it," Derek orders them.

"We just need to be on high alert all the time, at least until they leave," Kelly concurs wisely.

Hannah trusts him so implicitly to keep her and her entire family safe.

"Exactly," Derek says. "Sue wants to work in the garden so that they can continue with their canning, and I told her that Cory can help her which means that we'll need to watch the shed when he does."

"Sounds good to me. Just so long as their group is being watched at all times. That's all that matters to me," Kelly says stiffly.

"I've gotta go out and tell John some of this and just make sure he's on the same page," Derek announces.

"Man, you need to sleep," Kelly advises with a chuckle.

"I will. I also need to tell him about the one faucet in the hog barn. It needs some work," her brother-in-law informs them.

"Ok, *then* it's off to bed, mister," Sue scolds her husband.

Her laugh is squelched as he must pull her close for a kiss. There is soft whispering between the two of them before they leave the hall altogether. This also means that she is alone with Kelly. He takes her only available hand into his own and then takes baby Jacob from her. It doesn't even faze Hannah. All of the men are like this at the farm. They hold the kids, help with them when they can and offer up their affection freely.

"Let someone else collect the eggs for a while, ok?" he asks but mostly demands.

"I'll be fine, Kelly. It's one of the only outdoor chores that I can help with," Hannah argues softly.

"They aren't listening to our orders, Hannah. You're at an obvious disadvantage than the rest of us. I don't want you walking into the coop and have one of those men already be in there," he tells her.

"Ok, I won't do it until we know whether or not we can trust them," she concedes as his sound judgment is pretty hard to argue against. It isn't as if she'd see if someone sneaked up on her.

"Thanks, Hannah. I just have to keep you safe until they're gone is all," he replies.

"You need to catch up on sleep, too, Kelly. You were up before me this morning and that's supposed to be your sleeping time," she reminds him.

"I'm good. We're all used to keeping bad hours while we're on a mission," he tells as he presses a kiss to her forehead.

"Alright," she says in a tone that clearly doesn't convey that anything about it is actually 'alright' at all. "I'm going to feed him and help Grams get a tray of food ready for Reagan and her nurse."

A knock at the front door alerts them both and Kelly hands her Jacob again.

"Who is it?" she asks him as they travel toward the front of the house. She knows that Kelly can see who might be at the door because the top half of it is glass.

"Looks like the twin of that sick boy in the shed," he relays as he opens the door.

"Hello, sir," comes a very small voice from the other side of the threshold.

"What do you want?" Kelly says with a bit of gruff.

Hannah jabs the back of his arm.

"Where... where's my brother, sir? I'd like to see him. I mean, if that's ok with you. I'd really like to see Garrett," the boy says.

There is such worry in his young voice that it breaks Hannah's heart.

"Uh... sure, kid. Let me take you to him, ok?" Kelly says with a truckload more sympathy this time.

This young boy must look tragic and sad to have brought about such a quick change of attitude in her big fierce lover.

He quickly adds, "Stay right here and I'll be back in a sec."

He shuts the door again and turns to Hannah. She feels his large hands on the sides of her face as he presses a quick kiss to her mouth.

40

"Be careful today, ok?"

"Yes, sir," she says jokingly as if he's her commanding officer.

He chuckles, chucks her under the chin and leaves the house with the boy whose twin brother lies dying in their medical facility which is not much more than a pole building with a cement floor.

"Come on, kid," Kelly says, his voice fading.

"Oh, thank-you, sir," the boy's reply comes on a squeal.

Hannah needs to find time today to read some Scripture and pray harder for this young boy's brother. To lose a sibling at such a young age would have to be one of the hardest things a child could possibly endure. She's not sure if this boy has any other family left, other than his father. His father sure doesn't seem to be much of a shoulder to lean on. Sometimes Hannah has learned to read between the lines, read the unspoken things that people tell her. She isn't stupid, and she's a whole heck of a lot more intuitive than most people have always thought of her, with the exception of her family. She'd realized that Frank, father of these twin boys, is a hard, terrible man by what Kelly *hadn't* told her this morning. Kelly's omissions about the occurrence out at the shed at dawn had told her all she needed to know about this Frank. He is a bad father, a loud and intimidating person and someone she needs to steer clear of while he is on their farm.

Chapter Four
Reagan

Sam is tending to the pregnant woman near the back of the small building, wiping her brow with a wet cloth. They talk periodically but not directly to Reagan and when she walks closer to them from time to time, they stop talking altogether. Sam is wearing her protective gear again. They both are, but Reagan wonders if any of it will be enough. These people have lost four of their own group to whatever this is, so it leaves to reason that perhaps a thin, paper mask isn't exactly going to beat back a thousand year old disease. However, she has to give her best effort to try and help them if she can. Grandpa was right. They need to hold on to their last vestiges of humanity, no matter how difficult that becomes.

And a short while later, Kelly comes back to report that the visitors have retrieved their water and have gone directly back to their campsite. Of course, having Derek escort them with his rifle had probably encouraged them not to wander. Kelly has with him a guest for Garrett, and it's his twin brother who they've found out is named Huntley. He favors more of the Native American features with darker skin and hair than his brother and at second glance, Reagan realizes that they are not identical twins at all, but fraternal. His large eyes tilt at the corners, and he has what promises to be the high cheekbones of an American Indian. Unlike his brother who is sick, Huntley wears his hair much longer and down to his shoulders.

Reagan puts the protective gear on Huntley, making sure to tighten down the metal part on the nose piece so that no germs get through there. It almost seems ridiculous to do, though, because they have all been traveling with the two sick patients for what was probably quite some time. However, they can't be overly careful anymore.

"I've got him, Kelly. You guys stay out of here," Reagan tells Kelly and John. John has not left her alone in the shed. He's been standing for the last hour near the door.

Sam comes over to stand next to her, and Huntley hugs the girl's waist tightly as if afraid to let her go.

"I can take him in to see his brother, doctor," the girl offers kindly.

The kid seems nice even though she has sad, mournful eyes. It'll be a shame to send her away with those miscreants when they leave, hopefully soon.

"Sure," Reagan allows her to take the boy with the long, greasy hair. Then she removes her latex gloves and goes to the door opening to the shed where the two Rangers still stand.

"Hey, bro, you need to run in and grab some grub because we've got to get that hay cut in the top pasture," Kelly instructs. "Let's leave Cory here, and me and you will cut it while Derek gets some sleep. If we use both tractors, it won't take more than a couple hours at the most. Derek can work it tomorrow and hopefully sometime this weekend we'll bale it if it doesn't rain."

Kelly tells him, and John nods but reluctantly.

"It'll be ok, John. We can see the whole farm from up there, bro. She'll be ok."

John's eyes snap up to Kelly's and he grimaces hard. Reagan would like to inform them both that she can manage just fine on her own but doesn't. Something about saying this doesn't feel right. She doesn't feel safe at all on the farm now. John doesn't answer his friend but nods again.

"Um, I'll just go get Cory. I think he's in the barn with Derek. Then your brother can hit the sack for a while," Kelly tells them both and jogs away.

"You gonna be ok?" John asks after Kelly is out of earshot.

Reagan nods stubbornly but feels like telling him not to leave her for some reason. These visitors have brought back some bad memories, memories that were just starting to fade the tiniest bit.

He continues on a frown, "Ok, I won't be gone long. Got your pistol?"

"You brought it out to me earlier, remember? It's under my gown. Grandpa's shotgun is in the shed behind this door, too," she tells him. He nods but frowns.

"I'll hear the shots," he reasons to himself.

John grasps her hand for a brief second and gives it a gentle squeeze, but Reagan doesn't try to pull away. Having John near just seems to make her feel safer, protected. And his touch is reassuring, not revolting in this moment. His touch also makes her feel more than just safe and protected, but Reagan doesn't want to think about those sensations.

"Yeah," she answers quietly, and they stand there awkwardly, not wanting to part. John's thumb strokes her knuckles before he releases her. It's like that damn electricity again, and Reagan's glad when he lets her go.

"I'll be relieved when they're gone," John complains and a line pinches between his strong brows.

"Yeah," Reagan repeats because she completely agrees and there's nothing else that needs said about it.

He finally leaves as Cory jogs up, but John does turn to glance over his shoulder at her, not once but twice. Her resistance to being away from John probably comes from the fact that they'd spent so much time together the last week and he'd saved her ass in the city multiple times, Reagan reasons. She doesn't want to think about what any of it means any further than that.

"What's up?" Cory asks pleasantly.

He's trying to make small talk, but Reagan just rolls her eyes at him and turns away.

"He wants to know if he can stay in here, Doctor," Sam inquires quietly for the young boy.

"Not all day, but an hour or so at a time might be ok," Reagan returns. She notices that the sick child does not look at all better and is back to the breathing pattern of short breaths in and long exhalations that usually signify the body is shutting down. Sometimes this can go on for days. Reagan is hoping that in those days she'll be able to pump the kid with enough steroids and antibodies to kill the germ and restore his life.

The woman on the other cot, Jennifer, has not awakened for more than a few minutes at a time. Reagan consults her chart, noticing that Grandpa ran pain killers and a light sedative through her

IV line. It's not the normal procedure for handling a pregnant woman because the drugs could have negative consequences on the baby in utero, but given the situation there's not much of a choice. It's best to keep the patients sedated and not coughing up blood while the medicines run through their bodies undisturbed. It also helps reduce the spread of infection when they aren't spewing phlegm and blood from their lungs all over the room.

Together Reagan and Sam do their best to clean Garrett with a warm wet rag, and Reagan uses scissors to carefully cut away the part of his shirt and the sheet that he's coughed blood onto. She discards them in a plastic bag that she will order to be burned. The bedding will need to be burned when these two are done in the med shed. They cannot afford the danger of these types of contaminants on the farm.

The boy's brother sits quietly in a chair at Garrett's side and holds his hand through his latex glove that is too big for him. Reagan feels sorrier for the kid than she can say. If one of her sisters had become this ill as a child, she wouldn't have handled it so well. Hannah going blind hadn't killed her. This could very well kill this young boy.

"Huntley, are you ok?" Sam asks him.

Reagan realizes as the boy lifts his gaze toward them that his eyes are a light hazel green and not the brown she'd expected. They stand out against his dark skin tone. He only nods in response.

"Frank was over here this morning. Where did he go?" Sam asks.

Her inquiry of the boys' father is tinged with a tad of fearful trepidation that is barely concealed.

"He's back at the RV," Huntley answers.

Reagan can detect the most subtle hint of the broken lilt of the American Indian dialect. His mother must have been full-blooded because their piece of shit father sure isn't.

"He doesn't even know I'm here. I snuck off."

"Oh no," Sam worries.

Cory has come to linger in the doorway which immediately causes Sam to step closer to Reagan. She can hardly blame her, though, because Cory is starting to look like the rest of the men around here: a broad-shouldered, muscular bull, and it seems he is growing taller every day.

"It's ok. You can be here. If Frank says anything, I'll say I sent for you," Reagan tells them both.

"Thank-you, miss. Frank doesn't like it when we don't listen. He can get real mad sometimes," Huntley explains.

Yeah, I'll bet he does, Reagan thinks to herself. Frank needs to spend some quality bonding time with John, Derek and Kelly or just John judging by the reaction he had to Frank earlier.

"Is he your real dad or stepdad?" Reagan asks.

"He's our real dad," the boy asks as if he's surprised by the question.

"I just meant because you call him by his first name," Reagan explains.

"Oh, it's just what we've always called him. Our mom's name was Laura, but her Navajo name was Anaba," Huntley explains.

A deep sadness touches his pale eyes.

"Where is she now, Huntley?" Reagan asks as she takes his brother's pulse and blood pressure.

"She's walking in the Spirit World with our Grandfather," he replies and looks away from Reagan.

"Did she die when this started?" The boy nods a reply. "I'm very sorry to hear that."

"Their mom was beautiful. Huntley has a picture of her in his bag out in the RV. She was at some ceremonial dance, and she had on a really cool costume," Sam supplies with a soft smile, exposing perfectly straight white teeth.

Reagan is hit with a sudden, unexpected case of dejavu, but she doesn't have time to work it out. Sam is obviously close with these two boys, so she may be helpful with getting information about these people.

"And your parents, Sam? Are they out there with that group?" Reagan prods again, trying desperately to get this girl to tell her something about the dynamic of these people.

However, Sam shuts down, hugs her arms across her front and shakes her head with downcast eyes. Those bastards out at the camp have this girl on silent lockdown, and Reagan is afraid that she is being abused by them. If that's the case, John and Kelly will beat the tar out of whoever's doing it. Reagan won't even have to ask

46

them to do it. Huntley also looks away again and doesn't volunteer any information, so Reagan goes back to her patient. She figures it's all going come out in the wash which will probably be sooner rather than later.

"In a few hours we'll give Garrett another breathing treatment. Jennifer, too. Hopefully she'll awaken enough to take some broth or even eat a little bread or something," Reagan complains with worry. Jennifer had improved just slightly yesterday, but she's worse today.

"There's a really nice boy out there named Simon," Huntley offers Reagan out of the blue.

"Oh yeah? Is he one of those teenagers?" Reagan turns around and asks him. Hopefully if she can get some sort of information from these children, then she'll be able to relay it to her family so that they can decide if these people who have descended upon their farm are any sort of a threat.

"Yes, ma'am," Sam cuts in. "He's not that one with the black hair. Simon has red hair and freckles. He's… sweet. He's a really nice guy. He tries to help us when he can."

"Help you how?" Reagan asks. Sam looks at her feet, refusing to answer. "How does he help you? Like help you with chores or scavenging for food. What?"

"I don't know. He just tries to help," she answers evasively. Her mood has soured slightly.

"Are either of you related to him?" Reagan presses to get more information on any of them which she can share with her family.

"No, he's related to the other boy. They're cousins," Huntley tells her. "Bobby's older, though, and he likes to beat up on Simon and…"

"Huntley!" Sam says on a sharp breath.

"What?" Huntley asks innocently. "It's true. Besides, they can't hear us in here."

"No, they can't. You're right, and you see that big kid over there? His name's Cory, and he's our guard while we're in here, so you're safe with me," Reagan reassures them both. Huntley seems relieved, but Sam is reticent, wary. Her bright blue eyes dart to Cory periodically and then quickly retreat.

"This place reminds me of my Grandpa's place, 'cept for it's a lot more greener," Huntley states honestly because he doesn't know any better. "He lived in the desert on a reservation, and mom took us sometimes to see him. Once when she left Frank, we got to stay with Grandpa for a couple months. That was really fun. He was cool. But then Frank came and got us and made us go back home with him."

"Who are those other people out there?" Reagan asks either of them that will talk, likely Huntley.

"The lady with the dark hair, her name is Amber and the other one is named Jasmine. She has the bleached blonde hair with the black roots," Sam surprisingly volunteers.

"Yeah, guess it's hard to get in to the hairdresser now," Reagan states and inadvertently looks again at Sam's messed up haircut. It makes the girl self-conscious because she fingers the choppy ends and looks down. Great. Now Reagan feels like shit. She hadn't meant to hurt the kid's feelings. This is the reason she's so much better with books and cadaver dissection. "Are either of those women related to either of you?"

"Not us," Sam says. "But Amber, the one with the dark hair, she's Bobby's mom and also Simon's aunt. His parents are both dead. His dad is in the government or something, and his mom was a nurse. But he's an orphan now, too."

Reagan follows Sam's line of sight. She's staring nervously at the door where Cory has come to stand briefly before walking away again. Reagan suspects that he is also listening to everything the kids are relaying.

"Are you an orphan, Sam? Or are any of those people out there your parents?" Reagan presses again, and Sam just shakes her head, leaving Reagan to wonder exactly what she means by it.

"Reagan, Grams is coming," Cory says from the door frame and slings his rifle behind him.

"Don't let her come in here, Cory," Reagan calls back sternly.

"Yes, ma'am," Cory says seriously. "Looks like she's bringing food."

The clock on the wall reads 8:45, past the family breakfast meal. Their normal customs will likely go by the wayside while these people are on their property. All of their schedules have been rearranged, their lives interrupted.

48

"Breakfast, kids. Everyone, come out and eat something," Grams calls from the door.

She hands Cory a giant serving tray with dishes and cups, silverware and a metal pitcher.

"Yes, ma'am," Cory answers.

Reagan knows better than to argue, either.

"I heard that we have a couple guests out here with you, Reagan, so we sent extra. You kids come on out here and eat, too," Grams orders and wipes her hands on her apron.

Sam and Huntley just look at each other.

"It's cool. She always cooks a lot," Cory explains.

But the kids appear hesitant and unsure of themselves.

"You have to eat something, and if you aren't going back over to your camp, then you'll just have to eat with us. So come on. Take off your gear, set it over there and then I'll show you how to scrub up at the sink," Reagan charges them into motion.

A few minutes later they join Cory on the cement pad and sit patiently while Grams makes them each a plate of food big enough for two people.

"Later I'll bring out some broth for your patients, Reagan," Grams adds with her usual kindness.

"Thanks, Grams," Reagan says and leads her grandmother a few feet away. "Don't bring any for the boy. He's not able to wake up enough to take food orally. We're just pumping him full of fluids through the IV," she returns too quietly for Huntley to overhear.

Her grandmother nods with a sad grimace and lingers a moment before returning to the house to help Hannah with the children.

Cory has propped his rifle between his legs and sits next to Huntley followed by Sam and then Reagan all in a line on the long, single step cement stoop. Huntley tears into his biscuit and gravy as if it's the first time he's eaten in days and then greedily moves on to the eggs. Sam barely holds herself back, as well, although she does show a slightly higher modicum of dignity.

"Were you guys hungry?" Reagan asks lightly. Sam glances sideways at her and nods nervously.

"Grams makes the best food around so eat up," Cory adds to make them feel more comfortable.

Huntley doesn't need encouragement. He's half through his plate of food already. Reagan's not sure if he's come up for air long enough to even take a drink of his milk.

"Yeah, my sister Hannah and our grandmother do all of the cooking, and I take care of the horses and the medical stuff. We all have jobs around here," Reagan explains.

"What do you do? Shoot people with your gun?" Huntley asks Cory.

The teen starts laughing with unabashed good humor, which is highly unusual coming from the normally stoic kid.

"No, dude. I don't go around shooting people," Cory says on a laugh through his bit of biscuit. "My brother's the big guy, and I have a younger sister here about your age, I'd say. She's probably inside with the other kids. I help out with the tractors and take care of the cows and kind of anything else I can learn to be more helpful."

"Cool. Are those the horses over there?" Huntley asks, peering into the sun toward the pasture.

"Yep. They're kind of fun to ride. I've been learning. Miss Reagan over there teaches everyone how to ride. Do you know how?" Cory asks.

He's making conversation better than Reagan would've given him credit for. Cory is usually pretty quiet. Perhaps he's just needed a few peers close to his own age to talk with. He is the oldest kid on the farm with absolutely no teenagers with whom to hang out.

Huntley shakes his head and answers, "Nah, but Sam…"

He is cut off by Sam nudging his arm. She shakes her head.

"Do you ride, Sam?" Cory asks her.

The girl shrugs one shoulder and looks down at her plate.

Cory is also smart enough to know that the family needs information about these people. Cory has a wisdom beyond his seventeen years, and Reagan's not sure if it is newly acquired since losing his parents or if he was always like this. He has a calm, quiet demeanor about him, much like Kelly.

"Here, Huntley, have some of mine," Sam says and attempts to scrape some of her food onto the boy's plate. Reagan grins.

It's touching to say the least that a kid her age would think of someone other than herself.

"Oh, hey, wait. You don't have to do that. Look, we've got plenty for him to have seconds," Cory stops her with his hand at the edge of her plate.

He brings the bowl of scrambled eggs around from behind him and scoops more onto Huntley's plate.

Cory says, "See? It's ok. You don't have to share. Just eat your food, ok?"

"Ok, thanks. This is a lot, though. We don't eat this much... *ever*," Sam says with a sneer on the last word.

Her fair skin is bruised on her forearm, and Reagan knows enough to know that the four, fading marks there are a healing bruise from a person's hand. She'd done some work researching domestic violence and had even worked for a summer at the E.R. in Nashville while on break from school. Reagan has seen this form of bruising on domestically abused women. It is hard to speculate where this girl could've been man handled. Perhaps she'd been in a scuffle while searching an abandoned home. Perhaps she'd really just fallen or injured herself. The one speculation that Reagan fears the most is that someone within her group of traveling companions could've possibly done this to her.

"What do you guys do for food? Is it in the RV?" Cory asks casually.

Reagan allows him to guide the conversation, hoping that it will help the kids to feel more comfortable to talk to him about their situation.

"Nah, we just drive around and look for places to find food. Us kids have to get out and go in places..." Huntley starts, but Sam stops him.

"Huntley!" she hisses.

Cory looks at Reagan over Sam's bent head. There will be much to discuss later this evening if the family can all dine together. If they can't dine together, then a meeting will need to be called for the adults.

"Do they have food out there now?" Cory asks.

"Yeah, some," Huntley answers.

Sam shakes her head as if she can't believe the boy is telling some big secret to strangers.

"How long do you think it will last?" Reagan asks Sam quietly and notices movement over at the camp. The two women are hanging clothing on the line that they've erected, and they have the campfire going again, presumably for cooking whatever food they do have. The woman with the blonde hair is dressed in micro short shorts and a shirt that is cut off through the center exposing her tan, flat stomach. Three of the men are simply sitting in fold-out lawn chairs doing absolutely nothing. Some of the others are absent, leaving Reagan to wonder where they could be. Maybe, if they are smart, they are only in the RV's so as not to earn the wrath of three Rangers.

"Maybe a few days or so," Sam almost whispers and is clearly uncomfortable.

"It'll last longer if we aren't eating it. Even though they don't give us much," Huntley grumbles the last comment under his breath.

Cory swiftly stands, alerting Reagan by his posture that someone is coming from the new group.

A young man, the red-headed teen, approaches as Huntley dashes over to hug him about his waist. The young teen returns Huntley's hug without embarrassment or shame.

"Simon!" Huntley says as the older boy presses him to his stomach.

He's a tall young man and certainly does have a messy mop of dark auburn hair and freckles that splatter his nose and cheeks. He is dressed conservatively, not like the rest of his group.

"Hi, I'm Simon."

The boy extends a hand in a half salute wave but then holds both hands up in a supplication of passive surrender.

He says, "I was just checking on Garrett. I was worried. I… I know we're not supposed to come over here and I don't mean any disrespect or anything, but I wanted to see if there was anything I could do to help."

Simon offers this to Reagan who has also stood. The boy has kind blue eyes and is holding a baseball cap and twisting it nervously in his hands. His eyes are mostly downcast, and he seems shy and reserved. No wonder he got beat up a lot. Reagan's pretty sure that she could kick his ass. The world is even less sympathetic than it used to be. Behaving meekly isn't going to help this kid get ahead.

"Simon, I'm Reagan McClane, and I'm a doctor, too, like my grandfather. This is Cory. He also lives here," she introduces the two boys so that they don't have tension between each other. Although if they are going to have a pissing contest, then Cory would clearly come out as the alpha male victor. This kid doesn't look like he has a mean bone in his body.

"Can I see Garrett? Or is there anything I can do to help with him?" Simon asks with genuine care.

"I'm sorry, but I don't think it's a good idea to spend time in there with him. He is very ill, as you probably know," Reagan explains. "We're doing all we can to help him. He has an IV with strong meds running through him. The lady, Jennifer, also has an IV full of medicine. The boy hasn't changed. His condition is still extremely unstable. And if we've correctly diagnosed him, then it's also very contagious."

Simon is visibly distraught at the news of Garrett still being so ill after receiving medical care for two solid days. His features are set in a deep and melancholy grimace.

Cory had seemed wary of Simon at first, but as soon as the other kid had opened his mouth and Simon's soft voice and guarded mannerisms came out, he'd relaxed. Cory is also a fairly good judge of character for someone so young. Of course after the shit he'd been through to stay alive, it is no wonder. He is extremely distrustful of the new guests, just as much as his hard, older brother.

"Simon, they have food. Like real food," Huntley exclaims with the unabashed excitement that only a child can show.

"That's good, kid. You should eat. You need to eat, little buddy," Simon says.

Reagan notices that he does not make any attempt to beg a plate for himself.

It used to be highly unusual for a teenager to befriend a kid who can't possibly be much more than ten years old. These are strange new times they are living in.

"We've got plenty. You want some?" Cory offers.

Reagan is strangely proud of him. Cory is so good-looking and just has a cool way about him that he just had to have been popular in school, and yet, here he is being nice to this obvious misfit. The fact that they are both orphans of this new world is what

Cory probably sees as linking them in any small way together in it. The fact that they are also the only two of three boys around doesn't hurt, either. Cory doesn't seem like the kind of boy who would've been cruel to weaker, unpopular kids before the apocalypse anyways.

"No, thank-you," Simon rejects the offer and shoves his hand into the pocket of his faded, baggy jeans that are covered in rips and tears.

The kid is skin and bones thin and looks unhealthy. He is wearing brown leather loafers with tassels. That was not a current teen fashion trend in any state that she knew of anytime in the last hundred years. This kid does not at all fit in with these people with whom he is traveling. He seems like a congressman's kid, like he could be on the cover of a yachting magazine or an ad for Ralph Lauren clothing, except for the dirty gray t-shirt he wears. The dead giveaway that he doesn't fit in with the band of hooligans is the lack of lewd tattoos and body piercings that the group seems to have received on some sort of bulk rate discount. John explained to her last night that some of the tattoos the visitors sport are gang related and prison associated. Another clue is the fact that Simon isn't eyeing up Reagan as if he's trying to get an x-ray of her through her clothing. Perhaps she's just being paranoid about that part, however, since she's uncomfortable around most men. Simon doesn't leer. He mostly looks at the ground.

"Here, Simon. I'm done," Sam says and shoves her plate forcefully into the boy's space.

He has no choice but to take it because it is either accept the plate or wear it on his shirt. He gives a gracious nod to Sam who turns her back to him and sits again. Simon doesn't sit, but he does inhale the second-hand plate of food like it's the nectar of the gods.

"Wow, this is awesome. I haven't had food like this since... forever," Simon acknowledges.

It pisses Reagan off that he keeps looking over his shoulder nervously toward the camp as if he's afraid to get caught eating.

"Yeah, that's what I said when we first came here," Cory remembers.

"This place is really something. It's very beautiful, picturesque even in this valley the way that your farm is positioned in it, Dr. McClane," Simon comments.

Reagan recognizes that the boy is educated by his tone and clear diction and the way that he motions with his hands as if he's taken quite a few speech and debate classes in school.

"Thanks. It's been passed down from family time and again. How did you come to be with this group?" Reagan asks.

"Amber out there is my aunt. She has dark hair, the one hanging those clothes," he indicates.

Reagan spots the woman of whom he speaks. Kelly had not been impressed with this woman yesterday and he'd made his opinion of her known.

"Uh, yeah, I see her," Reagan says with a nod. Amber looks like a real piece of work.

"My parents are both dead. Well, my dad may not be actually. He was a senator from our state. But he was in London on business when everything went bad, so he had no way of getting home and we hadn't heard from him or his staff in over four months. We all heard about London being bombed. I don't know...," he trails off sadly.

"I'm sorry, Simon," Reagan acknowledges and lays a hand briefly to his sinewy, thin forearm.

"Mother and I held a private memorial service for just the two of us at our home. We needed, *she* needed the closure. My mom was a surgical nurse and was killed shortly after it all fell apart when the hospital where she worked was raided. I told her to stop going to work, but she wouldn't. Most of the doctors and nurses left and never came back. But she felt a responsibility to try and help people. Some of the workers were still going but not many. I went to the hospital to look for her when she didn't come home. There were fires everywhere. They'd been raided. I found her, though..."

His eyes tear up, but he forces them not to fall. He glances away for just a moment and then back at them. Reagan feels sorrier than she can say for this orphaned kid. She also feels sorry for his dead mother because what almost happened to her at the university is probably what had happened to Simon's mom. She's learned a lot about some types of men since the apocalypse started. She's learned that some of them are beasts. She's also learned how John deals with them.

"I'm very sorry, Simon," Reagan says with much understanding.

"Thanks. I guess everyone has lost someone since this all started. My Aunt Amber lived nearby, and she took me with them even though we really never had much to do with her before or were around her family very often. She was my mother's sister, and I don't believe they got along very well. We didn't have any other family in the area, though, so I was kind of stuck. I thought about just staying in our home, but I had nothing to protect myself, no guns, no weapons of any kind. I didn't figure I'd last too long."

"What about your dad's family?" Cory asks as he finishes his breakfast, setting a completely empty plate on the platter.

His plates are always empty. He is definitely a growing boy. Reagan just grins. She hopes the family can always grow enough food to take care of everyone on the farm.

"My dad's family was all from the New England states, and so they are likely dead, as well. We didn't hear from any of them after the first tsunami. I had a sister but…" he doesn't finish.

Reagan figures that it's because it is too difficult for him to discuss. These kids dealing with shit that is so beyond their years is enough to make her wince.

After a long pause, Simon continues, "When I first went with Aunt Amber, it was just her and her son and two of the guys. We met up with the other caravan later. They knew each other or at least some of them did anyways," Simon answers openly and honestly.

Reagan has hope that she can pry more information from him.

"What about those men? Who are those men? I've counted five, not counting our worthless uncle and the other teenager Bobby that Huntley told us about," Reagan inquires.

"Yes, that's correct. Bobby is my cousin, Aunt Amber's son. There's Frank, he's the twins' dad. Buzz, he's the bald one with the tattoos, kind of short. He's not so bad most of the time. Then there's Levon and Rick, they're the African American men, and they are cousins, I believe. They were friends of Buzz, who is your great-uncle's friend. Rick's cool, but Levon… he, he can get kind of crazy. Then Willy, the Mexican man who is quiet and, well, he's just different. Then there's just me and Bobby."

He says the last name with open derision and looks at Sam who, in turn, looks away.

"I'll take Huntley back in to sit with his brother if you don't mind, doctor," Sam suggests.

Reagan nods to her. What was that all about? Is Bobby some sort of bully or something? And what did Simon mean that Levon could get 'crazy?'

"How dangerous are they, Simon?" Reagan asks point blank. They don't have time for social trivialities.

Simon doesn't immediately answer and sighs heavily instead. He looks toward the campsite again and clams up. He is being cautious for some reason, a reason Reagan would like to understand better. The other teen boy Bobby is coming toward them, and Simon quickly hands Cory the plate.

"Thanks for the food. I'll come back later if I can," he murmurs quickly and leaves them.

He meets Bobby about halfway across the yard, and the other young man shoves Simon almost knocking him down as he barks commands at him and calls him "prep school boy." Simon hunches his shoulders, returns the ball cap back to his head and goes back to the camp.

Cory and she exchange a look of understanding, and Cory nods. They return to their assigned jobs without discussing the shoving of Simon as no words are necessary. Reagan highly doubts that it is simply cousin rivalry that is going on with those two boys. If anything, the current screwed up world events should've brought them closer together. Bobby could be a problem.

A short time later as Reagan is caring for the sick again, she has time to reflect on everything that has transpired and her short conversations with the kids. Simon had gone back to his camp, after being insulted and ridiculed by the other boy. She'd watched as he resumed his chores, which looked to be carrying more water from the barn, helping the women with laundry and cooking and anything else they ordered him to do.

Neither Reagan nor Cory failed to notice, however, that Bobby, had openly disliked Simon either being with them or that he just didn't like the McClane family in general. Why would any of them be hostile toward her or her family? They are letting them stay on their farm for a while. It's strange to Reagan, but none of them seems appreciative of this fact. Bobby had taken a second to send a few nasty looks toward everyone standing outside the med shed. He had even taken two malevolent steps toward them until Cory had picked up the rifle again that he'd just rested against the wall of the building. This time it had been enough to make the other boy turn and walk back to his camp. This time.

Chapter Five
John

At the end of the day, after chores and after dinner, John takes his sack full of explosives making equipment and Reagan to the back of the horse barn where he can work in secrecy on his demos without the prying eyes of their new friends. Reagan had given the whole accounting to the family of the information she'd gleaned from Huntley, Sam, and a new kid that John hasn't met yet named Simon, who sounds bookish and awkward which aren't the worst qualities to have anymore. John has left the outer lights in the main aisle turned off, and he and Reagan are in the back of the barn near the tack room where he's laid out most of his loot on an ancient, oak work table covered with scratches and divots. Three single light bulbs illuminate the work surface they've established.

"This is a lot of crap," Reagan observes.

She rubs the back of her neck, trying to massage out the kinks of fatigue.

"You tired, boss?" he asks her with genuine concern and a frown.

"No, I'm just tense because I missed my run this morning," she answers nonsensically.

"And you just pulled a fourteen hour shift watching over patients in our medical facility. It's ok to be tired. You don't have to do this, either. If you want to take Jacob upstairs and go to bed that's cool," John offers, and she shakes her head.

Sue and Hannah have been on Jacob duty all day, and John had only seen him briefly at dinner where Reagan had held him this time. The kid likes her, or at least he likes grabbing fists full of her curly hair. He can't blame him. John would like to do the same thing, but not for the same reason as Jacob who likes slobbering into it. John's reasons for wanting to sink his fists into Reagan's hair are a lot more lascivious in nature.

Reagan had changed again after dinner because Jacob had smeared the front of her shirt with mashed potatoes and gravy, though she'd changed into sterile, clean clothes before it, as well. John had realized during dinner how much they need another high-chair so that they don't have to wear most of Jacob's meal, and a crib would be great so that Reagan doesn't have to have bony baby elbows and knees in her back and side all night.

When they'd all come in for dinner, sweaty and dirty from cutting hay and firewood, welding a section of steel in the milking parlor that had worn through, doing the evening milking and feedings and also taking turns all day on patrols and spying on the visitors, Sue had announced that dinner was to be corn on the cob, mashed potatoes and meatloaf. She told John that she'd found out what his favorite meal was and had requested it from Hannah and Grams that morning just for him, which was very thoughtful. When he'd asked her why, she'd just smiled and walked away. He hadn't understood her and still doesn't, but heck, he's never understood most women. His dear sister-in-law is certainly no exception.

Reagan huffs beside him.

"No, I'm not going to bed. I want to learn this. You seem to be good at getting yourself stabbed and shot a lot, so somebody else around here should know how to do this," she teases with a smirk, glancing up at him through her long lashes.

John chuckles and would like to snatch her into his arms for a disciplinary kiss but checks that idea for fear of the .45 on her thigh. He hates to admit it, but strapped to her muscular, tan thigh it's actually sexy as hell. Combine that with the tight black V-neck, matching shorts and a pair of flip flops on her bare feet and it's almost too much for him to withstand tossing her down in the hay. He just wishes she'd dress a little more like Hannah while the visitors are here, and it's a topic that he's planning on broaching with her. He does not, however, anticipate it going well.

"Wow, thanks," John says to her, to which she shrugs playfully. He definitely likes tired Reagan better than ready for a fight and alert Reagan. This version is more relaxed, less on edge.

"How are the patients doing anyways? You and Doc didn't bring it up at dinner. Everyone was too busy asking about everything you found out today about the hadji," John inquires as he inspects one of the switches on the table.

"They are about the same, no better. What the heck is hadji?" she asks.

"Remember hadj? Hadji, hadj- same thing. It's just what we called the Muslim terrorists all over the world that we were after. During the Vietnam War the soldiers would call the enemy Charlies, and during the first and second Iraq wars they called the enemy hadjis or just hadj. It sounds better than targets one through five. Don't you agree? I don't think Grams or Hannah wants to hear us talking about target one or target two, but to us that's what they are," John explains knowing that if this was any other woman, he'd never have explained even that much. But Reagan isn't like any other woman he knows or has ever known. She can handle a good dose of violence.

"Oh, as far as I'm concerned you can call them targets."

John shouts laughter to the empty barn. She is so tempestuous. And she makes him laugh a lot, even though she doesn't necessarily mean to be funny.

"Yeah, I'm sure you would be ok with it, boss," he agrees with her, and she grins crookedly at him.

"Well they're just deadbeats, most of them. And I think they're going to end up being more trouble in the end than they're worth," Reagan concludes wisely.

John couldn't agree more. But this is Grams's brother they are also contemplating.

"Yeah, I'd say you're right about that," he concurs again.

"I'm always right," she mocks with a cocky shake of her head.

"Yeah, I'm getting that," he says with a smile, which makes Reagan look away.

"Ok, what do we do first?" she asks.

She's rearing to go of course.

"Patience, woman," John jokes, holding up his hands to her, and she slugs his arm. Ok, maybe she isn't quite tired enough yet. "I need to lay this all out and see what I've got. This was so much easier in the Army. We had all the good toys then," John says with an ornery grin.

"I bet," she agrees.

She gives him a small grin. It's progress.

Then she adds, "How come you didn't steal, I mean borrow, some Army loot like grenades and crap when you left?"

"Uh… we did. How do you think we got home?" John asks her, and Reagan nods with a frown as it dawns on her what he's saying. Out of pure habit, he takes a pack of cigarettes out of his cargo pocket and lights one up.

"What the hell? You're smoking in a barn full of hay?" she complains loudly.

"Worried about my health? Did you see all my bullet holes and wound scars?"

"No, I'm worried about you burning down the barn!" she argues and sets her hands on her hips.

John pauses a long moment to examine those curvy hips and inhales a long draw. A slow smile of appreciation spreads across his features.

"Hm," he drawls as he considers her, mostly her figure, though she probably doesn't realize it.

"What? Why are you looking at me like that? Are you even listening to me, John?" she demands impatiently.

The toe tapping commences.

"Sure, barn burning, nagging, the usual," he jokes, and she predictably frowns hard when he laughs.

He turns back to the table and holds his cigarette with his lips while he picks up different objects to explain them, ignoring her roll of the eyes move.

"Ok, see these pressure switches? We need to get them wired to the nine volt batteries that will connect to the squib that will be the explosive to complete the circuit. The circuit is like a big circle that needs completed," he explains and Reagan nods, completely tuned into him. "Pressure switches sense when there is weight on them. So it will click to complete the circuit when weight hits them either from a car or a person… and boom. The Iraqi terrorists used them to make improvised explosive devices, IED's. Utilizing their cell phones, they could detonate them. They made roadside bombs during the second war we had with them. Pussies. Hid behind their women and blew up our caravans. Real tough guys. These explosives are simple, probably why even *they* could figure them out. It's amateur hour stuff really. But they can be effective in diverting people away from the farm if we need them to," John explains.

"I think we should actually put them *on* the driveway after these assholes leave, not beside it," Reagan says with her usual lust for violence and bedlam.

John cocks his head to the side and gives a firm disapproving look. He's given the same look to Arianna a few times when she's fighting with her brother, who is way too nice to just haul off and tackle her when she's being bratty.

"Boss, how do you think Grams would like that?" he asks as Reagan looks away and shrugs. "Or Hannah? She's not like us. She'd be pretty darn upset if we went blasting away at every person that came down the drive. Trust me, if it was just us men on this farm, that's exactly how we'd handle it. But we have to think of Grams and Hannah and the kids. And most importantly we need to consider your grandpa. This is his farm, after all."

"Maybe they just need to toughen up. It's not like we have the luxury of making new friends and being all welcoming and shit anymore. Peace and love and happy-joy bullshit kinda' went out the window when the neighbors got attacked and lost half of their family in one night. Anyone that comes down that lane should be treated like a threat," she argues.

"We will, but we still need to be diplomatic about it, boss. Plus we might accidentally blow up your boyfriend," John hints and takes the cigarette out of his mouth for a moment.

"What? What boyfriend?" Reagan asks testily.

She's glaring at his cigarette.

"Mr. Reynolds?" John refers to his arch nemesis Chet, the neighbor who is too good-looking to be sniffing around here.

"Chet Reynolds is not my boyfriend. I told you that before," she counters and picks up a switch to inspect it.

He can only wonder what is whirring through her little super brain. He'd been amazed by her this morning when she'd saved that kid with Doc and then diagnosed the sickness. Later, he'd heard Doc discussing it with Sue, and he'd told her how he thought Reagan was probably right and how brilliant she was about medicine. Sue had countered with a joke about Reagan not knowing shit for dealing with people, just their illnesses. Doc had laughed heartily and agreed.

63

"Am I?" John asks playfully and gets a nasty glare, one of her many.

"Are you what?" she asks in her usual clueless, guileless demeanor.

"Am I your boyfriend, woman?" John presses further, earning a snort.

"Can we just get on with this? You're getting on my nerves, as usual."

John stares at her another minute before continuing. "Ok, have it your way. You always do," he remarks and gets a saucy smirk in return. Then she gestures toward the table of materials. "Fine. Then we'll pack fertilizer and diesel fuel and the squibs all inside of those old coffee cans. We'll do that out in the field, though, once we've got the switches and batteries rigged. We can work on those tomorrow. The last thing we do is wire in the squib so that static electricity or anything doesn't set it off. That's the final phase- arming it. And we'll use those pipes over there to also make some other similar explosives. The pressure wave or shock wave will be what kills people, not the actual explosive. Or we can put some shrapnel in for kicks if you'd like. Kind of makes a big mess, though," he tells her, and she smiles ruefully.

"Cool, so what were the rubber bands for? I saw you grab a ton of them in that craft store. Are we gonna shoot them at the bad-guys if we run out of bullets?" she inquires in her smartass tone.

John laughs loudly again, though he is actually trying to be quiet so as not to draw attention to them from the visitors' camp.

"Reagan McClane, somebody shoulda' spanked you a lot more growing up," he jokes with her, and she actually laughs once.

"Feel free to try if you feel lucky, punk," she quotes the classic Clint Eastwood movie line.

He laughs again and chucks her under the chin. His thumb stays there, though. Darn that top lip and its beckoning fullness. John looks at her sensual mouth and takes a meaningful step toward her. Even though they'd shared one, fatigue-ridden kiss in her closet when they'd returned from the city doesn't mean that she'll ever condone it again.

"I thought I smelled a cigarette…"

A woman's voice comes from around the corner, interrupting his plan of kissing Reagan. A second later the bleach blonde from the visitors' group appears, and Reagan tenses.

"Smokin' and neckin' in the barn? Boy this brings back some memories."

"You aren't supposed to be in here," John says coldly, hoping she'll go away. Not surprisingly, she doesn't leave but ambles closer.

She has four inches of black roots showing and what might be considered a rather pretty face by some men. Her shirt is cut off, barely concealing her braless breasts which are an obvious enhancement job due to the size and perkiness. She's thin, sexual and moves like a feline, and she's about five or six inches taller than Reagan. Minus the bad hair, she might have been the type of woman that John probably would've had a one night stand with on one of his leave weekends before this all happened. And the way she is looking at him, he's pretty sure he could do so again. Subtlety is not this woman's forte.

"I don't mean any harm. I was just getting water again and smelled the smoke. Got an extra?" she asks with no pretenses at being shy.

John doesn't want to be the world's biggest ass, so he takes out another cigarette and lights it for her, holding his hand near her mouth so the flame can catch.

"Thanks. Oh man, is that great or what? I haven't had a smoke in like two months."

John just nods and gives her a pained but brief grin.

"Watcha' two doing out here?" she asks peering around them.

"Making bombs to blow shit… and people up," Reagan says tersely.

She really doesn't like this chic. Well, in this woman's defense, Reagan doesn't really like most people. The boss is glaring daggers.

"That's just lovely," the woman remarks.

She speaks with slow intonations as if she has been drinking and arches an eyebrow toward John. She extends a hand to him. There is a rose tattooed on the base of her thumb, the vines twining down toward the tip.

"I'm Jasmine."

"Is that your stage name?" Reagan cuts in rudely.

John begrudgingly shakes Jasmine's hand. He is taken aback by Reagan's crass accusation but not completely surprised.

"Actually it wasn't," the woman returns.

She hits Reagan with a glare of her own, but it disappears from her face as quickly as it had appeared.

"My stage name was Kitten if you have to know."

"Shocker," Reagan returns and rolls her eyes.

"What about you? You ever do a little dancing?"

"What?" Reagan asks on a shocked gasp and half-chuckle.

"You've got a hot bod for it. You're a little short, but nothing a good pair of pumps couldn't have fixed. Bet you could've made a lot of money," Jasmine says kindly, too kindly.

She's literally checking Reagan out with more than a little interest in her gaze. Maybe he's guessed this one wrong. Perhaps she isn't interested in him, after all.

"No."

Reagan is grinding her teeth. John can actually hear it.

"She's a doctor," John defends her and leans a hip against the table and fiddles with the wiring he's still holding.

"A doctor? Aren't you a little young to be a doctor? You can't be more than eighteen" Jasmine-Kitten asks in disbelief and steps closer to John.

"She's twenty-two and she's a super genius, whiz kid," John boasts proudly, and Reagan looks astonished by this. Does she not understand his esteem of her? Well, she does now.

"Oh really? Hm, such a waste," the stripper answers on a frown.

She's starting to show her Kitten side. Being a genius doctor is a waste and being a stripper would've been a more life-affirming career choice? She puffs her cigarette and strums her fingers idly against her bare thigh below her denim micro-shorts. She's wearing blue and red cowboy boots, and John just bets that this was her former work uniform.

"You can go now," Reagan suggests coldly.

"And what about you, handsome?" Jasmine asks without acknowledging Reagan's dismissal. "What did you do before all hell broke loose? Were you a male model or an actor or an *entertainer* like me?"

66

She sneers slightly at Reagan as she emphasizes her word of choice to describe her former career. Her left eyebrow has two rings piercing it, and John can just make out part of a tattoo that must wind around behind her neck. She sports another on her slim ankle of a dragon.

"No, I was a Master Sergeant in the Army," John answers, although he's not sure why he's even wasting his time talking to this trollop.

Upon further inspection of Jasmine's face, John can tell that she's wearing makeup- a little reddish-colored lip gloss, silvery eye shadow, and mascara that has smudged slightly under her right eye. He's not used to looking at women with make-up on anymore. John is pretty sure that none of the women at the farm wear makeup. At least he doesn't think they do. Back in the day when he'd visited with Sue and Derek a few times, he'd not noticed her wearing it then, either. But Sue's pretty. It's not like her or any of the McClane women need make-up anyways. It's actually refreshing not looking at the heavy, plaster-of-Paris goop on women's faces. Once he witnessed Reagan applying some sort of lip balm. He's fairly certain it was just ChapStick, though.

"Yeah? You look like you work out a lot. I like that in a guy. I like working out, too. Maybe we should work out together some time," she suggests and licks her lower lip suggestively.

Then again, perhaps she is here for him as he'd originally suspected. She's eyeing his crotch with not too subtle implication. Her eyebrows rise with further suggestion.

John looks at Reagan and replies, "I'm pretty busy around here so probably not gonna happen."

"Oh, I get it. You two are a couple or something. It's cool," Jasmine says.

John's not quite sure what she thinks is 'cool.'

"We're not a couple," Reagan corrects her.

John could strangle her for saying it. He quickly amends her mistake, "Yes, we are."

"Sound like you two don't know what you are. I'll tell ya' what, if my man looked like you, I'd know he was my man. That's for sure," Jasmine offers.

Coming from her, it doesn't make John feel all that great.

"We have a kid together, too," John clarifies, and Reagan looks at him as if she'd like to punch him.

"Yeah? I had a kid once, too" she laments and her eyes take on a flash of regret, but it quickly flutters away.

"Did you forget it somewhere?" Reagan asks snidely.

That was harsh even for her, and John lets her know it by giving her a chiding glance. She just looks at her feet.

"No, his prick of a dad took my boy with him when he left me four years ago. He was only two at the time. He probably don't remember me now if he's even still alive. They moved to Portland," Jasmine explains.

"Maine or Oregon?" Reagan asks.

"What do you mean?"

"Never mind," Reagan says on an exasperated sigh and another roll of the green eyes.

Why is it that she is so darned cute when she does that and also so sassy? John stamps out his cigarette butt on his boot sole.

"Need some help? I can be *real* helpful."

This kitten is purring, leading John to think maybe she could also possibly be in heat.

"I'm sure you can," Reagan says.

Her own kitty claws start extending. Jasmine steps closer and touches John on his bicep with her fingertip.

"Thanks, but I think we've got it under control," John says and would like to step away, but there's nowhere to go without running over Reagan beside him.

"Sometimes it can be fun to lose control," Jasmine suggests without the slightest trace of restrained subtlety.

"Maybe another time," John says trying to get rid of her.

"Why don't you go back to your tent," Reagan spits.

John notices her emphasis on the word 'tent' to be purposely insulting. This woman used to dance around without her clothes on for a dollar. Pride isn't going to get in her way of much.

"You know where to find me," Kitten purrs again.

She touches John square in the middle of his chest with her index finger. Jasmine spins like she's working a pole and saunters off with a vulgar wiggle, blowing a kiss over her shoulder at him. A full minute goes by before John peeks around the corner to make sure she's gone. She's making her way across the yard toward their camp, but she is not carrying anything to transport water. John decides not to share this information with Reagan. When he goes back to the table, the boss is seething.

"I can be *real helpful.* Argh. What a bimbo!" Reagan says in an awful, imitating voice of Kitten. "I'll just bet she can be helpful."

"She is special," John concedes, deciding to go with this to see where it leads, though he knows they should get right to work, having wasted too much time with the professional dancer.

Reagan runs her finger down his bicep and then his chest and prances around in front of him emulating Jasmine the stripper further. Then she does a fake giggle.

"Are you a model? Oh!"

"Ok, boss. So she isn't a brain surgeon like you, but she was nice and obviously not a threat," John says. If she touches him like that again, he is going to kiss her and she's not going to like it one bit. When the stripper had done it, John had felt nothing. When Reagan had done it without even doing it seriously, he'd gotten a surge of lust that shot straight to his groin, though he's positive she has no idea of it.

"Target six," Reagan says on an angry pucker and a defiant crossing of the arms across the chest.

"Wait a minute. Are you jealous?" he asks with skepticism and blinks hard.

"What? No!" she retorts angrily and way too hurriedly.

She is jealous, a little. John's quite sure of it.

"Hold the phone, I think you are," John counters and leans against the table again, crossing his arms over his chest, too. Reagan for some reason is staring at his arms, and her lips part slightly.

"Get real. Why would I be jealous? If you want to have sex with her, then go for it but don't come whining for antibiotics when you catch something," Reagan says sarcastically.

She starts picking up their supplies to give them a mock examination. John's got her number. She acts like this when she's nervous and usually avoiding him. Or trying to.

"That's a bit assuming don't you think? You don't know anything about her. That's kind of judgmental of you, boss," John says in jest mostly. Of course Jasmine is a skank. It was written all over her... everything.

"No, I think I can figure that one out. I may not be as worldly as you or a man whore like you…"

"Hey!"

"What? And you aren't… or weren't before this shit happened?"

"Have you seen me screwing around since coming here?" John asks.

"There's not exactly a plethora of tail to chase around here. And yeah, I've got you figured out. You were a playboy womanizer before. I can tell," Reagan judges.

She's right, but he sure as heck isn't going to admit to it. He doesn't like her thinking badly of him. She's the only woman he's ever wanted to impress, and the only one he's ever encountered who isn't.

"There's only one girl I've been chasing, and she's kind of dense when it comes to how I feel about her. Or else she's in denial. I'm not sure which," John throws an insult her way and takes a step toward her. She backs down and glances away. "And look, it's not a bad idea, boss, to let these people think you're with me."

"Why would I want to do that? Jasmine has obviously got her eye on you. Maybe you can take her up on her offer. Hey, maybe you can go with her when she leaves, too!" Reagan chides loudly.

Man, she is jealous because she won't drop it. He tries to redirect her anger.

"We don't know what those men out there are like, but they seem like sewer sludge. I'm just saying it might be a good thing if you stuck close to me most of the time while they're here. Let them think we're a couple."

"I can take care of myself. Besides most of the time I'll likely be in the med shed," she says stubbornly and juts out her chin.

It's John's turn to grind his teeth. Why does she always have to be so bull-headed?

"Fine, do what you want. You always do," John says through his teeth. "And another thing, you need to dress more conservatively than you do while they're here. Let's not give them a reason to step out of line and make me kill them. I'd rather Grams and the kids and your own little sister *not* see that side of me, babe. It was bad enough that you had to."

Reagan frowns hard and won't make eye contact. "No shit. That wasn't exactly pleasant, Doctor Death," she taunts, using his military nickname.

John doesn't encourage her sassy mouth, but continues on while ignoring her comment. "Just try to cover up a little more while they're here, 'kay?"

"What? I'm not exactly dressed like your stripper friend," Reagan says impatiently.

"She's not my friend. She is a stripper, though, or was," John jokes.

"Yes, she has many lovely talents, I'm sure. But I'm not parading around here ninety percent naked like her," she argues petulantly.

"No, but could you at least wear some jeans or a baggier shirt or something, Reagan? Would it kill you to listen to me just this once?"

"It's hot. In case you haven't noticed it's the end of summer and still hot?"

"Yeah, I know," John runs a hand through his hair in frustration. She is like talking to a brick wall. "But those scumbags were checking you and Hannah out, Reagan. And even Sue. It's bad enough that you wear that stuff around me and I have to look at your body in your tiny shorts and tank tops. I've got a strict moral code that I live by. I don't think those guys have any morals or a code."

"They were looking at us like that?" Reagan asks quietly.

Her troubled eyes drift off to the side, staring at nothing. Her hand goes to the hem of her shirt where it meets her shorts and nervously fidgets. John places his hand over hers, and Reagan's eyes dart to his. He can read the fear there. It's almost always there. It's just sometimes more suppressed than other times.

"Hey, I don't want to scare you. That's not why I'm telling you this. I just want you to be careful. Don't worry. This is just like the city. Nobody's gonna hurt you, ok?" John reassures her, and she nods without blinking as she stares directly into his eyes. Instead of jerking her hand back, she slides it slowly from his. More progress.

"Let's just work on the demos, ok?" John asks her, softening his tone.

"Yeah," she answers shakily.

They work together for an hour. John explains in more detail how the demos will work and how to assemble them. As usual, she catches on quickly, freakishly so. He takes his time to thoroughly expound on the different items, the way they go together and how they will perform to keep the farm more secure.

"For the record, I don't want to have sex with Jasmine the Kitten, ok?" John confirms with a smirk, and she grimaces at him like he's being disgusting.

"Do what you want. I don't know why the hell you think I care what you do. I don't! I'm not your mom," Reagan returns.

"No kidding. Thanks for the update. I don't want you to be my mom, idiot," he uses one of her favorite insults against her. Her eyes bulge as she purses her lips in anger. Kelly was right. Sometimes being a dick does work more effectively.

Before she can even let out a retort, Kelly comes into their work area, and Reagan splits for the house and to check on her grandpa who is on medical duty. According to his watch it's nearly 22:30. John doesn't even like her walking from the barn to the house or the med shed unescorted, but Cory should be on guard duty and making his rounds while Derek catches his first dose of sleep before he starts. Kelly will be relieved by John, and he and Derek will start watch at 04:00.

"Hey, bro," Kelly says as he comes over to the table. "Everything ok with the little Doc?"

"Yeah, same old same old with that situation. How's the haj pack?" John inquires of the visitors.

"Looks like they're staying where they should. You notice anything?" Kelly asks.

His friend picks up a switch and begins wiring it. Most of the men in their unit know basic demos, but John just had a wider range interest in them. He'd studied with the best in the Army and had become an expert.

"Not much. Sounds like a couple of them need their skulls cracked from what Reagan told us at dinner, but they've been quiet so far. Not sure if that'll last or not," he tells his friend.

"Yeah, me either. Uncle Peter, or piece of shit as Doc calls him, came and got the two kids that were hangin' around the med shed and made them go back to the camp. Doc said he thinks they keep them around to make them do all the work, but we're not sure

72

on that just yet. But it seems to me that mostly the men out there sit on their asses. Saw that woman come this way earlier. Did she come back here?"

"Uh huh," John responds noncommittally.

"What did she want?"

John doesn't answer but gives Kelly a very telling look.

"Ohhh, that would be why the little Doc looked so pissed. Well, more than normal."

"Yeah, I guess. It's not like I'm gonna act on it, though. She's not exactly my type, not anymore," John reveals unnecessarily to his oldest friend who knows him so well already.

"Yeah, heard you were more into the intellectual types now," Kelly says with a laugh.

"Yeah, that's really gonna get me somewhere, huh?"

"Maybe, you never know. How did it go in the city with her? I mean I know you told me and Derek about killing those dudes and all that but how was the trip with her?"

"Not great. She got to see some of my special talents, and I don't think she liked it. I think it scared the crap out of her actually," John relays as he wires into a battery.

"I'm sure she understands, though. She's smart as hell. Kind of intimidating, and not just for her nasty mouth," Kelly jokes.

John laughs with him and nods.

"I don't know, man. I just don't know if she's ever gonna be able to let whatever happened to her go. She's pretty messed up," John confides. This is the first time he and Kelly have ever talked like this. Heck, it's the first time he's ever talked about a woman or his feelings about one with someone because before Reagan there hadn't been one worth talking about.

"She'll come around. If anyone can help her, it's you. Not me, bro. And not your brother, either. That dude would probably tell her to run ten miles or something. He's not exactly Mr. Touchy Feely. But he is good in a tight spot, and there's nobody other than you or Cory that I'd trust with my life," Kelly says.

John appreciates the compliment about his brother.

"Or Hannah's?" John pries with a knowing smile. His friend doesn't answer.

Finally, without looking up from his battery, after a few long moments of silence, Kelly finally admits, "Yeah, or Hannah's."

"What's going on with that situation, huh?" John teases as he turns the table on Kelly.

"Nothing. Nothing new," Kelly tells him evasively. "What are we turning gay or something? We're talking about our feelings and women and shit like a couple of bitches."

John laughs loudly at his friend's crudeness.

"I'm actually wanting to spoon with someone right now," John says with deadly earnestness and then laughs.

"I'm thinking about taking up fuckin' flower arranging," Kelly says.

They both laugh gregariously.

Kelly adds, "I'm outta here, bro. Gonna go check on the hadj dipshits."

"Yeah, me, too. Gotta get my beauty sleep. Think I'll do a mani-pedi and a facial before I go to bed," John says as they leave the barn together with the bag loaded.

"I always knew you were queer," Kelly says.

They laugh again, bump fists and part ways. His giant friend stealthily moves through the buildings and barely makes a sound. What John didn't tell Kelly is that there wasn't anyone he'd rather have watch his back, not even Derek.

When he gets to the third floor attic space after taking a quick shower and wrapping in a towel, he spies Jacob dead asleep in Reagan's bed, and she is at her desk still reading. The lights out rule has been bumped back an hour to dissuade the visitors in becoming curious about their use of electricity, but Reagan is reading by an extremely faint light, and she has drawn the blinds and draperies on the windows. He checks the book she's reading and sees that it's *Micropathology* something or other. Her slightly damp hair is coiled into a bun on top of her head and held there with chopsticks. She's wearing what appears to be only a baggy, thin shirt and panties. How can she be so completely unaware of what she does to him?

"Are you done hovering over my shoulder?" she asks.

She does this without pausing in reading because she turns the page and makes a note on the pad beside her.

"Maybe," he returns.

"You need to go put on some clothes."

She points without turning toward the closet where she's finally allotted him a tiny amount of space for his newly acquired clothing and shoes.

"So do you. And why should I? Does it bother you?" he taunts. A drip from his hair hits her naked thigh and makes her jump. He'd like to demonstrate for her exactly how much her outfit bothers him.

"Go!" she says almost loudly enough to wake Jacob.

John chuckles and pinches her earlobe between his thumb and index finger lightly before he leaves for the closet.

He changes quickly into boxers and cotton shorts that hang low and crookedly on his hips. He hangs the towel on the hook she's told him he can use. It's kind of hard to argue about more space when he is still basically a guest and an unwanted resident of the bedroom's owner. When he's finished in the closet, he goes to the small area between the living room and her desk where he commences with push-ups.

"What are you doing? Aren't you tired?" she asks and turns to face him.

What he'd like to tell her is that what he's doing is enjoying the view of her bare legs, but he doesn't because he's not totally ignorant and would like to keep his manhood intact.

"If you only knew what a day in my life used to be like, you wouldn't question a hundred push-ups," he tells her and she continues to stare.

"You should get some rest because your shift starts in less than four hours," she reprimands.

John easily ignores her mothering.

"We used to work out all the time in the Army just for fun. I'm not getting regular workouts anymore, so I figured I'd better stay frosty," he informs her. It's either this or sex with her, he'd also like to tell her.

"You are working out. It's just a different kind. You guys are working hard around here and none of you are getting a lot of sleep, either."

He'd like to offer up another workout that she hasn't considered which he'd like to add to his daily activity. It's as if her silky, tanned skin is beckoning him, daring him to touch it.

"You worried about me?" John asks as he switches to one arm for ten counts and then the other.

"No," she says too dramatically to be believable.

"How are the patients? Did you talk to your grandpa?"

"Yes, I talked to him. They aren't doing any better. As a matter of fact, the woman is worse. It will be a miracle if her body doesn't abort that pregnancy. She's thin, dehydrated, malnourished, but we got her to eat a little bit," she grinds out with a goodly amount of helpless anger and frustration.

She rakes a hand roughly through her curls. She sighs long and loud.

"The boy, on the other hand, is the same. It doesn't seem good to me. That's why I'm reading this. I'm hoping I can find an answer that will help."

Reagan goes back to the book and back to chewing the end of her pencil.

"That sucks. I don't want that kid to die. His brother is gonna be devastated. I would've been at that age if Derek would've died," he tells her honestly. No kid should ever have to deal with the death of a sibling. However, no kid should have to deal with any of the crap they are all dealing with now. Heck, most of the time this crap is too heavy for adults to handle.

"I know. I want to let him spend time with his brother, but I don't want the kid to see his brother die or be there if it happens," Reagan says.

She's showing more compassion than John had thought her possible. It's a good sign.

"Yeah, that's a tough call. What about those other kids? Sam and Simon?" John asks her as he finishes his last set of twenty.

"They both seem cool. Fucked up and getting dealt the shit end of the stick from those morons out there I think. But they're nice for all they've been through would be my guess," Reagan says.

She swivels in her chair to face him as he finishes and stands again.

"What do you think the family's gonna do? About those kids that are with the group?" John clarifies.

Reagan doesn't answer right away but rubs her shoulder and neck and then a hand over her face. She's beat.

"I don't know," she says after a moment. "I can't exactly get clear information from Sam, and Simon hardly comes around. I just don't know what the situation is with some of them."

John thinks for a moment before answering. "I sure wish we did. I don't like having a bunch of strangers running around here all day long. Frank's obviously a dick. Grams's brother is a stoner. And some of the other ones look like ex-cons. It's not exactly making me feel comfortable having them here, especially not with you three women on the farm."

"What's that mean? Like we're wimpy or something?" she asks snippily.

"No, I just mean that I don't like them being around you and your sisters. You're all good-looking women, boss. I don't want them to get any ideas."

"I can handle myself," she argues as usual.

"Yeah? You sure about that?" John returns testily. Sometimes her bull-headedness is irritating. "What about Hannah and Sue? Can they handle themselves?"

Reagan doesn't answer. He's apparently hit a nerve with this comment. Good. She needs to get shaken up a bit. These people could be dangerous to the well-being of the farm. They could be dangerous to the family if they find a way to get to weapons. Reagan wearily rubs at her neck again.

"Want a shoulder rub?" he offers and her eyes let him know that she thinks he's out of his mind. "Hey, I know you think I'm not able to control my baser urges, but trust me I can. Plus, I'm pooped, so you're off the hook for tonight. Just turn your skinny butt around, and I'll rub the tension out for you before we go to bed."

"I go to bed and you go to bed, not *we* go to bed," she makes sure to correct.

John smirks at her. She's so stinking cute.

"Yeah, that's what I meant," he teases and twirls his finger in the air to show her to copy it. She shakes her head. "Quit being a wimp. Turn around."

"I'm not a wimp."

She takes the bait like John knew she would.

"If you say so," he tugs the line.

"Fine."

She gets hooked so easily and turns back to her book. John places his hands tentatively on her thin shoulders fully expecting her to jump or cringe from his touch, but she doesn't. Another small victory.

He rubs and gets an instant, "Ow! Geesh, that hurts. You aren't rubbing Kelly's shoulders!"

"Sorry, forgot how scrawny you are," John apologizes with a chuckle and rubs her thin neck and shoulders more gently this time. "You're so critical. Do I need to remind you that this is a free massage? Just try to sit still and let me help."

Reagan is so tense she's like rubbing steel and wire, but he eventually gets the kinks worked out, causing her to loosen up slightly. She's been so stressed out lately, and John's been worrying about her. First the city trip, which was beyond harrowing, and now these people living on the farm has sent her into pressure-cooker mode.

After a few minutes, John believes she's forgotten that his hands are on her at all because she makes another notation and flips about ten pages, looking for something. He allows his hands to travel up the back of her neck into her hair where he rubs out more knots. Then it's back down to the shoulders, but he never travels elsewhere because he doesn't want to freak her out. This is serious progress in the no touching rule. He's tired, sleep-deprived and he knows he has to get up soon for his watch, but this is well worth losing a little shut-eye over.

Reagan rubs her forehead and squints her eyes tightly.

"Got a headache?" John asks to which she nods absentmindedly.

"I just can't figure this out. It's so fucking frustrating," she growls angrily.

"Hey, potty mouth, you'll get it. Good grief, Reagan. You impress me every day with the stuff you know about medicine. If anyone is gonna be able to save those two, it's you, honey," John tells her honestly and, like an idiot, without thinking bends and presses an encouraging kiss to the side of her neck. That bolts her straight out of the chair.

"What the fuck was that?" she nearly yells.

John blinks twice in surprise at her. Jacob stirs and fusses once but goes right back to sleep.

78

"I'm... I'm sorry. It was just... I wasn't thinking. Sorry, boss. It just seemed...I don't know how to describe it to you. I was just trying to comfort you. I don't know. Crap. I was just trying to make you feel better. Sorry, Reagan. Don't be mad. It won't happen again, ok?" John pleads and puts his hands up, palms toward her.

She's staring at his hands, the same hands that she'd watched him kill men with just a few days ago. Her breathing is faster, her chest rising and falling at an accelerated rate. He takes a step toward her as she takes two in retreat. Her eyes dart to her desk, and John knows that she's looking at her .45. Great. Now they're back to square one again.

"Let's just go to bed, ok? You to yours and me to mine," he tries a joke but crashes and burns.

When he turns his back, he catches in his peripheral vision as she snatches the .45 from the desk. She can move fast when she wants to. The light on the desk is clicked off next.

She slinks around him and practically dives into her bed where she stashes the gun under her pillow. She's not taking her eyes off of him. Even in the dark John knows instinctively that she's watching him. He sighs heavily.

"Reagan, don't you think if I was going to do something like force myself on you that I would've done it in the cabin or during any of the three hundred hours of trail riding we did to get to the city?" he says, sarcastically making light of that trail ride from Hell.

She won't answer him, but John hopes that in her big nerd brain that she's reasoning out what he's just told her. She should be able to make sense of it that way. There have been plenty of opportunities for him to just take what he wanted from her. And want her he does. She is practically all he thinks of anymore. But he doesn't want her on his terms. He needs her to want to be with him and to let go of the fear she carries with her. John is beginning to lose hope that it will ever happen.

Chapter Six
Kelly

Last night before his watch shift had started, even though he should've been catching forty winks, Kelly had sat on the front porch swing with Hannah and talked with her for a while. It also gave him the perfect opportunity to keep an eye on the visitors. John and Derek had still been up, but the rest of the family, including her grandmother, had retired. Doc had been in the shed with the sick patients, so Kelly had felt like it was safe to steal away with Hannah for a few minutes of discreet alone time.

It had been great. It had been great talking, holding hands, occasionally risking a kiss and getting to know her even better. She is by far the most interesting woman he's ever met in his entire life. She is so intelligent and talented and funny. She actually makes him laugh out loud sometimes. He hasn't done that for a while. Her generosity of spirit is almost shocking to him. He'd lost his generosity toward his fellow man. Twelve solid years of fighting in wars had killed that within him. The current events of the world aren't exactly helping with that or instilling some newfound humanitarian drive within him, either. Kelly still doesn't believe that he deserves her. But, unfortunately for Hannah's lack of better character assessment, she's chosen him, and Kelly couldn't be happier.

For the first time in a long time, he actually feels happy. There aren't any desert countries to fly off to and sweat his ass off fighting terrorists; no mountainous regions to drop in by helicopter for a quick mission of intel gathering or sniper style shooting of some turd; no swampy, mosquito-infested, third world marshlands to sneak into for a snatch and grab of a drug dealer. There just isn't any more warring for shit that they didn't need involved with in the first place.

His purpose on this earth finally makes perfect sense. There is just Hannah, and she is all he'll ever need, all he never even knew he needed. His one goal in life is to keep her and his young siblings safe. If in doing so he also keeps her family safe, then that's just fine with him. But she is now priority number one.

It had been great just talking quietly on the porch, watching fireflies dance about in the night sky. It had been great until he'd spied a couple of the men from the visitors' group wandering around in the pitch dark equipment shed. There was even a clanging of metal on metal as they must've been rummaging through things. He'd quickly snatched up his night vision goggles to ascertain who it might be. His rifle was also at his side in case he needed it.

Derek had appeared at the side of the house before Kelly could even rise from the swing and had gone straight to them after a quick nod to Kelly. After a few minutes of what sounded like heated accusation and unveiled threats on Derek's part, the men had returned to their camp. It had been great. Past tense. It hadn't been so great after that because he'd been left too unsettled to sit any longer with Hannah and had sent her in to bed. Not before he'd stolen a kiss at her bedroom door, of course. Then it was back outside with John and Derek.

Now as he drags his ass out of bed and up the basement stairs at eight a.m. after about a whopping five hours of sleep for the third night in a row, the first thing he sees is Great-uncle Peter at the island in the kitchen, Hannah at the back counter and Grams cooking at the stove. Not exactly the greeting he'd been hoping for this morning. The only redeeming moment is when John comes in the back door. He's probably headed upstairs for a few hours of rest since he's been up since four.

"Good morning, Kelly," Grams offers up a sunny greeting.

He merely grin-grimaces and nods once. She simply smiles and turns back to her recipe box while continuing on with their conversation as if Peter being in the kitchen is nothing out of the ordinary. The man is her brother, after all, which puts Kelly in a bad conundrum since he'd like to throw his ass off the back porch. He sizes up the other man and his smaller stature and is fairly sure he could get some hang time with this lump.

"Peter was just reminding me of something our mother used to make for as when we were children. It's a pound cake, and I just know I have that recipe around here somewhere."

John has halted right inside the back door as if he can't believe what he's seeing, either. His scowl is one of downright anger, pure anger that is unsheathed for all to see. What the hell is that about? He allows the screen door to shut quietly behind him without taking his blue eyes off of Grams's brother.

Peter ignores John and gives Kelly a wolfish smile, revealing three missing teeth.

He says, "Maryanne, that sure would taste good. Haven't had Mom's pound cake in years. Haven't had much to eat at all lately."

"Why's that?" Kelly asks as Hannah hands him a plate of breakfast leftovers. It matches the empty one in front of Peter.

His woman's great-uncle asks for and receives seconds from Grams. Suddenly even the smell of the women's cooking cannot bring back Kelly's appetite. He forces himself to eat, but he refuses to sit at the center island near Peter. He takes up a defensive stance near Hannah and consumes his food while standing.

""Cuz, man, there ain't crap for food at our camp," he whines for sympathy.

"So go on a run for it. You can hit the cities for food and supplies. Hit abandoned homes," John practically demands in an unfriendly tone. "Take up residence in one of those homes," his friend hints with zero subtlety.

"It ain't as easy as it looks, man," Peter whines again. "It's real dangerous out there, Maryanne. Couple of the dudes we was traveling with got killed raiding homes."

"Yeah? Try raiding the ones that don't still have people living in them. That might work a little better for you," John says with open antagonism.

Kelly almost feels bad for Grams's brother. He's also wondering if Grams is getting pissed at John, but she doesn't show it or seem to be. Peter doesn't answer, and John has moved toward the stove where Grams serves him a plate of warm breakfast food. His friend of so many years also stands while eating his breakfast.

"Peter, do you and your friends out there have enough food to last for a while or do you need to go and get food somewhere?" Hannah asks firmly.

This surprises Kelly. It surprises him that she doesn't just propose to give them all of the food from the pantry, the garden, the cellar and the storage of canned goods along with offering the basement bunk rooms for sleeping.

Peter repeats Hannah's words as if astonished by them, "Go get food?"

"Right. Go and get food as in go out to the city and search for supplies like food," Kelly elucidates.

John jumps in with his own suggestion. "Might be a good idea anyways. You and your group could scout around for a new place to live while you're at it."

"This place here is fine for right now if you ask me," Peter counters smoothly.

"But Grandpa has made it clear that your friends can't stay here, Uncle Peter," Hannah says, shocking everyone in the room.

Peter will not be put off, however. He shifts his argument to the one weak link in the family.

"It's dangerous as all get out, Maryanne. We even talked to a group that was from South Carolina. They said there ain't crap over there no more. The ocean level rose so much that everyone just drownded, man. There ain't no cities left over there. And we heard California is just as bad. Frank's brother lived in Vancouver and he said it's real bad there, too. But then he went and got killed the first week into this crap. Frank found that out from his other brother. We met up with him and his group in Ohio, but they decided to split for the west instead of come here with us. That's where we was gonna' go, but not now. That's when I remembered this place. I knew you'd let us stay here, Maryanne," he drones.

John softly groans with irritation beside Kelly. He's glad that Peter didn't bring a whole other group to the farm, too. Thank God for small miracles. Keeping an eye on the small group he's with is proving difficult enough.

"You aren't staying here. Not forever," John corrects the great-uncle.

"We'll see," Peter mumbles.

He shoots a glance toward John and Kelly that has an underlying malice to it. John looks ready to strangle this weasel. Kelly is also not thrilled with the living arrangement on the farm, but this type of behavior from John is unusual. His friend is usually a cut-up, the life of the party, the funny guy. Kelly's seen this other side many times before, though, and it didn't usually end well for whomever John was aiming his wrath. Back then it was usually an interrogation suspect or a tense, mission type of situation that brought this out of him, so it had been apropos. Now it somehow makes sense again. His friend has a lot to lose on this farm.

John badgers on, "No, we won't see. Doc already laid down the rules. When the sick are better, your caravan is out of here. There's no renegotiation."

"I haven't talked to Herb about it yet, but I see it as we could be helpful around here if we stayed on," Peter argues stupidly.

Kelly almost laughs. How the hell could they possibly be helpful? They've not offered to lift a finger since they've been here, not even to take care of their own sick people or children.

John looks ready to yank Peter off of his stool at the island to take him out back for a good old-fashioned ass whipping. Kelly is also not feeling the love where Peter is concerned.

"Doc has all the help he needs now with us staying on the farm," Kelly interjects.

"Yeah, but you ain't family and I am," Peter says with way too much confidence.

"They're family, too, Uncle Peter," Hannah says defensively.

She goes back to mixing and measuring some concoction or another at the counter.

"They ain't family, Hannah," he argues again with less patience and more temper showing.

"Derek is married to Sue, Peter. Don't you remember?" Grams asks. "And John is his brother and Kelly and the kids are like family. They take care of a lot around here."

"They're very helpful on the farm," Hannah says more quietly this time.

"Well, we'd be *more* help if the rest of us stayed on the farm," Peter responds.

He shovels in his food as if he hasn't eaten in a while.

"It's not happening, man," John says with more force.

This gains his friend a quick glare from Grams's brother.

84

"Besides, why did you bring all those people here in the first place?" Kelly asks with a touch of accusation. "You coulda' just came by yourself."

"'Cuz they're my friends, man. We watch each other's backs," he answers and then adds. "Plus, like I said, we were hoping to help out."

Kelly doesn't believe this for a minute. This man until now has made no effort to be helpful one bit. John even harrumphs rudely beside him.

"We've got it under control. The harvest is about done, so we really wouldn't need help now anyways," Kelly says coldly. "The sooner you guys find your own place to hole up the better. It'll take some time to get established somewhere, and then next planting season you'll have a lot to work out... amongst yourselves."

"You could maybe find a farm nearby, Peter," Grams comments with more than a little suggestion.

This is surprising, to say the least, coming from Grams. Kelly had not thought she would have it in her to turn away her own brother. She has obviously had a slight change of heart regarding extended stays of unwanted family members on the farm.

Peter reddens in the face slightly.

"What about if we get sick again? Or what if we get shot or something, Maryanne? What then, huh? It ain't like you can get to a doctor anymore. The hospitals are gone, Maryanne, gone!"

"Herb and I have been talking about it, and he may set his practice back up in town," she tells them all.

This is the first Kelly's hearing of this. It's not at all a good idea. As a matter of fact, it would be highly dangerous to even consider something like that this soon.

"What?" John asks with the same level of shock.

"He said that he and Reagan could go to town once a week and offer free medical care for a while until things get back to normal," Grams says.

She just keeps chopping tomatoes like it's no big deal what she's just informed them of.

"No way," John blurts. "There's no way she's going to town once a week. Doc either. It's not safe."

"Honey, there aren't any doctors around to help the sick or injured," Grams tries at soothing John. "Like Peter said, the hospitals are closed. The urgent cares are gone. The doctors have all abandoned their practices. People will need medical care, John."

"I'm well aware of what's going on out there, Grams, but it just isn't safe for either of them to just set up shop like nothing at all has happened," John debates further.

"Herb and Reagan have been talking about it for a few weeks now…" Grams starts again, only to be interrupted by John.

"No!" he says more firmly.

Kelly stays his friend with a hand to his thick forearm. John makes brief eye contact but pushes on with the discussion. His ire isn't geared toward Grams, Kelly knows. He's just frustrated at the topic. However, Kelly doesn't want John to upset her. They all care about Grams as if she were their own grandmother.

"Grams, I just came back from the city with her. I don't want to have to tell you how many times she could've been killed. I say no. This isn't happening."

"They aren't talking about setting up in Clarksville," Hannah offers to lighten the mood and be more hopeful. "Grandpa meant going back to his own practice in our small town of Pleasant View. Perhaps in the spring it will start to improve. Maybe they can do it then, Grams."

"That's really not any better, Hannah," Kelly concurs with John, who looks fit to be tied. Hannah won't be put off, though.

"People like Uncle Peter and his friends could come to the practice in the springtime to seek medical care. It would also give them time to consider this idea and to prepare the practice again for use. I'm sure that it has been looted…"

"Oh, yeah," Peter jumps in. "It's been ransacked! We drove past it. I even stopped in to see if there was any… medicine stuff that we could use to help our sick people. But let me tell ya' someone got there long before we did. That place was trashed."

Kelly is quite sure that Peter and his group helped add to the overall ransacked feel of the practice that had no doubt once been Doc's pride and joy. And he seriously doubts if Peter or some of the others with him were searching for antibiotics at Doc's building in town to treat their ill travel mates. He's seen enough of the visitors' behavior to realize that most of them are former and likely still even

86

current drug addicts. The pot smell near their camp at night is sometimes nauseating when he's doing his perimeter checks. Where the hell had they found enough of a stash to last this long? Perhaps one of them had been a dealer or grower.

"They could have a few of you stand guard while they take care of the sick," Hannah tries again to soothe the situation. She is quick to amend her statement and add, "I mean, in the spring when things improve more."

John doesn't answer. He's fuming quietly and biting his lower lip hard enough to draw blood if he doesn't stop. His protectiveness over Reagan almost beats out Kelly's need to hover near Hannah at all times.

"See? It will all work itself out," Grams blesses the grim situation. Then she goes on the offensive with her brother again. "But, Peter, you should not have brought people so ill to our farm. We could all be killed by this sickness. You knew that Sue and Derek had small children and now they have a new baby, as well."

"It's just a cold, Maryanne. It ain't no big deal like that," her brother reveals his ignorance again.

"A cold?" John almost shouts. "Dude, that *cold* has already killed four people in your group! Are you serious?"

"Maybe they had something else, something different. I don't know," Peter says and then comes back with, "Hey, it's probably 'cuz we ain't got much for food. Yeah, they are probably just tired or malnourishmented or something."

His love of the English language is also apparent as Kelly listens to him yammer on about their low food supplies, how hard it is out there, how difficult it is to find food, blah, blah bullshit. John and Reagan went to the city for a few days and brought back supplies, some of which were food items.

"Are you out of food completely, Peter?" Grams asks with a bit of exasperation.

No wonder. She's likely been carrying this deadbeat her whole life. Kelly's only been around him less than a full week and already he wants to kick his ass and then kick it to the curb for good measure.

"No, we've still got some. Kids found some berries in the woods near the drive the other day, too. We had them pick some and cooked them in pancakes. But a hot shower sure would feel great about now," he hints.

"We don't have hot water. No electric to the hot water tanks, dude. Sorry," John lies easily.

Neither Grams nor Hannah contradict this falsehood, and for that, Kelly is thankful.

"Hm, really? Well, that sucks I guess," he laments.

"I can offer you a bar of soap, though," Grams says kindly.

She's too kind in Kelly's opinion. This guy doesn't deserve shit.

Hannah adds, "It's good soap. You can even wash your laundry with it."

Peter is visibly disappointed that the offer isn't more, but he nods with reluctance anyways.

"You can take that bucket of tomatoes if you'd like. The ones in the sink?" Grams declares with a gesture toward the wide, ceramic sink. "Share them with your friends, Peter. You can share the soap, too. There's plenty of both to go around. The vitamins in the tomatoes will help you and your friends stay healthy."

"Aww, Maryanne, you know I never liked tomatoes," he whines.

This guy is unreal. Here the world has gone to shit, he's obviously malnourished and he's upset about a free food handout? Unbelievable.

"Just eat them anyway, Peter. They're good for you. Now if you don't mind, I have a lot of work to do. We *all* do," she says firmly, dismissing him from her kitchen in this single scolding.

"Ok, Maryanne. Thanks for the breakfast," Peter replies.

He gathers the soap and the tomatoes and leaves through the front door. John follows him, locking it after he is gone.

"You ok, Grams?" Kelly asks her. It seems like this interaction with her brother has left her downtrodden and tired. Maybe Hannah was right. Maybe Grams needs more rest.

She sighs and nods before answering.

"Sure, Kelly. I'm just fine, dear. My brother has just always been... well, like that."

"If it helps any, they always say that there's one in every family," John tells her as he comes back into the kitchen.

She laughs softly, but it doesn't reach her eyes.

"Kel, talk to you outside?" John requests with a nod to the back door.

Kelly nods in return and they leave Hannah and Grams in the kitchen to their duties. He'd like nothing better than to pull her close, hug her for comfort and give her a quick peck. However, there are simply too many witnesses about.

Once he and John are in the backyard near the chicken coop, his friend lays it out.

"I already told that dick first thing this morning not to go in the house," he says angrily.

His friend runs a hand through his hair roughly, making it stand on end.

"What do you mean?" Kelly asks him.

"Peter!" John hisses. "I ran into him trying to go in the front door of the house, and we had it out already about it. He said that he was going in to visit his sister, and I told him no. We argued and he left- or so I thought he did. He must've sneaked around back when we weren't watching and Grams let him in back there. Probably because she didn't know I already told him to beat it."

"Shit," Kelly swears with exhaustion. The situation with these guests of theirs is tiring already. He peers toward the visitors' camp, spying one of them coming out of the woods carrying a basket just as Peter is arriving there.

"I don't care if he is family. I don't trust him," John asserts with a grimace.

They both silently observe as Peter shows the others in his group the bucket of tomatoes and the bar of soap. Kelly has watched and then aided with the laundry soap preparation in the mudroom. First they boil down the bar of yellow soap, which Hannah says is great for combatting itchy poison ivy outbreaks, as well. Then they mix it with a five gallon bucket full of hot water and a cup of some other type of laundry washing formula mixed with Borax. It's a very old recipe for laundry soap and costs only about a penny per load, not that the cost matters anymore. However, the fact that it lasts five times longer than traditional laundry soap will help them get by during these hard times.

Two of the men from the group are visibly arguing, bitching at Peter, who doesn't seem to be sticking up for himself too much.

This group as a whole is obviously not being led by Great-uncle Peter. The men complaining are gesturing wildly with their hands and arms in a full-on vent. Kelly would like to know what this is all about. Are they angry about Peter not bringing more food back to the camp? Was Peter supposed to have negotiated a permanent stay on the farm? Hot showers for everyone? Who knows? One of the men even shoves Peter to the shoulder roughly. Levon and Frank are the two men who are being so verbally combative with the uncle. Peter is starting to get louder, and the event looks like it is about to become explosive. Just in the nick of time, Levon's cousin, Rick, comes to intervene on Uncle Peter's behalf and peace seems to be restored, temporarily.

"I don't trust *any* of them, my friend," Kelly says calmly as he continues to stare at the group.

Frank slaps the stripper Jasmine on her ass and yanks her toward the RV. Whether or not she wants to go with him, Kelly's not sure, but she does. Frank slams the door to the bus, and neither of them comes back out. Kelly doesn't see the other woman at all. Also, a few of the men are missing. That kid, Bobby, who seems aggressive for someone so young is missing and so is Willy. This man is strange, and Kelly and John have been wondering about his mental faculties. He's quirky, slightly off and definitely eccentric. The other day, he was talking to himself, and John said that he was doing it again the day he'd caught him in the hog barn. Sometimes he babbles in Spanish, which neither he nor John speak, so it makes it difficult to figure out what the hell he's talking about. According to John, though, when he rambles in English, it doesn't make a whole lot more sense.

"Just keep a keen eye, Kelly," John warns prophetically.

It is completely unnecessary.

"Yep," he agrees readily with his friend as he adjusts the sling of his rifle to sit more comfortably against his shoulder.

He also double checks the holster on his hip that contains his 9 mill as he and John walk toward the cow barn. The safety is set on his sidearm, but Kelly wonders if it will be for much longer.

Chapter Seven
Sue

Two days later at 8:20 a.m. Garrett, twin brother of Huntley, passes away on Reagan's shift, though Grandpa is called to help her. At Reagan's demands, they work frantically at the end to bring the boy back. Sue, Hannah and Grams stand near the building and when Reagan comes out, she looks like a feral animal as she throws her contaminated garments, mask and gloves to the ground and takes off at a full sprint toward her running path. Grams quietly weeps beside Sue, and Hannah is all out sobbing. Reagan is not wearing her gun or her knife which prompts Sue to find John immediately.

"John, Derek," Sue says when she locates them near the cattle barn. They are working on the water pump which has been malfunctioning. "She's gone. Garrett just passed, and Reagan's taken off for the woods by herself."

"Damn her!" John swears.

Her brother-in-law throws his pipe wrench against the side of the barn in anger before he runs off to catch up with her wild sister.

Sue has never seen him like this. He's such a mild-mannered, fun-loving person. But Reagan seems to bring this out of him.

"The boy died?" her husband asks for confirmation.

Sue nods and feels tears pool in her eyes. He crosses the distance between them and gathers her into his arms where she cries quietly for the little boy that none of them knew. Again, he's her pillar of strength.

After a few moments, she settles and Derek pulls back and asks, "Where's your grandpa?"

"I think he was going to go and tell their father, Frank," Sue explains.

"Not without one of us he's not," Derek says fiercely.

Together they run back toward the med shed. Even before they get there Sue can hear arguing and loud voices. Kelly and Cory are already with her grandfather, however. And it's a good thing because so is the boy's father and two of the other men from their camp.

"You fucking killed him, old man. You're a shitty fucking doctor," Frank bursts forth in a rage.

It's shocking since this man hasn't once gone into the med shed or even asked permission to see his son. He stands next to Uncle Peter who mostly diverts his gaze toward the ground and refuses to make eye contact. Her great-uncle has also not asked to visit with his pregnant girlfriend Jennifer, either.

Sue had been outside with Grams and Uncle Peter near the coop yesterday when her grandmother had made the offer to let him visit with Jennifer. For being his supposed girlfriend, he hardly seemed to care what happened to the pregnant woman. Sue only remembers her great-uncle ever having had one girlfriend that she knows of. He'd brought her to the farm once. It had been rather memorable. Sue was seventeen at the time and had not been impressed. The woman had been some sort of drug addict, as well, and had kept itching her arms. That's one thing Sue definitely remembers about that woman. But yesterday, Peter's visage had contorted into a look of pure disgust, and he'd had to use the excuse of not wanting to spread germs as a valid reason to not visit his current girlfriend Jennifer in the shed. Then he'd taken the loaf of pound cake Grams had given him, tucked it under his shirt and promptly departed. He'd slinked back to one of the RV's and crept furtively into it. Sue does not believe that he meant to share that loaf of sweet bread with anyone at his camp. Some friend he is to his compadres.

Frank is still ranting at her grandfather, "You dumbass! You killed my kid!"

Derek strides straight up to Frank and shoves him roughly, causing him to fall to the ground. The other man falls very hard, and Sue almost feels sorry for him. Derek doesn't like anyone to disrespect the family, especially Grandpa, and she knows that John

92

has told him that this man has already done so once and was warned not to repeat it. Kelly and Cory both look disappointed that they didn't get the chance to do it.

Frank's other son Huntley is standing with Samantha near the side of the house, and it surprises Sue that the little boy doesn't rush forward to defend his father. One of the other men from the visitors' group steps forward as if to jump in on this fight, but Kelly simply puts a hand to the man's chest and gives him one firm shove backward. Given the sheer size of Kelly, it's enough to make the stalky African-American man back down. Sue believes his name to be Levon. But he does glare at Kelly and Cory and then Derek in turn when none of them are looking. It leaves an unsettling feeling in Sue's stomach. It's so curious that none of the visitors seems appreciative of their temporary residency on the farm.

Kelly and Cory move closer to Derek, and Kelly even tugs at her husband's arm to hold him back. But Sue can't seem to get over the glare that Levon is still spewing toward the two Rangers and Cory. There is so much open hostility in his glare that she fears for Derek. Levon realizes that she's cautiously regarding him and his amber eyes next meet Sue's. His expression toward her is not like that of the look he pinned on the three men in her family. Sue's not completely naïve when it comes to this look in a man's eyes. His gaze makes her shudder and inch closer to Derek.

"You get up and run your mouth again, I'll break your jaw the next time," Derek cautions in an eerily low voice to the father who slowly gets to his feet.

Sue has not seen Derek react so violently before or speak to someone like that, and even she knows that Frank had better stop acting out.

Kelly jumps in to help, "Now Doc did everything he could for your boy. What the hell did you think him and Reagan have been doing out here twenty-four hours a day for the last week?"

Frank nods and doesn't meet her husband's eyes or any of the other men's eyes in her family for that matter. Uncle Peter is also not moving toward Derek for a confrontation with the man who just shoved his friend. After seeing Derek's explosive reaction, however, she can't blame them.

"I'm sorry, Frank. I truly am," Grandpa explains patiently and professionally. "My granddaughter and I did everything we could for him. If it wasn't for her, your son probably would've died the first night you people came here. There isn't a better doctor in the country than her on studying diseases. He was just too far along for us to save."

Sue wonders how many times in his life that her grandfather has had to give similar speeches to waiting family members. She could've never been a doctor.

"Ok," Franks says with resignation. "Ok, man."

"We can hold a service and bury him here on the farm if you'd like," Grandpa suggests as Hannah and Grams draw closer.

"Whatever," Frank emotes childishly.

"We'll prepare the body, and the men here can give you shovels to dig and show you where," Grandpa offers.

Grandpa's eyes belie his calm demeanor, but unless someone knew him it wouldn't be obvious. There's grief and remorse written there that breaks Sue's heart.

"Go back to your camp and we'll come and get you with the shovels," Kelly adds.

It's apparent to Sue that Kelly doesn't want them going into any of the barns with them to retrieve the shovels. Grandpa has a lot of tools and equipment in the buildings that the men don't want these intruders to find and get any ideas of stealing.

"Come on, Frank. Guess we'll wait to be summoned," Levon says to Frank in a horrible, fuming voice.

Again, he gives Sue the creepy-crawlies up her spine. This man has cool, light-colored eyes, a strong jaw line and shoulder length dread locks. There is bulk to his shoulders and forearms, and he seems like he could be a formidable opponent if he wanted to be. A shiver passes through Sue when he looks overly long at her. By the reaction of Derek, her husband has also noticed Levon's highly scrutinizing stare because she watches his fist clench at his side.

"Grandpa, can I help?" Sue asks when the visitors finally retreat to their camp.

"No, honey. I don't want anyone in there. I'll do it myself. When Reagan returns and the site has been prepared, you can retrieve my Bible for me, and we'll speak over this boy before he is buried. Kelly, I'll call for you when he's ready and have you carry him. He doesn't weigh much. But I want to wrap him and clean him so that the germs don't get on any of you," Grandpa tells her and turns to go.

Sue crosses the yard to Sam who is still standing with Huntley, who in turn has his face buried in the girl's stomach. Hannah and Grams are with them and are both trying to comfort the kids. Grams is explaining, without too many of the finer details, what will take place with Garrett. Huntley sobs quietly, and Sam is barely containing herself as she presses the boy against her side. Her eyes are red-rimmed and bloodshot, the blue color of them on fire in bold contrast.

"Why don't you both have a seat on the back porch, and I'll make a pot of hot tea?" Grams offers kindly.

Sue understands that it is all she *can* offer at this point. The boy has just lost his brother and likely his best friend in the world so what can anyone offer him?

She follows them and sits on the porch swing taking note that Huntley and Sam sit together on a wicker sofa across from her rather than either of them join her. Huntley is no longer crying but they all, Sue included, have red, puffy faces and look fatigued by this horrid new tragedy. There is so much death everywhere in this world. Cory also joins them but sits on the porch step near them. He has not shed any tears, but Cory has been through so much that maybe all he can feel is numbness when someone loses a loved one. He'd been in the same house when his parents had been murdered and had discovered their bodies. His despair and grief have taken hold and grown a root of hardness within him that Sue knows will be his hardship to bear for many years.

In the distance, Kelly and Derek are carrying shovels and pick axes toward the visitors' campsite. When she looks up, Sam's eyes have followed hers and the tears flow again. Sue quickly decides that she ought to distract the kids if at all possible and clears her voice to speak.

"Um…Sam, are you from New Mexico, as well, dear?" she softly asks of the girl as Hannah brings out a plate of cinnamon scones, along with a pint of blueberry jam, setting them on the wicker table. Sam regards her sister and her cane with curiosity. "Sam and

Huntley this is my sister, Hannah, in case you haven't been introduced yet."

"Hello," Hannah says warmly and extends a hand, palm out.

Sam doesn't take it but regards Sue anxiously. The girl has clearly never been around a blind person before.

"She just wants to introduce herself the way that she does. She can't see you, so this is how she deals with meeting new people if you don't mind," Sue explains as Hannah smiles gently toward the general area of the sofa.

"Hello," Hannah repeats and holds out her arm again, bending over toward them.

This time Sam takes Hannah's hand in hers tentatively.

Sam mumbles a faint, "Hi."

"There you are," Hannah says and smiles fully, allowing her hand to glide up the girl's arm and onto her face.

Poor Hannah, she has no sense of personal boundaries. Sam's eyes widen as Hannah lightly touches her face. Sue knows she should stop her sister's intrusiveness, but this is the only way Hannie knows.

"Oh, you're quite pretty, aren't you?"

"No, ma'am," Sam answers awkwardly and sniffs.

"Yes, she is, Hannie," Sue corrects as Sam blushes. Hannah's fingers trace Sam's head, and she frowns.

"What happened to your hair?" she asks bluntly.

Her sister runs her fingertips through the girl's hair and pulls at the tips of Sam's bizarre, jagged cut.

"Hannah!" Sue scolds her little sister who can be too forward sometimes.

"What? Her hair is messed up. Did you do this yourself?"

"Yes," Sam says, squirming under Hannah's scrutiny. "I couldn't find scissors."

"What did you use, a weed-whacker? We can have Grams fix it for you, honey. Not I or it will look like you did it with a weed-whacker and then a chainsaw!" Hannah jokes.

This makes Sam actually smile and Huntley chuckle once.

"No, she cut it with a knife, and it wasn't very sharp, either," Huntley offers up.

"It's ok. I don't want to be a bother. Neither of us does," Sam refers to Huntley who reverts to staring at his shoes.

"It isn't a bother," Grams says from the doorway.

She carries out a tray with a china tea pot and small tea cups. Sue jumps up to help.

Grams continues, "I used to cut hair professionally until I married Dr. McClane. I miss it sometimes, but the girls let me cut theirs and so do the men around here. I actually like your hair. It just needs a little snipping here and there, honey. You have such a tiny face, like a porcelain doll, that it suits you just fine."

"And Huntley? May I introduce myself to you, sir?" Hannah asks.

She makes her way carefully around the table without bumping it, the scones or the cups full of tea. Grams is serving the tea with sugar and honey to the kids, Cory included, and Sue makes her own, adding a splash of milk.

"Sure, I guess," Huntley tells Hannah with a pathetic shrug.

Sue has to look away because she's afraid she'll start crying again. The boy looks so lost, sad, abandoned and about a thousand other forms of depressing.

But Hannah works her magic and touches his arm first, remarking about a scar that Huntley tells her he got from bumping into Frank's cigarette two years ago, and then trails up to his face. Sue hopes to high heaven that his story is true about it being an accident.

"Oh, you're a rather handsome boy. Very strong bone structure. And your hair is long. You are Native American, I've heard?" Hannah asks, and Huntley gives a subtle nod. "I can't tell your response. Yes?"

Hannah asks and holds her hand on the top of the boy's head so that she can feel his answer.

Her sister says, "Well, I'd bet your hair would look so neat with some braids in the front, and we could tie the ends with leather and beads and a feather. You'd make a rather dashing chief."

He doesn't say anything, but he does give a half smile full of more sadness and fatigue than a boy of ten years should feel.

Huntley finally answers, "My mom used to braid it."

Sue weeps again. She mentally berates her impotence to make it stop. She needs to be strong for these kids. They will need her and Hannah and Grams to get through this. They sure as hell won't get any help from Frank.

"You just drink your tea and have a scone, ok? It'll make you feel better, honey. We'll do your hair another day," Hannah tells him and then squats where she lays a hand to his dark mocha cheek. "Huntley, I am very sorry about your brother. I know how much you're hurting. But we're all here for you, ok? You don't have to go through this alone, sweetie."

Huntley flings himself into Hannah's arms and hugs her tightly. She simply strokes the boy's back and coos and whispers to him as he cries softly until he's cried himself out. She has a way about her, a gentle, reassuring way about her that just makes everyone in her presence feel immeasurably better. When he's finished, Hannah dries his cheeks with a linen handkerchief pulled from the wide pocket of her apron. Then she rises again and takes a seat on the swing since there is one available while Grams sits on her favorite rocking chair.

They sit for a while all sipping tea and eating scones, even the new kids, while Grandpa and the visitors prepare the body and the grave site. Sue tries to get the kids to talk again so that the family can better understand what is going on with their group and more importantly to distract them from the death of Huntley's twin brother. Nobody has been able to speak with either of them for a few days because they are being kept away from the family by what Grandpa believes is no accident.

"So, Sam, are you from New Mexico, or are you from one of the other states that your group has traveled through?" Sue asks again, and the girl looks at her teacup.

"No, ma'am," she says without giving away details.

Grams prods gently, "Are any of those people out there your family, dear?"

"No, ma'am," Sam answers honestly.

Her eyes jump anxiously toward Cory. He looks away, out toward the horse pasture.

"Do you have family elsewhere? Where are your mother and father, dear?" Grams inquires as she rocks.

Samantha would do well to learn that Grams is like a dog with a bone when she wants to be.

"They're… gone, ma'am. I don't have any family left," Sam tells them. "Thank you for the tea, but we should go."

98

"Wait, you don't have to go," Sue says regretfully. Now she feels terrible because she hadn't been trying to scare her off but was just trying to get to know about them.

"We need to go. They get mad when we're over here," Sam says and looks furtively over her shoulder.

"At least take these. Just hide them and share with whoever you want or whoever you don't want, either," Grams says.

She uses the linen napkins which are embroidered with purple violets around the edges to wrap the remaining scones. Sometimes Sue forgets just how intuitive her Grams can be.

"No, we couldn't..." Sam tries to protest.

Grams firmly presses them into Sam's frail, bony hands and closes hers over the girl's.

"I insist. And you come back whenever you can. Both of you come back and that Simon boy is welcome over here, too," Grams tells the girl who tears up and nods.

"Thank you, Mrs. McClane," Sam says and nods again.

Sam has a split lower lip that has partially closed up and healed over. Sue's not sure, however, if it is from an injury or from being hit or which was the more likely scenario.

The little waif takes Huntley's hand and entreats, "Come on, Huntley. We better get over there."

"I'll walk you back," Cory offers and rises.

Sam shakes her head and scoots uneasily around him to get down the stairs. She's the most timid kid Sue has ever known, and she's left to wonder at the origins of it, and the split lip. Cory trails after them but stops at the edge of the porch. He doesn't come back to sit again, though, but stands there watching the other two kids make it back to their camp. He's going to be so much like the other men of the family.

"What the heck is going on with these people? Are they abusing those kids? Because if they are, then man we should let our guys take care of them," Sue seethes.

"Calm down, Sue," Grams says gently. "It'll all come out in the wash. We can't make assumptions against these people. That boy's father is one of them."

"I know but I don't think Sam wants to be with them or is being held against her will or something. Don't you? Did you see her lip? Her lower lip looked like someone smacked her," Sue rambles impatiently.

"Maybe. But maybe not. We can't just say that to them and accuse them of something we're unsure of. Like I said, we'll figure it out sooner rather than later, I believe," Grams says wisely.

The children come out to tell Sue that both of the babies are awake from their naps. But mostly they've come to ask to play in the back yard with the dogs which have become their constant companions. This is the first day that they have finally been allowed to play outdoors since the caravan arrived. They'd simply been too stir-crazy to stay indoors another day. So far it has been fine, no problems have arisen and the visitors have not bothered them. Two of the men from the visitors' group even walk out to the barn with buckets to fill, and when they come back through, passing the playing McClane kids, they make no notice of them. At least that sets Sue's heart a bit more at ease. They had kept right on going toward their camp and talking the whole time. It is a good thing that they take no interest in her children or in Em. If they had been staring at or suspicious around the kids, then Sue would have been forced to call Derek out to shoot them on the spot.

A commotion at the far end of the cattle barn alerts Sue, and she shields her eyes against the sun's glare. When she finds the source of the noise, she's not surprised in the least. It's John and Reagan, and her sister is yelling at him to go away and he's standing there taking it, of course. Where does he get his patience?

A few hours later, the family walks to the grave site which has been designated right inside the woods at the edge of the meadow nearest the driveway. Simon is leaning on a shovel looking sweaty and dirty. Frank has not broken a sweat. He is either a highly conditioned man to hard work, or he's made Simon do most of the work digging his son's grave. This area of the farm is peaceful, tranquil and covered in tiny clusters of white Baby's Breath flora and thick with forest ferns. The visitors have all assembled, and the McClane family has gathered, as well, with the exception of Reagan who volunteered to stay behind in the med shed to look after Jennifer. John is standing post at the door for her, and when Sue had glanced over at him before she left, he'd seemed angry and sullen.

Grandpa speaks a few Bible verses and blesses the boy whose brother weeps beside Sam, and not near his own father. Their grandfather gives Frank the chance to speak a few words for his dead son, but the man declines. When the ceremony is finished, Huntley surprises everyone when he breaks into a lovely, haunting song in his native Navaho language. He makes unusual hand gestures and motions with his arms, and this single act of showing respect to his deceased brother is so poignant that Sue's tears start anew. He must feel a great deal of responsibility toward his brother to do this tribute of honor and manage to get through the song so bravely.

When he is done singing, he takes a knife out of his pocket and cuts a tip of his hair off and tosses it into the open grave where his twin rests. Then he squats and pokes his finger in the rich, black dirt and smudges his forehead and under his eyes with it, leaving dark streaks. If anyone finds his ceremonial show of respect to his great nation of elders bizarre, then no one says anything. To Sue, it is simply beautiful and moving and proves how close he was to his mother and grandfather and their customs as Native Americans.

Kelly and Derek stand watch with their rifles slung on their backs while the men cover in the hole as the rest of the group leaves the grave site. Simon is walking back with them because Derek had taken the shovel from the teenager and shoved it into Rick's hands whether he'd wanted it or not. The poor kid looks dead on his feet, and Sue is glad that her husband had also recognized it. This kind act toward this boy had earned a deadly glare from Frank, Rick and Rick's cousin, Levon, who already likes to glare with hatred at everyone all the time.

A while later, everyone in the McClane family is back at their usual duties and chores, and the men keep watch. The overall mood of the farm is melancholy and glum.

The children are in the barn because one of the goats that Reagan brought home from the Johnson's farm gave birth yesterday to two kids. Her sister hadn't known when she'd taken them that one was pregnant, but it was fortuitous because when Isaac is done breastfeeding, Sue eventually wants to put him on goat's milk which was advised by Grandpa because of the added nutrients and higher calorie content than cow's milk. The visitors have allowed Huntley to go with her children to see the new goats, which is surprising, but Frank doesn't seem to care much for him anyway nor had he shed a single tear over Garrett during the service. They have not, however, permitted Samantha to return to the family, and as Sue picks corn she observes the girl making trip after trip with Simon to the barn for heavy buckets of water.

Voices near the end of the cattle barn catch Sue's attention. She crosses over two rows to peer between the corn toward the source and just about falls on her face when she spies Kelly and Hannah kissing. She also sees Kelly hugging and comforting Hannah as she is probably still distraught over the death of Garrett. They obviously think they are hidden from the rest of the family, and they would've been right if nobody had been picking corn. Their secret is safe with her, though, because she knows how much Hannah loves Kelly, and if he has finally come to terms with his feelings for her youngest sister, then Sue's happy for them. It might not be so easy to find happiness anymore.

"Sue!" Cory calls from somewhere in the corn field toward the center.

She makes her way there and calls back to him. When she finds him, Sue stares up at him. The kid has grown at least two inches over the summer.

"What is it, Cory?" she asks. He appears distressed.

"I just talked to Simon and Sam- well mostly Simon because that Sam girl won't really talk to me. Anyways, he said that they're almost out of food at the camp. He said him and Sam and Huntley haven't eaten since they got here 'cept for what we've given them. He said the women over there have been making pancakes for four days straight, and I guess they're about out of even that," Cory tells her.

This isn't good at all. And why are they eating the food and not feeding the kids first? What is wrong with these people?

"Ok, let me find Grams and Grandpa and Derek and talk to them about this," she tells him, and he hefts her sack full of corn for her. He's like that. He's a good kid just like his brother, even if Kelly is not exactly a teenager but a grown man. Hannah can attest to Kelly's character better than anyone else at the farm, and the thought makes Sue grin with her new secret.

"Doc and Reagan are with the woman in the med shed, and Grams is watching the kids in the barn. Derek and John are setting up demolitions in the outer field and at the end of the driveway again," Cory tells her.

"Uh, where's Isaac? Grams was supposed to be keeping an eye on him while I picked corn," Sue asks nervously.

"Oh, sorry. Yeah, Em's got him out at the barn with Grams. Thought everyone forgot about him? He's a loud little dude. Kind of hard to forget him," Cory says with a grin.

"You aren't lying! Hey, let's just go and get Grams and talk to Grandpa about it with them until the guys get back. I'll go get Grams and meet you over by the med shed," Sue says, getting a nod from Cory.

It only takes a minute to find Grams because she can hear the high decibel voices of the children as they excitedly talk and giggle over the baby goats. They are awfully cute bounding around on their brand new legs and she hates to drag the children away, but she quietly explains the situation with the visitors' food depletion to Grams.

"Em, do you think you can keep an eye on the littler kids while I talk with Grams over at the med shed? Maybe Huntley could help you? Just let Jacob crawl around in the grass, and I'll take Isaac," Sue asks, and Huntley nods and puffs his chest just a tad with pride.

Grams is holding Jacob who is bobbing up and down on her hip while he watches the goats. Sue has always wondered what little ones at this age think when they look at animals. It can't possibly make sense to their baby brains. He squeals loudly again.

They leave the barn and meet up with Cory, Reagan and Grandpa. A very suspicious-looking Kelly and Hannah also join the group a moment later, and he releases her hand when they get there. Nice try. Derek and John jog up to the shed. How the heck do they have the energy for running after working hard all the time on the farm? Conditioned bodies, she supposes.

She and Cory relay what is going on with the visitors, and Sue hangs back while suggestions come forth.

Reagan says, "Good. We'll feed the three kids with us and the rest can die for all I care."

Grams gives her a look, so her sister retreats back into the shed as if she could also care less what other opinions are put forward. She is bitterer today than normal, and Sue knows it's because of Garrett. It is sad to see her sister turn so hard and do it with such ease. Sometimes she thinks Reagan is getting better and then other times, like now, she slips right back into that well of coldness.

Grams suggests, "We have the goat in the barn that is producing milk now. We were planning on taking one milking a day off of her, so they could do it if they want to. But they'll need to let the babies get the rest of her milk each day."

"They aren't going in any of the barns," John says roughly.

He's in an extremely sour mood. Apparently he is still sore with Reagan for taking off without her gun. Either that or they have argued about something, which would not be at all surprising.

"No, we would have to tie her out there by their camp," Grandpa agrees. "The apple orchard is in full swing, so if they'd like to pick apples, that would be fine with me. We have a dozen trees out there, and we've never used all of the apples they yield."

"And we could let them pick those last two rows of corn after I finish the row I'm on," Sue notes and Grandpa nods in agreement. "We don't need that corn, and it was just going to be canned or eaten the rest of the summer as fresh corn. With the amount that we have out there it may have needed to be given to the livestock anyways. The cellar is so jammed full."

"We could take eggs each day and give them a basket," Hannah says while toying with her braid. "We're getting over four dozen a day, and the fridge is overflowing with them. Plus, in the barn I have twenty-two hens with their peeps that will be in production in about four months."

She looks like a woman well-kissed and is standing so close to Kelly that it is hard to tell where she ends and he begins. If Grandpa notices, he doesn't say anything.

"Ok, fine, but that's all. We don't want them to get too comfortable. If Jennifer lives and turns the corner soon, I want them gone from here," Grandpa remarks sternly.

Grams doesn't argue. Perhaps she's seen the negative side of these people, especially if they are being cruel to the kids.

"Agreed," Derek says.

John echoes his brother.

"How is the woman doing, Herb?" Grams asks.

He runs a hand through his white hair and removes his eyeglasses.

"Not any better. She has moments where she wakes and is lucid and we can give her broth and she speaks a bit, but then she's right back out or coughing up blood. She is going downhill no matter what drug concoction Reagan gives her. Surprisingly, the fetal heartbeat is still steady and strong, but the mother is no better, I'm sorry to report," Grandpa expounds and pinches the bridge of his nose between his thick, gray brows.

Sue lays a hand on his shoulder for comfort.

"That's too bad," Kelly says kindly.

They all nod in agreement.

"Let's go tell the deadbeats what we're willing to give them," Derek says to Kelly and Cory as the group breaks apart to go about their work.

"Derek, wait!" Grandpa calls out, and everyone turns and walks back. "Tell them that if they want the provisions, then Samantha, Huntley and Simon must be allowed to earn keep for the rest of them or something. Just think of some way to get those kids back over here. And if that other teen boy can act like he has some sense, then we'll give him some chores, too. I don't really want to force them into hard labor, mind you. They seem under weight enough as it is. I'm just thinking of a way to get them away from those others. I've been observing them and I don't like the way they are with those kids. They aren't taking care of them, and they are just using them for doing the work that *they* should be doing."

Sue is quite sure that her grandfather has been observing them. It's what he does best, introspective observation, which is why he was always such a fantastic doctor.

Derek and Kelly give curt nods and leave to speak with their unwanted guests. Sue is just hoping that neither of them shoot the visitors during this discussion. Not all of them seem so bad to Sue.

The bleach blonde stripper had cried at the funeral for Garrett and one of the men, the other African American man named Rick had, at the very least, comforted her. The shorter, Hispanic man, who she found out is named Willy doesn't seem threatening. He just has a few strange ticks like blinking rapidly and bobbing his head, but that isn't a reason to fear him, even though Derek has told her that the man talks to himself. The teen boy that Grandpa was referencing for minding his manners if he works with their group is the one named Bobby. He has cold, almost black eyes and he'd sneered at Sam throughout the funeral. Sue disliked him instantaneously because of this. How could anyone be mean to Samantha? She is a sweet young girl who was just on the cusp of womanhood when this shit all fell apart. Her mannerisms are quiet and delicate. Everything about her seemed light and graceful. She moves with an innate femininity. Then there is Buzz, the bald, short, skinny man with tattoos all over his head. Luckily he also appears to be meek like the man who had comforted the blonde during the funeral. Some of the others, however, have a menacing way about them that makes Sue highly uncomfortable.

Last night in their bedroom, Derek had shown Sue how to use the knife that he insisted she wear on her hip everywhere she went from now on and also a few self-defense moves that she's pretty sure she'll never be able to do if she is ever attacked. Unless of course someone was threatening her babies, then she'd kill anyone she had to and without hesitation.

As she walks toward the house lost in thought, someone touches her arm, making her jump. It's only John.

"Sue, can I talk with you?" he asks.

She stops to face him directly. "Sure, John. What is it?"

John tosses an apprehensive glance toward the med shed.

"Not here," he says.

"Let's go over on the front porch. Besides, we should probably watch this go down with Derek and Kelly and the visitors in case all hell breaks loose," Sue tells him, and John grins and nods.

"It would be the shortest all-hell-breaking-loose moment in history if you ask me," John says with his usual good humor.

The late day sun glints off of the gold streaks in his messy hair. He's such a handsome man, but she's never been able to see him as anything other than something akin to a brother.

"Aren't you worried about them? I was kind of wondering why you didn't go out there, too," Sue asks as they sit on the front porch swing together. She takes a second to pull her rubber band out of her hair and sweep up the loose tendrils of mahogany waves more securely again.

"Nah, they've got this one just fine without me. They don't need my help with a group of losers like that. What are they gonna do, overthrow Rangers with harsh language and pancake batter?" John jokes easily to which Sue laughs.

Shielding her eyes against the sun, Sue can see her husband and Kelly explaining the new rules of the visitors' temporary stay on the farm, and a few of them are complaining. They are no doubt protesting having to work harder- or about having to milk a goat, she's not sure which. She and John swing a few moments. He leans forward and rests his elbows on his knees, clasping his hands together and making the porch swing stop moving altogether.

"Tell me what happened," John finally says quietly as he looks at the ground and then out on the horizon.

Sue sighs heavily. She kind of had a feeling this is what he wanted to talk about.

"John, it's not my place. I…" Sue starts to explain, but John interrupts her.

"Please tell me. I just want to help her," John requests pleadingly.

"Oh, John, I don't think you can," Sue tells him and lays her hand against his back to soothe him. It doesn't work.

"Nobody will talk about it. I have to know if I'm going to help her at all. I just need to know. You have to understand that, Sue," John asks again and looks directly at Sue.

She sighs again, this time feeling the full weight of the burdening secrecy Reagan has sworn everyone to.

"Please," he begs brokenly.

"I don't know everything. I can only tell you what I know because of the snippets I overheard and the way she came home that day," Sue admits as John nods in encouragement.

"She came home in March. When things started falling apart overseas with the nukes and the wars and… well, everything, Grandpa called her days and even weeks before and begged her and then threatened her, but she wouldn't leave the school because she's so damn stubborn. I mean, that's not the shocking part," Sue says with a smile that John returns. "I don't know exactly what happened because Grandpa wouldn't let me in the room- you know, because I can't stand the sight of blood and stuff," she says with a chuff. John just smiles gently and places his hand on her shoulder briefly.

Sue continues, "Reagan owned a small Jeep but came down that lane in a black Volkswagen car. Grandpa called everyone out of the house when he saw it coming down the lane because we didn't know who might be in it. It could've been someone bad. It was weaving all over the drive. Do you see that oak tree there?" Sue points to the one in the front yard to their right. It's a grand old tree with a tire swing hanging from a thick branch. It has many deep, protruding roots, and a massive top full of wide leaves that have turned into brilliant splashes of orange and yellow for fall. John nods.

"Yeah," John answers with confusion.

Sue figures that he's probably wondering why she is pointing out trees.

"She slowed down, slower and slower and coasted right into it. If you look closely, you'll see black paint on the one side. That's from that car. When we realized it was her, we all ran out there and…," Sue shivers, and her eyes pool with tears. She looks away from John and bites her lip, hard. She has to get through this before anyone, especially Reagan, comes out here and finds them. "It was horrible, John. I've never seen anything like that, not even in a scary movie. The whole car, the whole inside of that car was just…," her voice cracks and tears stream down her face. John holds her hand.

He squeezes her hand firmly which gives her enough courage to keep going. "It was covered in blood, her blood. And when we opened the door, she just fell out of it onto the ground. Grandpa grabbed her up. Yeah, Grandpa," she says lightly, and John smiles at her. "He carried her straight into the house and put her in Hannah's room because it was closest. It also has the best lighting what with all the windows for him to see better."

"Did she wake up?" John asks.

"Yeah, here and there. There was a note on the seat of the car that she'd written for Grandpa in case she made it home. It said all her wounds and vitals and medical stuff. She'd taken the time to write everything down: the medicines she'd given herself, her wounds and the medical terminology to describe where they were on her body like abdomen this and that, and medicine dosages, and how many stitches…," Sue tells him but has a hard time finishing. Some of this is difficult to remember because the pain is just too great.

"You mean to tell me that she gave herself stitches?" John asks disbelievingly.

108

Sue nods and sniffs, wipes at her cheeks with the back of her hand.

"I know that they weren't good, and she didn't get them all in correctly. Grandpa gave us small updates and was yelling orders from Hannah's room. I've never, *never* seen him like that. He's been a doctor half his life. You know Grandpa. He doesn't raise his voice, but he was yelling that day. It was horrible. His voice was… so worried, panicked like I've never heard before. He was scared."

"I can imagine," John confirms and grimaces deeply.

Sue realizes that this is probably hard for him to hear. But he'll never fully understand Reagan if he doesn't.

"She told Grandpa that she was attacked, and her friend was killed and so was Grandpa's best friend, Dr. Krue," Sue says.

"Yeah, Dr. Krue. I know that name," John says with a nod. His blue eyes seem haunted.

"Yeah, he'd come down here sometimes during summer break. He was a very sweet old man. Eccentric, but sweet nonetheless. He and Grandpa and Reagan would stay up late into the morning hours discussing diseases and surgery and weird stuff like they always did. Anyways, the college was overrun with crime, and they were attacked. I don't know what happened there. That's the part I can't tell you. I think Grandpa knows, but I don't think he'd ever tell you, John. He's like that. I saw him in the middle of the night crying in the hallway when he thought we'd all gone to bed. He was the only one up with her. He'd sent us all to bed. But he must've lost it and didn't want her to wake up and see him, so he went to the hall. Don't ever tell him I told you that. He's so prideful."

"I understand. I would never say anything. He just loves her so much. He loves all three of you girls," John asks. "What else do you know?"

"When he was working on her, he was shouting things from the other room, making Grams take notes on a notepad for him so he could compare it with her note she brought home. He said that she put on her note that she was stabbed three times and had multiple lacerations and that she'd been choked. But Grandpa shouted to Grams that there were six stab wounds, four deep or some other term for deep and three superficial, whatever that means. I think it means not deep. How do you get stabbed superficially?"

109

Sue tries to make light, but she can see a deadly fury coming over John's face.

"Choked too?" John asks tightly, which is not a good sign with so many of the visitors being on the farm and also not being wanted on this farm by any of the Rangers.

"Yes, Grandpa said that her windpipe was nearly crushed. That's why she's so raspy sometimes. She's always had a little gravel to her voice but not anything like it is now. If you ever notice, she takes very small bites of food. Grandpa said she would have to always be careful not to choke because there's no way of doing reconstructive surgery on her," Sue adds and watches Derek and Kelly take two of the men from the group past the house to the barns. She doesn't think John even notices or cares.

"Was she...?" John asks with a great deal of hesitation.

Sue knows what he is asking.

"No, Grandpa said there was no sign of rape, thank God," Sue explains. "I think he checked her when she was out on the morphine or something. I feel bad for him that he even had to, but he had to know in case she needed care."

John nods solemnly and finally releases her hand.

"Yeah, she could've contracted a disease. He had to do it," John justifies and hangs his head a moment.

Sue rubs his back again, giving him time to collect himself.

"How did you guys do a blood transfusion on her when none of you match?" John asks.

Sue knows that he's obviously remembering his own brother's dilemma and Reagan being the only one who could help. Now he can finally understand why none of them wanted her to donate for Derek.

"He didn't. Grandpa said he needed to, but that she would have to either survive it on her own or she wouldn't because there wasn't any other choice. He said our dad was a match to Reagan but not any of us. Grams and especially Hannie were total wrecks. You don't understand how bad it was, John. You can't unless you were there. There were so many buckets of blood-soaked rags, and her screams were like something I don't ever want to hear again for the rest of my life. Grandpa used as much local anesthesia shots as he had- that's why there wasn't much for Derek. He told Grams that he had to re-open some of the stitching she did and re-sew them

110

because they weren't right. I can only assume that was because she was doing it on the run or something or in the dark because Reagan is very neat and precise with stitches. Derek barely has a scar and neither does Cory on his leg."

"Yeah, she's a fine doctor," John praises and looks out at the visitors with a contemptuous glare. "She probably couldn't do it 'cuz she was too injured and in shock."

Sue nods. "Yeah, maybe. I hadn't thought of that."

John just frowns and pats her hand.

Sue continues on, "She was sick for weeks and ended up getting a pretty bad infection. She was so weak. She spent thirteen days in bed. Grandpa pumped her full of a lot of medicines and had to give her oxygen which is why we don't have any of that left, either. She could hardly breathe for a few days because of her throat being squeezed so hard. It was a terrifying, raspy sound. John, from what I overheard Reagan explaining, or trying to explain to Grandpa that day, I think there was more than one person who attacked her."

With this new information, John looks like he's going to be sick right here on the porch. He swallows hard.

"How the heck did she get away from more than one person? She's so small," he asks when he is composed again.

"I don't know. That whole scene at the school is what I don't know. But at least I've been able to tell you why she is the way she is. It's why she doesn't like people touching her. For a few months afterward she would wake up screaming. I'd run upstairs to her room, after we got her moved up there because she had to use Hannie's room for the first month. When I'd try to comfort her, she'd push me away, and sometimes when I got to her room I'd find her in the back of her closet hiding and holding her knife or pistol."

"Jesus," John swears with disgust and frustration.

Sue is taken aback. She doesn't think she's ever heard John take the Lord's name in vain.

"But she was so cut up it was sickening. She won't even show me. The only person she would let change her bandages as she recovered was Grandpa. Look, honey, I'm not gonna lie. She's not the same person she used to be. She's changed... completely. Reagan used to be fun, like you. She had an ornery sense of humor and liked to laugh and joke with Derek when he was home. Don't get me wrong, she's always been a little feisty, but she never had so much hatred in her heart for everything and everyone. She would've never said to let the visitors out there starve to death. That's Reagan 2.0. The old Reagan would've wanted to feed them and take care of their sick because all she ever wanted to do was heal people. She's so damned smart, but she can't figure out how to fix this problem inside of her. I know about PTSD. Trust me, as a wife of a career military man you get to learn a lot of things you don't think you'll ever need to know. They make the wives go to classes and lectures when the men get deployed so that we can recognize problems when they come home. Luckily Derek never experienced anything like that. Well, not that he would ever let me find out, that is. But I think for sure Reagan has some form of post-traumatic stress. You know what's crazy? She probably already knows it, too. And if she can't fix it being the super brain she is, then how the hell are we supposed to help her?"

"Yeah, but I gotta try," John says.

His determination is something that Sue appreciates more than she can ever say.

"I'll be honest, John, since you came here I have been seeing small changes in her. I've seen you touch her here and there for a second, and she doesn't flinch like she used to. That has to be progress, right?" Sue asks with hope. She wants her sister back so badly.

"Maybe. Sometimes I think she's getting better, but then she'll just snap again. I don't know how to fix someone with PTSD. I just know what it is and what the signs are. Heck, Reagan could probably recite a whole medical reference book on it, but she doesn't know how to apply practical application to it," John says.

There is humor in his voice, and Sue is relieved that his darkness has lifted just slightly. Sue chuckles once to lighten the mood.

"Thanks for telling me what you know, though. I think it will help me to help her."

"If you want to understand more about that day, go and look at that car. It's down behind the barn. I think you guys might've parked that Hummer out there, too. I fully believe if it wouldn't have drawn attention, then Grandpa would've burned that damn car," Sue recommends softly so that no one will overhear. "I love you, John, and I know why you want to help her which only makes me love you more. You'll always be my adopted brother whether you can fix my real sister or not."

Sue pecks him on the cheek, pats his thigh once and goes inside. She watches from the window as John sits another few minutes with his head down in a pose of tension and rage. His handsome face is pensive, tortured and desperate for a solution. Sue can tell how much John loves her sister. Most men would've easily given up on her already and not had the resolve to deal with her. But not John. He is so much like Derek, and yet so different. But one thing is for sure. The Harrison men don't back down when the situation gets too difficult.

Before long, he plucks his baseball cap from the porch railing and leaves the area. She sends up a silent prayer to give John the strength to help her sister and the patience to not give up on her.

Chapter Eight
Hannah

Murmured conversation comes from behind the house as she and Grams are preparing breakfast together in the kitchen the following morning, early morning.

"Sounds like the kids are here, Hannah," Grams says to her. "Oh, Hannah. I wish you could see this. That boy, Simon, is holding Huntley's hand. What a sweet boy he is to look after him like that. They aren't even related I don't think."

A knock sounds at the door to the kitchen a second later, and Grams goes to answer it, momentarily leaving her biscuit cutting.

By 'kids', Hannah knows she means Simon, Huntley and Sam. They are here for their chore assignments but little do they know that the family just wants to help them out and not vice versa. And the fact that Simon would be holding Huntley's hand is also not surprising in the least. It seems from what Hannah can conclude, it's that all of the kids on the farm, including their own, feel the need to stick together, cling on to one another. There is a closeness between the children, from the young to the older teens that might not have ever developed before the apocalypse. They've all seen so much death and despair to know enough to hold fast to each other because they might be all that they have some day.

"Good morning, children," Grams greets them.

Hannah rolls her eyes. From what she's learned, two of them aren't exactly children but teenagers. Sam is fourteen or fifteen and Simon is sixteen if she's heard correctly.

Grams just continues on, "Simon dear, why don't you head out to the cattle barn? I believe Cory is going that way. He can show you where Kelly might need you."

"Yes, ma'am," Simon answers.

Hannah can hear Cory leave his chair at the island. Simon has not entered any farther into the kitchen than one step.

"Ok, Grams. I'll take him with me. Just let me put my other boot on. I help my brother do the milking, and then we clean out the milking area and shovel... you know, crap and stuff," Cory explains shyly.

"That's cool. We're glad to help," the other boy says.

His voice is deep, not as much as Cory's, but very refined, gentleman-like. Reagan told her the other day that he is a dork, but Hannah knows that her sister's opinions of people tend to be a tad on the harsh side.

A quick shuffling is following by Simon's voice murmuring soothingly again, "It's ok, bud. I won't be gone long, alright?"

This young man is obviously speaking to Huntley who is probably afraid to be left alone in the care of virtual strangers. He's lost his best friend and mother to this horrific new world, and is likely turning to Sam and Simon for comfort because he certainly isn't going to get any from his wretched father Frank.

Grams just chatters while bustling about the kitchen. "Then you two come back in and I'll have breakfast for you. You teens can sit here at the island," Grams says.

Hannah isn't sure why she doesn't just sit them at the table with the rest of the family, but she also doesn't ask her in front of them. Does she not fully trust them yet? Hannah does. They seem harmless enough to her. Some of the others out at the camp, not so much.

"Yes, ma'am," Cory answers, and Simon echoes him.

The other two kids are quiet, probably awaiting their own assignments. Hannah continues to cut out biscuits and place them on the baking sheets.

Cory blurts with teen enthusiasm, "Come on, dude."

With that directive, the teen boys are out the back door again and gone. Hannah can hear them through the open kitchen window above the sink, chatting all the way to the barn. If these three weren't early risers before, they will be soon enough. Farm work doesn't exactly start at the crack of 10:30, and the animals are used to morning feedings that start between 5:00 and 6:00 a.m. Sometimes

115

the kids sleep until 7:00 or 7:30 but not today. They are all up and out, probably enjoying the last pleasant weather of the summer. Nobody argues, though. They sleep great when they play hard and work even harder outside all day.

"Huntley honey, why don't you go out to the chicken coop and help the other kids collect eggs. They're already out there, sweetie," Grams suggests. "There are a couple of small shovels by the door, and the chicken poo needs cleaned out every morning and put into the wheelbarrow. The kids will show you where it gets taken. The compost pile behind the horse barn is where it goes, but they'll show you, ok?"

"Yes, ma'am. I'll help," Huntley promises.

"Then it will be about time to come in for breakfast. So if I can trust you to round up the other children for breakfast then go on and head out there, dear," Grams orders gently.

Huntley agrees to the deal and leaves immediately and is probably glad to get away from a kitchen full of women. For a boy who has just lost his brother, he seems happy to be away from the group with whom he is traveling. He is more eager to spend time with the strange company of the McClane kids than with his own father.

"Now, what to do with Miss Samantha?" Grams asks lightheartedly.

Hannah cannot gauge the girl's response, though, because she does not verbalize it. She rarely verbalizes much of anything according to Reagan.

Grams prods further, "Well, dear, what would you like to do?"

"I can do whatever you'd like me to do, Mrs. McClane," Sam finally offers kindly.

"My husband says you make quite the nurse, young lady," Grams praises.

Again no response. This girl isn't much of a talker.

Grams just keeps pushing, "Would you like to help out at the med shed? Or if you'd like, my eldest granddaughter is working in the greenhouse with plants. We'll try to keep many of our plants going all the way through until the first snow and even some after, like the lettuces and cabbages."

116

"Um, I think I'd like to work in the medical facility if that's ok," Sam says.

This doesn't come as a surprise to Hannah. Apparently Samantha is very helpful and takes direction well, follows orders clearly and does whatever is asked of her. Grandpa and Reagan have both praised her abilities.

Sam quickly adds, "But I would like to learn about the plants sometime, too, if I can, Mrs. McClane."

"Sure, the more you learn then the bigger help you'll be to us, dear. Now run along and join my granddaughter. Oh and just ignore her crassness. Sometimes she's a bit rough around the edges, but we still love her just the same," Grams tells her.

"Oh, no, ma'am. She's fine. She's nice, actually. I like being around her. She's so smart, and I've learned so much just listening to her. She even showed me how to take a blood pressure reading," Sam exclaims with enthusiasm.

Hannah just about slices through her finger with the biscuit cutter. Reagan nice? Hm, this girl has extremely impaired judgment.

"Uh, ok, honey, whatever you say. But just make sure you both come back in here for breakfast in one hour, ok? My granddaughter doesn't like to be bothered with eating and by the looks of you, neither do you. So I'm putting you in charge of getting her in here," Grams orders.

"Yes, ma'am," Sam agrees. "I'll bring her on time, ma'am."

The back screen door opens and shuts whisper quiet as Sam makes her exit. This is not the norm around the farm. That screen door gets slammed about four hundred times a day.

"I think she's going to fit in just fine around here. Don't you, Hannie?" Grams asks.

She has come back to join Hannah at the island.

"Yes, I agree, Grams. She's helpful and respectful. I didn't hear that Bobby kid. Was he not with them?"

"No, he wasn't," Grams says with a touch of derision. "Guess he isn't interested in helping out around here. Oh well. That's up to him. The offer was made, and if he'd rather be out there with that band of hooligans, then that speaks to the boy's character better than anything else."

Black and white. It's how Grams sees things. It's also how the love of her life sees things and why she cares so much for him.

She'd managed to sneak back to his room only once more since the arrival of the visitors where they'd made love twice before he took her to her own room again. Kelly is so tender and loving, yet fierce when he needs to be. Hannah likes to think of him as her gentle barbarian. Thinking of him throughout the day is the only way she gets through most of her days. Their quick, stolen kisses and secretive caresses keep her going and, unfortunately, also keep her extremely frustrated. She'd begged him to just be out in the open with their relationship and let her tell everyone, but he'd said the time wasn't right, especially with the visitors on the farm. But, oh, those moments of pure bliss with him made Hannah just ache to be with Kelly every second of the day. She can only hope that he pines for her in the same way.

"Hannah?" Grams asks like she's asked it more than once.

"Yes?" Hannah stammers out.

"Did you start the sausage?" Grams asks.

Grams is standing closer to her than she'd realized. She must've moved around the island to be next to her. And like a doofus, she'd been in a daze thinking of Kelly and his muscular arms as he'd cradled her body against his.

"Uh… no, sorry. I was distracted," Hannah admits and stops what she's doing.

"Well, honey, you've been stirring those same peaches in that bowl for about ten minutes. Where's your mind lately, Hannah McClane?" Grams asks without criticism but with concerned worry.

"Sorry, Grams. I guess it's the visitors that have me distracted," she lies, but not well because her blush would probably betray her to someone with sight- or common sense.

"Uh huh, the visitors," Grams says sarcastically.

Her grandmother takes the big ceramic bowl full of sliced peaches and sugar that will go into a crock for cobbler after tonight's dinner.

She adds, "Just start the sausage, love."

"Ok," Hannah mumbles as she feels her way for the stove and the package of sausage which Grams has already opened for her.

"What do you think about Samantha?" Grams asks as she preps something at the island.

118

Hannah thinks on her question a moment before answering, "I think she seems nice. Shy, but nice just the same. Don't you?"

"Yes, she's a good girl, I'd say. But something is wrong with her," Grams clarifies and runs water in the wide porcelain sink.

"What do you mean, Grams?" Hannah inquires. This statement is confusing. "Do you mean like she's disabled or sick or something?"

"No, honey," Grams states. "I just mean that something isn't quite right with her. She's very sad."

"Well, she did say that her family is gone," Hannah remembers from their conversation with her on the back porch after Garrett's funeral.

"No, I know grief. I've felt grief, like when we lost your brother. Sometimes I feel grief for your father, but I'm also still trying to hold out hope that he's alive. But that isn't what's wrong with Sam. She's sad from grief, but there's something else, too," Grams insists as the water is turned off again.

"What do you think it is?" Hannah asks her sagely grandmother, who seems to have all the answers.

"I think it's fear," Grams says slowly and calmly.

Her words send a panicky tremor down Hannah's spine. They don't speak more on it, and for this Hannah is glad. She doesn't want to dwell on whatever could be causing this young, sweet-tempered girl to look so terrible that her Grams would label it as fear.

A short while later Grams starts putting breakfast platters on the dinner table, knowing full well that the chores should be done in but a moment. And sure enough, the sounds of shoes being dropped on the back porch soon follow as people file into the house. Grams has set three place settings at the island for the teens, and Huntley will eat in the dining room with everyone else, including the smaller kids in the McClane pack. Hannah believes that perhaps her grandparents are still not sure of the two teens and where their loyalties might lay.

"This smells great, girls," Derek announces kindly.

He's coming downstairs from his room where he was finishing what short-lived amount of sleep he and the other men can get.

Soon after, John also joins the melee in the kitchen. Grandpa had gotten on his case last night and forced him to get a full night's sleep. Whether or not John had actually listened and not started his watch shift until four a.m. she'll never know.

Sue is showing the new kids where they can wash up in the guest bathroom nearest the kitchen. Reagan is the last to enter the room. She comes right in complaining which makes John chuckle. He sure woke up in a good mood if he found Reagan's complaints, first thing upon waking, humorous.

"Reagan McClane, shoes, young lady!" Grams yells at her.

Reagan throws her likely dirty shoes loudly onto the back porch.

"I'm not hungry!" she says vehemently, of course. "I don't have time to eat. I'm in the middle of something out there! I have to..."

"You'll sit your scrawny butt down and eat like the rest of us, young lady!"

And with that, the argument is over. Grams is about the only person Reagan will listen to.

She just keeps on railing at Reagan, "You'll be no good to that woman or her care if you're fuzzy-brained and exhausted from lack of nutrition."

"Good morning, Grams," Kelly says.

Grams pecks his cheek, which Hannah can hear. Her Grams also has a soft spot for Kelly.

"Good morning, Kelly. Hope you all are hungry, boys," Grams says as if they are all little boys and not giant men and growing teenage boys.

Kelly just chuckles and returns with, "Smells fantastic. We're starving. Aren't we, guys?"

Kelly is asking Cory and Simon because they both perk up and verbally agree.

Cory even adds, "Simon's good with the animals. He catches on quick, too."

Her honey moves furtively closer to her and eventually lands beside her near the stove where he snatches a sausage link. The noise and chaos of the children escalate to deafening levels.

"Hey," Hannah scolds in a hushed tone. "Did you come over here to see me or for the meat?"

"Would it be wrong if I said both?" Kelly teases her gently.

"I guess not," Hannah concedes with mock irritation, and he tugs her braid once.

"Let me help you," he says and tries to take her spatula.

"No!" Hannah halts him. "I do this every day, Mr. Alexander. I don't need help. Quit worrying about me and go wash up."

He groans softly and pats her bottom with a playful spank which makes her squelch a yelp. Apparently everyone in the kitchen is more preoccupied with either washing up, carrying dishes full of food to the table or already in the dining room or else he would never have done something so bold. She can tell that Kelly leaves her with great unwillingness. He is such a worrywart.

Cory and Simon are chatting almost non-stop about how cool the farm is and what features and animals they like about it. To Hannah, it's just always been her home, and she'd never really had the opportunity to ponder whether or not it was 'cool.' Sam is quiet, however, and the boys are not trying very hard to help her fit in with them. Typical boys in their own worlds.

Hannah is overcome with the urge to use the restroom and sets the platter of sausages on the island. She prays that the two teen boys don't eat all of them before she gets back to take them to the dining room. Once she makes it to her own bedroom she relieves herself in her bathroom and tears spring to her eyes as she feels an urge to bear down even after her bladder is emptied. When she's done, Hannah washes her hands and leaves her bedroom where she runs into Kelly's chest. He kisses her forehead which makes her smile.

"Hey, are you alright? The kids said you split out of the kitchen really fast, and Cory was concerned," he asks as he grasps her shoulders in his large hands.

"That's so kind of Cory. But, yes, I'm just fine. It was nothing. You need to stop worrying about me!" she says with a broad smile and is surprised when she feels Kelly's mouth swoop down onto hers for a long, lingering and rather delicious kiss. She is breathless as usual when Kelly finally pulls back, and she is clinging to him feebly.

"We'd better get back. I hear Sue asking for you," Kelly tells her.

Funny, she hadn't heard anything other than her own panting. Kelly Alexander is a bad influence on her. And she loves that about him!

He doesn't miss a beat and takes her hand in his to lead her back to the kitchen where the boys are still talking and Sam is still quiet.

"Sam, why don't you join us in the dining room?" Hannah knows that this is going to get rejected by the girl who doesn't like to intrude. "I think my sisters could use the help with some of the younger kids if you can manage that."

"Oh, um, ok, Miss Hannah," Sam says.

Her voice contains relief. She is probably glad to be getting away from the boys. Hannah can hardly blame the poor girl.

They join the rest of the family, minus Grandpa who is sleeping since he covered the med shed all night while Reagan slept. Hannah knows that they have both been going on caffeine in large quantities in order to provide medical care around the clock.

"Can we find a seat for Sam, everyone? I didn't figure she wanted to sit in the kitchen while the boys do guy talk. She's going to get reflux. They're on to cars and motors, ugh," Hannah explains as Kelly laughs beside her.

"Here, Sam, sit over here by me. Scoot down, Justin," Em suggests.

Naturally Em would want Sam to sit next to her because Sam's older and so much more hip than all the other kids just like Em is so much more sophisticated than everyone else in Ari's opinion.

"Ok, thanks," Sam returns softly.

When she scoots her seat out and then back in, she doesn't allow it to scrape against the hardwood floor like most everyone does.

The conversation at the breakfast table starts up and mostly covers the crops, the greenhouse activity, milk production, the usual. Nobody discusses the visitors because of Huntley and Sam being present at the table since there is a slim possibility that these children could take information back to their guests that the family may not want them to know. They keep the conversation light, casual and try to include Sam in it.

122

"What subjects did you like in school, Sam?" Sue asks when the discussion of crop rotations is over.

"Oh, um," Sam starts and is barely audible. "I guess I like English, writing mostly. I also like art, but that wasn't a subject I studied at school."

"Oh really?" Sue says as if she's concocting something. "And what about you, Huntley? What did you like in school?"

The young boy takes a while longer to answer. "Um, I guess I like lunch."

At this answer, everyone laughs and Kelly and Derek heartily agree with him.

Sue starts again. "We are going to need to get school going around here and very soon. As soon as the weather turns and the crops are finished, that is."

"School? Really? Are you doing it here on this farm?" Sam asks with confusion.

"Sure. Grandpa and I were talking about schooling just the other day. He would like some of the children to learn medicine and some veterinary care, but then there will be the basic subjects that everyone still needs to learn. We'll also supplement the kids' educations with learning how to can, tend crops and animals, that kind of thing," Sue explains, and Grams concurs.

"Hannah and Reagan can also teach whoever wants to learn music, too. It will be a good way to keep the kids busy in the winter," Grams adds.

Reagan snorts rudely, and John warns her to be nice. She snorts again.

"Oh, well that will be nice for the kids who live here," Sam laments.

There is obvious sadness in her voice because she thinks she won't be able to stay on.

"Well, I actually hate English and anything to do with it. I always loved math the most," Sue tells her. "And just like you, I love art. We'll have to sketch together some time."

"Yeah?" Sam asks just to be kind.

There is a heaviness in her voice. Grams was right, nothing new there. Something is very wrong with this girl.

"And Herb could always use more help in the med shed, obviously. You've been a very valuable asset around here, Sam," Grams illustrates.

"Thank you, ma'am," Sam says. "I'm happy to help."

"What about English? I just want to know if you'll be teaching that or if I'm going to get stuck with it?" Sue asks impatiently.

"Sure, Miss Sue, I can help. While we're here I'll teach the kids for you," Sam offers generously.

"Why are you able to work around the sickness out there with Reagan?" Derek asks unexpectedly. "I would hate to see you get sick. How come you haven't caught this?"

His question is so out of the blue that the girl blurts out her answer without her usual guardedness.

"Um, my mom took me and my brothers and sister to get vaccinated over in Nashville. My uncle was a pediatrician at a big hospital there, and he told her to bring us when the wars started overseas to get everything he could give us. He was really smart like...," Sam stops abruptly.

She must realize she is revealing way too much.

"So you aren't from the Southwest like the rest of your group?" Derek asks bluntly.

He's quite good at getting people to say things they don't want to say, and Hannah isn't sure she wants know the origins of this ability. Sam is quiet again, but then she finally answers.

"No, sir," she says honestly but will provide no more.

Hannah feels that same urge to urinate again. She excuses herself and rushes to the guest bathroom nearest the dining room because she is afraid she won't make it to her own. It is more painful this time, and the urge to bear down is awful, bringing tears to her eyes. When she comes out, Kelly is waiting for her again.

"What's going on, Hannah?" he asks quietly so as not to be overheard by the rest of the family.

"I'm not sure. Just not feeling great, Kelly. Don't worry," she says, trying to allay his concerns.

"I do worry. That's my job," he says trying to lighten the mood.

He gently lays a hand against her cheek. Hannah can hear the meal winding down in the dining room and soon they will be accosted by a hoard of people moving through the hallway.

"Did Grams ask Sam and Huntley if they want to stay on here when their group leaves? I was kind of wondering if that was the direction they were going with that conversation," she asks her lover as his hand continues to caress her cheek.

"No, not yet. But, yeah, I think that's what the plan is. We'll probably find out at the next family meeting tomorrow," Kelly says.

She nods against his hand. He steps quickly back from her because his brother has come into the hall with them.

"Hey, Kelly. Can I take Simon out and show him the horses and maybe ride for like an hour? We won't be too long. I know you need the hay brought in from that pasture. Me and Simon could do it if we can take the wagon and tractor out there by ourselves. Right, Simon?" Cory asks.

Hannah believes that he has more excitement than a boy of his age should have over picking up hay bales and riding horses.

"Yes, sir. I'll help get the hay. That's no problem," Simon jumps in.

"Yeah, sure, Cory. I just gotta help Derek and John with that wheel on the wagon first. Got a part messed up. Might need welded. We'll see. But you guys go out and mess with the horses, and we'll call you when we're ready," Kelly says.

Hannah wants to scream. Her stomach is hurting down low, and she is feeling like she is going to pee her pants, or dress in her case. Something is wrong. Hannah excuses herself to find Reagan while the guys go on about stupid tractors.

Sue brushes past her, and Hannah stops her sister. "Sue? Is Reagan still…"

"I'm here, Hannie. Whatcha' need?" Reagan asks.

Her beloved sister sets her hand on Hannah's shoulder for a brief second.

"Um," Hannah pauses to find Reagan's hand. She nearly drags her back the hall to her own bedroom where Hannah goes straight to the bathroom. "Just a minute. I'll be out… oooh."

"Hannah? Are you ok?" Reagan asks from beyond the partially closed door.

125

"No, I don't think so," Hannah answers her as the enormous tears fill her eyes again. This is so embarrassing… and painful.

"What's wrong?" Reagan asks.

Hannah can tell that that her sister has come into the bathroom. Hannah is bearing down and tearing up so much that she doesn't even care if her sister sees her on the toilet.

"Oh, Hannah. What is it, hon'?" Reagan asks.

She is squatted right beside Hannah. She finally stands and flushes. Then she moves around Reagan to wash her hands.

"I don't know, Reagan. It just hurts like… horrible when I pee, and I keep feeling like I have to go. But when I do, it's like nothing hardly. I mean it really hurts, and I really feel like I'm going to… pee my pants," Hannah says with a great deal of mortification.

"Oh, that's nothing to be embarrassed about. Sounds like a UTI or a bladder infection, something of that nature. They're quite common. Wait here. I'll go get some antibiotics and a cup for you to give me a sample, but it sounds like a bladder infection. I'll bring you a little something for the pain. You just wait here for me so you can keep using the restroom, and I'll tell everyone that you are just under the weather," Reagan offers.

"Thanks. This is so embarrassing," Hannah answers. Reagan's manner is kind and gentle. Perhaps she should tell John to fake an injury so her sister will be nicer to him, the poor guy.

Ten minutes later, her sister has properly diagnosed the urine sample that Hannah is able to give her after going to the bathroom two more times. She also takes her temperature and declares that Hannah is fever free, and according to Reagan, it's a good thing because it signifies that it is highly unlikely that the infection has spread to her kidneys.

"The stick shows a minor presence of bacterial infection, not too high, but enough to cause your symptoms. I don't have a lab to grow a culture and be more thorough. But if I was to just make a quick guess, I would say that this is just a minor UTI or bladder infection like I initially diagnosed. They aren't usually a big deal and clear up fairly quickly," Reagan monologues.

Hannah's pretty sure that her darling sister is mostly talking to herself because she buzzes about the room doing who knows what.

"What can I do?" Hannah asks her brilliant sister.

126

"Just take it easy today and probably tomorrow. It will take a few hours for the antibiotics to kick in. I'm giving you a low dose of painkiller for the discomfort, too. By tomorrow you'll feel better, but just stay on the antibiotics for the three full days anyways. Sometimes you can treat these types of infections homeopathically, but since we have the antibiotics and I don't like seeing you in pain…"

Reagan ruffles the hair on Hannah's head.

"…you're getting the antibodies, kiddo."

"Thanks, Reagan. What would we do without you?" Hannah declares and holds her sister's hand and is surprised when Reagan doesn't pull away.

"I just can't figure how you got this. We eat so healthy around here. It's crazy. Sometimes I have heard of patients who consume too many tomato based products or just tomatoes themselves or oranges, anything acidic, causing a bladder infection or urinary tract infection. But it's not like we're eating ten damn oranges a day!" Reagan exclaims.

This is how her brain works. She can't just treat something without knowing every minute detail of the problem or figuring it out. If Hannah wasn't so miserable, she'd probably laugh.

"It's just weird. I can't put my finger on it. Bladder infections used to be called the honeymoon sickness because women who weren't used to sexual activity or who didn't know about going pee after sex would get these and end up in an E.R. on their honeymoons. Here, take these," Reagan says with a disbelieving chuff.

She hands Hannah pills and a glass of water to wash them down.

"Um," Hannah says nervously as her face flames. "Hm." Oh God, that's what had caused this infection. Why hadn't Kelly told her any of that stuff? Perhaps he didn't know, either. He'd never want to see her get hurt. He doesn't even like her going in any of the barns without him, so she highly doubts that he knows the pee-after-sex rule.

"What?" Reagan asks straightforwardly as usual.

"Um, it's just that… you know about what you said…," Hannah searches for the right way to tell her sister.

"What? Just spit it out, Hannah," Reagan asks more impatiently this time.

They are sitting on Hannah's bed together.

"Well, don't get mad. Reagan, I mean it. Don't get mad. And you have to promise not to tell Grams or Grandpa. Ohhh, or anyone," Hannah frets, her brows pinching together of their own volition at her distress.

"I won't. Ok, I promise," Reagan assures her. "What's going on, Hannie?"

"Oh, goodness. Don't call me 'Hannie' right now, ok?"

"Ok, just tell me what's wrong," Reagan implores.

Her sister squeezes her hand reassuringly.

"I think I might have honeymoon syndrome," Hannah finally blurts. Reagan is unnaturally silent.

"Honeymoon *sickness*," Reagan corrects. "What do you mean, Hannah? I just explained to you what honeymoon sickness is."

"I know and I'm telling you that *that* is what's wrong," Hannah explains it to her genius sister more clearly.

"What do you mean? Like sex?"

"Shh, don't talk so loudly. Yes, like… sex," Hannah says with a great deal of humiliation as her cheeks burn with embarrassment.

"What?" Reagan nearly screams.

"Reagan, quiet! You'll wake Grandpa," Hannah warns under her breath. That is the last thing she and Kelly need. If anybody finds out about them, it could be detrimental. But Grandpa discovering her amoral conduct would be particularly devastating. She's not sure she could handle him being disappointed in her.

"Who?" Reagan asks with deadly fury in her voice.

"What do you mean who? You are so unaware sometimes, Reagan. For being a brilliant doctor, sis, you sure can be pretty lost when it comes to people. I'm talking about Kelly, of course!" Hannah says in a rush. "I love him. And he loves me and it's so wonderful, Reagan. I am crazy about him. He's so special and tender. We love each other very much, and he makes me so happy. We just don't want anyone to know just yet. When things settle down and the visitors leave, that will be a better time. We're just waiting until they leave."

There is no answer. No response from her sister who is downright terrifyingly protective of her sometimes. Hannah's having

128

a flashback to the feed mill scene in town when they were younger and her sister had punched a boy twice her size for teasing Hannah for being blind.

"Don't say anything to anyone. You promised," Hannah reminds her. Reagan slips her hand from Hannah's grip.

"What? Oh yeah, right. I remember. I won't tell anyone. Does anyone else know?" Reagan's voice has become deadpan.

Hannah prays that it is just because she is still processing.

"No!" Hannah whispers dubiously. Is her sister crazy?

"Ok," Reagan says calmly. "You just lie down and rest, Hannie. I've got to get back to the med shed, ok? That woman is sicker today. I'll make an excuse to everyone for you. I'll bring you some dinner later tonight. Take it easy unless you start to feel better, then you can come out and join everyone. But I don't want you to overdo it today. Promise?"

"Sure, sis," Hannah accommodates her, and Reagan insists on making her lie down on her bed. Then her loving sister bends and kisses her forehead tenderly, touches her hair and moves away.

A few minutes after Reagan leaves her bedroom, Hannah realizes that her sister had not even asked anything about Kelly or their relationship or the sex for goodness sake! Neither of them had ever done it before, so she should have wanted a first-hand accounting or some small snippet of detail. But, no, she'd just left so calmly. She'd also not told Hannah whether or not she could resume sexual activity anytime soon, either.

Chapter Nine
John

"You fucker!" Reagan screams like a banshee.

She comes at a full tilt run and jumps onto Kelly's back before he can get himself all the way erect.

They were working on the wagon wheel he, Derek and Kelly, and Kelly was bent over tightening a bolt. She must have stalked up on them before she started the running assault because John had not heard or seen her until the yell. Now John's friend has a lunatic on his back who is trying to punch him and rip out his hair.

"Jesus!" Kelly screeches.

He tries to dislodge her from his back without hurting her.

"Reagan, what the hell?" Derek yells, as well.

She and Kelly whirl around two complete turns before John is able to grab her by the waist and yank her off of his friend. But she immediately jerks free and jumps at Kelly again from the front. She manages to land a solid punch to his massive square jaw. John knows that it hurt her hand more than Kelly's large jaw.

"Ow, fuck!"

Her expletive leaves nothing to the imagination as she shakes her hand and holds her tiny wrist with the other.

"Are you ok?" Kelly asks in a strange turn of fate.

The concerned look on his friend's face is almost comical for having just been punched by the very person he's trying to console. Kelly even reaches for her only to have Reagan shove with both hands at his chest. It doesn't move him even an inch.

"Fuck off," she yells at him. "Ouch!"

The shove has obviously re-strained her small, injured wrist. John knows she's hurting because she shakes her hand vigorously trying to get away from the pain.

"Reagan, calm the hell down. What's wrong?" Derek shouts at her.

John tries to hold her back as she lunges for Kelly again, though the guy is worried for her.

"He knows what's wrong! How could you? You bastard!" Reagan shouts in an accusatory tone.

John regards his friend who is starting to look like he's figured out what is going on between them. She is struggling to be free as John holds her around the waist again.

"Let me go, John," she screeches.

"Not until you calm down," John says firmly as she wiggles and twists. She's harder to hold onto than he would've thought.

"What the hell is going on, Reagan?" Derek asks again.

"Stay out of it, Derek!" Reagan bellows at his brother.

She wriggles her skinny body free of John's grasp but doesn't lunge at Kelly again.

"You stay the fuck away from her, or I'll kill you. Do you hear me? You came into our home, and *you* did this. You disrespected my grandparents and my sister by doing this. She's sick. Did you know that, tough guy?" Reagan accuses.

Kelly is stunned. His eyes bulge, and he shakes his head.

"Wait, what do you mean she's sick? What's wrong with her?" Kelly asks with obvious worry.

He runs a hand through his shaggy hair and then the beard, which could also use a trim.

"Don't worry about it! I took care of her, which is more than I can say for you. She's sick and it's your fault and that's all you need to know about it. Just stay away from her!"

"I... I can't, Reagan. Trust me I tried, but I can't," he admits with a tinge of defeat. "I'm sorry. I'll make this right. It's just that everything has been crazy around here lately. I wasn't going to... I mean... shit."

Kelly is about as ineloquent as a man can be, and he looks freaked out, stressed out and about to come unglued. But he's not arguing with Reagan or getting pissed at her for the assault. As a matter of fact, he looks surprisingly understanding of her.

"Is this about Hannah?" Derek asks stupidly.

"Ya' think?" John asks. He wants to laugh and almost does, but he's afraid the tigress will attack him next. Derek sneers at John who just shakes his head at his clueless brother and laughs once.

"Stay the fuck away from her, Kelly. I swear to God!" Reagan hints at future attacks.

"Reagan, you don't understand," Kelly tries to explain.

Reagan won't hear any of what he has to say. She walks closer to him and sticks her index finger closer to his center chest area.

"Stay away from her or you'll force my hand, and I think we both know what that means," Reagan threatens with lethal intent.

"That's why I wanted to leave, but she didn't want me to, Reagan. I mean it. It just didn't happen the way I thought it would."

"Well I'm telling you how it's gonna end," she hisses and gets closer to him.

It must be so frustrating to be so short. With Kelly in his combat boots that make him an inch taller than his six five stature, Reagan only comes to the bottom of his chest. John notices that she gets on her tiptoes. Poor kid.

"No," Kelly says nonthreateningly.

"What did you just say?"

Oh boy, this isn't getting any better. Her small fists clench at her sides, and he decides he'd better step closer to her lest she attack Kelly again.

"Reagan, I'm in love with her, ok?"

Kelly actually sighs and then looks nervously from Derek to John as if he's embarrassed.

"There's a shocker," John quips sarcastically.

"Shut up, John!" Reagan barks at him and then swings back to Kelly. "And you, you can't be with her. Hannah is… she's…"

"Too good for me. I know."

His friend hangs his head dejectedly and jams one hand on his hip. This just isn't true. John is about to contradict him, but Reagan beats him to it.

"Exactly! So stay…" Reagan agrees meanly.

"Reagan! That's enough. That's unfair to Kelly," Derek scolds her like a big brother reprimanding his kid sister.

132

"Shut up, Derek! This is between him and me. He can go and find someone else. Not our Hannie," Reagan says irrationally.

She's ready to take on all three of them if she must and is jerking her small thumb toward the driveway as if she's suggesting that Kelly go and find someone off of the farm. Either that or she's pointing toward the visitors' camp which would not be an enticing proposition. Nasty.

"Reagan, that's ridiculous. This isn't actually between you and Kelly. It's between Kelly and Hannah. Don't put Hannah on a pedestal like that. Kelly cares about her, and he can take care of her better than anyone," Derek corrects her again.

Reagan hisses out, "Stay out of it. This has nothing to do with you Derek... or you."

She swivels and points directly at John.

"Hey, what did I do? *He's* the one molesting your sister," John jokes, and Kelly shakes his head at him and mouths the word "thanks."

"Jesus, John. That's really helping, ya' dick!" Derek gripes. "Look, Reagan, I know this is hard for you, but it's not like Kelly has forced himself on her. She obviously likes him, too. We've all seen it. Everyone but you has seen it, honey."

His brother is trying to appease Reagan, and it almost seems as if it's going to work.

"You're an asshole, Kelly," she says more quietly.

"I know," he accepts.

Unfortunately, the scuffle has drawn the attention of the two women from the camp as they were fetching water in buckets. The stripper, Kitten, and her cohort in crime, the toothless hadji girl as the Rangers have been referring to her, walk by with their water. Kitten is practically prancing.

"What do we have here, Jasmine?" toothless nag asks rhetorically of Kitten-Jasmine.

"This looks like a whole lot of man meat to me, Amber," Jasmine answers.

She purposely raises a suggestive eyebrow at John. He and the other two men are working without their shirts on like they do most days on the farm because they just get too hot. And it also ruins what few shirts they each have when they get grease on them or holes

133

and rips in them. John's not so sure he should've taken his off. He's starting to feel like what Kitten must've felt like on stage as the two women gawk at them. Both women have paused and are looking at the three of them like they could possibly sexually assault them. John is wishing he had a rape whistle.

"Oh yeah. Haven't seen nothing like you three in quite some time," toothless says as she bobs her head side to side.

"Fuck off, trailer trash!" Reagan yells at them violently.

The women both jump in surprise like they hadn't even considered Reagan standing there. In their defense, she is small. Both of these women from the visitors' group are considerably taller than the boss. However, if she feels confident enough to take on Kelly, then John's quite sure she could handle herself against Amber and Jasmine the Kitten.

"Geez, that wasn't necessary. We were just making a friendly observation, little one," Kitten says.

She is apparently unfazed by the insult. The other one, though, is glaring at Reagan as if she'd like to murder her. Jasmine licks her lips sexually and walks closer to John where she touches his bare chest with her middle finger running it down to the waistband of his faded jeans. He'd like to tell her that her fingernails are too long, and dirty to boot.

Reagan marches over and slaps Jasmine's hand down hard. The crack echoes in the barnyard.

"Go!" she barks at the woman who towers over her.

Reagan points her finger toward their campsite. Her and her bossy little fingers!

"Suit yourself, little one," she purrs.

Jasmine leans close and says so that only Reagan and John can hear, "You're always welcome to join us, sweetie."

"Get the fuck out of here before I use this on you," Reagan says.

Reagan fingers the pistol strapped to her sexy thigh. The women retreat and when they are out of earshot, only then does the group talk again. John is quite sure that Reagan McClane had not caught on to Jasmine's threesome insinuation. She doesn't even get John's more blatant and not at all subtle sexual innuendoes most of the time.

134

"Gross, I feel violated," John jokes to lighten the tension. Derek laughs and even Kelly chuckles once and shakes his head.

"Yeah, right," Reagan doubts. "I'm out of here. I need... I need... I'm going to run or something."

"I know what you need," John mumbles, and Derek and Kelly both laugh loudly this time. She just looks at him queerly, though. Of course.

"You got that right, little brother," Derek laughs again.

Reagan glowers at them like they are complete imbeciles and takes off at a sprint as she obviously doesn't get John's sexual insinuation. Sometimes for being so brilliant she is kind of dull-witted.

John catches up to her just past the barns on her running trail and follows along for a while, enjoying the view until the path widens enough for the both of them.

"How's your patient?" John asks her, easily keeping stride to her shorter one.

"Same. Sam's keeping an eye on her for me. Probably gonna die like all my patients," Reagan bites out angrily.

There is ice in her voice and she pants lightly from the run.

"Reagan, you're a fantastic doctor. None of this is your fault. You and your grandfather are doing everything you can for them," John defends her against her own criticism.

"Go back. I just want to be alone."

John snatches her by the arm, and they come to a halt.

"Let me go..."

"I'm kind of tired today, babe. Can we just walk for a while? Plus, you look hot," John lies smoothly.

"Then go back. I didn't tell you to come. And, of course, I'm hot. I'm wearing jeans for Christ's sake!" Reagan says crudely.

She continues to walk with him, albeit a fast walk. He's glad she's switched to jeans instead of wearing her tiny shorts around the visitors. She's obviously holding a hard grudge against him for telling her to dress differently for the time being, but John can take it. It's worth it to know that the men in the visitors' group won't be eyeing her up which would force his hand in shooting them.

"Take it easy on me. I'm getting old," he jokes with her, and she hits him with a snarky look as they climb a short hill together.

135

She slips once and automatically grabs for John's arm which is already there. It makes him feel like a demi-god.

"What the hell was he thinking?"

"Darwin? I've never gotten that one, either. Too many flaws in the theory. I mean look at these trees and that cardinal over there…" he is cut off from continuing his jesting as Reagan slugs his shoulder.

"Don't be a jerk. I'm not debating evolution, and you know it. I mean Kelly. What was he thinking? He can't be with Hannie," Reagan says.

They hike up to the top meadow where they stop a moment while she rubs at her wrist.

"Let me look at that, boss," John says and takes her fragile hand in his own.

"I'm the doctor, moron," Reagan insults him yet again.

"Yeah, but I've seen enough fights to know what I'm looking at and you haven't. You did give Kelly a pretty good slug, though, for a pipsqueak," John tells her and ignores her scowl. He bends her wrist backward and then down which makes her wince and makes John feel bad for doing so.

"Ow, damn it!" she exclaims.

"Yeah, 'ow.' You're too small to take on giants."

"So?" she returns immaturely.

Her pout is sexy even though John knows that she doesn't mean it to be.

"Now we haven't gone over throwing a punch so you shouldn't have tried that. I'm not saying that Kelly didn't deserve it. I mean, Hannah is your sister and all. But you just weren't ready to fight him. I'd say you've got a good sprain, but nothing seems broken. I'll help you wrap it when we get back."

Reagan looks up at him and John is momentarily distracted by how pretty she looks in the late summer sun in a meadow full of flowers and tall grasses that match her eyes. Her golden blonde hair is half down and half up from wrestling with Kelly, her cheeks are flushed from the run, and he's left to wonder if this is what she'd look like after sex. Before he tosses her down in the field and has his way with her, which he's sure she'd enjoy, John starts talking again.

"What did you do- pole vault onto his back? That was quite the leap!" he praises, which earns him a grin.

136

"He pissed me off. You don't know the half of it. He's very wrong in this, John."

She is almost beseeching him to hear her side.

"I'm with you, boss. You want me to beat him up, I will. Alright? Whatever you say I'm gonna do it, no questions," he tells her, and he's being completely honest, although he'd get his butt kicked.

"Really?" Reagan asks with surprise and wrinkles her nose. "He's your best friend."

"You're... my girl. That's just the way it is," John explains and hopes she doesn't freak. She does frown up at him, but she doesn't say he's insane for calling her it.

"I'm not asking you to do anything like that for me," Reagan tells him.

John lays his palm against her cheek briefly, and she swallows hard.

"I'd do anything you asked," he informs her. How can she have any doubt? He'd killed nearly a dozen men in the city to keep her safe. Of course she doesn't know the exact body count of the ones in the park, but she knows he'd killed people to protect her and he'd kill a dozen more if need be.

"Don't," she whispers, stops speaking and looks at her feet.

Surprisingly, she hasn't pulled her hand back yet, and John is rubbing his thumb over her delicate wrist bones. Her breathing is becoming shallower, and he very much wants to think it's because of his light touch that seems to be distracting her.

She continues quietly, "Don't fight with Kelly over me. He's your best friend. You two are like brothers."

"Reagan, Kelly loves her. He loves her a lot, like the for-life kind. Like your grandparents love each other. He's loyal as all get out, and he will take care of her," John tells her gently to help assuage her anger at the situation.

She frowns and puckers, and John gives her a lopsided grin. The urge to kiss her is almost too much.

"Look, whatever's happening between them I think we should let them be. They are both adults and just to give you some input on Kelly, he wasn't a womanizer. He never was even when we went on leave together and partied and stuff," John explains. He's waiting for her to call him a man whore again. If she does, he might just have to prove it right here. She does slip her hand free of his.

"Fine, I'll leave it be for now. But if I think he's just using her, then I'll tell Grandpa and he'll throw him out or shoot him. Or I'll shoot him," she finally settles down some and John laughs.

"Reagan, he's not using her. Believe me. He's not that kind of guy, not at all," John tells her as the frown lines and the crease between her brows finally let up. She is quiet for a few moments.

"You'd really beat up Kelly for me?" she asks mischievously.

"Come on," he tells her, and they walk some more. "I'd probably get my butt kicked, you know."

"Yeah, I was thinking the same thing. Unless, of course, you had your rifle. I've read about super high-power rifles for hunting big game. You might want to invest in one of those first," she teases.

John pokes her in the rib, earning him a small smile.

"We'd better get back to your patient. Wanna' finish or just go back the way we came?" John asks, and Reagan gives him a knowing grin before she sprints the long way home. There are so many other more preferable, delightful ways to burn calories that he'd like to show her.

Yesterday after dinner before he'd gone to catch some sleep and before his shift started, John went out behind the barns and found that black car. Though Sue had told him what it looked like he hadn't been prepared for what he'd found. It had been dark, but he'd taken a flashlight and what he saw was like nothing he'd seen in all his years of warring. Maybe it was because he wasn't used to looking at the aftermath of carnage since his team made their quick strikes and then split the scene. Or maybe it was because he actually cared about this victim. The weeds had grown up thick around the VW, and he'd had to really yank the door to get it to open past the foliage. The dome light had surprisingly come on when he'd pried the door open, and between that and the flashlight, it was more than he ever wanted to see. There was dried blood everywhere, literally everywhere. The driver's seat was completely coated with dark blotches. The console, even the passenger seat and the floor of the passenger's side had blood on them. The glove box, the steering wheel, the dash, all of the instrument panels were splashed or splattered with it. He'd found blood in the trunk and on the tailgate, as well. He'd also found the note on the floor of the driver's side.

138

Her grandfather must've put it in there when he moved her escape vehicle. It was also blood-splattered but was written in the same, no-nonsense manner in which Reagan spoke about any patient. Lateral this, quadrant that, a diagram of her abdomen with notes scribbled off to the side.

John had opened the glove box and found the registration of the car saying that it belonged to Dr. Krue, which is what he'd suspected. Along with the blood everywhere, John had found used sanitary napkins soaked with it and many bandages in the same condition. There were hypodermics, empty packets of clotting powder like he'd seen many times in the military, and pill bottles on the floor, most of which were empty. A map lay open with a red line that crossed through the states of Ohio and Kentucky to their own valley in Tennessee. They were not main freeways that were marked in red but back country roads. Smart. If she'd taken the highways to get home, she wouldn't have made it because the freeways, from John's own experience, had immediately become impassable and highly dangerous.

As John runs beside her back to the farm, he is amazed by her tenacity and her sheer will to live, coupled with her determination to get home that one, devastatingly, eventful night. He's glad that she did, however. His life has literally been turned upside down by Reagan McClane. But it's not the most unwelcome of experiences that he's had to deal with. Her spirit and toughness is what had kept her alive. Her sense of family had kept her going. Her courage had healed her. And John has come to respect and care for her more than he'd ever thought possible.

Chapter Ten
Sue

As soon as she gets Isaac and Jacob down for their morning naps, with a lot of help from Grams, Sue heads out to the garden to resume picking the last of the summer's crop of peppers and some of the sweet corn. She stops near the horse barn to talk with Derek first.

"What the heck was that all about?" she inquires after the shouting match between Kelly and Reagan.

"Uh, nothing really. She's just got it in her head that Kelly should stay away from Hannah."

Her tight-lipped husband answers her with a casual nonchalance. It didn't look like 'nothing' to Sue.

"I saw from the window in the music room. I was feeding Isaac," she tells him. The muscles on his forearm flex and strain as he tightens down a bolt under the tractor's open hood.

"It wasn't anything. I think they got it worked out," he says on a weary sigh.

Sue knows this man so well. She won't get anything more out of him on the subject.

"Honey, you need to go and get a few hours of sleep," she tells him. "You were up before breakfast and you haven't even gone to bed yet from your watch last night."

He scowls to himself. "I'm fine, Sue. I did sleep about an hour before I came down to breakfast."

"No, you aren't fine. You need sleep. We all do, Superman. You're dead on your feet. Look, Kelly and Cory are up and moving around. I'm sure John will be back soon. We're safe, Derek," she says softly, laying her hand on his forearm.

He yanks her to him, against his grease and grime and Sue could care less. His kiss holds quite a bit of promise. When he finally pulls back Sue smiles up into his brown eyes.

"I'll go in and sleep, but wake me up in two hours. And be careful," he says quietly. "I'll tell Cory to keep an eye out for you while you're in the garden."

"Got it, two hours," she says with sass. Derek just smirks down at her and gives her another quick kiss.

"I mean it, Sue. Don't let me sleep longer. I don't want the guys to have to hold down the fort throughout the daylight hours by themselves," he laments.

Sue simply nods and kisses his stubbly chin. "Aye-aye, Major Harrison," she quips which earns her a swat to her derriere.

After Derek leaves again, she picks up her basket for picking vegetables and goes straight to the aisle where peppers are located next to the tall, towering stalks of sweet corn. Cory comes out to help her, and she's more appreciative than she can say. He picks beans an aisle over from her, but they are still able to converse.

"What do you think of the new kids Sam and Simon?" she asks him after swiping the back of her hand across her brow to remove the sweat there. Sue is sure that she's left a trail of dirt there, as well, but she isn't out here for a beauty pageant.

"They seem cool," Cory says noncommittally.

He's not much of a talker most of the time.

"Yeah?" Sue pushes. "Even Simon?"

"Sure. I mean he's kind of shy, but he seems all right," he tells her.

He finally makes eye contact with her, but looks away just as fast. To say that he is unsure of himself around women is the understatement of the century.

"Do you think he could be dangerous?" Sue asks.

Cory chuckles, shakes his head and replies, "No. I don't think he's a threat to anyone, Miss Sue."

"I guess that's good, right?" she says to which he nods. Sue indicates toward her basket. "Mine's almost full."

"Yeah, mine, too," he tells her.

"What about Samantha?"

"She's ok," Cory says, but this time his statement is accompanied by a deep scowl.

Sue decides to press on this. "What is it, Cory?"

He shrugs, so Sue pushes again. This time it works and he answers, but stares at his hands.

"I dunno. She's kind of messed up, you know, like Miss Reagan?" Cory blushes and quickly amends his declaration. "I didn't mean it like that! Please don't tell her I said that. I'm so stupid. Sometimes I just say stuff that's so stupid. Miss Reagan's a great doctor..."

"Cory, it's fine. And just call me Sue." She lets him off the hook. "You're actually right. My sister is deeply troubled by some things that have happened to her. She's very distrustful of people. I think I also see that in Sam, just like you do. But don't worry, I wouldn't tell Reagan or Sam that you talked to me."

"Ok. I didn't mean any offense, Sue," he says quietly.

"None taken. I'm the one who asked what you thought of Sam and Simon. I really want to know your opinion of them, of any of them. You are a lot like Kelly. You're both a good judge of people. I trust your opinion a lot, Cory," she confides softly so as to set him at ease.

"Thanks, Sue," he returns. "They're both nice kids. I don't think they'll give anybody on the farm any trouble. And I don't think they like any of those people out there that they're traveling with. I get that vibe from Simon, not so much from Sam. She doesn't really talk to me much. That's kind of why I think she's like Reagan, you know? They don't like to talk to men."

If she'd thought he was a good judge of character before, then her assessment is now completely blown out of the water. Sue had grossly underestimated this kid's ability to form quality, adult opinions of people. He is very astute for someone so young. She decides to play devil's advocate to see what gets revealed.

"Maybe she's just shy," she throws out to him. Cory's eyes dart to hers and stay there.

"No, that's not it. There's something seriously wrong with her. It's almost like she tries to look ugly and dirty or something. The other day she had a big blob of mud on both of her cheeks, and when I pointed it out and handed her a handkerchief- one of the ones Grams gave me- she said no. She wouldn't wipe it off no matter what. I think that's weird."

"Strange," Sue contemplates.

"Then today she had a bunch of dirt and grass in her hair. I tried to pick some of it out for her and she jumped away and said no again. I don't know what's her deal, but she's kinda' weird. She seems smart, but then she acts strange like that," Cory informs her.

Sue nods. "My basket's overfull. I'm gonna run this back to the house, Cor," she tells him, stands and stretches her back.

Cory takes her basket before she can head to the house.

"Nah, I got it, Miss- I mean Sue. I'll take both of them back. Here, take my other empty one and I'll bring a couple more back."

"Thanks, Cory," she tells him and then places a hand on his shoulder. "You're a great help around here. We'd be hard-pressed without you."

He blushes again and splits for the house with barely a nod of acknowledgement about the complement. Speaking of shy! Sue chuckles to herself and returns to picking. After a moment, a shadow falls across the plants in front of her. He may be shy, but he sure is a fast runner to be back so quickly.

"Well, that was..." she turns and stops dead in her tracks.

Frank from the visitors' group is the one casting a shadow and not Cory. A second later, Levon comes toward her from the middle of the corn field. Frank is only standing one aisle of vegetables over from her. His casual stance makes her uneasy.

"Hey, little lady," he sneers while chewing a long, thin blade of grass.

"Um, hi," she returns but would rather not. "Aren't you supposed to..."

"Those hot peppers?" he interrupts.

She was about to order him back to his camp when he breaks in with a question of his own.

"What? No, they're sweet peppers actually," she says and before she can demand he return to his campsite, he steps over the row of cabbage to stand three feet from her.

"Sweet, huh?" he asks.

There is suggestion in that one word that Sue would rather not think about. She scowls at him, but it doesn't slow him down.

"Sounds pretty good to me, right, Levon?"

"Mm hm, yeah real sweet," Levon says.

Sue feels like throwing up. Frank is lean and lanky, but Levon is another thing altogether. He's almost as big as Kelly, but just not as heavily muscled or in such top condition as any of the Rangers. He takes his time perusing Sue up and down with disgusting implication. Damn! Now she wishes that she hadn't sent Derek in to catch some much needed sleep. She glances around. There's no one in sight. Where the hell did Kelly go off to?

He asks, "What's your name, little lady?"

"Sue," she answers through clenched teeth. Why are they over here?

"I'm Levon and…"

"We all know who you all are. Introductions aren't necessary. You just need to go…"

"What's the hurry? It's nice out today. Isn't it, Sue?" Frank asks as if chatting the weather is just the order of the day.

"You need to return to your camp, gentlemen," she tries at civility.

"Hey, hey why the hurry? We could hang out a while," Frank suggests as he takes a step closer.

"I'm busy. That's why," she informs them, though they don't look ready to leave.

"We could help. This is sure a lot of work for a fine ass lookin' woman like you, Sue," Frank offers with a grin.

His teeth are nicotine stained and gunky looking. His yellow tinted eye-glasses slip down a notch, and he pushes them back up. His hair is greasy. His general appearance is dirty and greasy. The black jeans he wears have tears and rips. The white t-shirt is dotted with stains. One particular spot looks like it could be a small blood splatter. Sue doesn't want to contemplate the origins of that spot.

"We're good when we work as a team," Levon remarks coolly.

His amber eyes penetrate straight into Sue's, leaving her feeling like she needs a hot shower to cleanse away his stare.

"We don't need any other help. But I'm sure that once you establish a place for you and your friends, you'll be able to work on your own gardens," she hints.

144

"This place suits us just fine. Don't it, Levon?" Frank asks of his associate.

"Sure does," his friend agrees and steps closer.

Sue is starting to feel caged in by these two even though she stands in an open field of over five acres. Levon sports the same dress code as his cohort of dirty and tattered but also has the added flair of unkempt, frizzy dreadlocks.

"That isn't happening. It's already been covered actually," she tries to say with an air of authority. Sue is hoping that her tone will dissuade them from pressing this point further. "Our grandfather and the men on the farm have already told you that you aren't staying here once your sick people are better."

"That woman ain't no concern of ours," Frank says rudely.

How can he be so crass about Jennifer in her state of sickness? She had been traveling with them. Isn't she one of their friends, as well? These people and their behavior are so hard for Sue to comprehend. Nothing they do or say makes sense.

"What do you mean? Isn't she related to any of you?" Sue questions. If she can get these two idiots to reveal anything about their group, then it might help her family to better understand them.

"Nah, she was just some slut Peter let tag along with us. Found her along the way like a stray cat," Levon says coldly.

This jerk behaves as if Jennifer's life isn't hanging in the balance. Jennifer had hardly seemed like a slut to Sue. From the small amount of information that Reagan and Grandpa had been able to get from the woman, she was educated and well-mannered. She seemed different than the rest of her group, as if she didn't quite fit with them just like Sam and Simon.

"Wasn't she his girlfriend?" Sue asks, but receives bawdy laughs from both men.

"Yeah, sure," Frank says on a smirk.

This remark of sarcasm confuses Sue. His attitude is pissing her off. He is just being deliberately cruel.

"She's carrying his baby," she states angrily and gets more of the same rude laughter.

"She's Peter's problem, not ours. We ain't got women of our own," Frank informs.

As if she couldn't have guessed at this one.

"What about the women in your group? Aren't either of them with either of you?"

"They're with whoever wants to be with 'em, sweetness," Frank says with a snort. "We're looking to add a new member to our group."

"What's that supposed to mean?" Sue asks testily.

"You could come out to the camp," Levon suggests.

Frank elucidates further, "Yeah, come out some night and hang out. You know, party with us. We can get some pretty good parties going."

"I'm sure you can," Sue agrees with a grimace.

"Got some pot left. A little coke, too," Levon adds.

"We don't do drugs on this farm, and if my grandfather finds this out, then you'll be escorted off of it!"

"Easy, sugar," Frank attempts to appease her. "We was just sayin' you could party with us and if you don't want to stay here, you could leave with us. We need more women with our group. We don't know shit for growing a garden. We need some women for other…well, you know what I mean, sugar."

"Well, then good luck with that when you leave our farm," Sue says directly, but the longer they still stand near her the more irritated she becomes. "I'm sure there are some free love, hippie types still roaming around out there, but you won't find any women on this farm who are interested. None at all!"

"This one's got some fire, Levon," Frank calls over her shoulder to the other man.

"Sure does. It's cool. We got no problem with that. Do we, Frank?"

"I'm sure my husband would, fellas," Sue interrupts.

"Yeah, and which one is he? The big one?" Frank inquires.

Sue knows he's asking if her husband is Kelly.

"Look, I'm married and my sisters are with the other two Army Ranger Special Forces guys on the farm. I don't think you should go looking for trouble around here, guys. If you do, you're bound to find it, and I don't think you're going to like the result," she explains, hoping they'll leave. They don't. Frank shrugs, smirks and reaches for her arm. He obviously doesn't understand what 'Army Ranger' means.

"Hey!"

A loud, angry bark comes from her left. Sue swings with relief toward the man yelling. It's Cory, and he's come back from the house. He is stalking with such purpose and has the pistol on his hip drawn and down to his side.

He shouts, "What are you two doing?"

"Easy, man. We was just chattin' up this hottie," Frank replies.

"She's Mrs. Harrison to you," her savior orders.

Thank God for Cory's good timing. Thank God he's big and intimidating like his brother.

"Chill out," Levon says.

There is more force and underlying hatred in Levon's tone this time. His eyes alight with fierce anger.

"No, I won't chill out. Get back to your camp. Don't ever talk to her again. You hear?" Cory grinds out angrily.

He pulls Sue gently by the arm until she's half behind him. She can't see over his shoulder because he's grown so tall. His lean teenager body is starting to fill out with more muscle. He will probably fill out even further because of all the hard work like cutting firewood, handling thousand pound cows and the construction projects and repair jobs that never seemed to end on the farm. She's not sure if these two men are intimidated by Cory, but she sure as hell would be.

"Watch your mouth, boy," Levon spits out menacingly.

"I ain't a boy and I sure as shit don't take orders from you, so get the fuck outta' here," Cory says.

He has a calm composure that she would not have thought him capable of.

"Alright, kid. Relax," Frank jumps in to intercede, tugging his friend along. "We're going, man. We didn't mean no harm."

"Just go," Sue tells them with more confidence than she feels.

"It's cool. We was just being friendly is all. We'll go," Frank relents.

They slowly walk back to their assigned area, but not before Levon tosses a couple of foul glares in Cory's direction.

As soon as they are gone Cory turns to her and starts apologizing. "I'm so sorry, Sue. I shouldn't have used that kind of language around you..."

147

"Seriously, Cory?" she says on a laugh. "You do know my sister Reagan, right?"

He laughs nervously and continues, "Yeah, I guess. But I'm sorry anyways."

"I know, Cory. It's cool. I won't tell Grams on you," she appeases him.

"I was thinking more like maybe we won't tell my brother. He'd kill me if he knew I talked like that in front of any of the women…"

Sue cuts him off and lays a hand to his shoulder. "Cory, you saved my ass there. I don't know what they had in mind, but it seemed pretty bad. I don't think I want to know, either."

"Were they threatening you?" Cory asks and his brow furrows with renewed fury.

"Not really," she says. "They were just kind of… I don't know, creepy."

"Like creepy how?"

"Just saying things that made me feel uncomfortable. Nothing you need to know about," she tells him, momentarily forgetting everything he's been through. He's hardly a kid anymore.

"We gotta tell the others. Warn them. Let them know that those two could be dangerous," he says.

He shows such maturity and a strong sense of responsibility that Sue is stunned anew. She'd been awestruck by how brave and assertive he'd been when he'd threatened those men. He'd not shown an ounce of uncertainty of himself or any fear of them. It had been quite amazing to behold in someone who always seems so quiet and reserved.

"I suppose we do," she concedes. "But I'm afraid of how they'll handle it. Derek can be rather possessive, and if Reagan hears of this, then she might just go out and shoot them all."

"She might anyways," Cory mumbles as they return to their harvesting.

Sue chuckles at Cory's quip. It's rare that he makes a joke or finds anything humorous. He doesn't, however, join in her laughter.

For the first time in a few days, the family all convenes for dinner at the same time. Derek has locked the med shed and turned off the lights inside so that Jennifer can rest. More importantly, he's locked the shed to make sure nobody from the visitors' group goes in there to loot for prescription drugs. John locks the front door to the house and Kelly double checks that the back and side doors are locked. It feels strange to barricade themselves in like this, but it's probably for the best.

"How is your patient doing, dear?" Grams asks of Reagan.

They all pass the baskets of bread, platters of baked chicken and serving bowls full of roasted root vegetables. Reagan snorts.

"Not great," her sister answers.

A second later she yawns, and John reaches over to take Jacob from her. Reagan's fatigue is obvious by the way she carries herself and the dark circles under her green eyes.

She arches her back before reciting her patient's progress, "Worked on pumping fluid into her today. Around four o'clock she became unresponsive, so I can't give her broth or food. She's on a full IV diet now with heavy steroids and antibiotics."

"The poor thing," Hannah says softly to which Grams agrees.

"We'll work with her again after dinner, Reagan," Grandpa suggests to which she nods.

Samantha is sitting with the family, but Simon and Cory are at the island in the kitchen again.

"First we need to have a meeting after dinner," Derek butts in. "There have been too many things going on around here that we need to communicate."

"Sounds fine to me, Derek," Grandpa acknowledges.

The conversation ebbs and flows around them until everyone is finished and then pitches in to make the clean-up work go quickly. Em and Samantha head for the music room, where the blinds and curtains are closed, watching the babies and smaller children. Cory and Simon are keeping an eye on the shed and the outside perimeter of the house from Cory's bedroom upstairs. Finally, the pocket doors to the dining room are pulled shut.

The men talk of the harvest season and what still needs to be done. Then Reagan and Grandpa talk about the medical safety precautions again while the visitors are on their property. John goes over the new demos that he and Kelly have set at the edge of the cattle pasture so that everyone is aware of them and where exactly they are located.

"A few of them have been caught wandering around," John brings up the visitors.

Nobody wonders of whom he is speaking.

John adds, "We need to be careful while they're still here."

When a break comes in conversation, Sue figures it's now or never.

"Cory and I had a slight problem in the garden today with a couple of those men," she doesn't need to expand much about who she is speaking. Everyone knows. Once she tells them their names, Derek and Kelly tense up. John makes a fist on the table in front of him. She explains it in detail as best as she can recall, but notices how Reagan's demeanor changes. John tries to touch her arm soothingly, but she jerks away.

"These creeps need to go. Now!" Reagan demands hostilely.

"Reagan, calm down," Grandpa commands quietly. It barely works. "We still have their sick traveling companion, whether those two men are concerned about her or not."

"So she can stay and they can get the hell out," Reagan says forcefully.

"I agree," John is quick to add.

"I don't think it will be long before she either turns the corner or...," Grandpa can't finish.

It is too much to deal with losing another person to this devastating sickness. Their family is being touched by the tragedy that this world is creating through war, disaster and disease.

"We can't just throw them all out. Perhaps they can go tomorrow to search for a new place to live while Jennifer is getting better," Grams adds with her usual optimism. Hannah nods.

"Plus the situation with those kids hasn't been figured out yet, either," Derek says.

Grandpa sighs. "Right. We can't throw them out and let them take Samantha, Huntley and Simon with them without knowing what's going on with them in that group. We need more information before we make a decision about them."

Grams jumps in, "I believe that if those children want to stay here, then we ought to make the offer. I don't want them to have to leave with my brother's group if they'd rather stay."

"I think that's a good idea, Grams," Hannah suggests cheerily. "I think they need our protection. The others will need to

150

just find another home to live in, or a farm like ours, or a building of some sorts. If they go tomorrow to find some place to make their new home, then perhaps they can leave the following day."

Sue nods in agreement with her youngest sister and adds a solid, verbal, "Absolutely."

"We just need to stay calm and keep better watch," Derek says.

He is speaking with his usual level-headedness. He hits Sue with a stern look before continuing.

"Nobody goes anywhere alone. Not even for a minute. They'll be gone in a few days anyways."

"Cory was right there with me. He only left for a second to get more baskets," Sue defends. "He did a really good job, Derek. Kelly, your brother is a tough kid."

Kelly doesn't comment, but nods gravely. She certainly doesn't want Cory to get in trouble with his big brother. The kid already feels so much responsibility, even the obligation to take care of Em.

"At the rate that our patient is declining, I don't expect an improvement. It's amazing that her body hasn't aborted her baby as it is. I think we're looking at maybe less than a week, don't you, Grandpa?" Reagan asks.

His only answer is a grim nod. Removing his eyeglass and setting them on the table, he leans back in his chair. Sighing heavily, he rakes a hand through his white hair.

"A few more days could be dangerous, boss," John says tightly.

He also looks exhausted. Sue wonders if he's even had a full night's sleep since they've returned from the city trip.

"I know, but Grandpa's right. She could pass tonight for all we know. Then you guys can throw those dicks out," Reagan relents.

In Sue's opinion, John still looks as if he'd like nothing better than to go out and shoot them. His fun-loving spirit is nowhere to be seen on his handsome features.

"Reagan," Grams admonishes.

"I just get the feeling that they don't think they *have* to leave," Kelly finally interjects. "From what we've heard from Sue tonight and the way Peter was talking the other day, I don't think they get it."

151

"Oh, they get it," Derek says with a snide smirk. "They just don't want to."

"Denial isn't going to help them," Reagan states.

John doesn't nod or agree with her. His posture is tense and he still seems angry which is highly unusual for him.

"Let us give it a day or two and then they can leave," Grandpa states with finality. "You men can talk to them tomorrow and let them know that it might be a good idea to leave for a few hours to find somewhere they can eventually settle. If they choose not to, that's fine, as well. It's up to them. But they will be leaving soon. Make no mistake about that."

The meeting wraps, the family goes about their own chores and business and Sue collects her children for bedtime preparations. Derek refuses to go to bed with her and instead decides to go back downstairs to help keep watch. He is uneasy and tense. She knows that he would like to just throw those people off the farm at gunpoint, but she also understands his hesitation. There is more than just the group of adults out there to consider. There are an additional three children to worry over as they puzzle out the pieces of this jigsaw that the visitors have brought to their farm. Her husband's stiff body posture and the firm set of his jaw let her know that he is truly uneasy over this situation. Sue returns that sentiment and lies awake for over an hour worrying about what their future may hold with these people on their farm.

Chapter Eleven
John

The next morning, the boss reports at breakfast, which he shares with her while sitting on the cement curb near the med shed, that the woman isn't doing better. She and Doc expect the pregnancy to miscarry even though she is far enough into her second trimester that the baby possibly could've survived if things hadn't fallen apart in the country. Unfortunately there are no neonatal intensive care units still available where this baby could have received proper medical attention, and they have no way of doing so on the farm.

Reagan's mood is sullen and angry, so John suggests a quick run before she goes back to work. Sam agrees to keep an eye on the shed, and Derek is only a few feet away working on a new solar panel that they'll take over to the Reynolds to show them how to manufacture one of their own. The plan is to also take one to the condo community that they've helped to establish for the same purpose. Those people need a source of power, as well. There are quite a few young children living in that condo and taking care of them will be made much easier with a source of power. The visitors, however, are holding up any sort of forward-moving progress until they get the heck off the farm. None of the men want to leave the farm for even a minute while those people are still on it.

Reagan leaves her pistol with Sam, which surprises John since she has had it strapped to her thigh or waist since he's met her. She even shows the skinny young girl how to use it just in case. By the looks of her, John doubts that she would do any such thing. The kick of that .45 would just about knock Sam on her butt she's so slight. John has his pistol and two extra mags which will be plenty enough to keep them safe. The run is only to help alleviate some of the stress and pressure Reagan has on her right now.

As they jog alongside of each other, John lets her keep to her own thoughts until they reach the steep ridge where he helps her to the top. She's replaced the shorts she used to wear with a pair of black Ohio State University sweatpants with the letters across her derriere. It only draws his attention there even more than normal, which is rather hard to do since her derriere is one of his favorite topics of interest. He is wearing his camo pants and no shirt since he'd been helping Kelly at the barn on one of the wagon's wheels.

"Have you learned any more from Sam about those people?" he asks as he tugs her to the top of the hill. This is where they normally slow down until they get to the well-trodden path again.

"Not really. She's pretty backwards. Of course, maybe she's not and she's just depressed or something. Or maybe they've threatened her not to talk to us."

"Do you think that could be it?" John asks, feeling his temper rise at the idea of Sam being cajoled by any of those people.

"I don't know, maybe. Some of those dudes seem like real shit-bags," she puts so delicately.

John just chuckles at her, earning a glare of wrath.

"You've got a point, even if it is a bit crude," he teases and gets a punch to his left shoulder. "That Huntley kid is a good little boy. Don't you think?"

"Yeah, unlike his shithead father," Reagan says on a snort of derision.

"No kidding. I don't trust that one at all," John admits as they come to the edge of the woods again. It's blessedly cooler with the leaves providing a blanketing of shade above them. So far the fall weather in Tennessee seems much milder than in his home state of Colorado.

"I don't think we should trust any of them, even the women. That dark-haired one, Amber, is always giving me and Sue nasty looks when we run into her outside or near the water pump at the barn. She's got a really bad attitude toward us. Kind of disrespectful if you ask me since she's squatting on our land," Reagan tells him.

She doesn't have to, though, because John has already noticed this. That woman is pea green with envy over the women on the farm, and he's not sure if it is some sort of predisposed problem within her or that she is just an angry person in general.

"I caught her giving a look to Hannah, too. Luckily poor Hannie couldn't tell," he says as they come across a fallen tree on their path. "This is gonna need cut up. Must've fallen in the last couple of days. I don't remember it being down. Watch out for that poison ivy, Reagan."

She climbs over the tree with his help, and John holds onto her hand as she hops to the ground in front of him. When he tries to continue holding her hand as they walk, Reagan predictably pulls away. She is so frustrating sometimes. She is also content to pretend the kiss in her closet weeks ago had never happened. The one, solitary time he'd tried to bring it up she'd shut down and walked away.

"I don't like Levon or Buzz, either. What the hell kind of name is Buzz anyways? Idiots," she condemns.

"I think Buzz Lightyear has a prison record. Some of those tattoos are the kind that are offered while in the clink. I bet some of those other men are also ex-cons," John says with a sigh. Why can't they just throw them out? His patience is wearing thin.

"Wouldn't surprise me. I'm sure Frank's been in trouble, before this I mean. Who knows what the hell they've all done since? Probably don't wanna' know," she expresses with a groan.

"Yeah," John simply agrees. She's more astute than most people, and sometimes he forgets this about her and her giant brain.

"And your stripper girlfriend had to have done something to lose her kid through the court system. It's very hard to take a kid from their mother," she reminds John.

"No kidding," he agrees, but frowns at the 'girlfriend' remark. He decides to let this one go.

"And Simon's stuck with that skank Amber because that's all the family he's got now," she goes on.

"What do you think your family is going to do about the kids?"

"I know Grams is going to want them to stay, but I don't know how we could do that. Huntley is that asshole Frank's kid; Sam is with who knows who because she sure as shit won't say; and

Simon is the nephew of Amber. I think we're screwed on this," Reagan remarks with distaste.

Kids are important to her, even the ones who aren't actually related to her. Everyone on the farm feels a certain sense of protectiveness and obligation to all kids. If their sense of honor had been strong before, then it has multiplied by a thousand since the world has torn itself apart.

"We'll figure something out. I think us guys are just waiting for your grandpa to make the call, and we'll get it all handled," he says with confidence.

"I know," Reagan returns quietly.

They come through the woods behind the farm. When they get to the barn, Cory is waiting for them with Simon, and he's holding a horse by its halter and lead rope. He looks worried.

"Reagan, I'm sorry. We were riding, and I didn't see a hole. Think it was a groundhog hole and she stepped in it and now she's limping and I'm really sorry," Cory blurs together in a rush.

Reagan takes the halter from him and her mouth purses with a concerned pucker.

"Let's get her inside and have a look out of this sun. The flies are getting her out here anyways," Reagan says calmly.

John follows her into the horse barn where Reagan hooks the limping mare to a cross tie. John quickly removes her saddle and pad. The bridle is next.

"Is she gonna be ok, Reagan? I'm really sorry. She didn't fall down or anything, just stumbled," Cory explains nervously.

The two boys are looking sick with guilt, but Reagan is more composed than John would've thought. He knows how much her horses mean to her. Simon, on the other hand, is literally sweating.

"Her ankle's a tad swelled," she explains. "She's pregnant. Did you know that? She's not that far along, so the fetus should be fine. We bred her before you guys got here. We'll have to play it by ear, but this happens. Horses step in holes all the time. Don't worry about it, Cory. I'll take care of her before I go back to the med shed. We've got it."

Her hands glide along the horse's leg and up higher and then down again. She's being unusually nice and very understanding.

"If you two were riding, then who's watching the shed?" John asks of Kelly's brother.

156

"Kel's over there with Doc," Cory answers quickly. "They're working on something outside the shed. Think Doc wants to make some improvements to the shed so that if something like this sickness the visitors brought happens again, they'll have a better facility to handle it."

John turns to Reagan, who is still working with the mare. She nods and confirms Cory's story.

"Yeah, we need something better than the shed for this sort of shit. This isn't gonna get it. We need more beds, more sanitizing equipment, supplies like that."

"Do we need to make another run for any of it?" John asks with concern.

"Probably," she answers nonchalantly. "It would help to have some of the supplies that were still at that hospital. Sterilized hospital gowns, dividing curtains, other equipment."

"Ok," he agrees. "But you aren't going this time."

"Whatever," she returns angrily and scowls up at him from her squatted position. "I didn't say I was. He wants to take the pick-up truck with the cattle trailer attached so you guys can haul more. I think Grandpa's talking about making the trek once those people are gone."

They all three look to Simon to see if they've offended him. He is just nodding right along with them as if he is with *them* and not the visitors. The boy has obviously made his choice if he gets to have an opinion on the matter.

"Ok, well then that's settled," John says. "We'll take care of her, Cory, if you and Simon want to head up to that pasture and get the hay brought in. Find Derek and ask him."

"Yes, sir. We'll get it done. Come on, Simon," Cory says to the other boy before they both take off at a jog.

"So is she really going to be ok, or were you just saying that?" John asks her once the boys are out of earshot.

"There's some heat coming out of it," she says.

She props on one knee by the horse's hoof. She has no fear of these animals that are about seven times the size of her.

Reagan murmurs nearly under her breath, "I do think she'll be ok, though. We won't be able to let anyone ride her for at least a week, maybe longer. She's gonna be sore for a few days, but we can

157

apply some medicine to it. Stay with her and I'll go get it from the cabinet in the cattle barn."

She flees from the barn before he can even comment. He sometimes wonders if she even wants anyone's comments, or if she ever realizes that there are other people in the same room with her. She has some definite quirks, but to John they just make her who she is, who he has come to care so deeply for.

When she returns with a tub of greenish-yellow goop, she takes off the lid and slathers it on the horse's ankle and calf area- or whatever technical horse terms they were called. After she's done, Reagan puts the mare in a stall, and at her direction, John gives her two flakes of hay to keep her busy. Then the boss uses the indoor hydrant and pump soap to rinse the liniment off of her fingers and palms, which she says can burn and irritate skin.

John hears male voices outside of the barn, and they aren't any that he recognizes from their family. He touches Reagan's arm and puts a finger to his lips.

"…bullshit they don't give us more," says one male voice.

"Yeah, I mean look at this place. And it's too fuckin' hot to be out here luggin' water back and forth, man," says another.

"Fuck yeah. I want those kids to get their asses back to our camp to do it again," says a third and deeper voice.

"I've got mine. See ya', fuckers."

This man leaves the group. Reagan moves to go past John, but he holds her back. Her green eyes meet his and John can see the uneasiness settling in. It makes John wonder how women out in the world, unprotected by a sanctuary like the McClane farm are surviving on their own. It creates a stabbing punch in his stomach that spreads like pin pricks throughout his body. Women shouldn't have to live in fear.

"Man, he's a dick," the first one says and the other laughs.

Apparently these people don't even like each other all that much. John's not too keen on any of them, either.

"This shitty weather's too hot to be doing all this work," says the first one again with the complaining.

"I'll tell you what's hot. That chic with the scar on her face, the one that Jasmine said is a doctor is the hot one."

At this comment Reagan sucks in a breath. John stills her with his hand on her shoulder as he feels a vein working in his neck from clenching his jaw so hard. This is the city trip all over again. This overhearing of men whispering lasciviously about women and sharing their sick thoughts in the apocalypse is enough to make John want to take out his knife again.

"Nah, too scrawny for me. I think that one, the taller one with the dark hair, is hot. Or that blind one. She's hot, and she wouldn't see me comin'," the man says on a laugh, referring to Sue and Hannah.

"She'd smell you first," the other one says, and they both laugh.

"Yeah, but I think they're both with two of those Army dudes. The only one I ever see by herself is my little, hot scarface," the second one says.

So far they haven't said anything threatening but are just commenting on the women in the McClane family. It's harmless but still angering John because when he looks behind him at her face she is clearly frightened. He's tired of her being scared of men. He'd like to just go out and shoot these two in the head but doesn't think that the grandparents would like it too well if these men's brains were on the barn wall.

"Come with me," John whispers, takes her hand in his and pulls her across the aisle to where they will be more visible. "Reagan, I'm going to do this so that they know you aren't by yourself here on the farm. They need to think you're with someone and not running around here all alone and unprotected. I'm going to attach you to the one person they don't want to mess with- me. Just trust me on this, ok?" John asks her and knows she has no idea what he's talking about because she frowns up at him. And she also has a look of complete and utter distrust on her lovely face.

"What are you talking about? I don't..." she asks more loudly than she should.

That's fine with John. He purposely wants to draw their attention and to do so even more, he slams a stall door, interrupting Reagan and making her jump. He's sure they must be peeking to see what the noise was, so he wastes no time. John slides his hands into the hair on either side of her face and pulls her up against him. She lets out a high-pitched, surprised squeal as John presses himself against her.

159

"Trust me, honey," he murmurs before his head lowers. Reagan shakes hers vehemently.

The wall behind her holds her immobile, and John pushes one hand to the back of her head so she doesn't bang it against the unforgiving steel grates of the stall door. Her eyes widen as his mouth descends toward hers and she realizes what he's about to do. She tries to shake her head again, but he holds fast to her and even clutches some of her hair in his fist. As soon as his lips touch ever so lightly against hers, John knows he's lost. She sucks in a deep breath and holds it as his mouth moves against hers. There is no fatigue this time brought on by twelve hours of horseback riding through the mountains and four days of high stress situations while in the city.

Hoping she'll follow suit, John closes his eyes. Surprisingly, her frizzy curls are silky soft and intertwined in his fingers. He really has no choice in the matter because he's having an out of body experience like none other. Her lips are soft and full, and she's totally stiff as a board beneath him probably from fear or shock or both. She's still trying to shake her head as he holds her more firmly to continue their kiss. His other hand leaves her face and slides around the narrow indent of her waist to her back where he pulls her tightly against the front of him. Reagan's hands descend onto his bare chest, either for support or because she wants to or because she's hoping to push him away, but he doesn't know or care. She isn't clawing at him, so it gives him all the encouragement he never needed. He can literally feel her soften, relax. His mouth molds so perfectly against hers, and he's finally able to savor that fuller top lip that makes him crazy with lust just looking at.

He's waited so long to kiss her, to hold her, and he'd wanted their next kiss to be so perfect, so planned and private. But with him and Reagan, there was never a right time for anything. Their first time was technically in her closet, but it had only lasted a mere three seconds. The first time he had actually wanted to kiss her was when she came down the drive ready to shoot him and then pretty much every day since he's wanted to, as well. Heck, he had even considered it in the Home Depot after he'd just killed three men. There is never going to be a right, perfect time for them. With the state of the world now, stolen moments are all anyone can expect out of this life.

John presses the kiss deeper, forcing her mouth to open against his own and when it does he plunges his tongue inside. Her

160

mouth is warm and sweet like the candy she's always eating. He's become a ravenous fool. Her response is a whimper, but she's not pushing him away. She's finally trying to kiss him back with all the experience she doesn't have. Her fingers flex and relax and flex and curl again against his chest and in his chest hair, more importantly. She probably doesn't know it, but her unsure touch against his bare skin is about to take this to a whole new level that she is likely not prepared for. His breathing is ragged and hers is becoming so, as well. Her fingers slide up over his chest and shoulders and sink into the hair at the base of his neck as his tongue plunges again. Reagan strains against him, forcing her breasts to push against his chest as she lets out a soft sound into his mouth. His hands are moving and traveling at a pace he can't control. They tangle in her messy curls, slide down to pull her hips against his, tighten around her small waist, and with every touch she either breathes harder or moans. It's more than he can bear. Everything about her is more than he can bear. Even her inexperienced, guileless kisses and the rough way she is pulling at his hair makes him mad with lust. It's like he's awakened a sleeping lioness as she arches against him.

Hooting and laughing at the end of the barn brings John back to reality, reminding him of the reason for doing this in the first place.

When he pulls back, John puts his forehead to the side of her cheek to conceal her from the men he knows are watching them. One deadly cold look and they take off, their cat calls ceasing on their retreat. The men were Buzz and Rick, who were the only ones in the visitors' group that John considers non-threatening. It doesn't matter. He's done what he set out to accomplish, but it has turned into so much more than he anticipated.

It takes a few moments for their breathing to calm down to slightly slower puffs, and she refuses to look at him when he raises his head. She's staring at his chest, which he'd forgotten is still bare and sweaty from their run.

"What... what was that?" she asks.

Her own chest continues to rise and fall at an elevated pace. Her hands have moved back to his shoulders as if she's afraid she'll fall.

"That was… I don't know," he says raggedly and honestly. Her eyebrows lift in question as she finally meets his hot gaze.

"Why did you do that?" she asks.

This time there is a touch of resentment and more than a trace of angry accusation in her voice. Her green eyes are aflame, and her pupils are dilated.

"I wanted those guys out there to think you're with me. That's why, but it's not the only reason," he owns up and presses his forehead to hers. John holds the side of her small face with one hand and allows his thumb to stroke her soft cheek. It's thrilling to be able to touch her the way he's wanted to for so long and not have her flinch.

"Why else?"

Of course she wants the full Q and A session after their kiss. She's not going to be able to blame this one on fatigue from riding a horse all day on a return trip from the city. However, she will probably do a full analysis report on it later in one of her notebooks.

"I've wanted to do that since I first met you," he tells her and wants so desperately to continue where they left off.

"I was pointing a gun at you and gonna shoot you the first time we met, so I don't think you're telling the truth," she says bluntly.

John chuckles at her candid response. Sliding his thumb roughly over her top lip, he grins down at her.

"Doesn't matter. I still wanted to. I want to again. If you would've shot me and then kissed me before I croaked, then I would've died a happy man," he says lightly and kisses the tip of her nose.

"You're so weird," she says harshly and her kiss-swollen lips pucker into a funny expression.

"Maybe," he admits as his thumb moves on from her cheek to her jaw and then the long line of her throat and is joined by his index finger. He fully plans to take the same path with his tongue in a moment. He allows them to travel to the base of her throat and onto her upper chest which is exposed because of her damn tank top which he told her not to wear. Her breathing accelerates again. "I may be weird, but it doesn't change the fact that I like kissing you and… I think you liked it, too." His voice sounds husky with

162

passion, and he hopes that it doesn't frighten her. It's frightening to him because he's not sure he's going to be able to stop this.

John flips his hand over so that the backs of his knuckles touch her as he skims over the outside of her breast down to her narrow waist. Once there, he comes around front and hooks his index finger into the waistband of her jeans and pulls her an inch closer, closer to the erection he still has. His other hand slides under her leg, and he hitches it up against his hip. He doesn't remove his hot palm from the underside of her thigh, however. She shivers delightfully, and John traces with his middle finger the tiny goose bumps that have erupted on her forearm.

He is about to carry her upstairs to the hay storage when they are interrupted. Reagan jumps away from him like she just got tasered.

"John?" Kelly calls from the door.

Reagan sprints away from him as Kelly stands rooted there in shock, his mouth agape. John's not sure how much of their interaction that Kelly has witnessed, but he also knows that Kelly won't say anything to anyone. He watches as she runs from the barn to the med shed and doesn't look back. Kelly looks to Reagan and then at John and back at Reagan again. Then without pausing, he goes right into his speech.

"We were looking for some help. We told them they should go on a scouting run to look for new living arrangements. But those dumbasses can't get the second RV started, and the uncle is whining about not being able to leave if it doesn't. Thought we'd better help or we'll never get rid of them. Derek said…,"

John stopped listening at 'dumbasses.'

He's still thinking about the way Reagan felt in his arms and her soft compliance when he'd kissed her. She hadn't cried or tried to get away from him. It makes him wonder if he couldn't have gotten away with kissing her the thousand other times that he'd wanted to. It also makes him wonder if she's also been attracted even just the slightest bit to him all this time, as well. And, no, she doesn't have huge, fake boobs and isn't tall like a supermodel with the perfectly straight hair and matching teeth. But she is his new standard of beautiful and alluring and has been since he came to live on this farm. There was always something about Reagan that he couldn't quite put his finger on that had attracted him to her. Perhaps it was her brain, her looks or maybe her feisty temper or a combination of everything about her. She is a mesmerizing creature, and he can't believe that nobody had snatched her up before he came along. However, he's glad for it because he intends to make Reagan his and killing off a current boyfriend would've been hard to explain to her family. If he'd been determined before, he is absolutely steadfast in his resolve after that kiss.

She'd smelled like a strange mix of honey and cookies, sugar cookies. Maybe what he was picking up on was a vanilla scent, but it was heavenly, she was heavenly. Her small body fit so perfectly against his, and he likes that he can pick her up easily without effort when he needs to. It could come in handy if he ever tosses her over his shoulder to take her off somewhere to be seduced.

Kelly simply keeps giving him updates on the happenings on the farm that John's missed during his time with Reagan on their run. His friend is chomping at the bit to get rid of the visitors. They all are.

He walks alongside Kelly toward the shed and they discuss the broken, piece of crap RV that they are obviously now going to have to work on. They also discuss an exit plan for their unwanted guests and the list of things that need to get done to make it happen. But John's mind wanders many times again to Reagan. If his friend notices his lack of attention, he doesn't cop to it.

Her slender yet curvy hips had literally been beckoning his hands to pull her closer. Her soft lips had molded so nicely against his. These nefarious thoughts aren't getting him anywhere, but they sure are entertaining. Reagan McClane had better watch out because he can't wait to get her alone again.

Chapter Twelve
Hannah

"This is where we store the flour. It's nice and cool and dry," Hannah patiently explains to Sam, who has come to work inside today on whatever they need her for. "Helps to keep out the bugs that would ruin it if they were to get into it."

"Ok," Sam says quietly.

Hannah instructed both of the teens yesterday about the need to be more verbal around her. Head shakes and nods don't exactly translate to the blind. It was something that Cory, Em and her love, Kelly, had had to learn, as well.

"Apples are in full harvest, so let's make a few apple pies," Hannah suggests. They are standing in the small pantry off of the kitchen, and this time Sam doesn't answer. "Can you help me with that, Sam?"

"Su…sure, Miss Hannah," Sam finally says softly.

"Or if you don't like apple, we could do peach. We have quite a few jars in the cellar of canned peaches, as well," Hannah offers.

"No, ma'am. Apple is just fine," Samantha answers. "I like apple pie. It's my favorite actually."

"Oh, ok. I just thought… well, you seemed…"

"I'm sorry. It's just that my mom used to make apple pie every fall," Sam confides. "It was my dad's favorite, too."

"Oh, Sam, I'm so sorry," Hannah expresses as she reaches for the girl's hand and finds it.

"It's ok," she whispers.

It's not at all ok, Hannah knows. This young girl has lost her family, and nobody knows why or how it happened other than that it probably occurred during the systematic crash of their country.

"If you ever want to talk about it, I'm here, Sam," she offers and gives the girl's bony hand a gentle squeeze. Sam sniffs hard.

"Thanks, Miss Hannah," Sam murmurs.

She turns away and pulls her frail hand back from Hannah's grasp.

Sam says sadly, "I don't think I want to talk about it. Not ever."

"That's fine, honey," Hannah tells her. "Nobody here would ever force you to talk about anything you don't want to, Sam. Let's just make some pies, ok? A good pie always makes everything seem a little better."

"Yes, ma'am," Sam agrees kindly.

"You can collect the items for me, and then we'll get started," Hannah instructs, and they work together for a few hours slicing apples, rolling out dough and making pies.

It's always been therapeutic for Hannah to work in her kitchen. Sometimes toiling away at tasks that take a lot of attention to detail is a good way to take the mind off of things that one doesn't wish to dwell on. Or, at least in Hannah's opinion, they do. And it seems to do the trick for Samantha, too, because she talks quietly with Hannah- not about her family- but at least she talks from time to time while they work. They discuss the baby peeps in the barn, the stinky pigs that they both dislike, all the while Hannah tries to keep the conversation light and pleasant until she sees an opportunity.

"Do you know anything about Huntley's father Frank?" Hannah asks her as they get the first pie into the hot oven. Soon the smell of cinnamon and apples will be filling the kitchen with a comforting, all-enveloping warmth.

"Um, a little," she mutters and turns on the water in the back sink.

"Can you tell me about him?" Hannah pursues this line of questioning with the girl in the hopes that they might learn more about their guests.

"He's… he's kind of mean," she says.

"Like how?" Hannah asks.

166

"I don't know," she mumbles and pauses for a moment before continuing. "He's kind of mean to Garrett and Huntley... well, only Huntley now. He has kind of a bad temper. Yells a lot and stuff like that."

Remembering the twin brother of Huntley is too much for Hannah and apparently too much for Sam, as well, because she doesn't elaborate further. They work side by side cleaning the kitchen, wiping countertops, dumping a bowl of scraps into the garbage bowl for the chickens and pigs.

"He's also unkind to the two women out there," Sam offers out of the blue.

"Oh, my. That's terrible, Sam," Hannah tells her and has stopped scrubbing. Another thought occurs to her. "Is he also... mean to you?"

There is a long pause, and Hannah isn't sure if the girl is shaking or nodding her head again like she used to answer. Habits like that are hard to break.

"Sam?"

"Oh, sorry, Hannah," the young girl apologizes. "No, he's not mean to me or anything. He pretty much leaves me alone."

"Why is that, do you think?"

Her answer is a short mumble of, "I dunno."

This reply is curious, but Hannah doesn't push. Hannah believes there is an actual answer as to why Frank leaves her alone, but she also knows that she isn't going to get that answer. She understands that opening up to people is difficult for Samantha for some reason. Hannah believes that the reason may be something that comes from bleaker origins and not by accident.

"And the others? What about Rick?" Hannah asks of the man who is a cousin of Levon's. She doesn't need to inquire about Levon. Everyone has pretty much figured that one out. He is a definite problem, but nobody has said much about his cousin, Rick.

"Rick is very nice, Miss Hannah," Sam comments with more feeling this time. "He tries to help us kids out by giving us extra food sometimes. One time he found a case of soda in a house and gave it all to us when nobody else was looking. We each had two cans. It was great. And another time he gave us a sack of M & M's and a box

167

of granola bars just for us that he found in a looted supermarket. The others didn't find out, either."

"Good, that's good I suppose," Hannah replies with confusion. Sam's whole soliloquy is baffling. Why would the others traveling with them care if the kids were given food first or given the only store of food items, especially junk food? The children were the only ones who could've possibly benefitted from the extra sugary calories. Why wouldn't the others have wanted them to have those things? "And what about the other men? There are two others, right? Billy and Buzz or something?"

"Willy, his name is Willy. And the other one is Buzz. He's kind of nice most of the time. He mostly keeps to himself. But Willy is..."

Sam doesn't finish but issues forth a disgusted sound. Hannah isn't sure she wants to know why he is so offensive that Sam cannot explain it or that she'd make an unladylike sound.

"What is it with Willy?" she presses anyways. The family desperately needs information about these people.

"He's... I don't know how to put it. I'm sorry. He's just kind of creepy or something," Sam tells her.

"Oh," Hannah returns with confusion. "And the women? Are they a problem at all?"

Sam pauses a few moments before answering. "Um, Jasmine is pretty nice. She... I don't know, I guess I feel sorry for her is all."

"Why is that?"

"She's sad a lot. I think her life before all this was bad, too. I think Jasmine's just had a bad life," Sam offers.

"And the other one? Her name is Amber?"

"Yes, ma'am. She's a lot like Frank. I think they knew each other or were friends or something before. She's mean like him," Sam says in a very hushed voice.

Hannah is amazed by Samantha's frankness. This is big for her. They normally can't get much more than a short, one word answer of "yes" or "no" from this girl.

"This is all helpful, Sam. We just want to make sure our family is safe," Hannah tells her. Then adds, "We want to keep you safe, too, honey."

"You can't," Sam says morosely and moves away from Hannah.

168

"What do you mean? We'll do whatever it takes…" Hannah is cut off as the screen door opens on its squeaky hinges and slams shut again, followed by the sounds of Simon and Cory in full conversation.

"Oh, hey, Hannah," Cory offers promptly.

His interruption abruptly ends her and Sam's private conversation.

"Hi, Cory. Simon?"

"Yes, ma'am. Hi. Sorry," Simon blusters with embarrassment over the non-verbal gaffe.

"Hey there," Hannah greets him.

"Hi, Sam," Cory adds, but Sam does not return the greeting.

If she nods any acknowledgement at all to Cory, then Hannah is unaware of it. But she highly doubts if Samantha does so because she is more withdrawn and reserved around Cory.

"We were just talking about our guests, those men out there in particular," Hannah informs them and immediately hears Sam's sharp intake of breath. "It's ok, Sam. Nothing is taken outside these walls. Same goes for you, Simon. If you feel like there's anything we should know about that group, then you need to speak up and tell someone. We just want to keep everyone safe."

"I understand, Miss McClane," Simon says so formally.

She and her sisters have given them liberty to use their given names, but Simon is reluctant to do so.

Since she's finished with the pies, Hannah starts on cutting up vegetables for this evening's meal of tacos and burritos. Grams said that they should start using up the store of last year's beef to make room in the freezer for the steer they'll be butchering soon. And they've all agreed that non-perishables like store-bought items should be used before they expire, thus the taco shells. All of the kids, even the teens, had been excited about the prospect of taco night. Hannah would much prefer a hot bowl of soup to ethnic food, but she also realizes the importance of conserving what they are able to of their home-canned goods in place of the items Grams had purchased from grocery stores that will not have nearly as long of a shelf life.

"Is there any of that chocolate cake left, Hannah?" Cory asks with a smile in his voice.

169

He has a sweet tooth like Reagan. Hannah smiles gently to herself and turns away to wash the mixing bowls in the sink.

"Yep, in the pantry, Cory," Hannah tells the boys. She hears Simon murmur, "cool."

"Can Simon have some, too?" Cory asks.

"Hm, I don't know. What has he been working on out there with you today?" Hannah teases.

"Um, well, we've been stacking hay in the horse barn," Cory says honestly.

"Cory, I'm just kidding!" she cries with laughter. "You don't have to work hard to deserve a little cake. Besides, Miss Samantha and I have made apple pies for dessert tonight. So we kind of need to finish off that cake anyways."

Cory and Simon chuckle with the nervous laughter of unsure teenage boys.

"Oh, ok," Cory concedes.

"Sam, would you like to dice those peppers, honey?" she asks to re-engage the girl again. "Or would you like to take a break and have some cake with the guys?"

"No, thank-you. I'd rather just help." Sam agrees. "I'm not quite... what do I do?"

For the next few minutes Hannah works with Sam, showing her how she'd like the vegetable base for the taco beef to be diced. When they get to jalapeno peppers, she dons a pair of thin, rubber gloves and cuts these herself so the girl doesn't have to. The boys devour cake and gulp milk with enthusiasm while chatting about fast cars, music and things that used to exist before this mess their country has turned into.

"Hey!"

Reagan's loud, gravelly bark comes from the door opening as it slams, making Hannah jump. Good grief! For being small and slight Reagan can sure cause a lot of noise.

Her sister just continues on in the same tone, "Nobody said it was cake time."

"I told them they'd better hurry before you got in here," Hannah teases. Cory laughs, but the other two remain silent.

"Man, sold out by my own sister," Reagan complains good-naturedly.

She does, however, plop herself down at the island and from the sounds of it begins tearing into her own cake. Hannah walks over, feels for Reagan and finds her. She pulls her toward her and plunks a kiss to the top of her sister's head. It's encouraging that Reagan doesn't pull back.

"How is it going with the repairs on the bus thing?" Hannah asks of Simon.

"The RV?" Cory asks to which Hannah nods.

"Not too good," Simon comments finally. "It's a fairly complex machine, Miss Hannah. I don't know that they will get it running again."

"That could be a big freagin' problem," Reagan swears through a mouthful of cake.

Her sister's manners are caveman-like sometimes. Hannah shoots her a scowl of disapproval which gets no response though she's quite sure Reagan saw it.

"Yes, it could," Hannah agrees readily. Those people need to get off their farm, and soon.

The back door opens and closes again, this time slightly less noisily.

"Hey, babe," John's sultry voice comes through crystal clear.

What the heck is he thinking? Reagan won't like him joking around like that. He chuckles quietly, leaving Hannah to wonder what her sister has just done.

"Don't go teaching these nice kids your bad habits like the one finger salute."

Never mind. Hannah understands perfectly clear.

"Yeah and if Grams catches you doing that, she'll chew your ear for sure," Kelly's baritone adds in.

Hannah lights up. She can't help it. She'd also like nothing better than to go to him and fling herself around him for a long, sweet kiss.

"I... I'm done. Excuse me," Reagan mumbles.

Her sister sets her dish in the sink with a clatter and dashes back out the door. That was rude even for her, leaving Hannah to wonder at her rash behavior. She's obviously missed something as usual.

"Good grief, I was just kidding. Grams isn't even around," Kelly extends apologetically.

John laughs once. "It's not you, bro."

Hannah finds this all intriguing but can't take the time to question John about it right now. She'd been in the middle of a high level interrogation. Sort of.

"So the RV repair isn't going well?" she asks of Kelly or John. They both sigh long and loud. "That good, huh?"

"Don't worry. We'll figure something out, Hannie," John says lightly.

"If we have to we can always go jack... I mean borrow a car from an abandoned house. We've got enough gas around here for a car fill-up," Kelly says, earning a laugh from John.

"I'll let you do that one, bro. I think the boss has seen enough of my special talents for a while," John says on another chuckle.

"So maybe you need to show her some other ones," Kelly says with a tinge of racy humor in his voice.

Hannah believes that this is a crude implication because the teen boys chuckle and John shouts with laughter. She gives Kelly a scowl of disapproval of his own to think about. It gets the same reaction as the one she'd offered to Reagan.

"Yeah, maybe I should. But we gotta get our guests moved on as soon as Jennifer is... better," John says about the sick woman in the med shed who nobody believes will get better at all.

"What is it, man? Simon?" Kelly asks.

"Nothing, sir," Simon says evasively.

He passes behind Hannah as he goes to the sink to rinse his dishes.

"Ready to go back at it?" Cory asks probably Simon because a moment later they are both out the door again.

"What's going on?" Hannah asks of Kelly. Sam is quiet as she continues to chop vegetables for Hannah.

"I don't know. He just had a funny look on his face when we were talking about the RV," Kelly tells them.

"Like what?" John asks.

Apparently he hadn't witnessed what Kelly had.

"Not sure. I'll see if he tells Cory later," Kelly tells them. "Do you know why he would've looked like that, Samantha?"

172

"Nnn... no, sir," Sam stutters.

She is especially afraid of Kelly. Hannah figures it is probably his size. He probably instills this fear in most people. If only they knew his softer side, the one only she knows.

"It's cool. No big deal. We're either gonna get it runnin' again or we're not. But one way or the other Peter's group isn't staying," Kelly tells them.

"Right. Let's hit it, bro," John agrees.

They are gone again in a flash. They've all been working on putting up hay, and Hannah knows what a monstrous job that can be. Grandpa used to have some of the neighbors' farm boys help him with it, and he'd either pay them or split the hay bounty with the other family.

"It's blessedly quiet again," Hannah says and then laughs. Sam gives a short chuckle. "That's usually how the kitchen is. I guess it's probably why I like it in here, too. People are always coming and going. Plus, they all get happy when Grams and I cook for them. That doesn't hurt, right? Making people happy?"

"Yeah, it's good I suppose," Sam says.

Hannah isn't sure she means it. She's not sure this girl has any happiness left inside.

"It's sometimes hard for people to find happiness now. I think if we can help with that in any small way, then we should," Hannah comments but gets no response. This girl is reclusive when she wants to be, which happens to be most of the time.

They work side by side cleaning the kitchen, doing the dishes, wiping counters and cutting peppers and celery. A cry from the music room alerts Hannah that one of the babies has awakened from their morning nap.

"Oh, goodness. Sam, can you get whichever one that is? I think that's Isaac. My hands are in these gloves and covered with hot pepper oils."

"Um, sure," the girl says and rushes from the room.

When she doesn't return after a long time, probably at least five or so minutes which is much longer than it takes to retrieve the baby, Hannah goes to find her. Her instincts stop her from going into the music room, and instead she waits right outside the door frame out of sight. She's glad that she does.

"...it's ok, baby. Shh. Don't cry. It's all right. See? Everything's going to be ok," Sam coos gently to Isaac in a child-like voice.

It sounds like she is pacing back and forth. Apparently her gentle soothing is doing the job because he isn't squawking for his bottle yet. Hannah goes back to the kitchen feeling just a tad bolstered by this single, simple act of kindness from this young girl who is a virtual stranger to their family. From what she hears coming from the music room, Hannah smiles with renewed hope for this sad, broken girl and for all of mankind who has been so tragically dealt a bad hand in this war on humanity.

Chapter Thirteen
John

"We need my portable ultrasound machine," Doc says.

They are amassed in the dining room the next evening, the children are in bed already, and the visitors' camp is silent. John sits next to Reagan and the med shed has been locked down for this. Grams is in the music room giving Isaac his last bottle for the night since Sue had insisted on being present at the meeting. Doc had called them all in at 23:00 for it.

"What for, Grandpa?" Sue inquires.

"Reagan and I would like to get a look at the baby Jennifer's carrying. The fetal heartbeat is still there. But I don't know if the baby is big enough to be viable on its own yet. If I could get an ultrasound, we'd have a better idea of what we could do."

"Do? Like what?" John asks.

Reagan answers beside him, "Grandpa's talking about a C-section. We might be able to perform a cesarean birth taking the baby out by surgery, and at least we'd be saving the baby. Jennifer is not likely to pull through this. Nothing and I mean nothing we are doing is helping her at all."

"How would that work, Doc?" Kelly asks. "Aren't x-ray machines super big and heavy?"

"No, not mine. Damn it," Doc swears with frustration and removes his glasses. "I forgot it at my practice. Hell, I don't even know if it's still there. Should've taken the damn thing with me when I cleaned out my office, but everything was so hectic. I just forgot it."

Reagan interrupts, "If not, Grandpa, then we could get one from the stat-care in town."

Doc nods with a grimace. "They do have one, but it's not as new as mine. Not portable and not nearly as small."

"How big are we talking, Herb?" Derek asks.

John and Derek are both supposed to be sleeping at this hour to prepare for their four a.m. watch shifts, but this is infinitely more important.

"It's not much bigger than a brief case. As a matter of fact, it's in a case. Easy to carry. I've used it on house-calls before," Doc explains.

Kelly nods and Derek follows suit.

"How could you possibly perform a surgery here?" John asks the inevitable.

"With what you and Reagan brought home from the city hospital, I'd be just fine. Reagan will assist if it comes to that," Doc adds.

Kelly nods again and says, "Ok. Let's go get it."

His friend is a cut and dry kind of guy. There are no wishy-washy decisions made by Sergeant Kelly Alexander. John forces down a chuckle.

"Hold on, Kel," Derek adds as John knew his brother would. "We need more intel. Plus, we need a plan."

"Right," Reagan jumps in. "I can take you guys- whoever's going- and…"

"Not happening," John interrupts firmly and gets a deadly glare from the boss. "We'll decide who goes. But one thing's for sure, you aren't!"

Before Reagan can reply, Doc agrees with him and expands on this thought process. "John's right, Reagan. You need to stay here on shift in the shed with our patient. Let the men take care of this."

"Yep, he's right, half pint," Kelly puts in and gets a sneer from Reagan.

"How far is it from here, Herb? I mean exactly how far?" Derek asks.

"'Bout seven miles. You'd need to go out through the cattle pasture and catch that oil well access road. It's rutted all to hell, but it's your best bet of sneaking out without alerting our friends."

John knows he means the visitors.

Sue says, "Yeah, and you could come out around the other end of town going that way. It might even be shorter than seven

176

miles if you go in from there. You know where his practice is, Derek. Remember? I took you there once?"

"Yeah, I remember," his brother replies.

John's not sure he wants his brother to leave the farm, though. He has too much to risk.

"I'll go," he puts in quickly. "Makes the most sense."

"Well you can't go alone," Derek adds.

"I'm going, too," Kelly is quick to state. "Let me go with him, Derek. I'm frosty, and I could use the change of scenery."

Derek thinks a few moments, contemplating his choices. He pulls rank on them, so they'll have to adhere to whatever decision he makes.

"You should go tonight," Derek finally says. "Go after midnight. Go as late as possible. It'll be a better chance that the visitors won't see you."

John breathes a sigh of relief before replying, "Right. Good idea. We'll go around 02:00. We'll take Doc's truck."

"Head out through that oil well road," Kelly concurs.

Derek frowns but nods. "That'll be fine. I'll tell you where the practice is. Write you out some directions."

"Wait. I'm not so sure this is a good idea," Reagan murmurs uneasily beside him.

She fidgets in her seat. John grasps her hand from the table and gives it a squeeze. He does it right in front of everyone without thinking.

"It'll be ok, boss," he says while looking directly into her eyes. "Don't worry."

She doesn't break his grasp or the eye contact for a long moment which surprises John. Finally her fingers wriggle loose and she pulls free.

"I don't like it," she says as her brows pinch together.

Kelly jumps in to help, "I'll take care of him, little Doc."

"I wouldn't ask this of you men if I thought there were any other options," Doc says on a weary sigh.

"It's fine, Doc. We'll be fine," John assures him and his concerned granddaughter. "And we'll get that machine."

"Don't worry, Herb," Derek says. "This is what we do. Right, team?"

"Hooah," John and Kelly both reply quietly but intensely. They reach around Reagan who sits between them and bump fists. She swats their hands out of her way.

The meeting concludes, the family breaks up and everyone leaves the dining room. Everyone but Reagan who stands beside him near the door. She's staring at her feet.

"I don't even know if this is going to make a difference," Reagan says whisper quiet.

"It's worth a shot, Reagan," John tells her. "We have to try."

She doesn't answer but nods and swallows hard. When she raises her gaze to his, she is also biting her lower lip.

"Want my .45?" she asks.

Nothing she says surprises him much anymore. He just chuckles once and pats the pistol on his hip.

"Got it covered, kid. And before you say it, I'll take two extra mags," he reassures her.

"Take a shotgun, too," she prods.

John just smiles at her and chucks her under the chin.

"Ok, boss. I'll take plenty of firepower," he confirms and takes her hand.

Reagan frowns at him and says, "I'm serious, John. Our town fell fast. Kind of like everywhere else, I guess. But it was torched pretty badly and there were a lot of scummy bastards from the big cities moving through there. It could be as bad as Clarksville."

John raises her hand to his mouth where he places a kiss to her soft palm which causes her to pull away.

"Noted," John adds more seriously.

He's very familiar with how bad it is everywhere. He'd been to many of the remaining areas of the country mid nose-dive and he'd been deployed to help keep the peace, which had failed terribly. He'd taken her a few weeks back to the city. He's been in war zones for the last twelve years. He's ready for this trip. He just doesn't have to fly halfway across the world to get there.

"Send me off with a kiss?" he queries with a grin and gets an immediate, testy scowl.

Reagan roughly jabs her bony index finger to the center of his forehead. It doesn't hurt, and instead John throws his head back and shouts laughter.

"Get your head in the game, idiot," she says in a huff.

178

She spins, leaving John standing there laughing.

A little after two a.m. Kelly and John sneak through the back of the property with Doc's pick-up truck. Nobody at the campsite stirs. Derek and Cory are both keeping watch until they return. They both have a short barrel shotgun, their M16's and John packs his .45 on his hip. Kelly's holster holds a 9mm Beretta model 92.

They use Derek and Doc's handwritten directions to make their way using the back roads least traveled, some of which are just gravel. It doesn't take long before they reach the small town where Doc had his practice, the family went to church and Reagan and Sue had attended public school. Kelly is driving and slows the truck to less than twenty miles per hour as they come toward the main drag of the town. They're moving northeast on Pleasant View Road. They know that this road will eventually turn into Church Street, the road where Doc's old practice is located.

This town is small, much smaller than Clarksville. So far, it's completely deserted, not the worst thing ever. Kelly kills the headlights and they slow even further. The gibbous moon is nearly full, making it much easier to see by. They pass a few abandoned homes, another condo community where no lights are lit, and three fast food restaurants. A baseball field where children once dreamed of making it to the majors has not been mowed the entire season. It resembles the cow pasture back at the farm.

No cars move about. No humans scurry to and fro like furtive rodents as they had in Clarksville. This is decidedly different from that city he'd taken Reagan and some of the bigger cities he's been through since the apocalypse. The truck slows to a crawl as they pass not one, but two pharmacies. One have them has been nearly burned to the ground. Some of the homes are also burned out. They are moving toward a more industrial area where the business district must be situated. Kelly veers around abandoned vehicles in the middle of the short city streets. A few appear to have been torched out.

"Look there," Kelly whispers and points to their left through the windshield.

John spies what his friend is showing him. There is a very faint, yellow glow coming from a two-story home with a wide, wrap-around porch and gingerbread trim. It is likely candlelight. But he sees no movement whatsoever. It makes John realize how important this small town would be to the McClane family and why Reagan and Doc would want to come here to set up his clinic again. There are bound to be others trying to survive. They will need medical care. They could need it now.

Kelly pulls down his night vision goggles and John follows suit. They are used to the dark and moving around in it. This isn't their first rodeo.

"Up there," John indicates with his right hand. "There's the feed mill. I see the grain silos."

"Yep, that's it," Kelly agrees.

He pulls the truck into the other lane, not worrying overly much about non-existent on-coming traffic.

"Let's pull around back and leave the truck there," John suggests. It's always good to have an exit strategy. Leaving their mode of transportation right outside of Doc's practice could get it hotwired and stolen should anyone notice it.

"Looks like a good spot," Kelly says as they pull onto the gravel lot.

He drives around back and puts the truck in park. There is a fairly good copse of trees to their immediate right and around the back of the property, as well. The old white building stands empty, the large delivery doors wide open. Doc's practice is nearly visible through the trees and overgrown shrubbery to their east.

An owl hoot-hoots and then screeches, the sound coming from the feed mill. It sends a chill of uneasiness down his spine. But John knows that she's probably just hunting a midnight snack of mouse or rat or some other type of rodent taking advantage of the lack of humans out and about in the feed mill nowadays. They are likely all looting and feeding off of the leftover ground corn and oats and birdseed still in the weathered building behind them.

"Ready, bro?" Kelly inquires and John gives a firm nod.

"Let's roll," he says.

They both exit the pick-up, shut their doors as silently as possible and move toward the trees. Kelly stashes the keys in his pocket. Their rifles are equipped with the silencers again to prevent drawing attraction should they need them. John's is slung over his back. He carries the short barrel shotgun- care of Doc- down in front of him. John highly doubts they'll need any of their weapons. Other

180

than the one slightly illuminated home, this town seems vacant, like a deserted ghost town from a movie set in the old west.

He taps Kelly's shoulder and whispers, "Reagan said there's a side entrance. Should be straight ahead."

Kelly nods as they move out of the cover of the tree line and onto the blacktopped parking lot of Doc's former practice. It's a small, gray or white building with a darkly shingled roof. Kelly indicates that he'll go forward to the side entrance and John signals to his right that he'll come in from the front. This is likely being overly cautious but, then again, erring on the side of overly cautious lately isn't such a bad idea.

John creeps to the side wall of the structure and peeks around front. No movement. No people. He rushes forward, jumps over the railing that encircles the small front porch. Doc has incorporated a covered porch system similar to the one at his farmhouse into the pleasing aesthetic of his office. A white plastic railing goes nearly all the way around. It gives the practice a quaint, homey feel. There are even three white rockers there, but one has been knocked over and now lies on its side. John wonders how many of Doc's patients have sat in these rockers while waiting to be called in for their children's stitches or school-season flu and cold bugs or vaccinations. This would've made them feel comfortable, at ease.

A wave of righteous angers ripples through John when he glimpses the wide front picture window of Doc's practice. It's been broken, busted into a dozen sharp edges by someone either throwing something heavy through it or from gunfire. He eases through the unlocked, open front door and swings left and then right. He's in the waiting room where it appears to have taken on mortar fire, though that is highly unlikely. There are papers strewn everywhere, tables and chairs overturned, the reception area trashed, computers behind the desk lying on the ground. This is a damn shame. He's glad Doc didn't come with them. This would break the man's heart.

John clears the waiting room, the reception area, two patient exam rooms and meets Kelly in the hall.

"All clear," John provides. "What's back there?"

"Same. Exam rooms, his office, x-ray room, lab, pill closet. All clear," Kelly confirms.

"Doc said he would've left the ultrasound machine in the x-ray room. Let's check it out," John supplies and they move together again.

They both flick on their flashlights to see better and push their goggles back to the tops of their heads. The x-ray room is also a mess, but it's not so chaotic that they can't make sense of the remaining equipment. There is an exam table, computers, a digital film developer, two metal carts- one knocked over- a plastic skeleton as well as a poster of which hangs askew on the wall, a telescopic camera for taking the pictures which has wires and tubing coming out of it and two lead-filled vests to protect the patient against x-rays not needed to their abdominal area. There is also a small stepstool and a padded stool on rolling wheels where Doc or his x-ray technician had probably sat many times. Unfortunately, it is now sticking halfway through the broken window separating the x-ray area from the small room where the technician would've stood and manipulated the computer to shoot pictures of a patient's bones.

Kelly calls, "Think I found it, bro."

John joins him in the center of the room and examines the case that his friend holds open. He remembers seeing one of these once in a field hospital. This is definitely what they need. And it's also fortunate because it can't weigh more than eight or ten pounds.

"Good job, man," John praises and shuts the case and locks the snaps into place.

"Guess the dope-heads didn't care too much about an x-ray," Kelly comments.

John smirks. "Yeah, guess not."

"Wait, where's the wand thingy?" Kelly asks. "Open that back up, dude."

"What do you mean?" John asks as he sets the case on the exam table and flips it open again.

"Look, there's no wand. There's supposed to be a thing that transmits the frequency or whatever. It's supposed to plug in back here. See?"

"How did you know this?" John asks.

"I remember when my stepmom had to get an ultrasound when she was pregnant with Em. Dad was out of town for work and she was on bed rest. So me and Cory took her since I was home on leave. I'm positive it's missing something. There should be a wand

182

with a cord attached to it that plugs in. How else would this thing work?"

"Right. Ok, well it's gotta be somewhere around here. Let's fan out and find it," John complies.

"It looks like a microphone," Kelly offers and John nods.

They search everywhere but come up with nothing. Even after rifling drawers, Doc's office, the pill closet- which is completely wiped out- they still don't find the attachment.

"Shit. This thing is useless without it, John," Kelly says twenty minutes later where they've ended up back in the x-ray room again.

"Crap!" John says and kicks the toe of his boot against the exam table's leg.

"Hey, half pint said something about an urgent care facility in this town. Maybe they've got one," Kelly says, referring to Reagan.

"Yeah, she did," John agrees. Now they have to find that place, too. "Let me radio back to the farm and see what they can tell us for a location on that place."

Regrettably, the urgent care building is nearly on the other side of town, which means more moving around and a longer night for both of them.

They decide to take the truck again and manage to find the stat care without too much difficulty. Kelly successfully weaves around abandoned cars, a dumpster rolled into the street, and debris and garbage which is piled up on some of the roads as if people still thought that they were going to get curbside service. John spies three more homes and one apartment complex where there is a faint light in one or two windows. As they come closer to Center Street where the medical building should be, a pale orange glow in the distance becomes more visible. Orange glows don't light themselves, and John tightens his grip on the shotgun.

Bulldozers and dump trucks wait for their owners to return to the job site off to John's left in a new housing development. It's overgrown, muddy and the foreman's trailer has sunk three inches into the slushy ground. A cement truck is parked near the curb, the slide still extended, a pile of hardened concrete on the ground behind it. The glow from the fire rests beyond this unfinished suburban development. It could be squatters taking up residence in one of these expensive homes, though some of them are still under construction, their framing not even completed.

They spot the stat care, but instead drive past it to go behind a twenty-four hour Laundromat housed in a strip mall. It's a narrow alley that opens on both ends. There is a pizza shop next to the laundry washing and dry-cleaning building where Kelly pulls the truck alongside the brick wall. It no longer wafts the delicious scents of mouth-watering pepperoni and Italian spices into the air. A rat scurries in front of John and disappears under the pizza shop's dumpster.

Kelly takes lead and they skirt around the plaza and jog toward the medical building. A strident bellow comes from the general direction of the fire a few hundred yards away. Two more shouts from different voices reverberate through the low lying valley. John's sure that he and Kelly haven't been spotted. It's too dark to see them without the iridescent radiance of streetlamps and the fluorescent lighting from building windows spilling out into the street.

The rear door to the clinic stands ajar, so they make good use of it and slip inside. Kelly sweeps left and John takes point. This medical facility is in the same sad shape as Doc's practice. It has been looted and vandalized nearly beyond recognition. Once they ascertain that the building is clear, Kelly splits to search for the missing piece of medical equipment while John spies on the fire and possible people through a nearby window in an exam room using his binoculars. He has a more direct view of them than he had from the truck and the alley.

Upon further observation, he can see a fairly large group of people, perhaps twenty or more. There are three pick-up trucks, two mini-vans, an RV and four or five pop up campers set up and open. What he doesn't see is children, but that wouldn't be unusual this late at night. As a matter of fact, John's not sure why any of them would be awake at this hour. It's nearly three a.m.

Kelly comes back to him after a short time and announces the good news of finding the wand for the machine.

"Looks like it'll fit," John notices.

"Gonna have to," Kelly states simply. "What's up out there?"

"Not sure yet," John says quietly and hands his friend the binoculars. "Strange that they aren't asleep at this hour."

184

"Yeah, maybe. Or maybe they're trying to keep watch. Why would they be set up out there when they could just use those houses?"

"Passing through?" John suggests.

"Could be," Kelly concurs as he returns the binoculars to John. "Wanna' check it out?"

John weighs this decision heavily before turning away from the window. "No. Let's get back. There's a lot at stake if we don't make it back. They're counting on us and if we don't show, then Derek'll be coming for us."

"Yep. Let's roll, brother," Kelly says and turns.

Three short bursts of automatic gunfire sounds off from the direction of the firelight and voices, and they both swing back to the window. The screaming of women echoes in the dark night. Another short burst followed by the blast of a shotgun also descends on them from the area of the makeshift campgrounds.

"Son of a bitch," Kelly says under his breath.

Now they have no choice but to get involved. If innocent people, especially women need their help, then it's their obligation to offer it. Without pause, he nods to Kelly, gets one in return and they move. John trots through the med center, out the front door and down the short street using the half-built homes as cover. Kelly's on his heels.

As they close in on the camp, one of the pick-up truck peels out, spraying gravel. The driver is shot straightaway through the rear window. It looks to be a headshot. His vehicle careens into a tall stack of plywood meant for building the outer walls of these homes. John can hear shouting but cannot make out the words. Two men yell raucously. Some of the women have resorted to sobbing and crying. He and Kelly move closer still and take cover in the last house on the street, one of the few that seems nearly completed. Letting themselves in through the front door, it's immediately clear that the home is empty. They ascend the stairs to the second floor and separate, both taking a position at a bedroom window to spy down upon the campers.

"...bastard got what he deserved!" shouts one of the men.

The light of the campfire- what John can now make out as multiple campfires- provides a source by which he can see them

185

more clearly. He pushes back his goggles again and silently monitors the situation. He'd rather not get into a firefight tonight since Doc is waiting on this medical equipment. He'd also like to not get shot tonight if it's possible.

Each group down below him has their own campfire, tents, backpacks, food supplies and vehicles set up in their own self-assigned areas. He still hasn't seen children. Surely there aren't any with this large group or they'd be awake and crying over the gunfire. The people all seem to know each other and are likely traveling in a long caravan. John decides on quiet observation for the time being.

"Hell yeah, he did. Trying to steal our food," one of the women interjects and snorts derisively.

"He made a pass at my wife yesterday," another man comments.

"He did the same to me," a petite woman says and wraps an arm around the first man.

A man in khakis, loafers and a button down, short-sleeved shirt comes out from behind one of the pop-up campers. He states with anger, "That is the last time we let an outsider join up with us. No more. It didn't work out the last time we did it, and it sure as hell didn't this time. No more."

They all call out in agreement or nod.

"Get his gun," another man beckons to a person who is searching the dead man's truck. "We could always use more guns."

"You got that right," a tall, robust man shouts.

"We'll move out in the morning. Everyone get back to bed. We have a long day ahead of us tomorrow," says the man in khakis.

Apparently they have things under control. Whatever has taken place with this group or within this group is settled. The gunfire is done, and things seem to be settling down. John backs away from the window and meets Kelly on the second floor landing.

Groups of people like this may be forming all over the country. It's not for him and Kelly to judge them and get involved in their business. If they feel like they've been wronged by someone, then they will have to handle their own problems. Intervening could lead to problems they don't need right now. Helpless people who are falling victim to creeps out there do need their assistance. Not these people. They seem to be doing fine on their own.

186

They jog back to the truck. John's glad to be leaving this town. He'll be even gladder to get back home. They get to the truck just in time to find three men trying to steal it.

"Hey!" Kelly shouts, effectively startling them.

When their lookout spins around to face Kelly, he's holding a shotgun of his own. The two others jump out of the truck's cab and are also holding weapons.

"Hey! Hey! Hey! Take it easy, man," Kelly bellows.

"Fuck off! This is our truck. Get outta here or we'll use these on you," the younger man, the lookout says.

He has way too much confidence in his abilities with that shotgun for being so young. He can't be more than twenty. The other man beside him looks older, maybe late thirties. He has a hunting rifle, maybe a 30.06 if John was to guess. It's difficult to be certain with night vision green skewing his vision. All three of the men hold flashlights, but do not have the benefit of military gear. The last man looks afraid. He's definitely in his twenties and has a skater-boy grunge appearance. His eyes dart nervously between his two comrades. He's not up for this. Doesn't matter. He's still a threat since he's holding a shotgun.

"This is our truck, young man," John says, trying to appease them and calm the situation. He even holds one hand out in front of him to stay them. "We came in it and we're leaving in it."

"Fuck that, man," the older guy says and swings the hunting rifle in their direction.

Kelly and John quickly separate, jump and take cover on the opposite sides of the alley, using the brick buildings to shield against the sudden onslaught of rifle fire and two reports of the shotgun. They both unscrew the silencers and stow them.

"Get lost, assholes!" one of them crudely shouts again between shots. "This truck's ours!"

Kelly signals to John that he's going to flank. John will need to provide suppressive, and more importantly distracting fire. He steals a quick glance around the corner, avoids getting shot and discovers two more men that have joined up with the group shooting at Kelly and him. They are also both armed. He hopes his friend doesn't run into any others on his way around back. John pops off a round from the shotgun.

The light pop of a .223 round, likely from Kelly's rifle comes from the front of the building. Obviously he's found more targets. John's going to need to do more than support fire. He's wishing he had a grenade. Rounds continue to ping and chip at the brick and mortar building at his back. He glances right, finds another man coming at him. He's also young, probably close to the same age as the other, but he has a pistol. So he's also a threat.

"Don't do it, kid," John shouts.

Unfortunately, he doesn't take John's advice and raises the revolver toward him instead. He's forced to take him out with the shotgun. With that done, he trots in the direction of the kid and blasts through the front door of the building, not bothering to look at the young man's prone body.

He's now in a former restaurant of some kind. He's looking for a good position to take up at a window. Knocking into chairs and tables as he goes, John finds the right area. Next, he slides the window up whisper-quiet so he doesn't have to shoot through it. Slinging the shotgun behind him, he pulls the M16 forward, clicks off the safety and takes aim. He can only get a visual on four of them.

After a deep breath in, he squeezes. Two targets disabled quickly enough. The other two have spotted him and are shooting in his direction. The outer brick wall provides a good cover as he slides left, pressing his back against it. The window's smashed to hell, but he's protected from taking a round. The front door swings in noisily. It's the missing perp, so John takes him out with two shots center mass.

The dead guy's friends will expect the shots John fired to have come from their partner. They expect John to be dead at this point, so John takes the opportunity to go through the back of the building and come out behind them.

Movement behind them catches his peripheral vision. It's Kelly. Neither of the bad-guys have heard him or his friend. John and Kelly take aim, fire simultaneously and finish off their enemies. Just like old times. It's kind of sad that these are fellow Americans, though. But they have responsibilities at the farm to get back to. There was no other way for this situation to come out differently. They'd warned these men. He's not going to get shot or lose Doc's truck or hike back to the farm. These men are takers, and there's no place for taking when the property belongs to the McClanes. They

188

are just like any other terrorist he's ever come across. He just doesn't like it that they were also Americans. John knows they can't dwell on it now. There's always plenty of downtime to worry about battles, decisions and choices. He just usually chooses not to.

Kelly walks over and puts John's hit out of his misery. His shot hadn't made a clean kill, which is unusual for him. But Kelly's calm as ever. This is his normal attitude in a skirmish. He's cool and decisive and the best point man John's ever known. They stand a moment, listening and waiting. Nobody else comes at them. The deafening firefight has left a soft ringing in John's ears. But there aren't any other signs of life moving about, especially none coming at them with weapons.

"Sorry it took me a while. Ran into some dicks on the way," Kelly relays to John.

"Yeah, I figured," John says with a friendly smirk. "Heard the shots. Any problems?"

"Nah, just these losers and few more of their buddies around the front."

"Good. This crap's getting old," John remarks with a tightening of his mouth.

"Let's get the hell outta here," his friend suggests.

John bumps his fist, and they get back into the truck. Kelly fires it up.

"Didn't even have our theme music to get ready for this one," Kelly remarks good naturedly.

"Yeah, bummer, man," John states as he stashes his shotgun between his legs.

Kelly says, "Coulda' thrown off our game."

"I think I broke a nail," John returns which earns a shout of laughter from Kelly. It's good to blow off the tension with some lightness. It's how they've always dealt with the heavy stuff.

"See? Gay."

They both laugh again and make slow, steady progress back out of the town of Pleasant View without any other delays or violent interactions with the new townsfolk. This town may have been where the girls attended public school and where Doc had established his medical practice, but this is no one's town anymore. This is like any other town across America: dangerous.

189

John breathes a sigh of relief when the farm comes into view. All joking aside, he's glad they are on their way home.

The 'theme song' Kelly referred to was always AC/DC's "Dirty Deeds Done Dirt Cheap." Always seemed fitting before. Still does.

Chapter Fourteen
Reagan

Three days have passed since John and Kelly had come home from Pleasant View. Reagan's sure she must've come out of the shed fifty times to peer down through the cattle pasture looking for them. She'd noticed that Derek had done the same thing from the back porch. Grandpa had been as calm as always. They'd all blown a collective sigh of relief when the faint, shadowy glimmer of the truck's headlights had come into view.

As soon as she'd seen John's face, Reagan had known something went down on their trip to town. They'd both denied anything happening, but Reagan saw the gun powder residue on their fingertips, the spent shotgun shell sticking out of John's back pocket. Plus they'd also brought back six additional guns with them. John had said they'd found them. Fat chance. Neither of their military rifles had their silencers still attached. Something went down for sure. He also wouldn't meet her eyes with his own. He'd lied. She's not sure she blames him. She's not sure she wants to know what happened.

She and Grandpa had utilized the ultrasound machine to ascertain the baby's size and approximate weight that same night that John and Kelly had returned with it. Sadly enough, though, the baby is just going to be way too small to save. Grandpa had said that there is a small possibility of performing the cesarean if she lives a few more weeks. That's not likely to happen.

Subsequently, four days have passed since her damn, fateful kiss in the barn with John. Avoidance is a wonderful and useful tool when applied to dealing with an embarrassing and regretful experience shared with someone with whom you don't wish to speak. Instead of turning in at a normal hour the last four nights since that kiss, Reagan has stayed until the wee hours of the morning in the med shed with Grandpa so that she wouldn't have to be alone with John in their shared bedroom. He'd taken Jacob and put him to bed in her bed where she found him every night propped and barricaded with pillows and found John fast asleep in his own until his watch shift rolled around. She knew he wouldn't be so bold as to bring it up in front of the family so when she was with them she was safe, off limits. However, the lack of sleep has finally gotten to her, and she's practically falling asleep standing upright in the med shed.

Her patient Jennifer Miller isn't going to make it. She is simply too weak to fight off the sickness within her body. Reagan and Grandpa had discussed it this morning when she'd come back out to relieve him. Her vitals are lower than just a few days ago, and her body is starting the process of shutting down just like Garrett's had despite the different drug concoctions they've been trying. Her baby's fetal heart rate is also low, almost undetectable. Great-uncle Peter has not come in to see her even once since their arrival. Some devoted boyfriend he is turning out to be.

It's still early in the day, but Sam has not joined Reagan as of yet, and she had not come from the visitors' camp this morning when Huntley and Simon had. The kids had joined the family a few days ago for taco night, and everyone had a blast. John had played a Spanish song on the guitar afterward in the music room, causing the little kids to dance around and act silly. It had been a welcome change from the dark and dreary days of which they've all succumbed to lately. Reagan is starting to get concerned that Sam isn't coming at all when she finally hears a commotion outside of the shed.

"...you will get some or I'll kick your skinny ass again, you hear?"

"Please don't make me, Bobby. These people have been so nice to us," Sam replies in a desperate, fearful plea.

When Reagan gets to the door, she sees the teen with the steely, dark eyes, Bobby, jerk roughly on Sam's upper arm. What neither of the two teens catch is Cory jump the railing on the back porch, and he's on them in a heartbeat.

"Let her go!" Cory threatens with a flint of grit in his eye.

192

"Yes, let her go. Now," Reagan says as she steps onto the cement stoop and removes her latex gloves. They will encumber her should she need to draw the .45 under her surgical gown.

"This ain't got nothing to do with you two, so piss off," Bobby barks.

This makes Reagan seriously worried for the punk's health as Cory steps closer.

"I said let her go, dickhead," Cory says with calm fortitude.

He's a big kid and Bobby is not nearly the size of Cory. However, Bobby has a fight in him that has come from a life of hardness if Reagan was to guess.

"She was told to do something, and we were just having a discussion about it. So mind your own damn business," Bobby sneers and gives Sam's arm a shove as he releases her.

The girl stumbles hard and almost falls, but Cory catches her at the last second. He sweeps her behind him with one arm, and Sam stays there, content to have Cory defend her.

"What did you want her to do?" Reagan asks coolly.

"None of your business, hot stuff," Bobby says.

He licks his lower lip and swipes a hand through his black hair. There is a piercing in his lower lip and two matching ones in his left ear.

"Don't talk to Dr. McClane like that," Cory defends her, as well.

He's never called her that before. He usually doesn't talk much at all to her for some reason.

"She ain't much of a doctor. Everyone around here keeps fuckin' dyin'," he says on an obnoxious laugh.

He's a very good-looking young man, but the coldness in his eyes make him appear hard, which he obviously is. For being younger than her, Bobby scares Reagan. The intensity of his mannerisms comes off as confident and too self-assured.

"You could, too, if you keep running your mouth," Cory threatens.

Reagan is shocked at the brevity of his comment. He is not the kind of kid who talks like that. He doesn't talk much to anyone, other than his brother or Simon.

"Yeah?"

"You still didn't say what you wanted Sam to do for you? Do you need something?" Reagan asks before the two teen boys start rolling around in the dirt trying to kill one another. Cory wears a pistol on his hip, but she's not sure how experienced he is with using one. They sure don't need it getting into Bobby's hands.

"Yeah, I need something. You could help me out with that, Dr.," Bobby jeers.

This comment and this young man make Reagan's skin crawl. He grabs at his crotch with further implication.

"I think I'm a little old for you," she replies snidely, trying to shut him down.

"I'm nineteen. How the hell old are you? You don't even look nineteen to me. You look young... and hot, just like Sam there. She's my girl- Sam. Isn't that right?" Bobby says.

For this lewd insinuation alone Reagan wants to shoot him before Cory gets the chance to. Sam does not look to agree with Bobby's assessment of their supposed relationship.

"Don't be a dick. Just go on back up to your camp with your friends," Reagan scolds him.

"Why don't you come with me?" Bobby leers. "We can have some fun up there. Maybe you should check out my dick. We always got something going on that's fun. Isn't that right, Sam?"

Now Reagan wants to retch. Her nurse is staring at the ground with humiliation and fear. Cory unfastens the buckle to his pistol and withdraws it from the holster, slowly, out of Bobby's line of vision.

"As much as I'd like to examine your... tiny dick, I don't have a microscope big enough to do the job. Now run along, little dick, and join the others before my friend Cory here puts some lead between your eyes," Reagan says in an overly cheerful voice and even gives a smile.

Bobby finally notices Cory's drawn pistol and visibly startles. He takes a cautious step back.

"You do what I told you to do, bitch," he says to Sam.

The petite teen has come to stand next to Reagan. She is literally cowering in fear.

"Get the hell out of here," Cory says more loudly, and the offensive, psychotic teen leaves.

"You ok, Sam?" Cory asks when the jerk is gone.

194

Reagan peers into the distance and discovers that Derek has been observing the confrontation from the cattle barn. He is looking down the scope of his rifle at them. Reagan gives him a thumbs up, and he nods once before going back to working on whatever it was that he was doing. It feels good to know that the men on the farm are always looking out for them, although Derek and John should be sleeping at this early hour. Neither of them seem to sleep much, or at least none of them have since the visitors had descended on the farm. And they never let their guards down, not even for a second.

"Yes, I'm ok. Thanks for that," Sam finally answers.

"Cory, why don't you hang out around here for a while till things settle down? Sam and I need to work in here on some sanitizing," Reagan asks, and the young man nods and takes a seat on the stoop. "Come on, Sam."

Once they are in the med shed farther from the door and out of earshot, she tries to talk to Sam who usually clams up. Reagan observes a dark purple bruise on her upper arm and a small, fresh cut on her upper lip. She'd like to tell Derek to snipe everyone out at that damn camp!

This girl knows so much about her traveling companions, but she sure as hell isn't forthcoming with very much information. Hannah had tried to speak with her the other day but hadn't really gleaned anything new or useful. She also knows that Simon is the same way from what Cory has related. After the girl has put on her safety gear and Reagan has put on a fresh pair of latex gloves, Reagan hands her stethoscope to Sam.

"How'd you get those bruises, Sam?" she asks bluntly, the only way she knows.

"Oh… um, I just tripped. I'm really clumsy, Dr. McClane," she lies badly and looks away.

This is bound to be a dead end street. Reagan is frustrated and angry but not at this poor kid.

"What was that about out there with Bobby?" she asks, but Sam looks away very fast. The young waif uses a cool, wet cloth to wipe Jennifer's forehead. "Won't you tell me?"

Sam shrugs. "He just wanted me to… take stuff."

"Take stuff like what? From us? Like steal from us?" Reagan asks in shock.

"Yeah. I guess so," Sam comes clean with defeat.

"What did he want you to steal? Food?"

The girl shakes her head as she records the patient's blood pressure on the chart.

"Drugs. He wants me to steal drugs. I think he used to do a lot of drugs or something, and now he wants me to steal drugs from you," Sam says rather openly.

"Hm, interesting. I guess I was right then," Reagan says.

"About what, Dr. McClane?"

"He really is a little dick," Reagan jokes, and Sam actually laughs once and nods. A few minutes later, though, Reagan goes at it again as she sanitizes the sink and back counter.

"What kind of drugs did he want you to get?" she asks Sam.

"Um, I don't even remember what the names were. I think painkillers or something. He sure knew a lot of their names. I've seen him smoking grass and cigarettes and drinking alcohol and once, last month, they found cocaine and all got high," Sam offers up.

"Nice. He's also a Mensa student, I see," Reagan gets another sad chuckle from the girl.

"I only know that because I went to a few parties when… well, before and some of the kids there were doing drugs. I don't do drugs. I swear," Sam says fervently.

Reagan believes her. The girl does not show any of the typical signs of drug abuse, malnourishment maybe, but not drug usage.

"Don't worry about it. I believe you. I'm a doctor, remember? I can tell users when I see them. It usually takes about four seconds to figure out a tweaker. I'll see if you can stay here tonight. Do you want to?"

The girl regards Reagan with so much bald, blatant hope and longing in her eyes that it almost hurts to look at her. Sam nods lightning fast.

"Yes, please," Sam says.

"Fine, it's settled. What are you going to do when it's time to leave with them?" Reagan asks frankly.

Sam shrugs and shakes her head. "Run away? Run into the woods?"

"Well, I don't think you'd get far. We have bear in these woods, you know. And what the hell would you eat? You gonna catch a chipmunk and skin it and eat it? I don't think so. You need to think about what you want to do. You have options now," Reagan says and doesn't make eye contact for fear of making the girl too nervous to talk.

"I don't have any options, Dr. McClane. My family is dead, and I can't abandon Huntley," Sam says pitifully.

Reagan finds it strange that a fifteen year old girl would feel such a strong sense of responsibility for a kid who isn't her actual sibling. She has more honor in her pinkie finger than the whole lot of the visitors out at their camp, which appears dead silent as most of them must still be sleeping. No wonder they don't get anything done.

"Sure you do. You can stay with us. Or you can go with those idiots out there when they leave," she offers and waits to see what her response will be. She's quiet for a long pause. When Reagan looks up, there are tears in Sam's bright blue eyes. Grams has fixed her choppy cut, and her dark hair is in a more comely, smooth bob style, trimmed short up to her chin. It makes her already large eyes seem huge set in her tiny face.

"Really? I could... stay here? On this farm? With you and your family? They would let me?" she asks tentatively.

"Yeah, if you want to. The family talked about it last night. We were planning on discussing it with each of you individually..."

"Wait. Who do you mean?" Sam interrupts which is rare from her.

"You and Simon and Huntley. Maybe Bobby about an hour ago, but he's for sure out now," Reagan says insensitively but doesn't care. She suspects this girl is suffering physical abuse at the hands of that punk. "We have a fairly strict no-dickheads-allowed policy on the farm." Sam smiles and then throws her arms around Reagan's shoulders.

"Oh, yes. Oh, yes. Thank-you, Dr. McClane. I know Simon and Huntley will want to stay, too. Thank-you, thank-you," she babbles.

Reagan's arms are at her sides.

"Sam? I'm not a hugger. Let go," she says firmly, and the girl drops her arms and steps back awkwardly.

"I'm sorry, Dr. McClane" Sam apologizes. "We won't be any trouble. We'll do whatever work you want us to. We'll..."

"Sam, we're not asking you to stay on to be our slaves. For shit's sake! Relax on the servitude thing. And just call me Reagan. Look, talk to Simon today if you see him alone. Don't discuss this with the creeps out there, though. We're not sure how this is gonna work yet, and they aren't getting the same deal. I mean, Huntley is Frank's kid. And Simon is that hag's nephew. So this may be hard for us to work out with them."

"Yes, ma'am," Sam agrees.

"Come on. Let's check on Jennifer again. She's not getting any better. I kind of figured you knew that already," Reagan tells her, and Sam nods slowly.

"She is so nice. Her husband was from France. She has a picture of him in the RV. He was an actor, stage stuff mostly. But he was so handsome, blond hair, blue eyes, Hollywood good-looking. That's where he was when this happened, in France I mean. And she said she hadn't heard from him in months. Of course, France is mostly gone now, so...," she trails off sadly.

"And now she's with our loser-drunk, Great-uncle Peter?" Reagan asks with sarcastic disbelief.

"Um, yeah," she says hesitantly as if she's afraid someone will hear. Then she shuts down and looks away.

"Sam, if you're staying with us, then you have to tell us what you know so that we can deal with these morons," Reagan pressures the girl.

"I'm sorry," she says and then continues. "Your uncle just said that she was his girlfriend when we got here so that your grandmother would let us stay. They picked her up a short time before me. She told me she was from Virginia. She'd gone home from Los Angeles to visit with her family before the first tsunami struck while her husband was in France. I don't know much about her other than that I don't think she was your uncle's real girlfriend."

"What's that mean? Isn't she pregnant with his baby?"

Sam shakes her head.

"No, that baby is her husband's, not your uncle's. He just... made her his girlfriend."

"What the hell's that supposed to mean? You mean like forced himself on her? Did someone 'make' you their girlfriend, Sam? Did any of them force themselves on you?" Reagan is ready to call Cory back with his pistol to go and take care of business. Sam won't answer her, and Reagan is left to imagine the worst. Her blue eyes dart around and then tear up.

A knock at the door alerts them both.

"Reagan?" Sue calls from the doorway and concludes their private conversation.

"Yeah? What is it?"

"Huntley is sick," Sue says with urgency.

Derek is behind her and carrying Huntley. Please, God, not again, Reagan prays silently. This is just too much.

"Shit. Bring him in and lay him on that cot. What are his symptoms?" Reagan asks, though she's sure she already knows them. They'd sanitized and re-bedded that bunk with clean linens and a sterile pillow. Reagan had hoped at the time to never have use of it again.

"He coughed a couple of times, and I thought it might just be because he was in the barn with the other kids. You know, hay dust or something? But then he said he was tired and when I felt his forehead, he was pretty warm," Sue accounts.

Just looking at Huntley, Reagan can tell that the boy is sick. His beautiful, caramel-tinted skin has turned an ashen gray, and he is coughing frequently.

"I'm going to listen to his chest. You guys get out of here. Sam, show them how to sanitize. Then leave ok, Sue?" Reagan tells her sister who nods. She repeats what she is going to do to Huntley so that he isn't afraid.

Reagan presses her stethoscope to the boy's chest and hears the tell-tale bubbling sounds that come with pneumonia.

"Am I going to die like my brother?" Huntley asks her bluntly.

Reagan's gaze jumps to his hazel eyes. Jesus, why are kids so damned honest? She clears her throat.

"How long have you felt sick, Huntley?" Reagan answers his morbid question with one of her own that will hopefully deter him.

"I started not feeling good last night, so Levon made me go sleep outside. He said he didn't want no sickness in the RV," Huntley tells her.

"Tell me again which one is Levon, Huntley?" Derek asks from the sink.

His underlying tone is menacingly dark. Reagan panics that he is about to do something violent and perhaps reckless.

"He's the black guy that's really big. He has messy, freaky hair. He's not a very nice man," the boy relays.

When Reagan looks over her shoulder at Derek, he gives her a knowing nod. She wonders if her brother-in-law is going to go and shoot Levon on the spot for making a kid, a sick kid, sleep outside when the weather is turning much cooler at night in this third week of September. She would've never thought Derek capable of such a thing since she'd only ever known him as her fun brother-in-law who told her humorous stories of his military life. But now that she knows his brother and what John is capable of after their city trip, she isn't so sure about Derek anymore.

"I noticed they also did a half ass job of picking the corn, too," Derek remarks quietly to Reagan. "There's still a bunch of ears still on the stalks like they just didn't feel like doing it."

"Pathetic," Sue says with disgust. "We're sanitized, Reagan, so we're going back out."

"That's a good idea, Sue. I think we're catching this early enough with Huntley. Make sure the kids sanitize in the house since they've been playing with him. I'm going to start him immediately on an IV and give him antibiotics and a steroid shot. His blood pressure's good, lung function's a little dirty, but this hasn't progressed on him to where I think I can't manage it with medications," she says.

"Thank God," Derek tells her. "Hey, everything ok with that punk earlier?"

There's no need for using a name on this topic.

"Yeah, he was just being a little dick," she tells him to which Derek snorts once and smiles. Sam smiles sadly, but then looks at the ground.

"Let me know if you need help with him," he tells her and Reagan gives him a nod this time.

Her brother-in-law leaves, but Reagan grabs Sue by the arm.

"You'd better go calm him down. I'm afraid he might do something," Reagan says quietly.

"Should I really though?" Sue asks with deadly intent before walking away.

200

Reagan couldn't agree more, but these decisions have to be made as a family. She knows her sister will talk Derek down from his ledge of hostility.

She gets right to starting an IV on Huntley which he protests, but Sam helps her with him. The steroid shot in the back of his hip area is next, and the little guy just about passes out from fear and anxiety.

"You're doing so great, Huntley. You're so brave. Why don't you tell me some more about your mother?" Sam coos to the boy.

Her feelings for this young boy are so transparent. She has clearly adopted him as her little brother. As Reagan goes about administering meds and taking vitals on Huntley and then documenting everything on a new patient sheet, Sam talks to the boy non-stop to further take his mind off of what's going on around him.

"I'm going to give him an Albuterol breathing treatment, Sam. You can help him with it like you did with Jennifer when she was awake, remember?" Reagan asks the girl as she hooks up the machine and dispenses the tiny vial of liquid medicine into the correct chamber.

"Yes, ma'am, I remember. I'll hold the tube for him," the girl agrees.

Her brilliant blue eyes are staring up into Reagan's with such blind faith that Reagan has to turn away from this kid for the second time today. There is a very real possibility that Huntley will also die, even though his sickness has not progressed the way the other two had. For a young teenager, Sam is more intuitive than she should be, and Reagan doesn't want the girl to read the doubt on her face.

"Good," Reagan says curtly and flips on the power switch to the machine. Reagan walks away from her to start documenting her findings on the boy's chart. When she's finished, she next moves to Jennifer's bed where the woman lies in the same non-alert, comatose state of which Garrett had finally succumbed.

Minutes turn to hours in the med shed as the sun sets and dinner is called for the McClane family, though Reagan does not want to leave. The curtain has been permanently drawn between the two patients so that Huntley should not see when Jennifer passes. The boy is sleeping deeply as Reagan listens once again to his lung function and is pleased that the bubbling sounds have settled substantially since earlier in the day. The breathing treatment coupled with the medicines, seems to be working. They are also making him sleep soundly which isn't a bad thing.

Reagan pushes a heavy table, with help from Sam, over beside his bed to prevent him from falling off. As deeply as he is sleeping it is doubtful that he will even stir. When they leave the shed, Reagan locks the door and turns off all but one low light. The lock hanging from the heavy chain should discourage any would-be drug thieves from entering, and if it doesn't, she can always send the men with their M16's over to further discourage such behavior.

Once they are inside the house and Grams has yelled at her once again to remove her shoes, Reagan rushes straight to the laundry room sink where she can scrub up. Although anyone who's been in the med shed has to sanitize before they leave, she and Grandpa have also told everyone to wash up in the house, as well. With a sickness of this magnitude it is better to err on the side of caution.

Reagan doesn't bother to turn on the lights in the laundry room, which will soon become the coats and muddy boots entrance when winter sets in. It will help to keep the kitchen hardwood floors clean during the muddier, wetter seasons to come. The small amount of light coming from the hallway and the window above the sink is good enough for her to see to wash her hands and forearms.

"Hey," a voice- that voice- from the door makes her jump.

The one person she'd been doing so well at avoiding is now standing in all his dirty, muscle-bound glory in the doorway. She steals a peek at him and has to turn away quickly. He's wearing a filthy, white tank and dirty, baggy, faded blue-jeans. Forget the guy in the three piece suit, Reagan couldn't have found another man in the world as sexy as she thinks John is right here, right now in his grungy work clothes standing with one hand suspended from the doorframe which he can easily reach. She suppresses a groan and feels her cheeks ignite.

"I heard Huntley's sick now, too."

Oh good, he is going to keep this civil and light and not bring up that ridiculously mind-blowing kiss in the barn.

He has probably forgotten all about their kiss already. He is likely experienced with everything of a sexual nature, and she has no experience whatsoever. They couldn't possibly be more ill-suited.

202

She'd been completely overwhelmed by their kiss and his surprising plan to give her one. His mouth had moved on hers with an all-encompassing fire, and she'd kissed him right back, sort of. It isn't like she's had a whole lot to compare it with, but it had been earth moving. Apparently for John, the kiss had been completely forgettable.

"Um, yeah. I think he'll be ok, but hell, what do I know?" she remarks and dries her hands and arms on the towel hanging beside the stainless steel wash sink.

"Are you serious?" he asks with surprise. "You're the smartest person I know. You're the smartest person I've ever even heard of, Reagan. You know more than I do about that stuff, more than any of us. Your grandpa is up, and he said that it was lucky to catch the sickness early like this. He said you'd probably be able to cure Huntley."

He praises so openly of her, which makes her furious and proud and uneasy all at the same time.

"Cure him? I'm not a magician," she says sarcastically as she hangs the towel and then neatly arranges it to avoid turning to face him. God, this shit is embarrassing. No wonder she'd avoided dealing with relationships of this type her entire life. Books and specimens on a slide are so much easier. "But I think he'll recover."

Reagan proceeds to give John the full medical run-down of Huntley's symptoms, the meds she's administered and his stats. It is all another useful diversionary tactic on her cowardly part, but she finds it preferable to looking at him as she puts her hand on the ledge of the sink and faces the wall instead. Why does her voice keep going up in octave and sound so breathless? And why the hell is she talking so fast? She sounds like some sort of freak medical recording.

"If I didn't know any better..." John says from right behind her.

This makes Reagan jump again. He places his hands on either side of hers on the sink and leans into the entire length of her backside.

"I'd think you were avoiding me, boss."

His cheek brushes sidelong against hers, and John nuzzles the spot below her ear. He doesn't kiss her there, but just pushes his nose and mouth against her which is so much worse than just a kiss. Then he inhales deeply. Reagan blinks rapidly as her breathing keeps pace with her blinks.

"I... I'm not avoiding you," she lies so badly. It doesn't sound the least bit convincing. Damn! His hands slide inward and cover hers. She looks at those hands with the long, capable fingers that are so tan from summer and completely engulfing hers. The contact is like a thousand needles hitting her skin. His hands are warm and sure. Reagan's are icy cold in comparison.

"Kind of feels like it," he murmurs against her neck.

He finally kisses her neck, making Reagan's knees about buckle. John slides a supportive arm about her waist and pulls her more tightly into the front of him where she is pretty sure she feels something very prominent pressing against her through both of their jeans.

"I miss you."

"Don't," Reagan whispers raggedly.

"Don't what? Don't do this?" John asks.

He kisses below her ear. It causes a shiver to run the entire length of her spine. Jesus, where did he learn to talk like this? Is he trying to melt her with his words and touches or does it just come naturally for someone like him? His breathing is ragged in her ear, leaving Reagan to wonder if he is also disturbed by her, though she is doing nothing but standing there, barely. Had he been serious all of those times when he'd come on to her and she'd thought he was being a wise-ass? How can she possibly appeal to someone like him?

His fist clenches and unclenches so hard and repeats the process in the soft, worn cotton of her shirt lying against her stomach. This will surely leave it a wrinkled mess. However, he does eventually release it again, but he doesn't move away. Then, as he kisses her neck and along her jaw line, John slides his hand north and cups her breast in his large palm. Every area of her Reagan's body is on fire, some areas more than others. His touch is firm but gentle, and he brushes his thumb over her nipple. An unfamiliar sound escapes her throat. Anyone could walk in on them. What the hell are they thinking? She feels lightheaded and dizzy. The thought hits her that perhaps she is sick, too. She feels feverish, weak. Who the hell cares? Her free hand reaches high up behind her and grasps the back of his neck, tangling in his hair there so that she can pull him more tightly to her. Where the hell has her self-control gone?

204

"Where are John and Reagan?" Grams calls from the hall somewhere near the dining area.

They break apart. Reagan finally turns to face him, and she can see for certain that John is as unequivocally disturbed by their encounter as she is. His stare is all-consuming in such a way that Reagan feels she cannot look away.

"Don't work in the med shed tonight," he demands and pleads at the same time.

She swallows hard.

"Reagan!" Sue yells from the outer rooms. "Hurry up!"

"We're coming," John calls back loudly.

Reagan has lost her ability to speak, think, reason clearly. This never happens. She's normally a lot more in control of herself than this.

"Don't work out there again tonight," he says more forcefully this time as the corners of his eyes pinch.

Reagan has to clear her throat before she can speak. "Wh... why?"

"You know why," he says hoarsely and advances on her again.

This time he grasps either side of her face, and his mouth swoops down onto hers with a thunderous intensity that staggers her back against the sink behind her. If John is worried about being seen kissing her, he has a funny way of showing it. His tongue plunders into her mouth as Reagan's body sags against him weakly. A cry of denial elicits unbidden from her mouth as he ends the kiss, and she has to bite her lower lip. After a moment too brief, he raises his head and those dark navy eyes bore into hers.

He whispers huskily, "I want to make love to you tonight."

Holy shit! Did he seriously just say that? What is wrong with him? People don't just go around talking like that in broad daylight... or dusk or in a house full of people. Reagan's answer is a sharp intake of breath.

"And you want me to make love to you. I can tell. Say you won't work out there tonight. I need you," John says.

He murmurs softly against her mouth as he kisses her again, but very briefly this time.

"I... I...," is all she can get out before Ari runs into the room interrupting them.

"Come on, Uncle John," she demands with a squeal. "Come on!"

She extends her baby hand toward John's who takes it without question and allows her to tug him toward the door. Though Ari is doing her best to gain John's attention, his gaze has not left Reagan's, and she has to finally tear her gaze away.

Once everyone is seated, the family- including the two new kids that they've managed to squeeze into areas at the table- joins hands for a prayer. This is the part that Reagan usually opts out of, but John takes her hand firmly in his under the table where he strokes his thumb roughly over the top. His touch is aggressive, unforgiving and impatient. This is a whole new side of John that almost frightens her with his open assertiveness. She has no idea what is covered in the prayer because she is remembering his hand on her breast. He is holding Jacob on his lap because they still have not found the time to go out and salvage a high-chair from one of the outlying neighborhoods.

After the prayer, Grams opens the family conversation with the option for Simon, Huntley and Sam to stay on with the family and by Simon's shocked reaction he hadn't known this was coming. Huntley is almost too young to make that decision, but Reagan is fairly confident that he'll want to stay, as well, once he is better enough to consult. Getting his shit-head father to agree to it might be another case altogether. Sam, having been prepped and happy to accept the offer from Reagan, is less surprised but also clearly thrilled to be hearing it brought up in front of the whole family. Both kids talk animatedly about how gracious and blah, blah, blah.

John has not released her hand under the table and is trying to balance Jacob on his knee and serve himself food at the same time. When Reagan can take no more of his not so gentle caress, she pulls her hand free and shoots him a warning look. He doesn't smile or smirk or grin at her like he normally does. His gaze is heavy, heated and fixed on her mouth. It also holds more promise than Reagan cares to explore. She quickly looks away.

"Are you going to tell your grandfather that you can't work with him tonight, or are you going to make me do it?" he asks quietly.

The conversations flow around them and the children talk and giggle.

"No, stop it," she answers and shakes her head. Her temperature has finally cooled a few degrees, and she can better manage her brain.

"No, you aren't working? Or no, you want me to tell him?" John demands.

Jacob bounces on his knee and grabs a handful of John's peas.

"No, I'm not telling him and neither are you. I need to be out there. Stop talking like that. Jennifer is probably..."

"Doc, I think Reagan needs the night off," he states.

His comment rudely and abruptly breaking into everyone's conversation, drawing their attention to both of them. Reagan would like to shrivel up and die on the spot as different members of the family are staring at them with strange looks.

He just keeps going, "She's been out there all day and almost every night for the past three nights."

"Shut up," she hisses at him and pulls at his forearm which he shirks off like she is just annoying him.

"She's exhausted, clearly," John remarks and this time does grin at her.

Grandpa is giving her a long, appraising look and then regards John.

"I'm fine. Don't be an ass," Reagan blurts before she realizes she's done so.

"Reagan," Grams warns in a threatening tone.

"I agree, John. Honey, you do need to rest. I've got it covered. You just take Jacob and get some sleep tonight, alright?" Grandpa says so kindly.

Ohhh, if only her grandfather knew why the knight in shining armor beside her is making such a big deal over her lack of rest, he would probably go and get his shotgun.

"But, Jennifer is likely..." she starts.

"I know, dear. But you being out there isn't going to stop it from happening," Grandpa interrupts this time with a deep grimace and returns to his meal.

Reagan tosses down her fork, which clangs on her plate, and seethes at John, not caring to hide her anger toward him. This is bullshit! He doesn't own her. He doesn't have the right to do this.

"You better eat up," he suggests after the conversation resumes.

The two teen boys talk animatedly about using the plows on the tractors today. As if that is something to be excited about. Her life is in an upheaval, and Simon and Cory are talking about damn tractors!

"Leave me alone," she says through her gritted teeth. John ignores her and feeds Jacob some of his roasted chicken.

"You're going to need your strength," he says.

He is so point blank, so deadpan, so sensual that Reagan's face ignites into a brilliant blush.

"…and what goes on around the house and the med shed and our patrol schedule needs to be kept under the strictest confidence," Grandpa is saying to Sam and Simon.

Both teenagers nod in agreement and swear their loyalty to the McClane clan. There was never really any doubt of their trustworthiness since the visitors seem to treat them so badly.

Simon speaks out, which is unusual for him. "They don't like it very well when we're over here. I mean, some of them don't."

"Let us handle that, Simon," Kelly tells him firmly.

Simon nods and looks to Sam who in turn looks down at her lap.

"Don't make me feed you," John threatens beside her.

How the hell had this turned so quickly between them? She hates him! She isn't attracted to him. He irritates the hell out of her. But, God, when he touches her it is like fire in her veins. And for some bizarre and unfathomable reason she doesn't want to kick his ass anymore when he touches her. His touch sends chills down her spine but not the bad kind.

"Stop…," she starts to correct him, but John picks up her fork and then they ensue in a battle over it.

"Give it!" she screeches which makes him finally release it. Again, everyone stops eating to stare at them which, in turn, makes her blush harder. He has no damn right to tell her to eat, or not work in the shed, or… have sex with him, either.

208

"Reagan McClane, what has gotten into you, young lady?" Grams asks in her most disapproving voice.

"Um, John had my fork," she mumbles ignorantly.

"Well that isn't a reason to act like a wild heathen at my dinner table. Now apologize to John," Grams orders.

Reagan's eyes about pop out her head.

"Go on, young lady. You need to set the example for these kids, not be the bad example."

"Ss... sorry," she stutters with a great deal of irritation.

"No, problem, boss. Oh, look, here's my fork," he lies and then shoots her another grin.

His damn grin is also slightly irresistible.

He winks and adds, "My mistake."

His blue eyes hold hers another second before she can turn away.

The dinner conversation continues again as Grandpa and Sue go over what they would like the children to learn in the coming school year. Grandpa is talking medicine while Sue suggests studying medicinal herbs, and plant and seed storage. Grams chimes in with canning, and Hannah comments about music.

"I... I'm not having... you know with you. So just forget it and leave me alone," Reagan tells John dismissively, even waving her hand like she's swatting an errant fly, hoping he'll cool his heels.

"What is 'you know'?" John asks.

His smirk is damned irritating, and Reagan refuses to take the bait. He leans closer, his mouth almost touching her ear. She can feel his hot breath there.

"I didn't say anything about 'you know.' I said I was going to make love to you, and I still am so finish your meal so we can get on with our night."

Reagan feels like she's about to pass out. She can't even look at him. Her cheeks feel overly hot. Her stomach does a flip. Why is he doing this? What has gotten into him? Why does he talk like that? *Who* talks like that? He'd always just stuck to playful flirtation which she'd assumed was just playful *joking* around her because she can't possibly appeal to him. She has so many flaws that nobody would want her. The long scar on her face is just the icing on the cake. God, she has to get herself out of this. Where is her knife when she needs it? How had she gotten herself into this is a better question? They'd only shared a few kisses counting the one at the barn, in her closet and now the one in the laundry room. The one in her closet hardly counts, either. They had both just been exhausted from the trip to the city. Hadn't they? It isn't like she is some temptress for Christ's sake!

"Who's up for music after dinner?" she blurts loudly and again gets the bizarre looks from her stunned family. Hannah doesn't miss a beat, though.

"Oh, that's a wonderful idea, Reagan!" her little sister says in her silly, Disney movie voice and claps her hands twice.

Kelly smiles down at Hannah with pride, though she is a total dork in Reagan's opinion. Shit! This isn't what Reagan really wants to do, either. She'd just blurted it out to get John off her case.

Hannie just continues on with her excitement, "We can play together. Or you could just play for us. It's been too long."

Yeah, no shit it's been too long, Reagan wants to scream! She doesn't like music anymore. It reminds her of a time when her life had been simple, not full of hate and death and blood and destruction. Jesus, now she has to join in on music night? This day just keeps getting better.

"Good, I want to hear you play again, Reagan," Grams says.

The meal is coming to a close with dessert that will surely hop up the little kids on sugar. Not getting the kids to go to bed could work in her favor.

"Great," she mumbles sarcastically and tries to pick at her apple cobbler as the family goes back to talking about ten different things at once.

"Well played," John says against her ear again, making her jump. "But you can delay the inevitable as long as you like. My shift doesn't start until four a.m."

Her arm breaks out in gooseflesh, and he obviously sees it because he runs his index finger horizontally across her forearm like he had that damn day in the barn. Being sleep deprived as it is, she's definitely not going to make it until four a.m. playing music.

When the dinner is cleared away and the children have cleaned the kitchen, everyone but Grandpa gathers in the music room to listen as Reagan takes a seat at the stupid, damn piano. She hasn't played in over six months. Sometimes she would let herself into the music room at the university with the huge grand piano and play when there weren't classes going on. John has set Jacob on the floor, and the baby is trying to eat all of the toys systematically. Sue sits with Jacob and the other kids and cradles Isaac at the same time. John comes to stand beside the piano. Unfortunately.

"Go away," she hisses as the rest of family sits around the room waiting for her to play.

"Do I make you nervous?" he asks.

His deep timbre is full of mischief and something else she can't quite put her finger on. Is it desire? She just wishes he'd quit looking at her like that- or at all.

"No!" she barks, lays her fingers lightly over the tops of the ivories, closes her eyes a moment and places her right foot to the right pedal. When she opens her eyes again, Reagan begins playing. She can forget about everyone else in the room, that is, everyone except for John. The music takes over her fingers, her mind and her body. It's the same as when she goes for a run, and it's why she's always used either one as an outlet when her mind felt too bogged down, too crowded with information.

"Beethoven's Moonlight Sonata," he remarks.

Everybody knows this song. It's not a surprise that he knows it.

"It's actually called Sonata…" she starts to inform him, but John interrupts her.

"I know. Piano Sonata number fourteen in C sharp or Sonata Quasi Una Fantasia," he answers eloquently.

She's never heard him talk like that before. It is a day of many first discoveries with John.

"How did…"

"My mom was a music teacher, remember?"

"Oh," Reagan says as the room fades away and her song crescendos and flows.

"Scooch," he orders.

John sits beside her on the piano bench whether she wants him to, which she doesn't, or not. His fingers start on the upper keys as he mimics with one hand what her right hand is playing in the treble keys. He surreptitiously places his left hand on her thigh where no one can see. But she can feel it because it's huge and hot through her jeans.

"Oh, how lovely," Hannah remarks and claps again.

Reagan has to admit it does put a rather interesting twist on the piece. But his fingers keep getting in her way. He's an accomplished piano player and his long fingers, those fingers that had been on her breast such a short while ago... her fingers misstep.

"What the hell?" she exclaims under her breath. That never happens.

"Distracted?" John asks.

He bumps his shoulder playfully against hers and continues to play until she catches up again.

"No," she grits her teeth and continues on, managing to finish without any more errors. Hannie claps and others follow suit.

"See? Proves my point. I knew you were gay," Kelly quips to John as he leads Hannah toward the piano.

Her duet partner slides his hand slyly off of her thigh again but not before he gives it a firm squeeze that sends a shockwave into the pit of her stomach. Grams is oblivious because she is holding Jacob, who keeps pulling at her long braid. John laughs as Hannah gives Kelly a disapproving look.

"Kelly, that's not nice," her sister scolds.

Kelly smiles down at her like she's just praised him. Ok, so he is smitten, but it certainly doesn't give him permission to defile her sister. Hannah's arm rests on Kelly's massive forearm, although there is no need for her to do so because the piano is right beside her.

"No, but it's true," Kelly says with a chuckle.

Reagan rises sneakily from her bench.

"No, don't stop, Reagan," Hannah begs.

Her damn dog ears had heard the bench squeak.

"I'm tired, Hannie. Why don't you play for us and sing something?" Reagan requests and finally after a few rounds of debating, Hannah relents. Em takes a seat on the bench next to Hannah and asks her a bunch of questions that Hannah patiently answers about music before she begins.

Jacob has crawled off of Grams's lap again as Reagan joins him on the floor on her knees. John is across the room, sitting on the sofa next to Kelly who is talking to him. However, John is staring intently at her. She's not even sure he hears what his friend is saying to him. Reagan is gazing so long at John that she doesn't look up in time to catch Jacob before he whacks her knee with a toy car.

"Ouch," she remarks and takes the truck from him. When she looks back at John, he is still watching her, but his familiar smirk is there. Good, it's better than the predatory stare he's been giving her like he's about to rip her clothes off.

"Jacob is so cute, Reagan," Sue remarks.

Reagan nods in total and complete agreement. "Yeah, he is, I guess," she replies as the little stinker chews on another toy, adding to the overall slobbered-on appearance of any toys in his perimeter. She glances up at John again. He is back to the stare. Jacob is supporting his upper body by balancing his hands on her thigh. Unfortunately, he also bites her thigh.

"Ouch!" she yelps loudly this time. "Damn, that hurt!" She doesn't even care if Grams gets mad this time. The kid has some teeth on him. Sue just chuckles.

"Yeah, they go through that biting phase. I've had mine draw blood before. It's best not to take your eyes off of him. They can be like raising wolves sometimes," Sue jokes with a laugh as she pats Isaac on the back.

"Yeah," Reagan says with a frown and looks up to find John walking toward her.

"You ok?" he inquires with concern.

Hannah is finishing her song which she has managed to get Em to sing along to. John squats beside her on his haunches. Reagan gapes at his wide thigh muscle that bulges against his jeans and fights the urge to lay her hand there as he had done to her only moments ago.

"She's fine," Sue says on another laugh. "She's just learned a lesson about not staring at your guy when you need to keep your eyes on your baby who's just discovered his own teeth."

Thankfully the rest of the family doesn't hear her. Reagan's about to answer her sister with an acidic retort over John not being her guy, but he beats her to it.

"Mm hm," John agrees.

He places his large palm on her thigh where Jacob had just bitten. His hand takes up over half of her upper leg. What the hell is he thinking? There are a hundred people in the room with them. Plus, his hot hand is making her lightheaded again.

"What? I wasn't doing that!" Reagan says with mortification and scoots back from him.

"Ready?" he asks.

He stands again and extends his hand to her. He swipes Jacob up with one muscular arm.

"Wh... what?" she croaks out.

"For bed. We need to get this dude a bath. He's wearing most of my dinner and his, and then you can get a shower and then I will. Your grandfather wants you to get some rest, remember?" John says easily.

Reagan doesn't take his hand but gets up on her own.

"Good-night everyone," he says so easily, so much like himself.

Reagan is left with no choice but to follow him from the music room and plod slowly up the stairs behind him. She knows what prisoners who've had to walk to their own gallows must have felt like.

She supposes it's not fair to make him bathe Jacob alone for the fourth night in a row. Behind her, the rest of the family is also dividing up and bidding their own farewells for the night. Reagan is vaguely aware that the family discussed at dinner that Simon could sleep in the basement guest room and Sam could take the last available room down there or sleep in the littler kids' room with them, which is what she chose. Reagan's wishing she would have thought to invite Sam to stay in her bedroom in the attic.

"I'll meet you in the bathroom and bring him some clean clothes... and ours," he adds.

They reach the second floor landing where he hands her Jacob and then presses a quick peck to her cheek, leaving her stunned, again. Though they've only been home from the city for a few weeks, Jacob is starting to gain a bit of weight, and Grandpa has given him a clean bill of health being the doctor with more pediatric experience.

Reagan shakes her head to snap out of her shock over John's quick kiss and marches straight for the bathroom where she runs warm water for the baby, only a few inches to conserve hot water for the other members of the family. Derek and Sue had come to the

214

dinner table with wet hair and so had their two kids, but the added two teens would probably appreciate their first hot shower in… who knows when? Once she gets Jacob in the tub, he splashes and giggles and splashes a whole lot more and soaks her. His laughter is infectious, and she smiles down at him but has to look away because her feelings for this kid are starting to scare her. He could be the next one to get sick.

"Derek said you had trouble with that Bobby kid today," John says as he closes the door behind him.

What the hell? She hadn't even heard him come in, and she startles again.

"Nothing I couldn't handle," she remarks and goes about washing the baby with her soapy hands. Jacob splashes harder, and she gets a face full of water, which she wipes on the sleeve of her shirt.

John squats beside her and picks up the bar of soap, lathering up and then helping to wash the squirmer.

"Cory told me about it, too. You need to tell me that stuff, babe. You know, so that I can take care of it," he informs her.

Like he has some claim on her! She just rolls her eyes at him and tries to look back at the baby, but he holds her gaze with his own again. John's strong fingers tangle with her wet ones, and they become slippery and sensual under his touch. She remembers how capable of killing a man these fingers and hands can be.

"What would you have done? Shot him? You kind of lose your shit pretty easily," Reagan says bluntly. He laughs softly but sobers quickly enough.

"I only lose my crap where you're concerned. I don't like anyone trying to mess with you," John professes honestly.

His statement makes her stomach do a flip over his protectiveness. "Well, then take your own advice and leave me alone," she comes back with wit.

"Can't. And I've recently discovered that you kind of like it when I mess with you," John returns with a confident grin. "Don't you?"

His question is not really a question at all. He's phrased it as a damn statement of fact. Reagan swallows hard and looks away.

"No, I don't!" she hisses vehemently at him, hoping he'll shut up.

"Want me to prove you wrong?" John asks and stares at her mouth.

"He's clean!" she announces abruptly and rinses Jacob and her hands, and John rinses his own. She picks up the baby with a towel as John drains the water from the tub. It is not lost on Reagan how this scene of domesticity is playing out, and it's odd but not in the most repulsive manner possible.

Reagan squats on her knees on the thick, gray rug in front of the tub and dries the baby who only wants to be free and crawl away from her. John helps her and again their hands and fingers brush against the other's, making shivers trail up and down Reagan's arms. The fact that every time she looks up at him he's staring at her and not at Jacob doesn't help. They manage to get the kid dressed in a fresh diaper and a white onesie with blue elephants on the background before he crawls away to bang on the cupboard door. Why are baby boys so violent and noisy? This kid will grow up and want to blow up shit, no doubt.

Reagan takes the cup sitting beside the tub and bends over on her knees to rinse the soapy residue from inside the tub wall. She's seen Sue do this after her kids' baths and figures it must be the thing to do. When she's done and turns back, John has removed his shirt and is closer to her and also kneeling. Before she can even question why he is undressing for his shower with her still in the room, he practically tackles her to the rug. John's arm slips behind her back as they go down, and his other hand cradles her head. His body covers hers before they even hit the floor, and his mouth moves greedily over hers.

"Stop!" she struggles for air, for freedom. "What are you doing?"

"Proving you wrong, remember?" he mocks.

His head bends and his chiseled mouth covers hers again. It's like drowning, this feeling she has when he kisses her so thoroughly. Her fingers tremble as she raises just her right hand to his bare shoulder. His hands sink into her messy head of hair as he groans into her mouth deeply. This behavior, this animalistic behavior is not like John ever behaves. This is primal, primitive, uncontainable.

216

"I can't breathe," she gasps finally as she places both hands against his chest that is covered in blonde and brown downy hair. She remembers so clearly back to the other day when her hands and fingers had explored with great detail this area of his body. He leans back but just slightly. Reagan shakes her head at him and raises her eyebrows with heightened awareness. "I can't breathe."

Jacob crawls over to them and lays his downy cheek against hers. Then he slobbers there, as well.

"Can't breathe, babe? That's the way it's supposed to be, silly," he jokes.

John kisses the corner of her mouth lightly and then her top lip and then Jacob's soft forehead. Why are her uneven lips so fascinating to him? She's always been embarrassed by them and used to wish she just looked like a normal girl with normal lips and straighter hair and even not so smart sometimes.

"Get your shower. I'm taking the squirt up to bed and then I'll shower. Don't take forever."

He pushes himself off of her without pressing into her body to do so and snatches up Jacob who giggles. Good, maybe he has a sugar high and won't go to sleep for them. She doesn't like this new, controlling John and his kissing her whenever he wants to and his sexual references. His final comment to her had felt like a death toll.

Reagan lies on the bathroom rug for at least ten minutes before she feels like she can even get up to take her shower. She has to find a way of not going to bed upstairs or with John.

Chapter Fifteen
Kelly

After dinner has wrapped, music time has ended, he's seen to Em's shower- which she'd protested- and got her off to bed, and locked the toolboxes, Kelly finally relaxes. Well, he does his best version of relaxing while sitting with his rifle on the front porch drinking a glass of milk and enjoying a slice of Hannah's heavenly apple pie. She is sitting next to him unashamedly on the swing, and he rocks them gently as she has her legs and feet tucked beneath her. In place of the usual apron she wears over her white dress, there is a thick, white cardigan to keep out the cool night air. Her feet are bare, as usual. Derek and Sue join them a moment later, but everyone else has gone to bed. Cory should be getting some rest, as well, before his shift starts at midnight.

"Kids all in bed?" Hannah asks of her sister.

"Yes, thank God," Sue returns with a chuckle. "Is it wrong to say that sometimes that's the best part of the day?"

Everyone laughs at this. Kelly's not sure because he's never technically had kids, but they do seem like a lot of work. Not only that, but he has the full responsibility of his step-siblings now which makes the work feel doubled.

"It'll settle down this winter when we don't have quite so much farm work to do on top of taking care of the kids and everything else," Derek reminds her.

Sue agrees, "Yeah, that will be a nice break."

They take the two wicker chairs opposite Kelly and Hannah. The porch is divided by the front stairs leading up to it. Those same stairs lead to the front lawn where the kids like to make use of the tire swing, something they haven't done for weeks since the visitors have come. Kelly doesn't fail to notice that the other couple also holds hands. He'd like to hold Hannah's. Unfortunately with it being a full moon and the dim shaft of light coming from somewhere inside the house spilling out the front window, it just doesn't feel safe to do in front of them. He doesn't want to deal with the situation with Hannah until their unwanted farm guests are gone. There is already enough shit to deal with around here.

"Simon and Sam are settled in downstairs," Sue tells them. "Huntley can bunk with my kids when he gets better if he chooses to. Sam's in there with them. I offered her to have her own room, but she refused it. Simon's in the other room by himself, though. He just seems like such a nice kid."

They all talk quietly in the semi-dark so as not to be overheard by the people out at the camp. Their guests have a low burning fire going, and a few of them seem to be doing a steady amount of partying, even though Kelly is not sure where they could still be getting alcohol or drugs having been cooped up on the farm for weeks. Apparently they'd hidden their stashes more cleverly than he would've given them credit for. Of course, good old Uncle Peter probably told them how to do it since he knows that the McClane farm is, for all intents and purposes, a dry town.

"Yeah, but I had a hard time getting Simon to stay the night in the house," Derek says. "He didn't feel comfortable sleeping here in the house with the rest of the family. Said they'll be pissed at him when they find out."

Everyone knows of whom Derek is referring. This reinforces Kelly's dislike of those people.

"Whatever for?" Hannah asks with her usual innocence.

"I don't know, but Sam was the same way," Sue explains. "She said they wouldn't like it. Seems strange to me. Of course as soon as I offered a hot shower, she chirped up. Guess they haven't had one of those for months. She said that most of the time they just wash up in a bucket of cold water and bathed a few times in a stream or lake when they came across them."

"Nice. Now why the hell didn't the men at least heat some water in the buckets for the kids? Sorry, Hannah," Derek says and quickly apologizes for swearing.

"It's ok, Derek," she forgives so readily. "I know what you mean. I don't understand that, either. Perhaps it would have helped to control the sickness from spreading. It's the least they could've done."

Sue explains again, "No, not even close. They didn't do anything to help with that. They haven't taken any preventative measures other than isolating the sick by making them sleep outside those buses in the cold. I guess according to Sam, they even made the pregnant woman sleep in a tent on the ground outside once she got sick."

"That's disgusting," Kelly says with venom. "It's been too cold at night for the past three or four weeks for that."

"Not to mention the rains that have hit so hard this summer," Hannah comments.

"We told them almost a week ago that they could go on a scouting run for a new place to live or to search for food and supplies, but they haven't gone once," Kelly adds.

"That's bullshit," Derek says under his breath.

"I know," Kelly agrees. "Why the heck aren't they making an effort to go out and get supplies and food? They can't just eat pancakes and the apples from the orchard here. That crap's gonna run out soon, and then what are they going to do?"

"Bum off of us would be my guess," Sue comments with derision.

Derek tells them all, "That ain't happening. Not when they've got able-bodied men out there who could easily be making runs for provisions. I don't know what their deal is, but they aren't staying and they aren't getting any more than we've already offered."

Kelly nods in the dark. "Right. I agree. I think they're getting way too comfortable as it is. They half-ass picked the corn anyways. It's not like if they stayed, they'd be any help. They gotta go for sure."

Sue continues, "Sam also said that it was usually her and Simon and the twins who had to get water for the adults. They also made them clean up the RV's and pack them when it was time to move on. And yes, Hannah, I agree completely. They could've been sanitizing themselves and those nasty RV's with hot water. Anything would have helped that."

Her disgust at the visitors and their lack of cleanliness is obvious. Kelly can attest to their spring-cleaning skills. He'd been in that RV looking for weapons that first day when they'd arrived, and it had been foul to say the least. He's pretty sure that some of these people have lived this way before the world fell to shit. And to expect kids to do everything including cleaning, cooking and from the snippets he's been able to understand, also raid houses for food and supplies is just beyond his comprehension. How would a kid know how to take safety precautions to not get themselves shot or killed? It's not like they are trained soldiers.

"And Simon's hands are blistered all the time and rough as a cattle rancher's," Kelly comments. "I know it isn't from the work he does with us 'cuz we gave him some leather work gloves to use like we do."

Derek scoffs in anger. "That skank probably only agreed to take in her nephew just so that they'd have another worker in the group. I sure as shit don't see any of the rest of them doing much."

"I know what you mean, man," Kelly agrees with a nod as he sets his empty saucer on the lacquered oak stand beside him. "That kid's too skinny for his height, too. And I bet it isn't just his natural physique. He's skinny like he's missed a lot of meals."

Hannah jumps in with enough anger to light a fire. "That's just ridiculous! How can they not be doing the same amount of work as children? And to not feed them adequate portions? I think you're right on that, Kelly. Sam told me in the kitchen the other day about hiding food from them when they got some here and there, so I think you're right. I think they've probably all missed a lot of meals. I guess only Rick has looked after them at all. Are they serious? I just assumed they were working just as hard as the kids and taking care of them since I can't see them for myself."

Sue scoffs this time. "Trust me, Hannie. You don't want to see what they do or what any of them looks like, honey. Besides, not everyone's like us. We wouldn't feed ourselves before our children or make them work harder than us, but that's not how everyone in the world is. Some people are real dirtbags, Hannah."

"Speaking of… here comes some of the hadj pack," Derek says quietly.

He rises from his seat, moving toward the top of the stairs. Kelly joins him there as Bobby the young punk, Rick and Uncle Peter amble up.

"Can we help you gentlemen?" Derek asks.

He shows more calmness than he must feel after that conversation about the way they treat the children.

"Where's the kids?" Uncle Peter asks.

There isn't much concern in his tone but also not a lot of malice, either, which is lucky for him.

"Huntley is in the sick bay now, in case you haven't heard, Uncle Peter," Sue tells him.

She has not risen from her chair. It is almost insulting, but Kelly's quite sure it also isn't by accident to be so.

"Yeah, we heard," Rick says. "Is he gonna be ok? Do you guys know how he's doing?"

"Reagan's been working with him most of the day, and Grandpa's on it now. He's doing better than the other two were," Sue explains.

This man actually seems genuinely concerned for Huntley. This is the one who'd sneaked food to the kids according to Hannah.

"Maybe if I can find some berries or pick some more of those apples, that'll help him if he can eat them. You know fruit's supposed to have vitamins and all," Rick offers.

Kelly detects a Southern accent. He wears his hair buzzed close to his head. He is about the same size as Derek, but lacks the bulk in his physique that comes with having food for survival.

Derek takes over with the patient update. "The docs have said that it's good to catch it this early on. I guess they have a better chance of stopping it with the medicine they have."

"Man, that's good news," Rick says. "That would've been bad if that little guy would've died like his brother."

"Oh yeah?" Sue asks from her seat. "Then why the hell did you guys make that kid sleep outside the RV last night when he said he didn't feel good?"

Rick is visibly puzzled by this information and looks to his partners for help.

When he gets none, he says "I don't know what you mean, ma'am."

"We were told that he slept out in the cold last night when he first came down with it," Derek states this and steps down one step lower.

"Sir, listen, I didn't know anything about that. I swear," Rick tells them with a pleading look on his dark face. His eyes soften, and he seems genuinely regretful. He whispers to his friends, "Did you guys know that?"

Neither of them responds, which gives Kelly all the answers he needs.

"What kind of medicine?" Peter inquires.

Kelly finds his offhand question strange.

"What?" Kelly asks. The squirrely uncle jams his hands into the front pockets of his dirty khakis. Apparently he is also not making good use of the soap his sister gave him.

"You said Herb and Reagan were giving him medicine. What kinds?" Peter asks again with more clarity.

"Medicine," Kelly answers him definitively so as to put an end to that line of questioning about what supplies they might have in the shed. It is nerve wracking enough worrying about these bums going into the shed for drugs that don't belong to them or can't help their need in the first place without having them verbally nosing after the specific types the family is harboring. The punk kid doesn't take the hint as easily.

"He asked you what kinds you got?" Bobby insists.

The kid has more gumption than he should, being in front of Kelly and Derek. This is the one who'd physically man-handled Samantha today and got mouthy with Reagan. Kelly noticed Sam's bruises at dinner but had not commented. He and John had made brief eye contact. It was all that was needed.

"I said medicine. That's all you need to know, kid," Kelly says firmly. "What are you, a pharmacist?"

"No, I just wanna' know in case the rest of us gets sick, too," Bobby returns on a blatant lie. "Got any painkillers out there?"

"Why?" Derek asks.

He can tell that the Major's patience is waning, so Kelly adds, "You got a case of the gout or something?"

The kid just shifts his weight from foot to foot and sniffs hard.

"Look, I was just concerned about where Sam and Simon might be," Rick interrupts a potential hot spot. "I just wanted to make sure they're ok."

"They're fine," Hannah says icily from the dark. "They'll be staying with us from now on while you're here because they are doing work for us, work that cancels out *your* rent."

Whoa! Kelly didn't think she had something so rude and nakedly insulting in her. Good. She needs to have a little righteous anger where these people are concerned. It might just keep her safer when Kelly isn't near her.

Rick stammers out a hasty answer, "Oh, ok. That's no prob. Hey, I just wanted to check on them. I mean, if I you need me to do work…"

"No, it isn't ok!" Bobby interjects.

The mouthy punk steps forward past Rick, who tries to stop him. The kid just flings off Rick's grasp in irritation and swears at him under his breath.

"And why is that?" Derek asks.

Kelly isn't sure this is going to end well. He takes a step closer to Derek.

"'Cuz she sleeps out there with the rest of us. That's why. Because I said so," Bobby stupidly argues and then nails his own coffin. "And what's it to you, old man?"

What the hell is wrong with this kid? Derek just laughs obnoxiously. He is hardly old at the age of thirty-two, but this juvenile delinquent apparently doesn't know what the 'old man' is capable of. He didn't climb to the status of Major by being a puss.

"You want me to show you what this old man can do to a scrawny lump of shit like you, kid?" Derek antagonizes.

"No way, man," Rick jumps in.

Rick stops it before it starts with a firm hand to Bobby's shoulder. He whispers something about "military" to the young man. The kid is fairly large for his age and probably used to bully other kids who were smaller than him. But he is in no way, shape or form any sort of match for Derek. Hell, Kelly's pretty sure Cory could kick this kid's ass. There is something caged and feral about Bobby, though. And he definitely seems like the kind of kid who had probably spent some quality time in juvey before this started. Cory is a lot softer around the edges and maybe too kind in general. He's going to talk to his kid brother tonight about staying away from this little bastard.

"The kids won't be back over to the camp anymore. Their duties here keep them busy," Kelly explains with a tad more patience.

"There's too much work for us to do out there without them," Peter whines.

"What?" Derek asks incredulously.

"Yeah, dude," Kelly agrees. "There's about five of you men and two women."

"I know, but it's a lot of work carrying water and trying to do everything else," he rambles on. "We're trying to work on the RV, getting it running and stuff."

"You'll manage, Uncle Peter," Sue conclusively settles it.

And because Kelly can't resist, "Why haven't any of you gone on a run?"

"What do you mean?" Rick asks.

"Go off the farm, on a run for supplies and food, or to scout out a new place to crash when you leave here?" Derek confirms the message.

"For one, you took our damn guns," Bobby says in a louder voice than everyone else.

"Don't get whiney," Derek tells him. "You'll get them back when you leave."

Bobby shoots Derek an instant glare filled with hatred for the reprimand.

"And if you wanted to go on a run, we could've given them back. But you don't have any bullets anyways, so how were they going to help you?" Kelly asks. None of them answer.

"You don't necessarily have to have your guns back to go on a supply run," Derek enlightens them.

"Well, we've been busy working on the RV," Peter says lamely.

Derek just crosses his arms over his chest. He is obviously not impressed. Kelly's a little concerned that he's about to give Great-uncle Peter a hundred push-ups for the stupidity of his comments.

"I never heard anything about it," Rick tells him and Derek.

"You were out pickin' apples like a bitch when they told us to go and look for someplace else to live," Bobby clarifies.

The punk also effectively insults him while he's at it. Rick doesn't say anything back, though he easily has a good thirty pounds on this kid and at least three inches of height.

"We probably should," Rick says with a nod. "We obviously ain't welcome to stay on here, so we should look for somewhere new before winter sets in on us, right?"

Again, there is no answer from Peter or Bobby, who apparently don't agree with Rick.

"Nah, Herb ain't gonna toss us to the curb," Peter says, showing his IQ again.

"Uncle Peter, Grandpa has made it very clear and so have the men that you guys can't stay here," Sue says.

Kelly notes the touch of sad kindness in her voice as if she is speaking to an imbecile.

"Aw, little Susan, he ain't gonna throw us out. He ain't like that. He ain't cold-hearted like that. He'll come around," Peter says.

Sue regards Kelly with an expression of shock. She clearly can't believe that they are trying to reason with this moron.

"It's happening, man. Deal with it however you need to, but it's happening," Derek tells them.

"You guys just think you're so much better than us, don't you?" Bobby asks and then spits on the ground.

"It's not a matter of being better than you, son," Derek tells the kid.

"I ain't your fucking son, asshole," Bobby retorts with spite.

"Well, punk, this is our farm, and we aren't leaving it and you *aren't* staying on it," Derek says harshly.

Maybe this is what they need to hear from them. Maybe this will bring it home. Kelly isn't convinced. Maybe he's just fatigued of this situation with these people and wishing they'd all get the hell out.

"Fuck all of you," Bobby says.

The kid spits again, trying to hit Derek. Lucky for him, it doesn't. Rick tries to stop him, but the kid shoves the bigger man with fury before walking away.

"Sorry," Rick says when he turns back to them. "It's cool. I get it. Heck, I don't know if I'd want strangers on my land, either. We'll leave when Huntley gets better."

"Not if we don't get the RV running," Peter interjects on a toothy, or toothless in some places, grin.

His comment is weird, but then again, most of his comments usually are. Kelly finds him unpleasant and repulsive on every level possible.

"We'll get you another vehicle if it doesn't get fixed soon," Kelly says as he leans his shoulder against the railing of the porch. The look of surprise on Peter's face is priceless.

"What? What do you mean?" he asks in an almost hysterical tone.

"You can go in a van or a bigger vehicle of some kind. We'll go out and get one for you," Derek tells him.

"No way. We ain't leaving in something else. That RV holds all our crap," Peter argues.

"Then we'll get you a delivery truck. But one way or another, you're leaving," Kelly offers with a grin of his own. Had Peter actually believed they'd be staying if the RV didn't start? Get real.

"We got all our stuff in the RV, though."

His argument is getting even worse. Kelly's patience is waning thinner.

"Well with eight of you it won't take long to pack. So if you can't get it running in the next couple of days, then we'll go out and get a vehicle for you," Derek tells the uncle.

"You ain't in charge around here, Derek," Peter says more brazenly.

His glazed-over eyes flash with bitterness in the moonlight.

Derek just smiles coolly. "Actually, I am," he returns. "Senior officer. I pull rank."

"That don't mean shit anymore," Peter says and stands slightly taller. "This is still Herb's farm. He's the one callin' the shots around here."

"Yep, that's right," Derek agrees. "But he's also put me in charge of security, so when I say it's time to move on in a new vehicle, you will."

"Where's Herb? I wanna' talk to him right now," Peter argues.

This time his tone is growing more hostile, threatening. Reagan had told him and John last week that Peter could be aggressive when he wanted to be. She also mentioned that her great-uncle had been in a lot of bar fights which he'd bragged about when the girls were younger and had probably more gullibly bought into his line of bullshit. This guy looks like he's had his ass kicked a lot in life, likely because of his smart mouth. But for some people, getting their ass kicked didn't matter as long as they also got their way, be it free drugs, a mooched beer in a bar or a free place to stay. It isn't happening this time, but if he wants a free ass kicking, then Kelly is happy to accommodate him.

"He's in the shed working with the sick," Derek says in an increasingly quieter tone.

Peter doesn't miss a beat, though. "Fine, I'll go out there and talk to him!"

Kelly steps down two steps, making Rick back up three. It's a good sign. This man has no fight in him. "No, you won't, Peter. He's busy and doesn't need to be bothered by you. The doc has been working twelve and fourteen hour shifts taking care of people. The last thing he needs is to be pestered," Kelly tells him.

"Then I'll go in and talk to Mary," Peter says with way too much confidence for his own good.

"Not happening," Derek says.

The major sidesteps closer to Kelly, effectively creating a wall of Rangers that Peter would have to come through to breech the house.

"She's my sister, Derek," Peter grinds out hastily. "I'll talk to her if I damn well want to. Sue, tell your husband to move!"

"Uncle Peter, Grams is asleep. She's tired from taking care of all the added responsibilities around here and helping with kids all day. Let her sleep," Sue tells him from her seat.

"She's probably tired from having all these extra people on the farm," Peter insinuates toward Kelly and Derek.

Derek just laughs at him again.

Hannah goes after this one. "Uncle Peter, these men have enabled our survival. Did you even know that some people attacked our neighbors, the Reynolds? Their father, mother and brother were killed. If it wasn't for Kelly, Derek and John we'd probably all be dead by now. And they help with the farm work and repairs."

"Plus, they go on runs for us to the cities for supplies like you guys *should* be doing," Sue accuses.

228

"Besides, Doc is taking care of your girlfriend," Kelly says with more accusation. "I'd think you wouldn't want to disturb him with this bullshit for that reason alone."

"What?" Peter asks confusedly.

His tweaked out brain is on overload. Kelly is wondering if perhaps a punch to the side of his head would help.

"Your girlfriend? Jennifer? Doc's patient?" Kelly reminds.

"Oh, yeah right. Her," Peter says with open disdain.

"We thought she was your girlfriend, Uncle Peter," Sue inquires with the same disoriented look that the rest of them are mirroring.

"Yeah, she is. She's my girlfriend," he blurts, but it lacks believability.

"Perhaps you can talk to Doc in the morning. You could even visit your supposed girlfriend," Kelly offers with false amiability that neither he nor the rest of their group feel. "Might make her feel better. You could hold her hand, help out in the shed. You know, be Doc's assistant." Peter visibly shivers with disgust.

"Yeah, Peter, you could help," Sue says with a smartass tone.

"Fine, I will!" Peter says in a huff.

Rick sort of ducks his head in an awkward nod, and the two men leave to rejoin their campsite where the punk, Bobby, has also returned. Kelly had made sure of it by watching that kid. He doesn't trust him at all.

Sue's voice knocks him out of his daze thinking about Bobby.

"I don't think we should've told him to bug Grandpa in the morning. He's too tired to deal with Peter with not getting sleep and all."

Kelly chuckles once at this before answering. "I don't think we need to worry about it."

"Why not?" Hannah asks.

"Because, silly, Reagan's on duty in the morning. You really think she's gonna put up with Peter's shit?" Kelly answers and they all laugh heartily at this. Nah, Reagan would give him some nasty clean-up duties out in the shed like swabbing up bodily fluids or something else disgusting until he left. She isn't exactly a patient person when it comes to her great-uncle.

"Hopefully he won't bother Grams," Sue finally says when they've all had their laugh.

"We'll keep an eye out for him coming toward the house," Kelly tells her. "Don't worry. I'll put Cory on it. He seems to do a pretty good job of keeping people away from you, too."

They laugh again and Sue agrees with him.

"No shit. Tough ass kid," Derek says. "Well, bro, we're off to bed. Try to hold down the fort without me."

Kelly chuckles once, razzes Derek and the other couple goes inside. He immediately takes up Hannah's hand in his own.

She must feel the tension coming from him. Her lovely features are marred with worry and stress. She strokes his hand soothingly.

"Everything will be ok," she says quietly.

Hannah kisses the backs of his knuckles. He wishes he could return this sentiment.

Chapter Sixteen
John

There is no way she is getting out of making love with him tonight, even if it means he has to tie her to the bed which is not out of the realm of possibilities anyways. When she'd come upstairs to their room dressed in the black OSU shorts and black tank he'd chosen for her, he'd just about had Jacob asleep in his bed not hers, which was calculated and on purpose. He also propped Jacob with pillows so that the kid doesn't take a spill onto his head in the middle of the night. Reagan's bed is bigger and more suited to his plans. And she'd taken one look at Jacob in John's bed and had made some ridiculous excuse of needing to study something in one of her creepy medical books. He knows his brother and wife have gone to bed because he passed them in the hallway on the second floor on their way to their own bedroom about an hour ago. But now his shower is done and he wears only loose cotton loungewear pants that hang loosely on his hips- and nothing else. As he ascends the stairs that lead to their third floor space, he has a few seconds to reflect on the sudden change in their relationship, the sudden and very welcomed change to their relationship.

He'd simply had enough. He's had enough of her indifference, her apparent *faked* indifference toward him. She isn't cold at all, John has found out. She literally melts in his arms and clings to him like a wanton woman when he kisses her. She may not like it when other people touch her, but she sure likes it when he does and John likes it even more. She is amazing, beautiful and passionate, although she doesn't know just how passionate. Tonight he'll show her exactly how passionate she can be. And he isn't about to let her back out of it for all the gold- or socks- in the world.

When he gets to their room, she is sitting at her desk and reading. She has put a hoodie on over her tank top, even though it's warm tonight.

"Nice hoodie," he remarks slyly.

"Um... I was kind of cold," she lies but gets angry and retorts against him saucily. "Is there something wrong with it?"

"Yeah, it's not on the floor with the rest of your clothes," he tells her truthfully, and she gasps and whips back around to her book.

"Watcha' reading?" John asks though he really doesn't care all that much. He goes straight to the balcony and hangs his towel.

"Study on cell dysplasia," she tells him without looking at him.

Yep, he was right. He doesn't care.

When he re-enters the room, he stalks straight toward her and takes her book, tossing it aside onto the desk.

"Hey!" she says.

Her protest is not loud enough to awaken Jacob who John has observed as sleeping soundly. She jumps out of her chair, and John grabs both of her wrists before she can start fighting against him. He yanks her to him and steals a quick kiss against her inhale of surprise.

"Wait. Just stop, ok?" she asks.

Reagan tries to shrink back from him.

"Why? So you can come up with some analytical, scientific reason why we don't do this? I don't think so, boss," John tells her firmly. Feeling her in his arms where she belongs is like heaven on earth. Finally.

"I don't... but, we're... you're not attracted to me," she says rather stupidly and looks at him with dread-filled green eyes.

"Really?" John asks and takes her hand, pressing it to the front of his pants. "Does that feel like I'm not attracted to you?" Her bewitching eyes widen, and she yanks her hand back like she's touched an open flame.

She stammers out a befuddled, "Uh."

"You've been avoiding me for days, and I'm done being dodged by you," he tells her as he pulls her a bit closer by tugging her lower back.

232

"No, I've just been busy. I... I'm not avoiding you," she lies so terribly.

Reagan squirms against him which isn't helping her, little does she know. John grins down at her.

"I've waited long enough. No more hiding from me. And no more avoiding me. Yes, I knew you were, so don't try to deny it," John tells her pointedly to which she scowls deeply.

"I'm not attracted to *you*, I mean," she tries again and bites her lower lip.

"Do you want me to prove that one wrong, too?" he asks huskily, raising his right eyebrow to show his skepticism as he allows his hand to skim down the front of her sweatshirt between her breasts. She's overcome by a chill. So is he. Reagan rapidly shakes her head at him and tries to pull back so John tightens his grip.

"Just stop, ok? Don't. This is... crazy. This is too fast. I can't think," Reagan admits.

"I know you can't. I like that. You think too much anyways. Why don't you let me do the thinking tonight? And too fast? I've wanted you since that day you tried to shoot me. And Lord help me, I'm not sure why exactly," he tells her and she puckers at him. John kisses her quickly and stuns her. Reagan jerks her head to the side.

"Me either, so let me go!" she retorts in a rage.

He has clearly offended her by saying that.

She retorts, "Go and sew your oats with Bambi."

"Kitten," he corrects with a smile, causing Reagan to get madder and try to jerk her arm free. Not happening. John tugs gently, and Reagan's in his arms again and he's stroking her back and then down over her bottom. He murmurs against her neck and ear. "Yeah, Kitten was the kind of chic I used to be into. I admit it. But then I met you. And darned if I can explain it but you're the only woman I want now. Doesn't make sense to me, either. You're too darn short, and I have stoop just to kiss you. You're mouthy and it makes me want to spank you, but we can explore that later. You're a super brain freak, and I'm just an Army grunt. You've got crazy, messed up hair all the time."

She touches her curls self-consciously, trying to smooth them. He smiles down at her, and she frowns harder up at him.

"See? I'm not your type..." she starts.

John ignores her easily enough and continues on, "But then I got to know you and it just made me want you more. You cuss like a sailor and do just about everything better than me. I'm about to show you that I can do something better than you, though," John promises and kisses her neck before he continues. "I like your green eyes and your curves and your bad fashion sense." John allows his hands to roam over her muscular rear again.

"It sounds like you're just complaining about me so just go fuck Bambi, I mean Kitten!" she corrects herself in a huff of impatience and wiggles to be free.

"That's what I used to do. But that's not what it's going to be between the two of us," he tells her honestly, and her eyes belie her surprise at his admission. "You're what I want now. Not anyone else, not ever. And, Reagan? I know that you want me, too. It's why you responded the way you did the other day."

She shakes her head, and her eyes widen with the fear of realization in this truth. She's certainly not ready to accept it, or him. But after tonight, she will be.

He pulls her up closer to him and whispers against her ear, giving her shivers. "Remember I told you the other day that I know what you need? Well, I do. I know what we both need. I'm going to consume every square inch of you until you pant and moan and beg me. And when you can't hold back any longer, I'm gonna make you lose control for me."

"I have to check on the mare!" she bluffs with absolute terror.

John is temporarily stunned while he digests what she's just said. Most of the time he never knows what she going to say next, and this time is no different.

"Ok," he says and steps back, shocking her right back.

"Ok?" she asks with a victorious smile.

She's so funny sometimes. She thinks she's won.

"Sure, let's go check the mare," he accepts and chucks her under the chin.

"No, just me. I'll be…"

"Not a chance. You aren't going out there at night. It's 22:30, babe. Not happening, but I'd be glad to escort you," he says and grabs a pair of his new loafers from under his bed where he verifies that Jacob's still out like a log. Jacob usually sleeps through the night

234

which is lucky for him and Reagan since they basically know squat about kids and babies. He also grabs a zippered hoodie and puts it on without a shirt underneath and straps his pistol to his waist. "Ready?" he asks her as she still stands where he left her, looking puzzled like she's trying to process something difficult in her brilliant mind. After another second, she nods.

When they get downstairs, Kelly is on patrol, raiding the fridge. There are no lights on, but the dim light of the refrigerator bulb is enough to guide their way.

"Find any hadj in there?" John teases, and Kelly laughs once before closing the door. His friend holds his M16 in one hand and a chicken drumstick in the other.

Reagan pulls on a pair of unattractive, black rubber barn boots that come to her bony knees. They look like they are about three sizes too big. But on her, she even manages to make them look sexy. At least she's covered her black socks.

"Where you two going?" Kelly asks suspiciously.

"Check on that injured mare," John explains as Kelly raises his eyebrows and nods slowly. John's fairly certain that his friend has a few other hypotheses but holds his tongue nonetheless.

"Good luck with that," his friend teases with a smirk.

"Later, dude," John says and takes Reagan by the hand to go to the horse barn. She doesn't pull away, but actually walks closely next to him. She's probably afraid of the visitors, but he's prepared to make the most of it anyways as he tugs her against his side. All of the outdoor lighting has been left off so as to dissuade their new friends from rummaging in the dark for things that don't belong to them and to help the men wearing night vision gear able to better see. He has brought only a small flashlight because he knows the lay of the property by heart after hours upon hours of patrols.

When they get to the barn, John opens and then recloses the wide, sliding barn door behind them and flicks on the two light switches which control a single row of four hanging bulbs down the middle aisle. She looks nervously at him before she heads over to the stall housing the mare.

John goes straight to the tack room and takes down a clean blanket, one of the blankets they'd used on their trip, while she is still preoccupying herself with the mare. Knowing Reagan as he does, she's probably checked on this horse four times today. And John had checked on her this morning and she wasn't even limping anymore. But if it makes Reagan feel better to delay their union, then he'll give her this one last ditch effort. He doesn't even follow her to the stall but stands near the door and, more importantly, the lighting controls.

"I think she's ok," Reagan says awkwardly.

When she comes out of the mare's stall and closes the door behind her, her eyes jump around but won't connect with his.

"Hm, good," John says and flicks off the one set of lights, leaving only two bulbs lit. He stalks toward Reagan and, without preamble, ducks and flips her over his shoulder.

"What the heck are you doing?" she asks hysterically from her upside down position. "Put me down!"

"Shh," he whispers which settles her for a moment until he gets to the ladder that leads to the hay loft above them.

"What... what are you doing? Stop!" she cries.

He climbs the ladder still holding her over his shoulder, the blanket under his arm and the flashlight between his teeth.

"Oh my God, stop. John, you're going to drop me!"

John just chuckles at her and continues. It only takes him about a minute to climb to the second story hay loft where he puts her gently to her feet and tosses the flashlight into the mound of hay behind her. He can tell by her expression that she's still shocked that he has carried her up the ladder. He'd carried his brother six miles. Her skinny butt felt like half the weight of Derek. Her eyes follow him with trepidation and widen when he unzips and also toss his hoodie near the flashlight. Next he spreads the thick wool blanket near the flashlight. It's better lit up here than he would've thought from just two light bulbs a floor below. But the cracks and gaps in the old, wooden floorboards allow just enough illumination to see her clearly.

"I... I want to go back to the house," she says with trepidation and twists her hands in front her.

John just gives her a shake of his head while he puckers his lips. Next he kicks the loafers off and tosses them near the other discarded items.

"Stop!"

He ignores her again. Next he sets his holster and pistol near the top of the blanket. Then John walks slowly toward her and takes

236

her slim shoulders between his hands, which forces her to finally look up at him.

"Please don't," Reagan pleads as her eyes tear up.

John just shakes his head again. The time for words, angry rants and pretty pleadings has long since come and gone.

"I know you aren't afraid of me anymore, Reagan. Right?" he asks her as he closes the gap and takes her hand.

"No," she confesses.

"It's ok to be scared. But just not to be scared of me," he says calmly.

"I don't want…"

"Yes, you do," he corrects her, and he stoops slowly, very slowly as his mouth captures hers with an intensity so strong he's afraid they'll burn down the barn.

She's so sweet and reserved and afraid to let anyone in that John gets lost in her little shivers and whimpers of fear and desire blended into what makes her who she is. His hands move into the curls at either side of her face, and he loses it when she cries out against his mouth and clings to his forearms. John sweeps her easily into his arms and deposits her on top of the blanket on the deep hay mound. She doesn't try to bolt which is encouraging as he rolls his hoodie and places it under her head.

"I don't want this," she says pathetically.

Is she trying to convince herself?

"You will in a minute," John promises and joins her on the blanket where he kisses and caresses her hip, the inside of her wrist, her face, her small waist, a bare thigh and whispers his naughty plans into her ear until she's breathy and panting just like he'd foretold earlier that she would be.

He easily slips off her ridiculous boots and then her hoodie over her head, but when he tries for the tank top in between kisses, she frantically grabs at his hand.

"No, don't. Please don't," she begs in earnest and shakes her head.

He knows this hesitancy is over her scar issue.

"You really think you look worse than me?" John asks her, and she frowns up at him with her emerald eyes and kiss-bruised lips.

Then she nods which just about kills John's resolve. "I can't even see all that great in here," he lies.

"I just… I look… disgusting. You have no idea," she hints.

Her self-loathing is making John more determined than ever to conquer this with her right now. He is laying half on and half beside her and teasing his fingers through her curls. Reagan's hands cover her face with embarrassment.

"Why don't you let me decide that for myself?" he asks and brushes a loose strand of curls back from her forehead.

Reagan pushes at his chest, and John just captures her hands in one of his and holds them. He kisses her again and whispers into her ear how beautiful he thinks she is. This isn't an exaggeration. Reagan is beautiful. She just doesn't know it which makes her even lovelier.

He decides to try a different tactic and lowers himself to where her shorts and tank meet along her lower stomach. Poking a finger under her shirt, he allows his fingers to lightly trace around before he nudges his lips into the same space. She tries to push him away, but John takes her hand and presses it against his cheek. He kisses and licks, and his fingers touch her lightly as he manages to get her top higher and higher. When he's fairly certain that she's thoroughly distracted, he finally releases her other hand. John can see her scars easily enough in the dim light, but they aren't anything compared to what he feels as a rage builds inside of him for what has happened to her. Putting his hands on either side of her hips, he lifts her to his mouth, kissing each of the thin slivers that bisect her stomach area. He pulls down one side of her shorts and kisses her hip bone. His hand slides under her shirt, travels up her stomach and covers one bare, braless breast. It is the only time he's ever been glad that she wasn't wearing a bra. Her breasts aren't huge, not like the stripper or any stripper's probably, but they are plenty big enough for John and they fill his hand so perfectly. Not to mention the fact that she makes delicate, tiny sounds in her throat as he caresses them which makes him love them even more. She has a hand buried in his hair now and is pulling it almost painfully. He doesn't remove her shirt. Not because he doesn't want to look at her, because he does. He doesn't remove her shirt because this night is about Reagan, not him. There will be plenty of other nights when he can gaze down upon her naked perfection.

238

"Is he dead?" he asks as he returns to her mouth and grinds himself against her pubic bone. It takes her a moment to respond, to come back to him.

"What? Who?" she asks incoherently, unaware of her surroundings.

Good, she's almost where he wants her.

"Whoever did that to you," he says against her mouth as his hand goes south and rests between her legs, against the thin cotton of her shorts.

"What? Yes, yes, he's dead," Reagan says when she can because his fingers are working against her through the shorts.

"Good, I didn't want to have to leave right now to go and find him," he tells her, making Reagan smile against his mouth like he knew she would. He was actually serious.

"Please," she pants.

It's a little better, but not quite there just yet as his fingers slide so easily under her shorts and then her panties where he can touch and tease her soft flesh at his leisure.

"Oh God. Please."

"Patience," he scolds and kisses her mouth, taking her with his tongue, plundering and claiming. Her hands are at his shoulders, against his chest muscles, in his hair and around his back, pulling at him. It makes him smile into her neck where he kisses and licks and feels her tremble and shimmy.

John pulls back onto his knees and is glad when she cries out in protest and grabs at him. He just half-smiles down at her. Her eyes are glazed over with passion. His fingers glide up her legs, teasing as they go until he reaches the waist band of her shorts. He whisks them and her panties away at the same time and discards his own pants near her clothing items. When he lies on top of her again, she paws aggressively at him. John presses himself between her thighs and then goes back to teasing her, but not with his fingers this time. It earns him a whole lot more whimpering and soft cries as she pushes up against his shaft. Her need is growing desperate. He intends for it to grow to inferno proportions. It's how he's felt for months.

"Now… now," she insists in between pants.

He'll have none of it, though he can tell she is more than ready. John ignores her and continues his onslaught against her sensitive skin before he nudges just an inch inside of her and then another. Jesus, this is going to be harder than he thought. The urge to plunge forward and take her with violent lust is almost overwhelming. He stops pushing and goes back to touching her everywhere and kissing her, which he could do all night.

"Now, do it now. I can't wait another second," she demands.

Reagan arches her hips against him, tugs at his hair and tries to pull him down. John just smiles and is brought back down to earth as he remembers this is for her tonight. It gives him the fortitude to hold back.

"Easy, Reagan. I don't want to hurt you. This is your first time," he states huskily.

"So? I don't care. Just do it. Hurry. I've been riding horses my whole life so I probably don't even have a hymen. Medical studies… ohhh, God. Just do it, now!" she orders.

She is trying to give him a short medical briefing which makes him turn his head to hide his smile so that she doesn't think he's laughing at her.

She pleads again, "Hurry."

"Hey," he raises himself to look down into her eyes. He holds either side of her lovely face. "You can be the boss everywhere else, but not in here. I've got this under control. When we make love, I'm the boss," John corrects her, and she slowly nods at him in the dark. Only then does he kiss her mouth thoroughly until she is right back to breathing fast.

He pushes forward this time slightly more forcefully and then a bit further again and again until he is deep inside of Reagan and has to grit his teeth to hold still while she adjusts to him. He feels for the first time in his life of wars and battles and killing like he's finally found home. She is so delicate and supple and relaxing against him as she pants into his ear and begs him not to stop.

"Are you ok?" he asks and brushes her hair back from her cheek as his elbows rest on the blanket on either side of her head. She nods and pulls him down. John's not even sure she heard the question. He cradles her head in his hands and kisses her eyelids, her chin, the tip of her nose and then her mouth again as he lets her body acclimate to his invasion.

She is kissing his neck and chest of her own volition, and John almost loses control. But he manages not to and pushes her

240

back against the hay as he withdraws and pushes inside of her again and again until she is wild with need and wrapping her legs around him. They are both covered in sweat, likely most of it is his, he realizes. When his hand slides between them and he touches her with expertise, she erupts violently around him and cries out which he takes into his mouth so as not to alert anyone. John joins her a second later and groans loudly.

"I love you, Reagan," he says into the base of her neck as he buries himself and finishes.

They lie still, panting, trying to catch their breath for what seems like forever, but he is careful not to squash her beneath him. After a while, John withdraws from her gently, slowly and rolls to his side, taking her with him. He's never letting her go again.

His fingertips trace up and down her soft, smooth back and lower to dip into the valley of her curvy hip. Every detail of her is perfect, even the way she molds against his side. Her skin is silky, flawless even with the scars that John wishes she'd never gotten in the first place. If only he'd been with her that day. He'd like to kill the guy again even as irrational as that sounds to him.

"That was...," she whispers throatily against his chest.

"Yeah, incredible. Just like I knew it would be," he acknowledges and presses a tender kiss to her forehead.

"You didn't know it would be... like that," she answers shyly.

"Oh, I knew. You were the one that didn't know," he smiles against her hair.

"How could you have known?" she asks disbelievingly.

"I just knew. I've been walking around with a hard-on for months, woman," he teases, and she pokes him in the stomach.

"Don't be crude," she reprimands.

"You didn't mind me being crude a few minutes ago," he teases further and kisses her on the mouth slowly, savoring her sweetness. John can feel her smile against his lips. Reagan lies back down against his chest. He'd like her to just lie still because he could look at her all night. But he knows she's not ready for that yet. They rest peacefully together for a while before she speaks again.

"If I'd have known it would be like that, I might've raped you," she says huskily.

John chuckles softly. "I might've let you," he agrees.

"Do I ever get to be the boss?" she asks.

Reagan rises on her elbow to look down at him. Her curls create a halo about her and tickle his side. There's mischief in her tone which is playful and nice to hear. She raises one eyebrow jauntily which makes John grin before he answers her.

"No," he says resolutely and pushes her head down on his chest. He can feel her smile against his pec muscle which makes him grin in turn. Her fingers do twirly circles on his abdomen. His fingers twine in her wild curls. Her thigh drapes casually over his. It's funny, but she hasn't flinched from him even once since they'd started, not even when he'd kissed her stomach.

"Never?" she asks a few minutes later.

She's dead serious. John grins at her because what the heck else can he do? She is so darn cute... and annoyingly tenacious.

"Maybe." John lets her think this. Never happening. Her fingers trail lower until they are into the hair on his stomach that leads to his groin. His hand flattens over hers to prevent further exploration.

"You said maybe," she sulks.

He puts his hand to the back of her head and pulls her down for a kiss. She's immediately out of sorts and more awkward being over him. Reagan is unsure of herself and back to being stiff and nervous.

"Not as easy as it looks, is it- being the boss? Got cocky, didn't you?" he teases when he pulls back. She frowns at him. "Maybe meant maybe someday. Not tonight."

Instead of scowling again, she kisses his chest and then his nipple which makes his pectoral muscles jump.

"Maybe you'll be the boss again tonight," she suggests and refuses to make eye contact with him, preferring instead to stare at his chest.

"Maybe," he teases on their word play, and she leans up for a tentative kiss. John rolls her to her back again. "I think that's enough for one night, Reagan."

"I don't."

"Do you have to argue about everything with me?" John asks and feels his body stirring again just being pressed against her bare skin. Reagan apparently feels the same way because she lifts her hips against him, making him mad with craving for her.

242

"Only when you're wrong," she taunts.

Reagan sucks in a breath as he slides his hand under her hip and pushes against the tender flesh at the apex of her legs. She pants readily and pulls his head down to her mouth. She kisses him like she has more experience than she actually does.

"You won't be able to walk tomorrow, honey," he says, trying to discourage her.

"So?" she puffs against his mouth. "Then you can carry me."

For some reason this logic sounds rational to John in his tortured state as he pushes inside of her a few inches. He passes a long period of time in bliss with her and then afterwards wonders how it had happened that he'd been talked into making love to her again when he clearly remembers so ardently being against it. He realizes that she has not returned his sentiment of love, but it doesn't matter to John. He'd needed to say it. He'd needed to tell her for quite some time, and now she knows his truth.

A little after midnight they return to the house, and John lives up to his promise and carries her the whole way, though she tries to protest, even up the two flights to the bathroom where he waits for her. He easily scoops her into his arms again and carries her to their bedroom where he spends the next three hours passed out from heavenly exhaustion with her. He's waited so long to be with her, to hold her, to make love to her like he did earlier that all he wants to do is hold her so tight she can never get away. He spoons her back as she curls into his front and falls fast asleep as a woman well-loved and spent. When his watch alarm goes off at four a.m. John hits the button and presses a kiss to his woman's neck, places their baby in the bed beside her and goes off to keep watch over both of them.

Chapter Seventeen
Reagan

Reagan blinks confusedly at the gray light filtering through the draperies and rolls to her side. Jacob is gone but a furtive peek to John's small bed, and she ascertains that he, as well. Reagan rolls to her other side again to glance at the alarm clock on her stand. Shit. She's slept in past nine. Why hadn't he awakened her?

As she swings her legs to the side of the bed, Reagan realizes how sore her inner thigh muscles and some other parts of her body are today. Damn! She hadn't accounted for this. She isn't the kind of person who likes to be laid up or slowed down by anything. On the other hand, she's also not sure she would trade last night's activities for a few less sore muscles in her body, either. She yanks open the curtains, allowing even drabber, drearier light to enter. Great. It's raining again. It doesn't completely dampen her spirits as she remembers last night with John. A sly grin creeps onto her features as she crosses the room to her closet.

She chooses sensible black cotton cargoes, a long-sleeved black tee, clean black socks and her .45 and balls it all under her arm. Then she has to cover her face to hide her embarrassment at her own thoughts of John's scarred, yet silky smooth skin, his dark blue eyes as they'd pierced hers with passion and the way he'd skimmed his fingers over her body with such vivid familiarity, as if he'd done it a thousand times. Perhaps he had in his mind. This thought makes her blush harder. Jesus, how is she going to face him in broad daylight?

After taking a quick shower in the second floor bathroom and trying unsuccessfully to do something with her hair other than just running a brush through it, Reagan dresses, straps on her pistol and brushes her teeth. Then she pulls her wet hair into a messy, disheveled bun on top of her head. It probably isn't the most attractive hairstyle going, but she reminds herself that she doesn't care. She has to remind herself this again when she takes it down and then pulls it back up again with uncertainty. Who cares what he thinks of her hair? This is ridiculous. She's fairly certain that John doesn't care what her hair looks like. Obviously it didn't disgust him enough to toss her out of his bed. The deep crimson stains on her cheeks stare back at her in the large mirror above the double sinks. She traces the white scar on her right cheek with her index finger and furrows her brow at it with deep resentment. She has no idea how John could find her attractive enough to have sex with her. Avoidance had been so much easier than having to now deal with this new, uncomfortable situation she is in. She knows nothing about what kind of woman John likes. Does he prefer someone who would wear makeup? Or maybe someone like Hannah who wears dresses all the time? Shit. This relationship bullshit is hard. What had they been thinking? Oh, right. She hadn't been thinking at all. His kisses and light touches had robbed her of that ability last night. Reagan scowls hard at herself one more time before leaving the bathroom. Grow up, she mentally scolds.

She bounds down the stairs to the first floor where most of the family has already gone outside. Grams is at the island cleaning up after the breakfast that Reagan has apparently missed, and Hannah is bouncing Jacob happily on her hip while rinsing dishes.

"Someone surely must've needed some rest," Grams says lightly.

"Yeah, guess I was pushing myself too hard or something," Reagan mumbles.

"Hungry?" Hannie asks from the sink. "We've got plenty of breakfast leftovers."

"Um, sure," Reagan replies as her stomach grumbles loudly. She helps herself to ham, fried potatoes and peach cobbler. She even pours a full glass of milk, which she doesn't usually care for all that much.

"Apparently a good night's sleep is what your appetite needed to get charged up, young lady," Grams comments.

Reagan chokes on a potato inelegantly. Her grandmother takes Jacob from Hannah so that her sister can finish with the dishes.

If only Grams knew the truth behind her voracious appetite. It was more like the sex Olympics in the barn last night that had brought it on.

"You ok?" Hannah asks.

"She's fine, Hannah. Just eating like she's in a timed competition is all," Grams falsely assumes.

Reagan doesn't correct her. There's no sense in getting into any of her relationship issues with her family members.

"Grandpa still with the patients?" she asks with concern. She is trying to scarf her food down because she feels guilty that he's been out there all night while she's slept in like a lazy-ass.

"No, honey," Grams answers. "He went to bed about an hour ago. Left Sam in charge. Said Huntley's doing much better already, showing some positive signs of… I don't know what. You'll have to read his notes."

Grams wipes her hands on her ever-present apron and retrieves a piece of paper from one of the two, large pockets on the front of it.

"Here, honey. You'll have to decipher his chicken scratchings."

Reagan scans the notes quickly, wanting to hurry out to the shed. Hannah and Grams talk around her, discussing chickens or something while she studies and eats. She is vaguely aware that Hannah clears her place setting when she finishes her meal. A moment later, the screen door slamming jolts her out of her study trance. The one person she'd like not to see today is standing there with his manly countenance and wet, dripping hair.

"It's rainin' cats and dogs out there," Grams confirms, although nobody needs her to when John is clearly drenched to the bone.

"Sure is, Grams," he agrees.

John uses the towel Grams is offering to pat his face and hair. He's also staring Reagan down, who is staring mouth agape like a besotted moron. His plain white t-shirt is clinging to his stomach muscles and chest.

"Boy, you sure did sleep late, boss," he mocks with a cocky grin and a quick flash of white teeth.

Reagan's sure that her face has turned scarlet again.

"Wh… what?" she croaks and expediently rises from her seat. She also trips over the leg of her stool, proving what a clumsy imbecile she is in front of John.

"She needed it," Grams adds. "She's been working so hard in the shed and out with the horses, too!"

Good grief. Her Grams is championing her, even though she'd flip her lid if she knew what Reagan had really been up to the previous evening. She gives John an almost imperceptible shake of her head to dissuade any intimate contact or talk in front of the family. He just chuffs once and smiles knowingly.

"I know, Grams. She's a classic workaholic," John agrees with a sly grin. "Hey, I'm going up to our room to get some dry duds 'cuz I gotta go over to that condo village to take our friends the schematics for the solar panels and to check on them."

Reagan's gaze shoots to his directly. "Are you going alone?"

"No, I'm taking Simon and Cory. It'll be good for them to learn the way- well, at least Simon since Cory should remember the way there. But the boys gotta learn how to work together as a team. It'll be a good training exercise for them."

"But the visitors are still here," Reagan argues as she folds Grandpa's notes and tucks them into the cargo pocket on her leg. "I don't think any of you should be leaving the farm until they're gone."

"It's fine, Reagan," John placates. "Derek and Kelly are out on watch, and I'll only be gone about an hour, maybe even less."

"I don't…"

"It's fine, boss," he repeats more firmly. "These people all need a way of harnessing energy before winter sets in. Remember, they have little kids in that village."

His deep voice is melting her insides. His comments are irritating, though. His reasoning is downright pissing her off.

"I think it's a good idea," Grams says.

"Come on. I need dry clothes, and I also need to talk to you about something."

John motions to her with his hand as he leaves the room. Reagan just gives him a queer look, and he motions again like she's a damn puppy.

"Fine," she grumbles and follows him from the room and up the two flights to their attic. John flings off his soaking wet shirt as they enter the room.

"What the heck do you need to talk to me about? Can't this wait? I need to…" Reagan's words are cut off as John turns on her, grabs her into his arms, lifting her clean off the ground and kissing her soundly.

He carries her, never breaking their kiss, to her bed where he comes down gently over her onto the soft mattress. His jeans are also wet, probably dampening her own pants, but Reagan hardly cares at the moment. His mouth moves insistently against hers, his tongue sampling from the hidden, secret recesses of her warm mouth. Soon Reagan forgets all about the med shed, her patients, her duties, him leaving the farm, everything.

His hands move about her face, her neck and skim down over the center of her chest until he wraps one around her waist. It effectively pulls her up closer to him where Reagan can smell the outdoors, rain and… everything that makes John smell the way he does, which happens to be sensual and intoxicating. She hooks her leg around the back of his muscular thigh.

Finally John leans away from her, but Reagan can barely focus and realizes her hands are at the waistband of his jeans. "Your skin is cold," she tells him.

"Care to warm me up?" he hints with a dazzling display of dimples.

Her fingers toy around with the button of his baggy jeans, but John's strong hand covers hers. He chuckles.

"Maybe later."

"Why later?" she asks with confusion. How can his breathing be so steady?

"Honey, you need some time to recoup after last night."

He kisses the side of her mouth once. Reagan tries to pull him closer.

"And I have to get going. Cory and Simon should be waiting for me."

"Then why the hell did you bring me up here?" Reagan fumes.

John hefts his weight to a standing position, pulling her along in one smooth motion where she slides down the front of him.

Reagan continues with her complaints. "I thought you needed to talk to me."

"I know," John divulges huskily.

He pulls her up against his bare chest where she plants both hands.

John adds, "I just wanted a few seconds alone with you, babe."

It is hardly a reason to get mad at him, but she's not quite sure she likes this power he has over her and her body's response to him. Of course, his skin does feel rather nice under her fingertips.

"More than a few seconds?" she asks. His answer is to look at the ceiling with a grin and then back down at her. Talking so intimately with him is difficult, but not as much as she would've thought. Plus, she does want him again which is so strange. Again with the irrational hormones lately.

"Yeah, maybe more than a few," he answers.

He kisses her lightly. Reagan's hands slide around his back where she tugs him roughly to her and kisses him back more aggressively.

He pulls back and says, "No! We can't. I told you that you need to recover first."

"I'm the doctor," she reminds him. "I say when I'm recovered and I'm saying it's now."

John laughs against her mouth before sliding his hands into the hair at the nape of her neck. Her haphazard bun is falling sideways on top of her head.

"No," he murmurs against her lips more decisively, even though he has not backed away. "I gotta go, sweetie."

Reagan's had enough. "Fine!" she bites out angrily, earning another chuckle.

"Hellion," he mocks. "I've created a monster."

"Yeah, no shit," she returns with anger anew and rants. "You shouldn't have done that last night because I didn't know what I was missing and now I do, damn it!"

"Potty mouth," John teases.

He swats her bottom lightly. He releases her and goes to their shared closet where he comes out with a dry, long-sleeved red flannel shirt which looks sexy as hell on him. The muscles of his back flex and move as he pulls it on.

Reagan frowns, bites her top lip and says, "Damn."

He whips around to face her, buttoning his shirt as he does so, leaving the top three undone.

"What? What's wrong?"

"What?" she squeaks out and then hastily clears her voice and adds, "Nothing."

John just puffs air through his nose and gives her a funny look as if he finds her bizarre but doesn't comment. She'd been mentally dreaming about the ruggedness of his appearance and had said the first idiotic thing that had come to her brain. Damn her brain!

Without saying anything, John takes her pistol out of her thigh holster and checks the magazine and safety without permission. Even the frown on his face is handsome. He jams it back into its holster, refastens the snap and takes her very firmly by the shoulders.

"Be careful while I'm gone, ok?" he demands.

His navy eyes are drowning her in their pools. What is the question he'd asked? She's not sure. All she can think about is his chiseled mouth and the strong square angles of his chin and deeply hollowed out cheekbones.

"Reagan?" he prompts, but his thumb is skimming over her top lip. Another few seconds pass. "Babe? Are you listening?"

"Yeah, careful," she repeats his directive as she leans up for another searing kiss which he obligingly gives her.

When John pulls back again, they are both out of breath and clinging to one another. Her hair has completely toppled down around her shoulders in a damp mess of chaos, probably with help from his roving fingers.

"I'll see you in a little bit, 'kay?" he promises.

Rubbing his lips against her forehead but not with an actual kiss, John breathes deeply. Sometimes the things he does are a little strange, but she doesn't exactly find them distasteful, either. All she can do is nod, so that's the answer she gives John.

They go back downstairs but instead of loitering, John takes off out the back door in a sprint to the truck where Cory and Simon are both waiting in the front seat for him. Reagan can see through the screen door that there are at least three rifles visibly poking up inside the cab of the truck. They'll be safe.

"What did John want, honey?" Grams calls from the music room.

She and Hannah are watching the children since it's raining so hard outside.

"Nothing important," she calls back, bowing her head. "Going out now."

Reagan doesn't wait for an answer because she doesn't want to pursue that line of questioning and instead runs straight for the shed, splashing mud on her pants as she goes. Kelly is standing just under the overhang of the roofline. It doesn't seem to bother him, but to Reagan the rain feels icy cold and miserable. She isn't much of a cold weather person. They give a curt greeting to one another before she goes inside. Samantha is already there, and she's making notations on a patient chart.

"Dr. McClane," she acknowledges with a nod. "Good morning."

"Hey, Sam," Reagan returns as she picks up the other clipboard. Sam is her usual bundle of nervous energy. At least she finally has on clean clothing. Today she wears a pair of jeans that Reagan had lent her and a red hoodie that reads in yellow letters: *Fox Run Academy.* Isn't that the pricey private school over near Clarksville?

"Dr. McClane?"

Sam interrupts Reagan's thoughts on that private school and what might've happened to it in the last six months.

"Should I start Huntley on another breathing treatment, ma'am?"

"Just Reagan, Sam. You go calling me Dr. McClane and I think Grandpa's in here with us. You call me ma'am and I'm looking for Grams," she corrects Sam for maybe the hundredth time. "And yes, let's get one rigged up. First I wanna' give his vitals a check, though. Did he eat anything yet this morning?"

"Yes, ma'am- I mean, Reagan. He actually ate a full breakfast for the first time. Your grandpa said it was ok to just let him eat what he would," Sam answers.

"Go ahead and start preparing his treatment. Make sure you notate it on the chart so that we know the exact time we gave it," Reagan tells her.

"Ok, ma'am- I mean, Reagan," Sam says unsurely.

The teen goes to the back counter for another small vial of Albuterol for the breathing machine.

"Sam?"

"Yes?"

"Relax. You're doing a good job. We wouldn't be able to care for them as well as we have without you," Reagan tells her and notices a shy, hidden smile come across the girl's features. Reagan can just barely make it out because of the mask covering her small face, but her eyes crinkle at the corners. It's only there for a fleeting moment, but it was there for that brief second which is all that matters.

Huntley is alert, lying on his side and awake.

"Hey, kiddo," Reagan greets him with a slight smile. His hazel green eyes stun her every time. Huntley's eyes are so startlingly different and not what one would expect against his caramel skin that they always surprise her. "How are you feeling?"

"Ok, I guess. Better," he replies softly.

She'll take 'better' any day of the week over the semi-comatose state of Jennifer and then Garrett before her. This boy will live.

"That's good. We need to get you better quickly. The other kids have been asking about you," she tells him honestly. Em and Justin had nagged her at least ten times each yesterday inquiring after their new friend.

"Really?" he asks with candid frankness that only a child can pull off.

"Yeah, of course. They like hanging out with you," she tells him as she takes his pulse, his blood pressure, his temperature, which is thankfully normal, and listens to his chest.

Reagan doesn't miss the sad expression on his tiny face. They've found out that he's only ten years old, but he seems small for his age. It could just be the malnutrition and the sickness that make him appear so small and frail, but it kicks Reagan's natural motherly instincts into high gear. She takes a seat on the chair next to his bed so that she can be closer to him for this conversation. She's not

252

worried about catching his illness because he isn't fevering and hasn't in over twenty-four hours.

"Huntley, do you like it here on our farm?" she asks quietly. A low reverberation of thunder echoes across the valley and rattles the building. The rain drums out a constant tapping on the metal roof.

"Sure. I like it, Miss Reagan," he replies softly.

His red-rimmed eyes let her know that he'll be ready for a mild fever reducer that will also help him sleep after his breathing treatment. Sometimes rest really was the best medicine. Sometimes it was the soft embrace of a mother. But this poor kid isn't going to get the latter. And he sure as hell wouldn't get the likes from his worthless, dirtbag of a father.

"Where do you think your group is going to go after this?" she asks him.

"Um, I don't know. Wherever my dad says probably," he answers.

Reagan removes her latex glove and takes his hand in her own. It feels too small and bony.

"Why is that? Is he kind of the leader of your group?"

"Yeah, basically, pretty much," he answers.

"Well, you know Samantha and Simon have made a pretty big decision recently while you've been sick," Reagan informs the boy. His interest is piqued, although he is too beat to do much about it. "They've decided to stay with us here on the farm when your group leaves."

His striking eyes immediately tear up. Reagan gives his hand a gentle squeeze. He clearly doesn't want to be separated from the two teens that have probably looked after him for who knows how many months.

"I want you to think about this, Huntley. I mean really think about it," she tells him as Sam comes to stand at the other side of his cot. She has the vial of liquid in her hand. "We'd really like it if you'd stay, too."

His face literally lights up. Perhaps freeing a person from a life of misery is also as good as a mother's touch when healing a child.

"Really?" he asks.

"Yep. My family likes you. The kids like you even more. And we'd *all* like it if you would also stay with us on this farm," Reagan tells him.

"Seriously?" he asks with two long blinks.

He tries to sit up, but Reagan lightly presses him back again.

"Rest, honey," she orders. "Think about what you'd like, Huntley. We don't want you to stay if you don't want to. You'd also be saying good-bye to your father, Frank. So you really need to be sure. You probably wouldn't ever see him again."

The boy's face does not fall at this statement. How sad. To be told that you'll never see your last, surviving parent again and to feel nothing remorseful about it is saddening to Reagan.

"He'll never let me stay here," Huntley finally says.

This time he does seem disheartened. He lowers his gaze and looks away.

"Let us worry about that. We'll deal with the big people stuff. You just worry about whether or not you'd even *want* to stay here," Reagan suggests.

Huntley takes one look at Sam and nods readily. "Oh yes, Miss Reagan. I want to stay. I really, really do."

Reagan smiles down at him before replying. "Just take a few days and think about it. Talk it over with Sam and even Simon if you want to. You don't have to give us an answer today. You're still getting better, so we don't expect you to think too much about it now. We just want you to concentrate on getting better for now, honey."

"Oh, I'm feeling a lot better already," he chirps up but then yawns widely.

Reagan and Sam both chuckle. It's short-lived for both of them, but they'd both done it nonetheless.

"Just think about it for a few days, ok?" Reagan requests. "Let Sam help you do another breathing treatment and then I want you to sleep for a while."

"Yes, ma'am. I'll sleep," he says on another yawn. "I'll be good. I promise."

Reagan stands and has to look away, has to appear busy with his chart. His last words break her heart. It's as if he's trying to prove to her that his behavior will be stellar enough to earn her approval to stay on their farm. Little do any of these wretched, young souls know

254

is that they've already wriggled their ways into all of the hearts of her family members. They've even managed to slink a few inches into her own, which she'd never guessed possible anymore.

"I'm going to the back to work with Jennifer. Call me if you need me," she mutters to Sam without turning back to them. Reagan can hear them quietly talking to each other before Sam starts the breathing machine a few minutes later.

Damn. No improvement is noted on Jennifer's chart. Reagan gets straight to work, not wasting another moment worrying about the future, or John, or their new, adopted orphan-baby or the visitors or anything else. The only thing that matters is the here and now and helping Huntley and Jennifer to get better from this sickness that is so fierce and to protect her family from contracting it.

The day flies by, the rain never ceases, and Kelly stands guard until John returns with Cory who takes up for his brother at the door to the shed. Reagan hadn't realized that she'd been holding in a nerve-wracking breath until she finally fully expels it upon John's return. The children aren't the only ones who have managed to inch their way into her heart. But she's not about to admit any of it to anyone any time soon. Hell, she's not even ready to admit it to herself yet.

Chapter Eighteen
Kelly

Two days after the death of Jennifer Miller-Durant as they now know her full name to be, there is a disquieting unease in the family as decisions need to be made about the visitors. Huntley is still in the med shed but improving every day. He is almost fully recovered with the help of the doctors' medicinal compilations. They buried the pregnant mother on the hill beside Garrett, and Doc had said kind words and read from the Bible again at her gravesite. Only the ex-stripper, Jasmine, had wept over this loss from the visitors' group. Not even Jennifer's supposed boyfriend, Great-uncle Peter, had seemed to care. He had cared that he'd had to help dig her grave, though, and had bitched about it. John had held back his brother from kicking Grams's brother's ass in front of the family. Kelly wanted to pound him to a pulp, too, but out of respect for Grams he'd held himself back. And out of respect for his gentle Hannah.

Hannah had told him about her bladder infection and turned three shades of red while doing so. Kelly had felt like a total jerk, although he hadn't known about women's issues and how such a thing can happen. He's not been with her for over a week. It just doesn't sit well with Kelly when he makes love to her because he knows it's wrong. He also knows how close Hannah's relationship with God is which makes him feel even worse. But his Hannah is growing increasingly frustrated with him. Little does she know, he grows increasingly frustrated just by looking at her during dinner, while she made food and glided so effortlessly around her kitchen, when she played with the kids on the floor, held Isaac or Jacob in her arms or was just sprinkling bits of grain to her stupid chickens. Or like they are currently: sitting shoulder to shoulder at the loud and sometimes boisterous breakfast table seated amongst their family and the new, extended family of Simon and Sam. The meal is finishing up and he is already wishing he didn't need to go out and cut wheat and that he could sit with her on the back porch swing and drink a glass of lemonade and hold her hand like when the world used to be normal.

As he hands his plate to Em in the kitchen, Doc walks up to him and says firmly, "Kelly, I'd like to see you in my office, please."

And with that, the older gentleman turns and walks toward the front of the grand home to his study, fully expecting Kelly to follow. He glances over at John, who shrugs, so he turns to follow Hannah's grandfather. Once he is in the man's study, Doc tells him to close the door.

"What is it, sir?" Kelly asks.

"Take a seat, Kelly," Doc says.

Herb sits behind his mahogany desk with the intricately carved legs and claw feet.

"Yes, sir," Kelly says and immediately sits in the plush chair in front of the desk.

"I have a few things I need to go over with you," Doc informs him and removes his glasses.

"Ok," Kelly says and for some reason feels a touch of apprehension at the formality of this meeting.

"I am going to ask our... guests, if you will, to leave in three days," Doc tells him.

Kelly nods. "I think that's wise, sir," he agrees.

"Yes, as do I. They are becoming more of a burden every day. Is their RV ready to leave?" he asks.

Kelly and Derek and even Cory have been helping them to repair the motorhome that has mechanical issues.

"I don't think we can fix it, sir. It's too computerized for us to figure out what's wrong and the things we've thought were broken, we fixed. And it's still a heap," Kelly informs the doc, and the man nods solemnly.

"No matter, they will still need to leave. They can leave it behind and go in the one that works. Besides, there are a lot less of them now and will be even fewer when they find out we intend to keep the three children," Doc says.

He picks up his pipe and lights it. The smell is nostalgic as Kelly remembers his own grandfather on his father's side who used to smoke a pipe or a cigar and tell him funny stories from his childhood.

"How do you want us to handle it if they don't want to leave the kids?" Kelly asks. He doesn't even bother asking how the doc wants it handled if they don't want to leave at all. Derek and John and Kelly will simply persuade them that it's in their best interest.

"I think I'll be able to work something out with them," Doc says cleverly as if he's holding a trick up his sleeve.

"Ok, you just give the order, sir. We're all willing to do whatever you say," Kelly tells him, and Doc nods knowingly.

"I know, Kelly," Doc says mindfully. "And I appreciate that. Without you men on this farm I have no doubts that those shitbirds out there would've overrun us."

Kelly chuffs.

"I don't know about that, sir. I've seen Reagan shoot, and I've got a feeling you can handle that shotgun just fine," Kelly praises.

"Yes, she's an accurate shot, that girl," Doc says with a chuckle of his own. "But I'd rather it doesn't come to such drastic measures. Later today, I'll have one of you fetch whichever of the visitors wants to hear what I have to say, and we'll hold a meeting near the front porch. It's where we welcomed them in. Seems right to ask them to leave the same way."

The doc is so old school and classic in his way of thinking.

"Ok, sir. We'll be there, right beside you in case it turns ugly," Kelly offers austerely.

"I know you will, son," Doc tells him and then adds strangely: "I wouldn't want anything to happen to Hannah."

Kelly's eyes snap up to meet the doc's. "Me neither, sir."

They sit for what seems like an eternity as Doc continues to puff on his pipe. It goes on so long that Kelly actually squirms in his chair and is about to ask if that is all he needs when the other man finally speaks again.

"Are you having sexual relations with my granddaughter, Kelly?" he asks stoically as if he's just chatting about crop rotation.

Fuck! That sure as hell wasn't what he thought Doc was going to say next. They'd been talking about the freak losers out at

258

the camp. Jesus, this guy is a lot more cunning than Kelly had given him credit for. He feels like a teenager again taking a girl out on a date and meeting her father for the first time. He's glad he still has the beard because he's sure his face has turned red. Kelly stares hard at his knees for a minute, wrestling with his thoughts, his conscience. Finally he raises his gaze to Herb's and answers.

"Yes, sir," Kelly confesses quietly.

"I'm glad you didn't lie to me, Kelly. I kind of already figured it out on my own," Doc discloses.

Kelly's positive that his look of shock must be all too readable on his face.

Doc adds, "I have my ways."

"I'm sorry, Dr. McClane. I never meant to disrespect you or your home. I wanted to leave. I did. I should've, but I didn't because somehow I just couldn't leave her," Kelly tries lamely to explain, but the only explanation is that he did have sex with Hannah.

"I know, Kelly," Doc says prophetically.

How does he know so much? Hannah may be more like her grandfather than Grams.

"I'm very sorry, sir," Kelly says again as Doc holds up his hand to shut him up.

"What are your intentions with Hannah, Kelly?" Doc asks point blank.

This makes Kelly have to look away and swallow.

"I don't know, sir. Hannah's so… good and pure. And I'm… just not. I understand if you want me to leave, Dr. McClane," Kelly explains. Herb sighs heavily.

"Leave? Do you think that would make Hannah happy? Because I sure don't. And as much as I don't approve of you having sexual relations with my granddaughter out of wedlock, I also don't want to have to mend her broken heart if you leave her," Doc explains.

He puffs that pipe again. Now the smell is making Kelly sick. It brings back the memories of his innocent youth before he'd become a stone cold killer.

"I just feel like I'm not good for her, Dr. McClane. I don't feel like I could ever be good enough for someone like her. Hannah deserves someone who is like her, someone who hasn't seen and done the things I have," Kelly tries to make Herb understand. The man just nods with a sagacious knowledge that Kelly may never understand.

"You're a man conflicted, Kelly. I recognize it in you because I have seen it in myself," Doc says.

He pauses while Kelly thinks about his words. Herb rises from his chair, walks over to a plaque on the wall and points to it.

"Boston General," he says.

Kelly nods, though he has no idea what the doctor is talking about.

"What I am about to tell you can never leave this room, Kelly," Doc explains. Kelly nods again. "It can never go beyond these four walls. You can never, *never* tell Hannah. It would crush her. You are partially right about her. Our Hannah is a delicate thing, but she's more of a fighter than you give her credit for, too, I think. But there are certain darknesses of the world, of my past that I've always kept her and her sisters sheltered from. My wife knows what I am about to tell you."

"Ok, sir. I swear I would never tell anything you told me not to, sir," Kelly promises in earnest.

"I believe you, son. You're a man of your word. And I also believe you have integrity, which will become a rare commodity in a man as this world further disintegrates."

His words of praise move Kelly more than he is willing to admit.

Doc continues calmly, "When I was a young pup out of med school, I didn't come straight back to the farm to set up my practice like most people think. I should have. But I was ambitious, thought I could take on the world and light it on fire with my brilliant medical mind. I was a fool, Kelly. And I paid the price because I sold my soul to the devil for fame, recognition and money, of course. I was working in the Boston General emergency room, a huge hospital. I met another doctor there who encouraged me to leave and join a practice with him and his friend who was also a doctor and older and already established. I left the E.R. and went into practice with these two men who were just as hungry as I was. We mostly treated pregnant women which was an easy transition for me because I minored in obstetrics and pediatric care. I was a lot like Reagan when I was young. I could learn and retain medical journals like a child

260

reads a comic book, or I guess nowadays, plays a video game," Doc jokes.

Kelly offers a grim smile because this story isn't going to have a happy ending. He can just tell. Doc's blue eyes are sad and full of regret.

"Anyway, we helped hundreds maybe thousands of women give birth to their babies. Made house calls on the rich women of the Boston elite. Had a very large practice. And we also performed abortions," Doc says and looks away from Kelly to stare at the plaque again. "I would've been better off at that damn E.R. At first I didn't think anything of it. I'd been raised in the church, attended regularly while growing up, but I never really thought anything of aborting babies because my scientific mind didn't think of them as children. They were just unwanted fetuses, not a life. That's when I met my Maryanne. I think she likes to tell people we met when I was in med school or we met after I started my practice here, but that's not the truth. She only says it so that she doesn't have to explain where I worked and what I was doing when we first met. She worked at a salon back then near my practice. She'd cut my hair a time or two. I was smitten from the moment I met her. Had to go back a lot of times for hair trimmings I didn't need. And when she found out over the course of dating that I performed abortions, I nearly lost her. You see, Maryanne lives her life and always has by the Good Book, and she has the strictest moral code of anyone I've ever known. Without my Maryanne, I might be working at that damn women's clinic still today, taking money for taking lives. I grew to regret the choices I made after we moved here and I set up my own family practice. And it didn't matter how many lives I saved, I never forgave myself for what I did up in Boston. I was young and stupid, you see. And I always figured that's why God never gave us all the children we wanted, Maryanne wanted. He was punishing me. I've never told my wife I felt like that about why we couldn't have more than one child, but she probably knows. I don't think there's much that she doesn't know. Hannah's so much like her, too."

Kelly is silent, and his hands shake. He doesn't even know what to say. There isn't anything to say. The doc is also so haunted by his own past, and Kelly has never known anyone but himself who was so troubled over the lives he's taken.

261

"So, you see? You aren't the only person who has ever led a conflicted life, Kelly. But the choice is yours to make as to what you want to do with it from here on out. Someday when I meet my maker I'll have to atone for my past, but you won't. You don't have any reason to feel guilty about your past, son. You did what any soldier does. You were trained to do a job. You defended our country. You should, at the very least, be proud of what you contributed to keeping our nation safe," Doc explains.

Kelly cannot answer. The emotion in his throat from this absolution is too much for Kelly to talk around. He just nods instead.

"I'll give you some time, not a lot of time, mind you. But I'll give you few weeks or so to decide what you want to do about Hannah, and I'll respect your decision," Doc says calmly.

Kelly thinks he's misheard him. "Sir?"

"I'm not a fool, Kelly. I know that Hannah can be very persuasive when she wants something. And my Hannah tends to not hold back her feelings, even if she should," Herb astutely remarks. "But I still don't appreciate the out of wedlock sexual contact."

"Yes, sir," Kelly says and feels like a rat bastard again.

"But for what it's worth, you have my blessing whether you should want it or not. I don't know a better man for the job," Doc says and goes to the door which he opens.

"Yes, sir," Kelly says because he knows when he's being dismissed. But before he can cross the threshold, Herb lays a hand on Kelly's shoulder.

"You're a good man, Kelly Alexander. I have faith that you'll do the right thing," Doc tells him quietly.

Kelly has to look at his feet and nod.

"Yes, sir," he says and leaves the room.

When he gets back to the kitchen, Kelly is surprised that Hannah isn't there, but Grams still is.

"She's with the children in the barn playing with the baby goats, Kelly," Grams says.

What the hell? He hadn't asked her where Hannah was. Does everyone know about them?

"Uh, thanks. I'm not looking for anyone, though. I need to… gonna take a run, ma'am," Kelly tells her and retrieves his running shoes that John found him in the city. He just needs to be alone for a while and clear his head, digest everything that he's just discussed

262

with Doc. Ten miles won't be enough time to think over what they've talked about, maybe twenty.

Before he hits the trail, however, he runs in to John who is hooking up the grain binder to the tractor for cutting the wheat. Then it will be put through an old-fashioned thresher that will take all of the men working together to operate. The stalky parts of the straw will be baled and used to bed down the horses and cattle this winter. The wheat will be processed in the hog barn where Doc keeps the wheat grinder. Some of it will be rough crushed and mixed with dried, field corn to feed to the horses and cows during the winter season, and some will be ground more finely for use by the family. Kelly knows more about wheat production than he ever thought he would need or would care to know. And he understands that it's going to be a tough, back-breaking process to bring in the field of wheat and then oats, but if they don't get it done, they could starve and so could the animals who provide them with transportation and food. In the spring, they'll replant again in a different pasture using the old grain drill in the equipment shed. And Doc talked the other day about planting winter wheat, whatever that is. He and Derek have been talking about taking the combine from the Johnson farm next year and using it instead, which would cut the time the job would take down by about eighty percent. But for this year they all need to learn how to do it the old way because eventually gasoline and diesel fuel could run out, and they have to stay alive somehow.

But despite all the hard work on the McClane farm, he likes his life here and so do his brother and sister. It is peaceful in this valley, secluded from the harshness outside of it. The life is simple, uncomplicated unless you count relationships.

"Hey, man, everything ok with Doc?" John asks.

He's lining the binder coupler up to the tractor.

"Uh, yeah. Everything's fine, dude. Don't worry about it," Kelly says as he helps John with the binder.

"Doc's equipment may be antiques but it all looks like it just came off the showroom floor," John remarks to which Kelly agrees.

After another ten minutes of struggling with the binder and then getting the tractor backed and lined up to it, they finish with the hook-up. Derek walks up to them from the cattle barn where he was working on a leaky water line. He's carrying a toolbox which will immediately get put away, no doubt.

"Thanks, bro. You comin'?" John asks Kelly.

"Nah, I think I'm gonna go for a run. Do a perimeter check," Kelly tells his friend. "Cory and Simon are watchin' the hadj."

"Hadj three and four are starting to get a little mouthy around here for my taste," Derek remarks.

"Yeah, a couple of them need their teeth knocked out," Kelly says, knowing which ones Derek is referring to. Hadj three is the bulky, black man named Levon who leers at Sue every chance he gets, and hadj four is Bobby the punk. Kelly has had enough of that kid.

"What teeth?" John asks.

All three men laugh. Leave it to John.

"You got that right," Derek chimes in and bumps fists with his brother. "Sue said that Peter was given a crate of our canned goods the other day to share with his friends and that they were wanting more already this morning. She also said she doesn't think they're milkin' that goat regularly."

"Lazy bastards," Kelly remarks. John is calm, quiet, the same way he gets before he kills someone. "Anyways, I'm headin' out."

"Sure, Kelly. I've got you covered in the wheat field. Derek can help and make sure it doesn't malfunction since none of us knows what the heck we're doing," John says as Derek jumps in.

"Yeah, no problem, man. You work your ass off around here, Kelly. Take a run," Derek agrees.

"Thanks, guys. Hey, John?" Kelly asks his friend, and John looks at him squarely and stops messing with the tractor. "You got that thing I wanted you to get for me in the city?"

"Coloring books for Em?" his friend asks on a laugh. "I'm just kidding, man. Yeah, I got it."

"I'm gonna need that," Kelly says to which John smiles approvingly. He is so easy to be around, his carefree friend, who also so easily kills bad people.

"What is it, a baby? John got one of those, too," Derek jokes, and John just goes with it.

"Yeah, yeah, I hear ya'," he replies with his usual good humor as he jumps down from the tractor seat.

"Yeah, man, what was up with that? I mean we know you like the little Doc and all, but that was kind of fast- even for you, lover-boy," Kelly razzes.

"Really fast," Derek adds. "Go to the city, come back with a baby. I think you missed a few steps somewhere in there, little brother."

"I wondered when you two were gonna get around to this," John remarks with a smile.

He wipes his face with the front of his shirt, removes it and hangs it on the tractor fender. He folds his arms patiently across his chest. Kelly notices a scratch on his friend's chest, but he doesn't comment. He's no fool. That isn't from a barn kitten.

John adds with good humor, "You two done?"

"Yeah, come on, Romeo. We'd better get this wheat cut before sundown. Looks like a bitch of a job," Derek says and leaves to return the tools.

"Doc wants us with him later," Kelly relays. "He's gonna tell the creeps they're leaving in three days whether they want to or not. And that we're keepin' the kids."

"Oh, good. This oughta' be fun," John says with a smartass grin. "Catch me after dinner tonight for that other thing, 'kay?"

"Sure, man. See ya'," Kelly says and takes off for his run.

An hour and a half later he joins Derek and John in the field because he feels too guilty leaving such hard work for the two of them. Naturally they tease him about missing them. It's always like this when he's around them. They say a lot without saying much at all, and he appreciates the quiet, male camaraderie of his two friends.

Before dinner is served, Grandpa has Derek tell Uncle Peter to bring his friends and come to the porch front. Kelly, John and Derek take up opposing points near the porch, close to their unwanted guests. Cory stands with his pistol beside Doc who is not brandishing a weapon. Kelly's sure that it's just leaning where it cannot be seen. The women have been asked to stay inside, though Kelly knows they are eavesdropping at windows. The visitors approach and look all too happy for a bunch of misfits about to get thrown out. They are probably hoping they are getting more free food that they haven't earned.

"Peter," Doc starts with a friendly salutation.

"What's up, Doc?" the idiot says.

He's mimicking the classic Bugs Bunny character, making his friends laugh. Kelly fails to find the humor. They really are dipshits. Their women amble up behind them, and Jasmine spends her time eyeing up John, as usual. Poor guy. John told him a few days ago that the stripper had cornered him again near the horse barn. Kelly had laughed at his hardship and punched him in the shoulder.

"We've been more than accommodating to you and your friends there, but now it's time for you to move on. We did what we could for your sick companions, but they're gone and in three days I'd like you to be, as well."

"Frank's kid is still sick, so how are we supposed to leave?" Peter asserts.

"He's on the mend and should be just fine very soon," Doc answers back.

"And what if one of us gets sick after you kick us out?" Amber accuses.

Kelly takes in her haggard appearance and stringy, dirty hair with disdain. They've been given soap and shampoo, but this woman is obviously not a big fan.

Doc doesn't even acknowledge her. "I'm giving you the three days so that you can pick apples and the rest of the corn you didn't pick. We'll give you some containers for your goat milk, but she'll need to stay behind because we have two babies who will need her milk," Doc says.

They all start bitching. Uncle Peter steps forward to take the lead but is interrupted by one of his friends.

"Amber's right," Buzz butts in. "What if we get sick next?"

He's normally quiet and hangs back in the shadows of his more mouthy traveling mates. Kelly still doesn't trust him.

Derek fills in the gap for these people with a quick, to-the-point explanation. "Then you'll be on your own. You can't come back here. Ever."

"Our other RV ain't runnin' yet, Herb," Uncle Dipshit whines.

"You have less people with whom you are traveling now, Peter, so you should all fit in just the one," Doc explains simply.

His analytic common sense is hard to argue against. Kelly had run six clicks earlier trying to outrun it and had failed.

266

"Hey, this is bullshit, man! We don't want to leave it behind," hadj three complains.

His light amber eyes grow ominous. His dread-locks look unkempt and dirty, just like the rest of him. He's managed to add on some bulk weight since coming to the farm. It is a sign that it is past time for them to leave.

"Yeah, you got more than enough space here for us," hadj one, or Uncle Peter, says.

"Yeah, man, we could live in those barns," Rick throws out.

He's generally a non-threatening man, but he's still been assigned the title of hadj seven. The other evening he hadn't argued against him and Derek, but now that his friends are with him Rick must be feeling buoyed by them.

"The barns house all of our animals, and we'll need them for hay storage and wintering the animals, Rick," Doc says patiently.

"Fucking assholes," the toothless hag hadji girl, Amber, bites out with remarkable anger.

Kelly levels a glare on her which shuts her up. She has the same cold, dark eyes as her son Bobby.

"Let us stay. We can be helpful, too. We can work," hadj five, or Buzz, says.

He's a zero threat factor and seems to hang out the most with Rick. Kelly, John and Derek have been gathering intel on this group since they'd first set foot on the farm. With help from Cory and sometimes Simon, they've gained a deeper perspective of the fairly wide range of behavioral patterns within their group. The intel includes: where the hadj pack goes on the farm, when they go there, movement within their own group, relationships within their group, how they treat the children and each other, what time they usually crash for the night, when they rise (usually late morning), and any other information they can get on them. It's the same type of vetting that the three Rangers have done in the past when dealing with the enemy. This is just a different threat, but they consider them no less of an enemy.

"I don't think that is what we're looking for," Doc tries to say nicely while also turning down the offer.

"Fuck this! We want to stay, man. You don't know what it's like out there. You can't just make us leave! It's fucked up, man," says Frank, Huntley's asshole of a dad.

"We know what's out there, dude," John says quietly. "But you don't belong here, either."

Frank levels a deadly glare on Kelly's best friend, which makes him want to pistol whip Huntley's mouthy father into senselessness. John now has the responsibility of baby Jacob, and Kelly's sure that he feels equally responsible for his brother's family, as well. He also understands John's protectiveness over the little Doc.

"You've survived this long," Derek adds in. "You'll all be just fine."

"There are plenty of empty farms and houses where the rest of you could establish your own home-front," Doc suggests.

Kelly's benefactor's tone is slightly less patient. Kelly also notices that Herb doesn't offer up the empty Johnson farm. Their abandoned farm is way too close to the McClane spread for anyone's comfort.

"We wanna' stay, gringos," says hadj six, the Latino man.

They've learned that he is a completely schizophrenic freak. He has bizarre ticks, and the men have caught him talking to himself when no one else is around. They believe he is mentally unstable, to say the least.

"Not happening," John says with absolute authority.

If Doc's patience is waning, John's is just completely gone.

Frank steps forward, "Fine you sons a' bitches. We'll leave! We'll get our shit together and in three days we'll leave. Send those fuckin' kids back out here so they can help!"

Derek steps forward, "Watch your mouth."

Frank takes a step back and looks Derek up and down nervously. His black jeans are tight which means that he has not lost weight during the apocalypse. It's also a possibility that he hadn't given food and liquid to his son, Garrett, and why they boy hadn't improved before coming to the farm. This is all speculation that pisses Kelly off further.

"I don't think that's going to be an option, Frank," Doc explains as he casually lights his pipe. "The children have decided they want to stay, and we'd be happy to keep them on."

268

"What the fu… That's my kid, old man. You ain't keepin' him," Frank yells.

He kicks the toe of his dusty cowboy boot into the gravel, causing it to spray.

"He wants to stay," John says through gritted teeth.

"No way. That's bullsh…" Frank is trying his damnedest not to swear since Derek had warned him. His ridiculous rant is interrupted by Jasmine.

"Hey, if the kids can stay, why can't I? I'm not going to cause any trouble for you, and I can cook, too," Jasmine offers.

Probably not like Hannah, Kelly thinks. His dad told him a long time ago to never trust a skinny cook with his meals. Hannah has just the right amount of curve for his taste. This chic is a skinny crackhead.

"We're full up with the three additional kids," Derek lies so easily.

"But I can be helpful with other things, too," she proposes to John, who is not even looking at her but at Hadj three, Levon.

There's bloodlust in John's eyes. Kelly's seen it many times before in his friend. They are literally staring each other down and the big black man's eyes are hungry for a fight. Levon and Frank are obviously the biggest threats in this group.

"I'm sorry, Jasmine, but the offer is only to the children," Doc says.

"What about me? You're gonna let Simon and Sam stay but not me?" Bobby, hadj four says.

Everyone is shocked, even the people in his own group. Is this dickhead serious?

"I'm sorry, Bobby, but we just don't feel like you'd be a good fit here, and like Derek said, we are out of space for any additional people to stay," Doc explains.

He's more patient than Kelly would be. If it had been up to himself, John and Derek, some of these people would've already been in holes on the hill.

"That's bullshit, man. You got like a mansion there," Bobby laments.

"Again, I'm sorry. But the answer is no," Doc says.

"Well, Sam's going with us. She's with me. She's my girlfriend," Bobby boldly announces.

Kelly gives a confused look to John who returns it. This is news to them.

"Samantha, would you come out here, please?" Doc asks over his shoulder.

A moment later the frail, dark-haired, porcelain doll that is Sam comes onto the porch. She stands overly close to Doc but not Cory. This kid is almost as fucked up as Reagan but not quite. Nobody is that bad.

"Samantha, this boy says that you two are together. Is this true?" Doc asks quietly.

Sam looks at the ground and shakes her head with such instant fear that Kelly is ready to shoot punk-ass Bobby where he stands. She won't look directly at Bobby. Kelly notices fresh bruises on her arm and a faded one on her cheekbone. Has he been raping her, too? Kelly sure as hell hopes not.

Bobby gives Doc a nasty glower with his evil black eyes. Kelly can just imagine the horrors that poor Sam has suffered at the hands of this jerkoff. He's much larger than Samantha. It would be very easy for him to overpower, bully and harm her. Kelly feels a vein pulse in his neck.

"Get your ass down here, bitch," Bobby barks loudly.

John stalks over and cold clocks the kid in the jaw. He falls very hard, and Kelly's almost positive he's out cold until he finally moves. John stands over him, and nobody moves or speaks. Kelly is almost afraid for the kid. If John is pushed too far, he'll simply shoot this piece of shit.

"Real men hit each other, not women, you little prick. Stay away from her and stay away from my woman, too," John says fiercely.

Kelly encourages his friend to back away by pulling on his shirt sleeve. If anyone on the farm was unsure of his feelings for Reagan, they sure as shit shouldn't be now. He is going to be the next one getting pulled into Doc's office, especially if Doc saw those claw marks on John's chest. Kelly noticed his friend wears his t-shirt again, a wise move. When Kelly glances at Doc, the man seems calm, unfazed. Old school. He simply tells Sam to go back inside.

270

"Well you ain't keepin' Simon and Huntley. They're our family," toothless hag Amber says from the crowd.

The group has subdued slightly after John's violent reaction. If they thought that was violent, they should see John cornered in a house by six or seven Muslims out in the middle of the Syrian desert.

Franks starts up again. "You sure as shit ain't keepin' my kid. He's my kid!"

"He doesn't want to leave with you," Derek tells the father of the year. "He feels very strongly about it, too. Doc and I both talked with him last night. He wants to stay here. Without you."

"Give me a break! You don't scare me, Army boy," Frank taunts. "Just because there ain't no law I can call no more doesn't give you the right to keep my kid."

"Frank, he doesn't want to leave the farm," Doc says, trying to soften the blow.

"Bullshit!" the man says and spits once.

It hits dangerously close to John's boot. Frank had better learn to tread a little lighter with Kelly's friend.

"Let me talk to him," Frank orders.

"No way," Derek answers firmly.

"He's my damn kid. Let me talk to him. Where is he?" the concerned father inquires.

For being so worried all of a sudden about Huntley being left behind, Frank hasn't once visited his sick son in the med shed nor has he inquired after him. He also never visited his little boy who'd succumbed to that sickness. That boy had died with only his twin brother and virtual strangers at his side.

"You aren't talking to anyone," John asserts. "He's staying. You're leaving. That's final."

"This is fucking bullshit," Amber cries angrily.

She tries to rush forward at John, but Rick smartly holds her back. At least one person in this group is halfway intelligent. Frank begins pacing back and forth in frustration. If Huntley belonged to Kelly, there wouldn't be enough men with guns to keep him from getting to him.

"What is it going to take, Frank?" Doc asks super cool and collected.

He's had this figured all along, Kelly realizes. The hadj pack looks from person to person within their group as a few of them mumble to one another. Frank argues a second but stops when Great-uncle Peter suggests something. They nod. The others nod.

"We want food and guns," Uncle Peter says.

Doc looks to Kelly.

"No guns," Kelly calls out to the crowd.

"You want our kids and you think we ain't gettin' guns in return? That shit's not happening!" hadji girl rants.

Where is Reagan when they needed her? She should've been allowed to come out.

"Yes," Kelly answers absolutely.

"This is even bigger bullshit," Frank swears, his voice rising in pitch.

"You keep mouthin' off and I can provide you with a bullet instead," John offers with clear intent.

The other man shuts up, which is smart on his part.

"We'll agree to food and perhaps one bottle of antibiotics but no weapons," Doc says from the porch.

Kelly knows that Doc is offering the medicine to placate for the guns. It's a tactically good move.

Doc adds, "And we'll give you back your weapons that you arrived with when you go."

John and Kelly have already removed the firing pins from their weapons anyways, so they are essentially returning non-functioning guns.

"Yeah, pills, get pills," Bobby whispers to the other men. "I know they're hoarding drugs, man. They gotta be. They're both doctors. They gotta have drugs here on this farm."

"We need more than one bottle. We need painkillers, too," Levon demands.

He even shifts his weight from foot to foot as if the prospect of free drugs is exciting. He and Bobby exchange grins.

"Fine, I'll package them myself," Doc agrees.

Kelly's starting to get pissed at these demands. They aren't in the position to make demands. They are more in position to get shot. They brought sickness to the farm that could've killed them all had Reagan and Doc not known how to take the proper preventative measures against it.

272

"And some of them peaches your women have been canning," the Mexican demands and then smiles weirdly.

His greasy black hair is disgusting, and he bobs his head and blinks rapidly- some of his many strange ticks. He's certifiable. How the hell does he know the women have been canning peaches? They'd finished with that weeks ago when the visitors had first come to the farm. Had he been sneaking around in those early days?

"Enough!" John barks. "We'll package two crates of food, painkillers and antibiotics and that's it. And we keep the kids."

His friend is getting low on tolerance and for John it means his finger is getting a little hairy on the trigger.

"Bargain," Uncle Peter says.

The uncle extends his hand for a shake, which nobody takes.

"Fine, fuckin' take my kid," Frank yells loudly. "I didn't ever like those fuckin' Injun kids anyways. Wimpy, whiny assed little brats. Injun blood is probably what made the other one too weak to fight off the sickne…"

Frank's speech is cut off as Derek rams the butt of his rifle into his soft gut. The guy doubles over onto his knees and vomits after he catches his breath.

"I couldn't take any more of that," Derek says.

He looks to Kelly and John, shaking his head as if he's hoping they aren't upset. John just purses his lips and nods, and Kelly shrugs as if to say: who gives a shit?

"Yeah, you guys are real tough, aren't you? With your guns?" spouts off hadj three, Levon.

The biggest guy in their group has been eyeing up Kelly's best friend for a tussle since the meeting had first started. Kelly is perfectly willing to take one for the team, though. Not that John would need his help. Levon's pale eyes are full of rancor.

Kelly hands his rifle to John and also the pistol on his hip and steps forward.

"No guns on me," he taunts the other man.

For a second, the other man looks stupid enough to take Kelly up on his offer to kick his ass, but his cousin Rick stops him. Levon looks from Kelly to John and then to Derek as if sizing them up.

Kelly clarifies something for him. "They won't step in."

Levon spits tobacco juice angrily at the ground near Kelly before turning away and shirking off his cousin's hand. Kelly just looks at the spot on the ground where the other man has marked and then at Levon and sees that the fight in this one isn't done yet. The storm is brewing; it's not over.

The two groups go back to their respective areas on the farm: the McClanes to their home for dinner and the hadj to their tents and RV for sulking, growing anger and resentment. Kelly paces back and forth across the front porch for a long time, though. He's lost his appetite and prefers the solace of solitude and watch duty for the time being. What the hell has the world come to when people sold their kids for drugs and peaches?

Chapter Nineteen
John

A family meeting is called after breakfast the next morning before Derek and Doc turn in for some much-needed sleep. John had caught up on his own yesterday afternoon. He'd come in after returning from the condo village again with Cory and Simon and had taken Jacob up with him to their attic space. They'd both zonked out like logs for a few hours in Reagan's bed. That kid let off sleep toxins or something because John had only meant to get the baby down for a nap while he worked in the closet on organizing the rest of the demo supplies. He'd awakened with Jacob tugging on his shirt and doing his baby babbling in his ear. Oh well, they all need to find sleep where they can until the visitors leave for good, which will be in a few days.

Now the adults are assembled in the dining room while Simon keeps an eye on the children in the music room. Cory watches over the shed and Samantha, who is acting as nurse while Reagan is inside for the meeting. She is seated next to him, which makes it difficult to follow along with Doc's conversation about the wheat grinding procedure. John has a firm hold of her hand under the table and is rubbing her soft palm with the pad of his thumb. The slow, steady rise and fall of her chest has increased, though he's sure that nobody has noticed. He can't help the grin that escapes his features as he remembers her practically attacking him last night. He'd tried to dissuade her manipulations so that she could let her body rest. It hadn't worked. She'd vented at first and then ran a hand over his chest, down his stomach and lower. It had been all the convincing

John had needed. He'd only laughed and complied with her voracious appetite. He truly had awakened a sleeping tigress.

"Right, John?" Kelly asks him.

"Yeah, sure," he agrees to something. Perhaps paying attention might be a good idea.

"Doc, do you think we should go out and get them another car or a van or something?" Derek asks.

"We could give them the Johnson's church car," Kelly offers. "Or we could run into one of the surrounding neighborhoods and jack a vehicle."

"You know how to do that?" Hannah asks with unveiled amazement.

Kelly just smiles at her. His friend is completely infatuated with Hannie. Poor guy. John knows the feeling all too well.

"You'd be surprised what we know how to do," Kelly answers.

Hannah doesn't respond but instead gives a funny little half frown.

Reagan snorts and butts in with, "I wouldn't."

"Moving on," John intervenes. He doesn't really want to go over any of his special talents in front of the family. It's bad enough that Reagan knows some of them. "They have plenty of room on that one RV since we're keeping the kids. I don't think we owe them anything else," John intervenes.

"Yeah, but they were acting like they might give us some trouble if they can't take the other RV when they go," Kelly says calmly. "I don't want any trouble with these idiots. Sorry, Grams. I didn't mean your brother."

"It's fine, Kelly. I understand, dear," she forgives so easily.

"I think they'll go peaceably without the extra vehicle," Doc says.

"Are you sure about that, Grandpa? They seemed pretty pissed yesterday," Reagan comments beside him.

She doesn't look up from what she's preoccupied with doing. Her hair is in a messy ponytail, and John is positive that she hasn't brushed it yet today. No matter. Reagan is perfect to him. She's also taking notes on some disease or something equally gross on a yellow legal pad. Her brain never rests. Heck, *she* barely ever rests. That's probably why she tends to crash so hard when she does. Last night as

276

they'd rested in each other's arms after making love, Reagan told him that she is planning on doubling her studying efforts. She doesn't like that the sickness in the shed has killed at least seven people for sure that they know of and possibly hundreds, maybe thousands more across what's left of their country. She's sure that more diseases of this nature will come their way some day. She's way too stubborn to go down without a mental fight. John had just been happy that she wasn't pulling away from him anymore or that she's not disgusted by his touch. She did return to her own, much larger bed after being with him in his small twin bed. Too much intimacy is still hard for her, but John finally has a little hope.

"I don't want any of the men leaving the farm in the next few days. Just until things settle back down," her grandfather suggests.

Derek also weighs in on this. "I think we should stick around for a few weeks afterward, too, just in case they decide to come back... or come back armed or something crazy like that."

"Agreed," Kelly says.

His friend looks immediately at Hannah who is sitting docilely like a white-haired angel. John's not sure what has transpired between the two of them, but he is sure that it isn't the same as what's happened between himself and Reagan. John and his friend don't talk about their sexual escapades. They never have. But he doesn't believe that Hannah and Kelly have a sexual relationship of any nature. He knows they hang out a lot and maybe his friend has stolen a kiss or two, but there can't be anything more than that between them. She's too innocent and religious for any sort of inappropriate relationship. Reagan on the other hand is no angel. He's not even sure if in her scientific mind she believes in God. She never speaks of such things.

"We just need to stay vigilant for the next few days," Derek tells them all, looking from man to man.

"I'll set the demos at the end of the lane and on the sides of the drive again after they leave," John volunteers. Reagan's eyes dart to his. "Yes, you can help."

At this, her lovely face lights up into a full smile, which blows him away because she rarely does so. Derek laughs.

"Good," Kelly says. "Even if they'd try to come back, they won't take us unaware. We'll be more secure after they leave."

277

"And we won't have to do the double man patrols twenty-four seven," Derek adds.

Sue nods and appears happy to hear this.

"Right," Doc agrees. "They won't give us too much cause for worry before they leave. Besides they should be fairly busy the next few days packing their belongings into the remaining RV and picking vegetables and apples."

Kelly chuffs as if he is disbelieving of them doing so.

"That's up to them," Derek says. "They can do it or not. We made the offer and if they choose not to help themselves to free food by doing a little hard work, then that's their own problem."

"We're only giving them the things that were negotiated and that's it. Anything else is up to them," Kelly affirms.

Hannah frowns. She is just too kind-hearted for people like the visitors who do not deserve to be the benefactors of her goodness of spirit. Hannah is so unlike Reagan in so many ways that it's sometimes hard for John to remember that they're sisters.

"It's not like they have a ton of shit to load up. They could've left today," Reagan swears.

However, it's not hard to remember how different they are. She gets the look from Grams

Doc explains his decision. "I felt like if we allowed them to stay long enough to make sure that Frank's son was well again, it might go more smoothly. At least that way he'd know his son was going to be ok."

Reagan snorts, writes something down. Sue must agree with Reagan because she chuffs with irritation and says, "I don't think he gives a crap, Grandpa. I think we're the only people on this entire farm who care about any of those three kids. Simon's aunt, Amber, didn't fight too hard to keep him. What the heck? She knows he's an orphan. Her own sister was his mother for goodness sake!"

"Yeah, and we still don't even know which one of those creeps Sam even belongs to," Kelly adds. "Cory tries to talk to her about it, but she just shuts down, won't talk to him. She's keeping some pretty big secrets if you ask me."

John nods. "Yeah, something isn't right there."

"I don't know if any of them are related to her or if they just picked her up somewhere along the way like they did Jennifer," Reagan adds.

278

She goes back to her book and flips to a new page. Her multitasking is something like John's never seen, and every time he sees her doing something like this it never fails to amaze him. She just goes right on scribbling notes while the conversation ebbs and flows around her. She is listening, though, because she comments along with the rest of them.

"Surely not," Grams says with wonder. "She must be related to *one* of them."

Reagan just shrugs before making another note. John can't make out most of what her words are, but the ones that he can read he can't understand their meaning anyway.

"I don't think it would've mattered," John confides what he's been thinking, what's been bothering him for the last day since they came to terms with their guests.

"What do you mean?" Derek asks him.

"They didn't care about taking those kids with them," he explains. "They were going to use them as a bargaining chip to get what they wanted. It's the same reason Peter came here in the first place with them. He knew that the moment we saw the sick kids and woman that Doc would never turn them away."

"Yeah, that's probably true," Kelly agrees.

Hannah reluctantly nods. Grams is quiet which makes John feel terrible for insulting her brother.

He tries to smooth over her damaged feelings by clarifying, "When Doc threw out the idea of an offer for the kids, they were all too compliant with it. Normal people would've had their kids in the RV and out the drive in a flash if that happened to them."

"Yeah, that was way too easy," Derek says with a grim nod.

"Kids tagging along with a group like that would just be a burden," Kelly confirms. "They only felt like they were a benefit when they could haul water or cook or do the laundry. Feeding them and taking care of them, especially the younger ones, was just a responsibility that none of them wanted."

"Frank sure didn't fight too hard for Huntley," Derek adds.

"He's probably glad we're going to keep him," Sue says sadly. "I can't imagine."

"Probably is glad," Doc concurs. "But I wanted to give the option anyways. I don't know what we would've been able to do about it if he wouldn't have yielded."

"Me, John and Kelly would've become more persuasive, Herb," Derek adds with a certain amount of confidence. "Besides, I don't think any of them will miss the kids for any reason other than for making them do all the work."

Doc sighs loudly. "I'll just be glad when they're gone."

Everyone agrees with either a nod or a verbal affirmation. Even Grams gives a curt nod.

"We still need to go over a schedule for the rest of the harvest," Derek says to Doc, who nods.

"Well the hay's done unless we'd get some unusual weather. But it's probably done for the season," Doc informs them. "The wheat still needs finished and we need to grind the corn for the livestock."

"Right," Kelly says. "We'll get on the wheat today."

"The garden will need finished out," Grams tells them.

"I know, Grams," Sue says. "I'm going to have Simon and Cory help me get some of the plants into the greenhouse for winter. The cabbages are still going, but I want to move the lettuces inside now."

"Good," Doc says. "If we'd get a hard frost too early, that would destroy your plants outside."

John makes the mistake of glancing down at Reagan's book. She's studying some nasty picture of a person's skin that looks like leprosy has taken over. No wonder she doesn't eat much.

"Gotta' butcher that cow, too," she adds in.

She's so ladylike. Well, she is beautiful and sexy so that makes up for her lack of femininity. Her small fingers work dexterously taking notes again without missing a beat.

She adds while still scribbling, "Should butcher a few more chickens, too. We only have six downstairs in the freezers."

"Yeah, and once the Reynolds finish their solar panels then they'll be ready for freezer meat again," Derek tells them.

"How did it go at the condo village the other day, John?" Doc questions.

"Went well," John tells them all. "Paul is going to start working on their own panels as soon as he can. Said his son could

280

help. I think they'll figure it out. They seem pretty smart. We'll be able to take meat to them if you want, Doc."

"The Reynolds will need to butcher at least two cows this fall according to Wayne," Doc says. "They're dry and not producing, so it's time for them to go. Nobody can afford to feed animals that don't produce anymore."

"What if Paul could find something to trade for a cow, Herb?" Derek asks. "Do you think he could keep one milk cow in the area around the condo community? I mean, heck, they could fence off a section of the golf course."

Everyone laughs. It's a good tension reliever. Plus, it is genuinely funny to think of a dairy cow having a whole golf course to herself.

"I don't see why not, Derek," Doc agrees. "I think it's a good idea to start establishing a trade flow within our small community."

Kelly starts in again. "Paul said that he could come out to their farm in the spring and work for them. You know, plowing, milking whatever they need help with."

"That's perfect," Grams says.

This is a positive feeling that everyone shares. Establishing a sense of community is going to be the first step toward rebuilding their country.

She continues, "And he could bring his wife sometimes, too. Bertie could sure use some company now and then."

"I know," Sue laments. "I feel bad that she's over there by herself with just the men."

"Until it's safer, you can't go over there just yet, honey," Derek puts in quickly.

Sue just nods. Doc reaches over and gives her hand a squeeze. The benevolence of the McClane family never fails to humble John.

"It'll get better, Sue," Doc tells her, to which she gives a pained grin. "I think that things will get better. People trading with one another, trusting each other again is a good, first step forward."

"I agree, sir," Kelly adds.

"And with that, I'm off to bed," Doc informs them.

His white hair is standing on end. There is a full day's growth of gray stubble on his chin and cheeks. He looks exhausted as all get out.

He rises, everyone follows suit, and they all leave the dining room. Hannah and Grams relieve Simon with the kids. Derek goes upstairs to catch some sleep while Kelly heads out to the shed to relieve Cory. It leaves him and Reagan alone in the kitchen.

Today she wears baggy jeans with the knees ripped through completely and a slim, long-sleeved white t-shirt. She looks fresh and adorable to John. Even the black socks aren't as offensive as they used to be. She tosses her work onto the island, not bothering to take it up to the attic. She's also a slob, which used to bug him, as well. Some things about her just make her the quirky Reagan he loves.

"Wanna' get in a run before I go to the shed?" she asks while looking at her feet.

She's never actually asked him before. He has to bite the inside of his cheek to suppress a smile.

"Sure," he says with a nonchalant nod. "Probably should just to do a perimeter check, right?"

"Yeah," she agrees. "Let me just check on Huntley real quick and I'll meet you out behind the horse barn near our path."

"Ok," he tells her and they separate. John likes it that she calls it their path. That has to mean something. It does to John.

Ten minutes later Reagan runs up to him near the back of the horse barn.

"How's Huntley?" he asks, and they start off at a fast walk. Naturally. She's not the sort to slow walk.

"He's doing great. I wasn't sure when Sue brought him in if he'd pull through, but I think because we caught it so early on with him that he's going to be ok. It gave the medicine more time to kill the virus."

"Good. Thank God," John says as they come closer to the edge of the forest. Her springy curls are coming loose of her ponytail.

"Yeah," she says quietly.

As they head up the first incline on the path, Molly yips and barks at their heels.

"Go on! Go back, Molly," Reagan scolds.

The mutt hangs her head and stops. She wags her tail with hopeful expectation.

"Aww, be nice, boss. She just wants to go, too. Don't ya,' girl? Come on, Molly," he calls to her. Reagan just huffs at him and continues on while shaking her head.

John reaches over and takes her hand. It would be nice to just walk their path today.

She asks with a great deal of disbelief, "What are you doing?"

"Holding your hand. What's it look like?" he teases with a smile. She tries to pull back, but John holds fast.

"Let's just get our run in, ok?" she says uncomfortably.

John just laughs once before they break apart and start jogging. Here and there the path is muddy and more deeply rutted from the bad rains the other day, but they still make fairly good time. When they come to the high meadow where the green grasses of summer and the rainbow of wildflowers are all turning to tans and browns with the colors of fall, John tugs her arm, pulling her to a stop.

He feigns the need for a break. "I need to walk for a while, boss. Getting out of shape," he jokes.

"Didn't seem out of shape last night," she jokes bawdily.

John laughs and sweeps her into his arms for a long kiss that ends with them in the meadow grasses rolling around like a couple of teenagers. The sun is warm and high today, unlike the rainy, chilly weather of the last few days. It caresses her tan skin delightfully, making it shimmery and lovely.

John kisses her deeply, pressing her into the natural flora around them. Reagan takes his hand and slides it under her white shirt. She doesn't seem to mind that it will be grass-stained and soiled from rolling around on the ground. Her curls tickle his nose and cheeks as he buries his face in her neck. Reagan's hands are at his back, clawing and pulling him closer. His hand closes around her breast, squeezing gently and teasing under the lace edge at the top of her bra.

"Yes," Reagan tells him.

It's more of an order than a request, and John knows it.

He grins against her mouth before answering, "Not here, sweetie."

"Yes, here," she argues.

Of course she argues. Somehow her solid logic seems to make sense as her mouth presses against the base of his neck and then near his ear. It sends a shiver through him. John has never felt like this with another woman, this desperate or frantic for another person in his life.

Reagan's hand slips under the hem of his white t-shirt where she runs her cold fingertips over his stomach muscles, making them jump and flex under her touch. Her cheeks are flushed to a lovely, deep pink. She whimpers against his neck as his hand moves over her hip to cup her bottom, tugging her against his erection. Her leg hooks around his like a coiling snake. John is about to unbutton her jeans when Molly's soft mewling jerks him from these thoughts, these thoughts that would lead to their nudity and satiated appetites for one another.

The dog is standing maybe twenty feet from them. Her hackles are raised with apprehension of something in the woods to their west. Perhaps it's just a deer.

"What is it?" Reagan asks.

John has leaned back slightly from her and has his head turned to look at Molly. Reagan is unaware of what is going on. He doesn't want to frighten her.

"John?"

"Not sure," he whispers and tugs her top back down, straightening it for her. Reagan leans up on her elbows, but John doesn't sit all the way up yet. He's still lying half on top of her, which also keeps her down below the long grasses.

Molly growls low in her throat. It's a foreboding yet threatening sound. John listens intently but hears nothing. He doesn't have the benefit of canine ears- or Hannah's. His mutt is on high alert.

"Do you think it's something?" Reagan whispers.

She's also feeling the dog's tension. John places his index finger to her lips.

"Stay low," he orders to which she nods.

They are far enough away from the wood-line that if someone would be in there, they shouldn't be able to see him and Reagan in the tall grass. This is also the reason he doesn't call to the dog.

284

John pulls his .45 from the holster on his hip, rolls off of Reagan, takes the binoculars out of his cargo pocket and scans the area carefully. Molly is still discomfited about something in those woods. Her head swings back and forth, to and fro. She is clearly upset. John doesn't hear or see anything, but it sure doesn't mean that nothing or nobody is out there.

After another two minutes, the dog comes back to John, licks his hand and lies on the ground near his feet. If someone or something was in the woods, they're gone now. Her usual calm demeanor is restored, and she even wags her tag once.

"Stay here. Keep her here with you," John tells Reagan and rises. She looks worried but does as she's told. John sprints into the woods at a wide angle, trying to flank any would-be trouble.

He runs for about a half mile but finds no one. It's frustrating but also a relief. On his way back to Reagan, John does spy a deer about a hundred yards to his south through his binoculars. He's not sure if Molly would react so strangely to just a deer, though. She's had to have seen hundreds since coming to the farm and he's never noticed her behave like that over anything before. He doesn't believe for a second that the doe he'd spotted has spooked his dog. She's smarter than that. When he takes Reagan back to the shed, John fully intends to grab Kelly and do a full perimeter check on horseback. If they have to go five miles out and track with Molly, then that's what he's willing to do. The safety of the family is the only thing that matters. The safety of Reagan being most important.

He collects her, all thoughts of sex in the open air long forgotten. She is also visibly shaken and afraid. John holds her hand as they head back to the farm. This time she doesn't pull away from him. This time he's more relieved that she doesn't, and John doesn't holster his weapon again, either.

When they finally get to the rear of the hog barn, having followed the path that leads there, they run into Weird Willy- as Derek has nicknamed him, and Bobby, the young punk. John is instantly uneasy and does not put his pistol away. The two men are loitering suspiciously behind the barn.

"What are you two doing back here?" John barks angrily. He's on edge after the hectic encounter in the meadow. Bobby's eyes are dazed and there appears to be the tiny end of a smoked blunt stamped out at his feet.

"Nothin,' what's it to you?" Bobby expresses out with a bad attitude.

"I don't see apples in your hands, so I'd say you're where you shouldn't be, kid," John tells him with more force. Reagan stands quietly beside him. Bobby's eyes travel up and down the length of her curvy, small figure more than once.

"We was just havin' a smoke is all," Willy answers, offering the remnants of what is left of another marijuana joint.

Where had they hidden their drugs? John and Kelly had checked that RV from top to bottom and not found drugs. Of course they'd been looking for weapons, but surely they should've found drugs, too. If these people have been crafty enough to hide drugs and possibly alcohol, too, had they also hidden weapons? This thought unnerves John.

"No, we don't want your drugs!" Reagan screeches at him.

"You shouldn't be back here," John tells them the obvious. "Get back to your camp."

"Yeah? And who's gonna make us?" Bobby taunts. "You and little hot ass there?"

John cannot believe his ears. He wraps a protective arm around Reagan's waist.

"Excuse me?" John demands with righteous disbelief.

"Sweet peaches," Willy remarks with wild eyes and a big grin.

Reagan and John look at each other. What the heck is he talking about? What a freak.

"Hey, Doc, I think I'm sick. Can you help me with that?" Bobby asks.

The punk is speaking to Reagan, completely ignoring John. She steps closer to John. The kid is jeering her, but John doesn't find it appropriate. She is apparently not fond of this kid.

"I don't think so," she returns.

Is she afraid of Bobby? John knows of the confrontation between the two of them over Sam.

"Really? You're supposed to be a doctor, took an oath and shit to help the sick. I think I need a special serum," Bobby hints.

Reagan smirks and answers, "I don't have a magic serum for little dick syndrome."

286

Or perhaps she isn't afraid of him.

Willie laughs loudly, but John does not. He is too busy glaring at Bobby who is looking like he'd like to slap Reagan. It's the same look he's probably given Sam many times right before he did so.

"Peachy, just peachy peaches," Willy adds to no one in particular.

Does he even make sense in his own head, John wonders? He's now tapping his fingers against the side of his temple and muttering incoherently. Freakshow.

"You think you're funny, huh?" Bobby asks with a sudden coolness in his black eyes.

Cory was right in his assessment of this jerk. He is psychotic. And Willy is definitely nuts. He's mumbling to himself and bobbing his head in a strange, jerky motion.

"Sure, why not?" Reagan pushes. John's not about to stop her. This kid is a little creep who deserves her wrath if not just for Sam's defense.

"I can show you what I like to do with mouthy, little bitches like you," Bobby informs them both.

Molly growls beside John. Her hackles have risen again. She bares her top row of pointy, sharp teeth. Even she doesn't like this kid, and she likes most everyone. John clicks off the safety on his .45. However, Reagan stays his hand with a soft chuckle. She knows all too well what he's capable of.

"Don't you talk to her like that, you piece of shit," he swears heartily. It's against his religion, but John figures that the situation warrants it. Kelly was right. It does work more effectively sometimes.

Bobby just gives a smart aleck chortle to John before brushing past him. He doesn't apologize to Reagan, but neither does he say anything else.

"Gotta go pluck some peaches," Willy tells them.

They have no idea why he is talking about peaches. 'Weird Willy' is now the most apropos nickname ever given to someone.

Bobby turns back at the corner of the barn and says, "Have a nice time in that field?"

It takes John a second to figure out what he is talking about. The kid grins maliciously and turns away, walking back to their campsite at his leisure.

"Jesus, do you think..." Reagan asks but can't finish.

"I don't know," John says quietly, pensively.

"How else would he have known?"

"I don't know," John repeats, although he does know. He just doesn't want to frighten her further.

That punk and Willie had been in the woods. That was the reason Molly had growled. It's the same reason she'd just growled at them again. She was trying in her own way to let John know of their threat. How had Kelly, Cory or Simon not seen them leave? They'd probably sneaked away while they were supposed to be picking corn or apples.

"Come on," he tells Reagan and tugs her along back to the shed where he deposits her.

He finds the other men and discusses what has just happened. It's basically harmless, but the fact that it had happened means that they've let their guards down too much. He'd thanked God earlier for Huntley's speedy recovery when in fact he should've been thanking Him that the visitors will be leaving in two days. Reagan was right. They should've made them leave the same day they'd been told they were vacating the farm.

Chapter Twenty
Reagan

The next morning Huntley is finally back on his feet and back in the house where he can rest and be around the other kids again which he seems happy about. Grandpa and Grams have talked to the boy again about staying on at the farm, and according to them, the kid was more excited to leave his birth father than a boy should be.

Grams and Hannah are preparing the two packing crates full of food items for the visitors to take with them when they leave tomorrow, but it's still early in the day and breakfast has just wrapped. Reagan is standing near the center island holding Jacob and helping pack items into the crate, as well. She and Grandpa have also spent most of the morning before breakfast in the med shed sanitizing the building and filling two pill bottles with everything from antacids and out of date allergy medicine samples left at Grandpa's practice from pharmaceutical reps to cholesterol meds and children's vitamins. There was no way in hell they were giving those creeps out there the real antibiotics and painkillers. It had actually been Grandpa's idea to put fake meds in the bottles, but when Reagan had tried to laugh and praise him, he'd only ignored her. It is still funny. She can't wait to tell John later. Why he is the first one she wants to tell anything to is still beyond her. But she can't get enough of him... or the sex.

Annoyingly, Reagan has a hard time accomplishing simple tasks because her damned, traitorous mind keeps slinking back to the memories of his hands on her body, his mouth on hers and on her body, and, in general, everything about him. She's never felt like this or been so distracted by another person in her life. They'd somehow found the time to have sex three more times in the last few days, though there was still work to be done and chores to manage. John's pursuit, his unbridled, unstoppable pursuit of her was relentless, and he never took no for an answer from her. However, she honestly hadn't put up much of a fight.

"What does this "B" stand for, Mrs. McClane?" Simon asks as he sets a fourth jar of peaches at the bottom of the crate.

Reagan startles out of her trance about John and his stomach muscles and perfect biceps and his many other perfect parts.

"Never you mind, Simon, and call me Grams. I've already told you that," Grams says and places two jars of green beans in the crate, as well.

"Sorry, ma'am," the redhead apologizes, avoiding eye contact.

Reagan rolls her eyes. What a dork. Reagan looks at the jars of peaches at the bottom of the crate and sees the "B" of which Simon speaks. It is a single letter written on the top of the metal lid in black permanent marker. That is strange.

"Do you need any more help, Grams?" Cory asks impatiently.

Grams sends them on their way. Simon and Cory take off for the barn and also to retrieve Sam who wants to ride a morning patrol with them. Reagan knows the two teens really just want to get out for a ride through the fall foliage, and she doesn't blame them. Grams goes off to collect a few more canned goods and some of the store-bought items that they don't need anyways that they have been packing into the crates as filler.

Hannah is humming for which Reagan can only guess why, though it seems like lately Kelly is ignoring her sister a lot. But nothing ever gets her insanely cheerful sister down. Reagan moves to the other side of the island to stand next to her.

"Where's Sue?" Reagan asks as Jacob lays his fuzzy head on her shoulder.

"Oh, she took Sam out to the greenhouse with her. She wanted to learn about the plants and how our greenhouse worked. She's such a nice girl," Hannah remarks.

"Looks like her lesson is gonna get cut short because the boys are taking her for a ride. And, Hannie, you think everyone's nice. Hell, you'd probably let those morons out there stay if we hadn't wanted to throw them out," Reagan tells her. Hannah slides her hand toward Reagan on the counter, finds her and takes Jacob, giving him a big kiss on his smushy cheek which he returns to Hannah with a fistful of slobber.

"Oh, no. They have to go. Kelly said they were a threat to our farm, so they do need to go," Hannah says firmly.

Reagan about drops to the deck.

"That's the meanest thing you've ever said, Hannie," Reagan remarks. "Maybe Kelly isn't such a bad influence on you after all."

"Well that one lady Jasmine seems kind of nice, so I sort of feel bad that she has to leave," Hannah says naively.

"You wouldn't if you saw the way she looks at the men around here, Kelly included," Reagan says.

"Oh? And why would you care how anyone looks at the men?" she asks with more intuition than a blind girl should have.

"I don't!" Reagan retorts quickly, too quickly.

The screen door slams behind her as John strides through it with a mega-watt smile and deep dimples. His damned good looks are sometimes irritating. His black t-shirt is a size too small for him and clings to his chest and stomach. Beggars can't be choosers in this new world where the local mall is likely now a local homeless shelter full of people meaning anyone or everyone harm who might wish to come there and do a little Saturday afternoon retail therapy for the latest fashion trends. His hair, which badly needs another trimming, is sun-kissed with light golden streaks. And the face? If Reagan stops to think about the severe cut of his angular jaw, the stubble there or the high cheekbones, she'll never get anything done.

"Reagan I need your help in the… cattle barn," he says and gives her a strange look and a cocky grin.

"Um, ok," Reagan agrees as he takes her hand because there is nobody around to see, and she's not even sure that he would care. But she sure as hell would. Luckily for John, every member of the McClane tribe is otherwise engaged with work, patrols or in the basement digging out useless junk to give to the visitors in exchange for their children. Derek and Kelly are overseeing the morons so that they don't try to steal the farm blind. So far the morning has been rather subdued, but, then again, it is only 9:30.

"I'll watch Jacob. Just go," Hannah says.

Her sister is sweet-talking to the baby who giggles back at her. Reagan is fairly sure that the kid is going to be a spoiled brat.

"Ok, let me just get my shoes and I'll meet you there," Reagan tells him as he leaves but not before he brushes her top lip with his thumb and kisses Jacob's forehead. It's strange how the men at the farm kiss and cuddle on the kids. She had even seen Kelly swinging Justin around and around in wide circles in the yard the other day, and he isn't even his uncle, not technically.

A few minutes later, Reagan is in the cattle barn searching for John. It would've been easier if he would've told her exactly where he needs help, but instead she's forced to search him out. Once she gets to the rear, older part of the barn where the cattle can come in out of the weather, a hand shoots out and grabs her wrist which makes her scream. It's only him, though.

"What the hell? You scared the…" she starts but is cut off as his mouth swoops down to take hers in a staggering kiss. He guides her backward until she is against the smooth, worn wood of the barn wall as he continues to ravage her mouth.

When he finally lifts his mouth from hers, she is gasping for air and has one leg hooked around his muscular thigh in a wanton manner. Reagan's hands slide up his chest, and she would like to rip his too-tight shirt to shreds. Why is it that she feels like this about him? Is this even normal? It sure seems abnormal, but it isn't as if she can discuss it with any of her family members, especially not her grandparents who'd raised the girls to believe in abstinence before marriage. She knows that when Sue had married Derek she'd been a virgin because she'd told Reagan as much.

And when John's hands are on her, it is like nothing she's ever experienced in her life, and it leaves her wanting more, wanting him. Her body is beginning to crave his touch, and when he does touch her, she can't breathe. But with John she doesn't feel the anxiety she normally feels when someone else touches her.

"What was that about?" Reagan asks. "What did you need me for?"

"That," he answers easily and grins down at her. "I just missed you. I've been watching the losers all morning, and it was getting old so I'm taking a break. Thought I'd check out the washroom in this barn. Wanna' help?"

He is obviously lying. They don't need to check out the washroom. He is trying to get her off alone.

"What? Are you serious? I have things I need to be doing," Reagan complains half-heartedly as she's actually having a hard time remembering what those things are.

John moves his hands to the wall on either side of her head and proceeds to kiss her neck, her ear, the base of her throat above her long-sleeved, button down, flannel shirt. It's nearly October, and the mild weather of the summer is almost at an end. The nights are cooler and damp, and the days take longer and longer to warm enough to where she can wear a tank top.

Reagan yanks him to her using her leg as her hands clutch at the front of his soft, worn cotton shirt. He seems a bit more oblivious of the cooler weather than she is, but it also gives her more opportunity to look at his body. John's fingers dip into the neckline of her shirt, and with one hand, he unfastens the top three buttons. She doesn't want to think about where he's developed this particular skill. He sinks his hand inside and cups her breast as his mouth moves on hers again. When he pulls back, she moans against the strained tendons of his neck.

"I love you," he whispers raggedly against her open mouth.

She hates it when he says this. It seems contrived, unbelievable. She'd like to explain endorphins, chemical reactions in the brain and physical attraction versus the ridiculous love thing to him, but she doesn't want him to stop kissing her, either. So instead, she does a small hop and is straddling him with her legs wrapped tightly around his waist. His hands move under her to support her weight. He slides them onto her bottom as he grinds himself against her, making her mad with need for him.

"We need a crib," John says.

"What?" Reagan asks him, furrowing her brow as she kisses the base of his throat. Why the hell is he talking about Jacob right now? Talk about a possible mood killer.

"I want him out of your bed and me in it," John tells her gutturally.

His mouth moves against her neck as he lifts her further into the air. Then he presses his mouth to her breast through her shirt.

He murmurs, "We have to make a run after they leave. I want to sleep *with* you, not near you."

"Yes," Reagan answers, sort of. What had he even said? She is mostly saying 'yes, don't stop what you're doing,' but he doesn't know this.

"And a high-chair so we don't have to hold him while we eat and get slopped on," John remarks as he kisses her neck.

Seriously? Is he going to go through the whole damn shopping list with her right now?

"High-chair, crib, got it," she repeats impatiently and John chuckles against her mouth.

She slides her hand between them to press against his erection. "Oh my God!" Reagan screeches and freezes.

"You haven't said that before," John jokes with a chuckle and pulls back. "I mean, I know it's kinda' big, but you already knew that…"

"What? Shut up. That isn't why I said that, stupid," she says meanly but doesn't care. He just chuckles at her again. "I was going to tell you where we could get a crib and a high-chair."

"Ok," he says with confusion as she squirms vigorously against him.

"Put me down. John, put me down now," she says in a rush, and he instantly sets her gently to her feet. Reagan walks away from him and starts pacing.

"Honey, what is it?" he asks with concern.

John puts a hand on her shoulder which she shrugs off. She needs to think for a second.

"Reagan, you're scaring me. Talk to me."

She paces back and forth ten or so feet and then stops, staring off to the side. John comes to stand directly in front of her and places both hands on her shoulders this time.

"Reagan?"

"That's it. I knew it. I *knew*. Come on. We need to go somewhere," she blurts as John still just looks at her with a blank expression.

"Babe, super genius, tell me what's going on," John asks of her. "You knew what? Ya' kinda' know just about everything, sweetie, so you gotta fill the rest of us in when you do this."

He strokes her cheek lightly, but Reagan knocks his hand away.

294

"We need to go back to that house. Take me. Take me there now," she demands. Frustratingly, John stands there looking confused. Reagan shakes her hands at him with exasperation.

She tries to speak more slowly, but her mind is buzzing, "That house. That house in the expensive... you know, the family? In the barn? The family that was executed in that fancy horse barn?" she asks so that he can get on the same page, and he finally nods. "Take me there, now, John. Please."

"Honey, we can't go anywhere right now. We need to stay here until those people leave," John tries to persuade her.

"No!" she says loudly. "We need to go there right now. It's important."

"Honey, I'll take you there tomorrow or the day after when these hadj are far away from here," John says and takes her hand in his as if appeasing a child.

"No!" Reagan says forcefully and yanks her hand free. She doesn't have time for this, for this pointless arguing. "Fine, I'll take myself."

"Whoa, no way, babe. Not happening. When they leave..."

"John, we may not be able to *let* them leave if I'm right about this," Reagan says with prophetic sincerity. John frowns down at her.

"Ok, ok. Let me tell the guys and get my rifle and the radio," John tells her and grabs her hand again.

After collecting extra guns and two radios, they run into Derek and Kelly near the horse barn entrance, and John explains the situation.

"No way," Derek protests. "Nobody is to be leaving the farm until those creeps are gone. Tomorrow morning you can go after they've left if it's that important."

"No, Derek. I need to go *now*," Reagan argues vehemently.

"I gotta take her, bro," John explains.

His brother sighs heavily and hangs his head for a moment. Kelly stands quietly awaiting a decision.

"How long are you going to be gone so I know when to come looking for you two?" Derek asks apprehensively.

He's made it quite clear that he doesn't like this. John looks to Reagan who holds a shotgun and is wearing her pistol on her thigh.

"We'll be back within an hour," she relays and heads for the pick-up truck.

Ten minutes later, after John has disabled the wiring on the driveway demos, they are driving at a fast pace down their gravel road that leads to the county road which houses the suburban properties. They are not obeying seatbelt laws and speed limit restrictions. Though John has not asked her again as to why they need to go to that house, he trusts her enough to just drive her there and not bombard her with any more questions about it. His absolute trust in her scares the shit out of Reagan and awakens something that she pushes down, deep down where she won't have to examine it too closely. When they turn onto the street where the executive homes were located, John slows down so that they can get a better look.

"I'm not even sure which one it was," John says with a confused expression marring his features.

Reagan can understand why because the weeds and native fescue have grown even taller than they were the first time they came. The trees have lost some of their leaves and have turned to fall reds, browns and oranges.

"There! It's that one with the circular drive and the horse fence," Reagan tells him as she points it out, and John pulls slowly down the driveway, coming to a stop near the house.

"Wait here for a second so I can check it out, make sure we're alone," John tells her.

He briefly places his hand on her thigh. Within a few minutes, he's back at her door which he opens.

He declares, "We're good. Nobody's around. I don't think there's anyone around for miles."

Reagan wastes no time and sprints up the front steps to the sophisticated mansion and through the stately front door that hangs dramatically off kilter on its one, solitary remaining hinge.

"Come on. Up here," Reagan says and runs up the stairs as John follows with his pistol drawn just in case and then takes the lead.

They pass the nursery again with the double set of cribs for the twin babies that once lived here, the room that had left her feeling depressed. Reagan squeezes past John as they traverse the long hall. The next room belonged to a girl.

She calls over her shoulder, "John, in here."

John enters first and looks around. It's dustier than the first time they were here, and Reagan was the only one who'd come up to this floor to raid for items while the men shopped the first floor. She goes straight to the dresser and picks up the photo of the girl and her friends and then the one of her standing next to her chestnut horse with her prize ribbon so proudly displayed. She's smiling ear to ear, showing her bright white, straight teeth. She's exuberant, elated with joy. Her big blue eyes shine with merriment.

"Look," Reagan orders and hands one to John.

He regards it pensively, and Reagan waits until it clicks for him.

"What? Why are you… oh, my God," John says. "It's Sam. This is Samantha, isn't it?"

Reagan nods. His blue eyes take on a deadly calm. He nods solemnly, but there is something dark coming over his features. She's seen this before.

"I knew I recognized her when we first met their group, but I couldn't put my finger on it," Reagan explains while she paces. "Plus we've been so damn busy I didn't have *time* to think about it. Look! Her hair used to be really long. She said she cut it off herself with a knife or something. Then she wore that riding academy shirt and she told us about her uncle in Nashville. Last week, she wore a shirt for a private school and I thought I recognized it as being a school near Clarksville. That must've been where she went to school. The signs were all there, John."

"Yeah, I guess they were. We just weren't looking closely enough."

"She also does weird shit like not brushing her hair and looking dirty all the time. I think she used to do it on purpose to make herself ugly. You know, before we let them stay with us? She doesn't do it anymore because I think she feels safe now. John, I think Bobby's been raping her," she says. John's eyes jump to hers and now they seem murderous. Reagan can hardly continue her explanation, but she also knows that he needs this information. "She's also had bruises on her that I've seen. On her face, on her arms. It just all started nagging at the back of my mind. But then I remembered earlier where we could get a high-chair and a crib for

Jacob because I remembered seeing the twin bedroom next to this one. And it just clicked and I knew this was where I'd seen her."

"Come on," he states.

John stashes Sam's photo in his pocket and tugs Reagan by the hand.

He says, "I'm glad you remembered this. And now I need to check out that murder scene in the barn again."

Reagan furrows her brow at him but follows along to the horse barn behind the house.

"Cover your mouth and nose, Reagan," John instructs her.

He wouldn't have had to because the smell is even worse than it had been before, probably because of the decaying horses. Reagan gags once.

They trek down the wide, center aisle to the back of the barn where John leaves her near a stall. He turns the corner toward the area where the dead bodies were in the earlier stages of decomposition. He comes back a moment later and holds out his hand, palm up which contains two different spent bullet casings.

"This is a .22 shell and this one's a 9 mill," John tells her and Reagan's eye flit to his. "They're all over the ground back there."

"What does that mean? I don't understand."

"Those two pistols we took off the hadj were a 9 mill Glock and a .22 caliber Colt," John explains.

He tugs her arm and they sprint to the truck.

"Do you think it's possible?" Reagan asks even though she knows it already. She knew it when she'd realized who Sam was and where she'd seen her before, but she hadn't wanted to vocalize it. The ramifications of this are too great to believe.

"No, I don't think it's possible. I think it's probable. That's why they've got Sam and definitely why she doesn't answer our questions. It's probably how Jennifer ended up with them and maybe Jasmine, too," John explains.

They speed along the county road and make a hard left to travel back toward their farm.

"Who do you think did it? All of them? Even Peter?" Reagan asks with a great deal of worry. "I mean I don't think Grams's dipshit brother Peter would be capable of murder."

"Really?" John proposes with a huge amount of doubt.

298

Reagan nods and frowns deeply. She replies softly, "Right. They are probably all cut from the same cloth."

"We're about to find out," John tells her.

When they arrive, she and John immediately find Derek at the front porch. He sits near Sue and Isaac while he keeps an eye on the visitors. John wastes no time getting straight to the point, and all traces of his good humor and charm are gone, replaced with nearly unbridled anger and malice.

"We have a problem," John tells his older brother who is on instant high alert.

"What's going on, John? Why the hell did you guys have to leave? What did you find?" Derek questions in rapid fire succession.

"Where's Sam?" John asks.

"She went riding with Cory and Simon. They should be back in a little bit, though, John," Sue answers.

Her sister is trying to keep her voice hopeful and light. But she does stand with baby Isaac, sensing the tension.

"Where's everyone else?" John demands.

"The grandparents are in the study and Hannah's in the back yard with the kids," Sue says in a rush.

"Sue, in a minute take the kids, Hannah and Grams inside when I leave here, and tell Doc to stay by the front door. Keep the whole house locked and don't come out till we come for you," John orders with enough grit that it scares Sue.

"Dude, what's goin' on?" Derek asks with apprehension in his brown eyes.

"I think those hadj scum killed Sam's family and took her. We found this picture of her," Reagan explains.

John digs in his pocket and hands the picture of Sam with her former girlfriends to Sue and Derek to study. The girl is wearing the same shirt with the logo for Fox Run Academy that she'd worn around Reagan while working in the shed. She'd been right about it when she had thought it was a school near Clarksville.

"Son of a bitch," Derek says on an exhale of exasperation.

John tells his brother, "Reagan recognized her from when we raided that house in the burbs. That really big house where the family was… in the barn? That was Sam's house. That was Sam's family."

"They've killed her family and taken her against her will, Sue," Reagan elucidates further.

"Oh my God, Derek," Sue exclaims, and her sister's eyes tear up. "No wonder she's so scared of them."

"It's also why she won't talk about her family or talk about those assholes out there, either," Reagan explains. Reagan can only imagine the horrors that Sam has had to endure from those people. Have the men been raping her? Has Bobby?

"They've probably warned her not to say anything to us," Derek figures.

His brow is furrowed in such a severe way that Reagan is starting to wonder just how alike he and his brother are. Is he also capable like John of murdering people who might harm them?

"Shell casings near the bodies match the guns we took from them. They might not be planning on leaving without a fight, after all. They might not be leaving," John says with cold intent.

"Yeah," Derek says simply.

He's a man of few words, but Reagan suspects he's a man of action when he needs to be.

"Where's all the hadj? Some of them are missing," John observes as he glances toward their camp.

How had he counted them up so fast? Reagan can hardly even keep track of them most of the time.

"Some of them are picking corn, and some are out in the apple orchard getting apples," Derek explains.

"Looks like the ones that we don't want out of our sights are the ones who are," John notes.

His brother nods solemnly. Reagan sees the two women, Great-uncle Peter and the skinny, tattooed guy named Buzz hanging around the camp. They appear to be packing. The stripper is milking the goat. The other five are missing.

"Sue, go. Go now. Give Isaac to Grams and go get the kids," Derek tells her.

Her brother-in-law sends Sue inside. Her sister looks worried sick. Reagan is also becoming so.

"We need to go find those teenagers, Reagan," John tells her as she nods in agreement. "Don't do anything till we get back with them and can talk to Sam, ok?"

"Right," Derek agrees with a nod. "We don't know who out there is responsible or if *all* of them are."

John nods and adds, "We'll go on horseback and try to meet up with them, get them back here."

"I'll find Kelly and get the hadj all rounded up," Derek says.

The two men nod in agreement, bump fists and separate.

Reagan and John dash for the horse barn. He is unusually quiet as she grabs Harry out of his stall, and John catches a high-spirited gelding from the pasture that he's never ridden. His usual mount is gone, probably with Cory or Simon since she's so well trained. Within minutes they have them saddled and ready to go. They take off at a fast trot and then break into a canter when they are clear of the farm. This day has quickly turned from good to bad. She'd been glad the visitors were leaving. Now they may need to stop them from doing so. As they ride, the situation begins to feel more and more desperate.

Chapter Twenty-one
Hannah

"Miss Hannah?" Huntley asks as he tugs at her dress.

"Yes, Huntley? Did you have fun seeing the baby goats?" she asks because he and Justin have just come from there. She is with Em, Ari and Jacob on the swings. Jacob squeals happily as she pushes him gently in the baby swing.

"Uh, sure," he answers.

"Why's your face red on the side?" Em asks Huntley presumably.

"Uh, I fell," Huntley says strangely. "I just tripped and fell."

"Where's Justin?" Hannah asks when she does not hear her nephew's normal rambunctious activity.

"He went to the house to get a snack," Huntley explains. "Miss Hannah?"

"Oh, yes, Huntley?"

"I need to…," he says but doesn't finish.

Hannah wishes she could see the boy's face. "Yes?"

"Kelly wants to see you in the hog barn."

"He does?" Hannah asks with surprise. Why would he want her to walk all the way out there? It is the furthest barn from the house, near the apple orchard, and the terrain is difficult for her.

"Uh, yeah. He said to hurry," Huntley says quickly.

"Oh, well then I'd better go. Em, can you take Jacob and Ari to Sue for me, honey?" she asks of the girl.

"Sure, Hannah. Come on, Huntley. We can play tag in the front yard after I give Jacob to Sue," Em says gleefully.

The lightness in Em's voice fills Hannah's heart with joy. She feels that maybe, just maybe Em will eventually find happiness again.

Hannah takes her cane and starts across the yard and then enters the paddock. When she is almost to the cattle barn, Hannah can hear Sue calling to the kids. They will just have to explain to her sister where she's going.

She trips three times but manages not to fall before she gets to the entrance of the hog barn. Poking her stick around in front of her, Hannah finds the man door and goes through it. She hates this barn. It smells like the pigs, it's always unfamiliar to her, and there's equipment in the center aisle that she never fails to bang her knees and thighs on.

"Kelly?" she calls softly. "Kelly, I'm here."

Suddenly, her cane is flung roughly away from her as if someone has kicked it. It's enough to startle her, and she lets out a yelp.

"Kelly?" she says with growing trepidation. Kelly would never throw or kick her cane from her.

"No, not Kelly. That's a faggoty name, you ask me," says a man's voice from behind her.

Hannah swallows hard. This is bad. This is really, really bad. This is the kind of stupid mistake that Reagan would yell at her for. The hairs on the back of her neck stand on end.

"Who's there?" she asks and hates how cowardly she sounds.

"Don't be scared. It's just me. It's Willy. Remember?"

Hannah has no idea who this man is. He's obviously one of those men from the camp, but she's not sure why she should know him.

He continues, "You brought me peaches. Sweet, sweet peaches. I bet you're a sweet peach, too, aren't you?"

"You're welcome for the peaches, but I need to get back to my family now," Hannah says and turns to leave but runs into the barn wall with her outstretched hands. Where is Kelly?

She didn't give this man peaches or anyone in their group peaches for that matter. She isn't exactly sure what he is talking about. She can tell by his accent that this is the Mexican man that Kelly's told her to stay away from when they get their water because he's strange.

"You don't need to run off, peach," Willy tells her in a creepy lilt.

Hannah has a dreadful feeling come over her. Kelly isn't here. He doesn't know she's out here, either. She's on her own.

"No, I do. They'll wonder where I am," Hannah says and slides her hand along the wall to find her way back out of the barn. "It was nice talking with you, but I should go. Good-bye."

"I said you don't need to run off!" he shouts with anger.

His tone scares Hannah. She continues to slide her hand along the rough, wooden wall.

"No, no. I really need to go," she tries to convince him.

"Get back here, bitch!" he retorts with evil venom and intent.

Willy grabs her from behind right as she is about to go back through the door she's found again. He hefts her off of the ground with one arm around her waist and carries her as she thrashes to be free. She can tell that he is not particularly tall, because her feet drag the ground from time to time. But he is much stronger than her.

"Stop!" she cries out feebly. "Please, stop this, sir! My family will be looking for me!"

"Shut your mouth," he warns with menace, not sounding at all like he had earlier.

They are moving toward the back of the barn where Hannah is not sure of her surroundings. Her leg bangs painfully into a piece of metal, probably machinery as she cries out and jerks free. Her captor drops her, and she tries to crawl away but runs her head into a wall or something before Willy is back on her again. He is carrying her farther into the barn. And he is laughing cruelly at her.

He charges forward, ignoring her pain and Hannah is flung roughly to the ground where she slides a few feet on her hands and knees. Her hands scrape painfully against the rough floor, and she bangs her head into something again, perhaps another wall and more forcefully this time. A slow, wet trickle begins running down her forehead, and Hannah knows that she is bleeding from hitting so hard. She touches her trembling fingertips to her head momentarily and pulls them away with her own wet blood coating them. She feels dizzy enough to vomit.

"Oh, peach. Oh, I didn't mean to do that."

Why is he suggesting that he didn't mean to do that? Of course he had. He'd done it on purpose. This man is irrational and crazy, and she needs to get away from him. His pleasant but more frightening voice is back.

"Listen to me, peach. Don't fight with me and that won't happen, ok?" Willy says in a bizarre placating tone. "You're such a peach, such a sweet thing."

Willy grasps Hannah's calf and forcefully yanks her backward toward him on her belly, and Hannah tries to grasp onto something, anything to prevent having to be close to him. Her fingernails scrape on the barn floor and some break painfully. His grip is so hard on her calf that Hannah has no doubt that she'll be bruised terribly. She also knows that if she doesn't get away from him, that a bruise on her leg will be the least of her worries, or injuries. She is vaguely aware that she is softly repeating the mantra "no, no, no" as if that will help her situation. How could she have been so foolish?

"See, I'm just supposed to get you so we can use the women to get what we want from the men. You were supposed to be our hostages. Then when your men give up their guns, yeah, we're going to kill them. But we ain't gonna kill any of you women. No way," Willy explains.

The disturbing man has an even stranger, creepier voice. He is certifiable. No man acts like this. Hannah reaches out and slices open the length of her palm on some jagged, sharp thing, which is probably metal sticking out of a grain bin or piece of farm machinery. She cries out against the pain in her palm. The man either doesn't notice or care.

"We're going to run this place. I'll be a king and you'll be my peach. Right, peach? We'll run this place right, the way it should be."

"Let me go," she pleads as Willy drags her the rest of the way to him and flips her onto her back causing Hannah to crack her head on the hard floor. She immediately starts striking out with her hands, and Willy lands a solid slap across her cheek which stuns her. He presses himself down onto her so that she cannot get away.

"No, peach. That was all your fault, ok? Ok, lovey? I told you not to do that. See? We're friends again. Right, peach?" Willy asks in all his insane glory.

His breath is foul. Hannah nods shakily as tears run down beside her face and disappear into her hairline. Her head is screaming with a severe migraine already. She's hoping that the man will stop hurting her if she doesn't keep fighting. He doesn't.

Willy rips the top of Hannah's dress as he starts talking to himself in an unusual gibberish that doesn't make any sense. Then he goes back to actually speaking to her as he roughly holds her down by her shoulder.

"We have us some time before they get back with that little senorita and kill off those boys in the woods. Little senorita Sam. She was a fighter, too, till Bobby got to her. He's young, but he's a good trainer. He's good at training dogs. You can be my dog, my little puppy."

"Please don't hurt Kelly. Please don't hurt my family," Hannah begs for her lover's life. Willy slaps her again, and Hannah figures it is probably best not to speak anymore because this man cannot be reasoned with.

"See? You don't learn, peach. But you will. I'm gonna train you like Bobby trained the girl. I tried to warn you not to act like that. You're going to be my girl, my good girl. Everyone else got a girl but not me. I need a new girl, too. You'll be my girl," Willy tells her.

He places his thick hand on her thigh over her dress.

"I can't be your anything. I'm with Kelly. We're together. I love him," Hannah tries a different tactic, only to receive more brutal treatment. His voice lowers in register as if he's become another person again.

"Shut your mouth! You'll love *me*! My girlfriends never love me. They never make it, either. They get bad. They go bad, just like my whore wife did. Then I have to discipline them, and they usually die. I don't know why they're so weak."

He starts back up with the incoherent babbling which is infinitely more frightening than the horrible words he says that she can understand. Hannah resorts to praying for her family instead of trying to reason with this criminally-minded, crazy man. They should've never let any of these people onto their farm. Why would her Great-uncle Peter even hang out with people like this? Hannah's not sure she wants to know.

Hannah is frightened out of her mind. This man is probably going to kill her. She will likely not make it to the negotiation phase of their plan. He's irrational and the things he says are so senseless that she's beginning to wonder at the kind of man he was before the apocalypse. Could he have been a serial killer? A rapist? Had he killed his wife?

306

He's still rambling above her and his hands move to her breasts, so harshly handling them that Hannah starts crying in earnest. Willy shoves her legs apart. He grinds himself against her between her legs.

"You motherfucker!" comes a deep, guttural voice behind Willy.

A splatter of something liquid hits her bare chest and neck as a primal grunt follows from the new assailant. Then Willy's body is yanked off of hers in one solid swoop.

"You think you can touch her? Fuck you, you creepy motherfucker!"

There are two punching type sounds and then gurgling sounds coming from Willy and then no sounds.

Hannah can hear him being dragged away from the scraping, shuffling sounds that come from the outer hall area. She pushes to a sitting position and scoots back on her bottom until she reaches the wall. Her hands reach behind her as she braces for another attack.

"Hannah," Kelly's voice comes through the dark to reach her.

Instinctively her hands extend outward, searching safety, searching Kelly. His deep voice has returned to the normal softness that Hannah has come to love. The voice she'd just heard had not sounded at all like her Kelly.

"Hannah, baby."

He pulls her up into his arms, and she clings limply to him crying and sobbing.

"Kelly!" she says on a gasp of relief. "Where is he?" she asks in fright.

"Baby, hold still for a sec," he orders to which she complies. "He's gone. You're safe now."

"What are you doing?" she asks in a panic as he moves away from her. Her hands, her legs, everything on her is shaking terribly.

"Getting a rag. You have blood on your face and neck," he explains and returns a second later.

He wipes roughly at her face and then neck and backs away from her again.

"Don't leave me!" she cries out.

"I'm not, Hannah. Come here," he says and pulls her to her feet.

Her legs can barely support her, they shake so badly. Her head is blaring with pain, and she feels like she's going to throw up from it. When she reaches out, his chest is bare.

"Put this on. Here, let me help you, baby."

Kelly pulls his shirt down over Hannah's head and helps her get her arms through the arm holes.

"I could see...," he says and stops.

She knows that her breasts and bra are showing where Willy had ripped her dress and that Kelly doesn't want to embarrass her further. Once he gets the shirt on, he fiercely hugs her to him.

"God, Hannah. When I couldn't find you I went crazy. Are you alright? I'm so sorry, baby."

"Where's... where's that man?" she asks with true terror.

"He's dead, baby. I killed him. You're safe now. He can't hurt you. I'm sorry it took me so long to find you. I'm sorry. This is all my fault. You're safe again, Hannah," he tells her and squeezes her to his chest.

Hannah nods and wraps her arms around him as Kelly holds her upright. Her voice quakes and threatens to crack when she speaks again.

"Kelly, they planned this. They are trying to kidnap us women or ransom us or something and then kill you men. They must have had Huntley tell me to come to the barn because he said you were out here and needed me," Hannah says in a rush.

Her head is spinning from hitting the floor, and the wound on her forehead is trickling blood again. Her mouth hurts just to talk from where Willy hit her twice, and she can taste blood. Kelly pulls back, skimming his hands lightly around on her face, her arms, checking her, Hannah's sure. He swears profusely at whatever he is seeing.

"We knew something was up. Derek's guarding the ones that we could find, and we knew when we couldn't find some of them that something was wrong. Their women and your uncle and that Frank asshole are up at the camp. And I found Rick out in the apple orchard right before I heard about you. That's what took me so long to get to you. I had to walk from the apple orchard with him up to the camp and then back to the house to check on you. That's when I found out you weren't there. And then Huntley told me that this Willy freak hit him and told him to tell you I was out here. If I hadn't

308

come back to the house to check on you, Jesus, I don't know what would've happened, Hannah. Reagan and John are out in the woods looking for the teenagers because there's a problem with them, too. Those people killed Sam's family and John's looking for her in the woods. She's riding with Cory and Simon. But we need to talk to her to find out more information about these bastards," he tells her and pulls her gently with him.

Then he just sweeps her up into his arms. When they go a few feet Kelly takes a giant step, and Hannah believes that he is probably stepping over the body of Willy.

"How?" Hannah asks when they reach the pasture where Kelly carries her at a faster walking pace.

"How what, honey?" he asks quietly as if he is trying to be.

"How did you kill him?" she asks and holds onto Kelly's shoulders tightly because now her beloved farm is not even safe from danger. They've allowed predators onto it.

"Baby, you don't need to know that," he tells her rather firmly.

Hannah knows that he won't tell her. Probably ever.

When they get to the house, Kelly carries her through the kitchen door and sets her softly to her feet. Grandpa is so upset over the state of what she looks like that Hannah is genuinely afraid he'll have a heart attack. He says a lot of swear words under his breath, but Grams doesn't reprimand him for it.

"Most of that blood on her isn't hers, Doc. Please, get it off of her quickly. It's from that damn, crazy Willy," Kelly tells her Grandpa. "Her hand is cut open. I think she hit her head or that bastard hit her because she seems unfocused. She could have a concussion...," her lover's voice cracks.

He moves away from her and the rest of the family, closer to the back door again if she hears correctly. Hannah hates for him to be so upset. She can hear water being run at the sink.

"Oh, Hannah," Sue says. "Are you all right?"

"I'm ok. Kelly saved me," Hannah says between sobs.

"I almost didn't," Kelly says with guilt.

He is very angry with himself. On the contrary, Hannah is very thankful for him.

"You did, Kelly. That's all that matters. I'll take care of her, son. Go now. Get out there with Derek," Grandpa tells him.

He assures Kelly once more that she'll be just fine because Kelly is reluctant to leave her. Her love touches her arm lightly. Sue wraps an arm around her shoulder for support. Hannah is more than glad for it.

Her lover leaves to look for the other missing men in the visitors' group, and Grandpa relocks the back door to the house with a fateful click.

Chapter Twenty-two
John

They move as quickly as they can on horseback on the steep hillsides, up one and down another and then canter across the high pasture to where the forest begins again. John leads the way into the woods and has to slow his gelding down multiple times. The horse is rambunctious, but one of the teenagers has taken his favorite mare. He's having trouble keeping this one under control. The gelding is obviously feeding off of John's tension. But he just has one of those tingling, hair-on-the-back-of-his-neck feelings and in the military those feelings were never wrong. These are the instincts that had kept him alive in dangerous situations.

"If the kids went the other way like Derek said, then we're heading in the right direction. I think we should meet up with them any minute," Reagan tells him.

But she doesn't need to do so because John knows these woods so well now.

"I think so, too," he says mostly to appease her. "Don't worry. We'll find them. Everything's gonna be fine."

This is another conciliation because John has his doubts, though he won't tell her this. These men have been wanting a fight, and they sure as heck don't want to leave the farm. He should've known the other day, when Frank had easily given up their argument of staying, that these people weren't leaving without a fight. And if John is right about it, then Frank is the one behind all of it. He's afraid to even consider that Grams's brother Peter is also manipulating this set of circumstances they're all in.

"Let's go through here," John says as they head north on a dry creek bed. His horse tosses its head impatiently.

"Ok, this will short cut us to the other trail that the kids probably took," Reagan calls to him.

They ride a few more minutes while John fights near constantly to keep his gelding under control. Even Reagan's horse is more excitable than what is normal. John just wants to find the three teenagers and get back to the farm so that they can talk to Sam with Grams and Doc present. And if she confirms that these people have killed her family and kept her captive all this time, then the men will have to take care of the visitors. They will have to take care of them the way that they take care of any terrorists they've ever encountered.

They are riding through a deep ravine encased by tall hills when John's horse spooks- very badly.

"John!" Reagan screams.

Her horse sidesteps about a million miles an hour, startling and stumbling sideways. Somehow it manages to stay upright. Crazily, Reagan is still in the saddle but is half on the side of Harry who doesn't like his rider's new position.

Simultaneously John's flighty gelding lets out a bone-chilling scream and rears, and he rears high, nearly falling over backward. John knows he isn't coming down the same way he went up because the horse has himself half on a hill and twisted. And as the horse falls onto its side, John sees hadj three with the amber eyes and the dirty dreadlocks coming out of the woods. He hears Reagan scream his name again, and there is nothing he can do as the horse falls hard and lands on John's leg, pinning him to the ground. He's upside down, angled going downhill. The pain in his hip is excruciating as the eight hundred pound horse crushes and grinds himself into his thigh and hip, unsuccessfully trying to right itself. If the beast decides to roll, John will be crushed and maybe even killed. Obviously horses were the good watch dogs that Reagan had once informed him of months earlier this summer. John just hadn't read the signs of their distress correctly because the animals has sensed an ambush was afoot. They'd likely heard people in the forest around them.

Harry runs in front of John's gelding. The horse is not carrying Reagan anymore, but John can hear her cussing and screaming. Somebody's got her. John's vision is blurry. He's not sure if he hit his head when he went down, but he feels like he got his bell

312

rung pretty good. He's been shell-shocked before from grenades and mortar fire, so he knows the feeling well.

The gelding tries once, twice and finally gets to his feet, using John as leverage and, more importantly, John's leg. Unfortunately, when the animal is back on its hooves, John's boot is hung up in the stirrup. Levon advances on him, jumping over a fallen tree. His menacing, fast approach is frightening John's horse even worse, though, and it bolts about twenty feet. The animal is dragging John through foliage, rocks and sticks that scrape his back and side as they go until it finally decides to stop. His foot finally comes free of the stirrup as the horse bucks once trying to rid itself of its fallen rider. John rolls to his side and springs up onto his haunches just in time to take a punch square to the jaw by Levon. Reagan screams again as John spits blood.

"Leave him alone, you asshole...," Reagan yells.

In John's peripheral vision he can finally see who has her. They are at the top of a small hill across from John who is still in the ravine. He must've dragged her up there, though she would've fought him tooth and nail like the banshee she can be. It's that punk Bobby and he's got her around the waist. Reagan's gun is also gone from her thigh which means she's either lost it or the kid has it. She's fighting him like a wild woman, but Bobby's much bigger than her. Most people are much bigger than her. Knowing that sadistic punk has her, gives John the fortitude to get up again.

His leg is badly injured or sprained or broken for all he knows, and he pathetically goes down again. He reaches to his hip for his pistol, but it's not there and has obviously come off during the fall or the dragging. Hadj three lunges at him, and John kneels because he can't do much else. The man has a dagger in his left hand that he wields with slightly more skill than John's opponents in the Home Depot had displayed. This man has been in knife fights before, but he isn't ex-military. John punches the guy to the low gut and blocks an oncoming stabbing meant for his chest. It successfully knocks the knife quite a distance away into the weeds and underbrush.

"Kill him, Levon! Kill that prick!" Bobby yells.

Reagan stomps his foot hard like John showed her to do. She gets loose, sprints a few feet away, but the kid grabs her again. Her foot stomp has enraged Bobby, and he shoves her to the ground.

"You want to take a look at my dick now, you little bitch? Yeah, let me show you what I can do with it. I was gonna wait till later after we killed your boyfriend over there, but…"

John is too distracted by this interaction and takes another blow to the side of his head by the man that he now knows is a part of the coup on the farm, the same man who'd been giving him the hard looks the other day when they'd been told to leave. This fight isn't going in his favor, making him feel weak. This isn't a feeling with which John is familiar and it pisses him off. He can't let Bobby rape Reagan or hurt her in any way. He's never felt so stinking helpless his whole life, and he vows that if he lives through this, he's going to shoot that stupid horse.

His radio is sounding off from somewhere either still attached to his saddle or in the dirt where it could've fallen. It's his brother's voice coming across the radio using their call signs, but John can't take the time to find it now as he deflects another punch and jabs Levon in the spleen. With John on one knee, the blow doesn't have the force behind it that he'd like, and he takes a shot to the side of his face.

"Not so tough now, are you, badass? When Bobby's done with your woman, I'll show her what a real man can do with a fine piece of ass like hers," Levon threatens.

The big man comes at John with a kick to his stomach which John partially deflects because he's busy unsheathing the one weapon he's still in possession of. John stabs it into the side of the other man's knee. Levon even screams but doesn't go down. He shoves John hard, making him land on his back and successfully dislodging the knife at the same time. That move should've taken Levon to the ground, but it didn't. Perhaps he is on drugs. They hadn't found these people's stash of drugs. John clenches his knife tightly so as not to drop it as he comes up onto one knee and then to his feet.

He can still hear Reagan fighting and screeching at that stupid kid, and it's making him sick. He manages to hobble a few feet away before Levon can make another move. By the grace of God, John spots his pistol in the fallen leaves and forest ground cover and clumsily hobbles over to it as quickly as he can manage.

A shot rings out loud and clear in the silence of the forest and John spins with his .45 ready to shoot. He watches as Levon staggers backward. He's been shot to the shoulder but not by John. The

314

surprised look on the man's face must mirror John's own. Three more rounds follow in lightning quick succession to the man's center mass and he falls dead. John turns to find Cory behind him on the other side of the ravine's hill holding his handgun with one hand. And he's still seated on John's favorite mare. He's glad that Cory took her because Lady is steady and easy to handle and doesn't take flight at the slightest rustle of leaf or, in this case, gun shot. Sam is riding behind him for some reason and not on her own horse. John's mare stands quietly under Cory, who looks unfazed and calm although he's just shot and killed a man. Good, it is a valuable quality to have nowadays. He'll be a lot like John when he gets older. And now to find his woman who is still swearing and yelling.

Cory swings a leg over the neck of the mare and helps Sam down, who he leaves with the horse. John hobbles to the hill where he can still hear Reagan. As he stalks as fast as a spreading wildfire to the top of that hill, leaving Cory behind, he is shocked as Simon stabs Bobby in the back from behind. Bobby the punk screams. That little piece of shit was on top of Reagan but, thankfully, she still looks fully clothed.

Simon drags Reagan out from under Bobby as the kid howls in pain. Simon literally picks Reagan up by the waist and then flings her over his shoulder. He is running toward the woods with her and surprising John that he is even strong enough to do it. John fires a bullet right into Bobby's heart, disabling the creep and putting him out of his misery.

Reagan is still yelling, and she's wrestled herself free from Simon and is running toward him. When she gets to John, she flings herself at him, making him stumble backward and hop twice to regain his balance on his one good leg. She's clinging to his neck, and somehow he doesn't fall down but manages to hold her and himself upright until she calms down and stops shaking.

"Are you ok, boss?" John asks hoarsely as his gun-free hand sinks into her hair. She nods, and John notices that she has a cut on her lip and blood and dirt on her forehead. "Were you thrown?"

"No that little fucker yanked me off when your horse reared. I didn't even see him. But I saw that other one. That's why I yelled your name, but it was too late."

Her legs wobble under her, and John does his best to hold her up. "Are you hurt, Reagan?" he repeats.

"No, I'm fine. But, John, you're hurt. That was bad. That was a really, really bad fall you took. We need to get back so I can take a look at you," she says quickly.

"I'm ok. I've been through worse," he pacifies her and strokes her cheek.

She dislodges herself from him as Simon comes out of the woods. He looks sheepishly at John before jumping into an unnecessary explanation of his actions.

"I'm sorry I grabbed her, sir. I just panicked. I just wasn't sure if Bobby would go down or come at us or get her again, and I'm sorry if I hurt you Dr. McClane. I know I was rough, but I'm sorry about that and…"

"You did good, Simon. Don't worry about it," John says. "She's safe and you helped me by getting her out of the way of my shot. I owe you, man."

The kid just looks at his feet. John lays a hand on Simon's skinny shoulder before they walk back down the hill. Cory is on the radio with his brother. His pistol is holstered again.

"Shit's happening back at the farm, too, John," Cory calls out.

John manages with Simon's help to hobble back down the hill. Sam is standing next to him holding the reins of Reagan's horse and theirs, and she looks scared out of her mind. Cory is holding her small hand in his in a protective manner. She is normally reserved and withdrawn around Cory, but perhaps she has seen some redeeming qualities in him this afternoon.

"Let's move," John says after he scans the area for other danger. He turns to Cory, "Make sure that pistol's safety is back on, man."

"I set it before I re-holstered it, John," he says simply.

"Good. Did you guys see anyone else?" John asks of their surroundings. Other men could be farther along on this path in their enchanting, serene, dangerous forest.

"No, it was just them. They already tried to get at us. That's why Sam's riding with me. She got thrown from her horse, and it took off. Come on, Sam," Cory orders.

He and Sam remount John's mare. John's nutty gelding is long gone like Sam's horse, so he gets on Reagan's. She swings up

316

behind him. He winces as he has to bend his leg to get his right boot into the stirrup.

"We already ran into them up on that other ridge, so we took off," Simon tells them as he remounts his black gelding with the one white ankle. "We were coming back to the farm to tell you guys, but we were trying to find Sam's mare, too. Cory didn't want them to find it and take off with it 'cuz then they'd have a horse to get away through the woods."

Simon's hands are shaking at the reins, but John notices that Cory's do not. Cory's also more tactilely intelligent than he'd given him credit for being if he had enough forethought to not want the hadj to get their hands on any of the horses.

"Yeah, somehow they got down into this valley before we did," Cory says. "That's when we saw from up on that hill back there what was going on, so we raced down here to help 'cuz we knew you guys wouldn't be expecting them. I'm sorry, John. I feel like this is my fault."

"What? No, man," John appeases him. "It's nobody's fault. These dirtballs were planning this, and we were stupid to let our guards down. Shoulda' shot these scumbags the first day. Give me the radio, Cory." The teenager hands it to him as they start the horses at a fast walk through the dry creek and up a hill.

"Derek," he says into the radio. No sense in pretenses now. There's too much at stake to be covert. "Come in, bro."

"Got ya', John," his brother comes through the static.

"Sit rep down there," he inquires after the farm.

"Area secure, hadj rounded up," Derek says. "Your status?"

"Ambush, two hadj down. We're three clicks out. Be back lickety and we're cleanin' house," John tells him, and he knows that his brother will understand exactly what all of this means.

"Roger that, out," Derek responds calmly.

When they come to the open fields again, they all take off at a canter. Every footstep of Reagan's horse jars John's hip, and it's agonizing but not as bad as some of the other injuries he's had in his life from battles.

As the horses pick their way at a slower pace along a stretch of the path that is too beat up for running, Reagan addresses the girl directly, "Sam, did these people kill your family?"

Of course the response comes as silence as Sam looks the other way, hiding her face behind Cory's back. John can tell that Reagan gets instantly pissed.

"Yes, ma'am," Simon replies for her as he pulls his horse up beside Reagan and John's.

Reagan whips her head the other way behind John, mimicking his own movement.

"Yes? They did, Simon?" she asks this again just to be sure.

"Yes, Dr. McClane, they did kill her family. I believe they took them out to her horse barn and shot them. I'm not sure exactly. They tied me up in the RV because I tried to help her family," Simon tells them.

"Where was Great-uncle Peter?" Reagan asks the teen directly.

John's not sure he wants to know the answer. The answer could be devastating to Grams and the rest of the family.

"He was in the other RV driving from house to house with Jasmine and Miss Jennifer and Rick and Buzz. They aren't too bad of guys. It was me, Willy and those two you just killed and that Frank jerk. Oh and my Aunt Amber. She knew what was going on," Simon explains. "But those other ones were somewhere else in the neighborhood when we raided Sam's house. They always sent us kids in first- probably in case someone started shooting. I went in with Huntley and his brother Garrett. I found Sam in the house as her family pulled in behind the RV Frank parked out in their driveway. I sent the twins back out to tell the group that nobody was inside. Her family must have gone somewhere in the neighborhood. Probably were scavenging for food or something. I told her to hide because I knew what Frank and the others would do to her family and her. I ran out and tried to stop it, but I couldn't do much. It was five of them against just me. They beat me up pretty bad that time. Huntley and Garrett were in the motorhome with me. That's where they tied me up so I couldn't stop them. The twins are too young and were too scared to do anything, especially against their dad. All I could do was sit there listening to the gunshots. And when they were done… with them in the barn, they went in the house and found her."

Simon shivers with bad memories as he explains and the barns come into view. John is sure this day is about to get worse.

"What about my patient, Jennifer Miller-Durant? Was she a captive of my uncle's? Or was she with him of her own free will? The only times she was awake enough in the shed to speak, she wouldn't talk to me about any of them," Reagan clarifies.

Her hands still shake as they clutch onto John's waist.

"I'm not sure, ma'am," Simon says quietly. "I think maybe she got with your uncle's group before my aunt joined up with them. I can't say for sure if they took her against her will or not. I'd guess that they did because of the way she acted. And she didn't do drugs and drink like them. She cried a lot, especially about her husband. Maybe she went with them on her own, but I don't know for sure. Your uncle wasn't nice to her, but he didn't hit her or anything, ma'am. He just… used her."

"Come on," John says and kicks Harry into a near gallop. Time to take out the trash.

As they come into the barnyard, Kelly and Derek meet them and explain briefly about an attack on Hannah and that Kelly has already killed the insane man named Willy. His friend has blood splattered on the front of his white t-shirt shirt and on his left cheek. There's even some on his hands. He's obviously killed Willy with his dagger.

He and the teens place the horses in stalls with their tack still on so that they can come back to them later to set them loose. There's simply no time to deal with the horses.

"Simon, please take Sam and go inside, son," John says, but Sam comes up to him and can barely meet his eyes.

"John?" she says in her tiny voice.

"Yeah, Sam? What is it?" he asks and lays a hand gently on her shoulder.

"I didn't go with my parents that day because I was staying behind to take care of the horses and the chores. My mom was sick, so I volunteered to take care of everything while they went to look for food and medicine in town. We never thought it wouldn't be safe. Our neighborhood wasn't that bad yet."

"I'm sorry, Sam," John tells her. The girls nods sadly, her huge blue eyes refusing to meet his.

"They took her, Mr. Harrison. She told me, Miss Jennifer did. She didn't want to be with them at all. They found her outside of an

319

abandoned FEMA camp. She must've been going there looking for help since she knew she was pregnant. They just pulled up on the road and grabbed her. Peter did it," Sam says.

A tear falls that she swipes angrily away.

"Simon, take her and keep the family away from the windows, preferably to the basement," John tells the boy with the splattering of freckles and the red hair.

Simon glances at the crowd of visitors and then back at John nervously as if contemplating something difficult.

"What is it?" John prompts him.

"Sir, it's just that... I don't know how to tell you," Simon stammers.

Kelly steps closer and lays a massive hand on the kid's skinny shoulder. "It's cool, man. Just spit it out. It can't be any worse than what we already know."

"They sabotaged the RV," Simon declares reluctantly and looks away and then at his leather loafers.

"What do you mean?" Reagan asks before pushing back a clump of dirty curls from her forehead.

"Well... they did some stuff to that one so that it wouldn't work," Simon tells them. "I overheard them the other day and they caught me. They threatened me not to tell you guys or they'd hurt..."

His eyes trail over to Sam and nobody has to guess with whom they had threatened Simon.

"Interesting," Kelly says with stoic calmness.

"I think they poured water in the gas tank and cut some of the wiring somewhere under the hood. I'm sorry I didn't tell you sooner. It's just that I didn't want anything more to happen..." he doesn't finish again.

They all know what he means. He has protectiveness over Sam and Huntley that is so obvious to see. Heck, everyone probably feels the same about Sam. She's just so frail and innocent and waif-like.

"Thanks for telling us the truth, Simon," Reagan says.

Her eyes jump to John's with even more hatred firing out of them than before.

"I guess they thought you'd let them stay if their vehicle wasn't running," Simon adds.

"Take Sam and go now, son," Kelly tells him.

Simon nods and goes directly to the waif. He leads Sam away, taking her hand in his while glancing nervously at the visitors' camp as if he's afraid they will suddenly charge at him.

John limps toward Reagan and levels her with an intense gaze. "Reagan, you'd better go in, too."

"I want to go with you, John," she says quietly.

He's so angry and most of it is at himself. Her beautiful face is smeared with dirt, and the cut on her lip still bleeding slightly. There's bruising on her cheekbone and her lower lip is also starting to swell like that dick hit her there. Leaves and twigs stick out of her hair which John wishes he had time to pick out. How could he have been so stupid? How can they have so underestimated these creeps?

"You're hurt. You need to go in to your grandpa and let him look at you," he says and uses his shirt sleeve to wipe at her mouth.

"I'm fine," she says.

She brushes his hand away and looks nervously at the other men of the group. She doesn't want them to think she's as fragile as she really is. She also probably doesn't want them to see them together as a couple in any way, either.

"This is going to be worse than the city, boss. You aren't going to want to see this. Reagan, you *really* aren't going to want to be up there," John tells her and watches as her eyes widen slightly.

"I can handle it. I want to be there. *Someone* from the family should be there," she says.

John nods, although he'd like to tell her to get her butt in the house. She's probably right about a McClane being present for this. And he can see the vicious fury in her green eyes.

"You might go in, too, Cory," Kelly tells his brother.

"He's ok, Kel. He's good to go," John tells his friend in an austere tone.

The kid is more than ok, he'll shoot whoever he's told to shoot and do it without remorse. And the 'good to go' comment tips Kelly to this fact. It's what he and Kelly have always referred to fellow soldiers whom they'd trusted to watch their backs, the ones who were battle-tested and ready like them, the natural killers. John's seen the killer in this kid's eyes, and he recognizes it because it's the same look he's seen in Kelly's. His friend gives John a perplexed look, but then he nods as understanding dawns. Cory's good to go.

"Ok, bro, let's roll," Kelly says.

He and Cory start walking as the others follow.

"You got their guns?" John asks his brother and watches as he pulls them out from behind him, out of the waistband of his jeans.

"Got 'em," Derek answers. "We took their crate of shit out to them earlier, and they were bitchin' already about it not being enough food."

"It isn't gonna matter in a minute," John tells his brother with a frown. Derek just nods.

Together they move as a group toward the campsite. Simon and Sam are welcomed into the back of the home by Doc who gives John a firm nod before he shuts and locks the door to his home. There is more perspicacity in that one look than there could be in a thousand words between them.

When they get to the campsite which is mostly packed up, Uncle Peter comes forward.

"Where's the rest of our group? Have you guys seen them?"

The men ignore him, and Derek tosses the guns onto the ground in front of him as the other squatters gather around and two of them come out of the RV. Even the women have come out.

"What's this "B" on the peaches mean? And there's two cans of green beans marked with a "B," too. Does that mean that they're bad?" toothless hadj, Amber, asks.

She is the woman that Simon said knew of the murdering of Sam's family and had done nothing to stop it.

"It means best," Reagan says snidely.

John is pretty sure that she's lying.

She just keeps right on going with it though, "Grams wants her guests to have the best."

"Where's our friends? Have ya'll seen 'em?" Buzz asks.

He rubs his bald head while shifting his weight from one skinny leg to the other. His eyes dart around nervously and end up on Kelly's rifle.

"Who owns these guns?" Derek asks impatiently.

"What? What the fuck you care now?" Huntley's father Frank demands. "We asked you a question, boy? Where's our friends? What happened to them?"

The way that he is acting tips John to the fact that Frank knew something was going to go down today.

322

"Who do these guns belong to?" Derek asks.

His brother chooses to ignore Frank and his open disdain and insults, and repeats his original line of questioning.

"Who used these guns?" John demands more firmly.

"That one there, the smaller pistol, that one is Levon's," Buzz answers with forthcoming honesty.

Nobody is surprised to hear this weapon belongs to the criminal-minded man who now lay dead in the woods.

"And the 9 mill? Whose gun is this?" John asks impatiently.

"It's mine, why the fuck you wanna' know? Did Bobby find Sam? Where the hell are they?" Frank barks.

"How did you guys come to be with Samantha?" Kelly interrogates.

His grip clenches on the forearm of his M16. His knuckles turn white. John's seen this many times. It usually happened right before they were air dropped into a hotspot.

Buzz seems confused, but the uncle glances away. Frank, on the other hand, boldly steps toward them.

"Why the fuck you wanna' know that? What's it to you?"

"Just answer the question, Frank," Derek demands. "How'd you guys get that girl? We know she just lives a few miles from here. So how come if you're from Arizona or wherever you're all from, do you guys have a teenage girl from a few miles away traveling with you?"

"Don't fucking worry about it, prick. That bitch was Bobby's little plaything, not ours. So what's it to you?" Frank snipes.

"Where's her family then?" Kelly barks angrily.

"Who knows? Who fucking cares?" Frank lies so blatantly.

"This 9 mill is the same one that was used on her parents and siblings, Frank. That's why I'm asking," Derek pursues with deadly antipathy.

John is not mirroring his brother's calmness. Frank's eyes widen and take on a new look of being caught in the headlights for the briefest of moments before turning angry again. John and Kelly both regard each other for a moment. They know a liar when they see one. They've done this a hundred times interrogating terrorists. The eyes never lie. Kelly nods and John returns it.

"So fucking what? You ain't the sheriff around here, asshole. I make my own rules. I do what I got to do to survive. Now I asked where's our friends, dickhead? Did Bobby find that little bitch or what? Where's Levon and Bobby, you assholes?" Frank shouts to everyone and flails his arms wildly.

"Same place you're going," John says and shoots the man two times point blank to the chest with his Kimber custom .45 and he falls hard. Some of the men in the Special Forces have guns custom made and donated to them from different gun manufacturers. John's has his name and squad engraved into it.

Jasmine screams and starts crying, and the other men back up abruptly. Buzz even trips over his own two feet and falls. He doesn't get to his feet but scuttles backward until he reaches Rick.

"You cold son of a bitch. What the hell's wrong with you, man?" Rick screams.

He runs to Frank and presses his fingers to the other man's neck. John would like to tell him that this isn't his first kill shot. There's no point in checking him. Rick is normally a quiet man, and he's not given them trouble yet. However, John reminds himself that this man is the cousin of the now dead Levon.

"This gun and the other one were used to kill Samantha's family," John tells him as he kicks the 9 mill toward them.

"No, man. You ain't got that right" Rick starts as he stands again. "Nobody killed them. We wouldn't do shit like that! Frank told us her family was already dead. He didn't…"

"He killed them and so did Willy and Levon and Bobby, and they're all dead now, too," Cory jumps in angrily.

"What? You killed them? You killed all of them? Oh my God!" Jasmine screeches. "No, they wouldn't do that. They wouldn't! They couldn't have killed her family! Could they?"

She is talking to herself, trying to convince herself, and her hands cover her ears. She squats in a hunched position in the gravel. She's hysterical and bawling. Buzz has moved closer to Rick again and literally cowers behind the bigger man.

Amber is unusually quiet and has retreated two steps. John keeps her in his periphery.

"And you knew about it, too, didn't you?" Kelly asks Amber and advances.

The woman stops retreating and juts out her chin defiantly.

Kelly keeps hammering his point, "You knew what they did to her family and you knew what Bobby did to Sam all this time, didn't you?"

"Yeah, so fucking what?" she finally responds with acid in her tone. "You sons a' bitches ain't got a clue. Fuck you. You sit around here playin' farm while the rest of us has had to scrap around for nothin' out there. Nothin'! We've had to kill and steal just to stay alive."

"Yes, you have. You've killed innocent, fucking people, you stupid bitch!" Derek shouts angrily.

He rarely loses his crap, but this situation has gotten so bad with these people. And they all know that this woman was a part of Sam's abduction, perhaps others, too. Perhaps some of the people that Great-uncle Peter had said succumbed to the sickness had also been their captives, their victims. Amber knew they were going to ambush Sam's family and kill them. She's as insane and sick as the men.

"How could you stand by and let them kill her family? Did any of them rape her, Amber?" Kelly demands.

"Fuck you, Army boy," Amber rails. "You don't know what it's like. That little fucking whore teased around *all* these men, and she had it all before the shit hit. You shoulda' seen her house! And her fancy, fuckin' snotty parents what thought they were better than us. Spoiled little rich bitch was what she was flirtin' with all the men in our camp. That bitch got what she deserved."

John watches as his friend walks away from her because Kelly is probably afraid he's going to lose control and do something violent. Kelly has a slightly higher amount of self-control than John and always has. John's next plan is to take Amber behind the bus to shoot her so that Kelly doesn't have to do it.

But suddenly the toothless skank comes at Kelly with a knife which he doesn't see because he'd underestimated her and turned his back to the enemy. A shot rings out behind and to the right of John, and when he turns to see, he's not surprised that it came from Cory's pistol. The young man has shot Amber in the head with his .9 mill.

Jasmine the stripper is crying in earnest and hugging her arms about her waist. When John looks to his left, Derek's pistol is also drawn.

"Oh my God. Oh my God. I didn't know anything. I swear!" Jasmine begs for her life.

Buzz and Rick begin doing the same. Buzz actually stars weeping like Jasmine. John glances over at Reagan. She's staring at her feet and shaking her head. She has paled considerably, but she's not trying to stop the killing.

"Hey, this is outta' control!" Uncle Peter shouts in a panic. "Hey, man. Reagan, tell these guys to calm down. Tell them, Reagan."

This is the first time he's spoken. It's not surprising, though. He usually slinks into the shadows like a rat.

"Did you rape Jennifer Miller-Durant, Uncle Peter?" Reagan asks calmly. "Did you rape my patient who died?"

Her repetition of the woman's identity is hammering it home to John that she took that woman's loss a lot harder than she let on. She wants all of them to remember her name. She wants everyone to know that she took this woman's care as her patient seriously. She is apparently not feeling too upset over the loss of Amber the toothless skank, though. The boss has a fierce sense of right and wrong, and she knows that what has been done to Sam is wrong. They all do.

"No way. No, Reagan. She was my girlfriend. I told you that. I told you," he pleads.

Great-uncle Peter's pleas lack an earnest believability because of the fear in his vacant eyes.

"How did she come to be with your group?" Derek interrogates.

"How? Um, she just did. Yeah, she was with our group. Wasn't she, guys?" he looks to the other two remaining men who won't answer.

"Was she?" Kelly demands of them.

Buzz and the stripper won't make eye contact, but Rick steps up and seems willing to talk.

"I… I don't know. She was already with him when me and Buzz got with the group," Rick answers and is more believable. "We didn't know they were doing anything like that. We thought Sam wanted to be with Bobby. We didn't figure it out till we got here that she didn't 'cuz she kept leaving us to hang out with you guys instead. And Jennifer, she was real quiet most of the time and then within a week or so of us joining up with the group she got sick. So I really

326

never talked to her. I swear. We were just with the group 'cuz we figured it would be safer that way. My cousin Levon told me to meet up with him in Cincinnati at Buzz's house right when everything fell apart. So that's where me and Buzz waited for him. We wasn't even sure if he'd make it, but he did. And he had all these people with him. It's just safer to stick together or join up with a group. It's too dangerous out there to be on your own anymore."

"She was with me, damn it!" Uncle Peter says angrily this time. "These jackasses don't know what they're talkin' about."

A bead of sweat rolls down his forehead and his eyes dart shiftily around.

"What was her age? Where was she from before this all started? What were her parents' names? Do you know anything about her? Or were you just using her like you use everyone, Peter?" Derek demands.

Great-uncle Peter looks at his feet and sweats harder.

"She was *with* me," he insists.

"That's not what we've heard," Reagan tells him.

This sucks. John wants to just shoot this piece of crap, but he's not sure how Herb and Maryanne would feel about it.

Reagan turns away from her uncle and the rest of his group. She tugs John's arm, and they walk a short distance away toward the machine shed while the other men keep their guns trained on the visitors. Her brows are pinched with stress, and she sighs heavily as if exhausted. The bruise on her cheek and lip and forehead are ripening into a dark purple which further incenses John. She says nothing but stands there for a few minutes quietly thinking.

"Kill him and send the rest on their way," she finally states decidedly.

John's jaw wants to drop to the ground, but he manages to keep it under control. "Are you sure, Reagan? He's your grandmother's brother. We could just send them all away."

"He raped her. I'm sure of it. I can tell he's lying. He's always been a piece of shit liar. Besides, Sam and Simon have already said as much," Reagan says on a sigh.

"We could just let him go, let him leave," John offers an alternative, although he doesn't really want to.

"No," she answers and shakes her head. "He'll come back someday. He'll come back the next time with guns and a lot more men."

John nods. "I know."

Her decision comes simply but not without a burdening heart. It's written all over her lovely features.

Reagan looks directly up at him and continues, "I wouldn't be surprised if he knew about the takeover today, either. Or what happened to Sam's family. They have probably done that to other families, and I'm sure he played a part in it. He came to this farm with these bastards to take it over. He just didn't think they'd meet with resistance from you guys. He could've come alone to seek shelter, but he didn't. He brought a violent mob here to overrun us. If you don't kill him, I fully believe that he'll come back another time. The next time he may bring fifty people here to overrun us."

Her super brain is kicking into high gear. John had thought the same thing about her uncle but had never voiced it to her. He tries to touch the side of her face to offer her comfort, but she pulls back sharply.

"Are you sure?" he asks one more time, giving her the chance to back out.

"Yeah, I'm sure. Grandpa would want it this way, too. Just do it. I'm going back to the house. I'll take Grandpa to the side and explain everything. Let the others go. I think they're just stupid assholes."

"I agree," John states.

"Hell, they're not even a threat to themselves. None of them has a killer instinct. They probably won't make it far," Reagan says.

"Got it," John tells her with a nod. Her eyes reflect his own coolness which is unsettling to see in her. He much prefers the dancing green eyes brought on by her laughter, but those moments with her are usually so few and far between.

Reagan walks to the house by herself and doesn't turn around. John's pistol rings out loud and clear in one clean shot again. The men send the three remaining visitors on their way, even after Jasmine begs to stay between sobs and bouts of hysteria. They don't waste any time getting the heck off of the McClane farm, and Cory and Kelly escort them out, following in Doc's pick-up truck. This has been a long and exhausting day, and it won't end for many hours still. He and the other men have a lot of burying to do.

Chapter Twenty-three
Reagan

There is no family dinner that night or the next. Everyone eats when they can for a few days because the men are gone in the woods burying the dead and cleaning up crime scenes. Cory and Simon are also helping with this whether they had wanted to or not. But both of them had not seemed to mind, neither had they complained. In a twenty-four hour period, both of them have turned from teen boys to men. The family is not permitted, children included, to be outside while they are gone. Reagan had explained what went down with the visitors' group to her grandfather, and he was more than understanding as if he knew that it would end this way. They agree not to tell Grams of her brother's death, though Reagan is sure that sometime in the future he will tell her. The visitor's campsite had been too hard to see clearly from the house, so she's sure that Grams hadn't witnessed the carnage. She's also sure that Grandpa had kept her from seeing, too. That's between the two of them and not for her to get involved.

Reagan is re-treating Hannah's injuries in her room, after she retrieved the supplies that she needed from the med shed. She's concerned about her sister and, more importantly, her sister's mental state.

"Grandpa was right. I don't think you needed stitches, Hannie," she tells her still-frightened sister as she inspects the wound on her forehead which Grandpa had cleaned.

He had given Hannah a quick clean-up job yesterday and that was about it. He couldn't run to the med shed during the attacks for his doctor's satchel or any medical supplies, but he had been able to clean, sterilize and lightly bandage Hannah. He relayed to Reagan an accurate report of Hannah's injuries and had told her that she hadn't been raped which was one small thing to be thankful for.

"The cut on your hand will heal, but you'll need to take it easy and not get it too dirty. And I don't think you have a concussion, either, sweetie. Just try to keep the bandaging on your hand nice and dry. No kitchen work for a few days! But I don't think it will infect."

"That's good, I suppose," Hannah says in an even softer voice than normal.

Her mouth is similarly swelled and bruised like her cheek from being slapped, and she winces when she speaks. She and Reagan have similar injuries, though to Reagan they are only minor ones compared to what had happened to her at her college.

"You'll be ok, Hannie. You're just going to be sore, and you're scratched up pretty good," Reagan tells her, trying to reassure her delicate sister.

She nods, but then the tears come and Reagan takes her in her arms and holds her sister. Her anger blooms anew at her sister's dead accoster.

"Oh, Hannah, don't cry," Reagan tries to console her tender sister. "You're safe now. You're safe."

After quite some time, Hannah pulls back and sniffs, "I'm such a baby. I wasn't even hurt like you were at your school, and here I'm blubbering like a baby. I slept downstairs with Kelly last night. Don't tell Grandpa. He'd probably be upset about it since he doesn't know about us yet. I was just too scared to be alone, Reagan."

"I won't say anything. I understand how scared you are. It's a normal reaction, Hannah. You were almost killed," Reagan explains and tries not to flinch at the idea of her beloved sister being hurt like this. "You've been through something very traumatic."

"If Kelly hadn't come out there, I would have been, Reagan," Hannah says and sniffs again.

"Yeah, well hell, I guess I can't hate him forever then," Reagan says on a chuff which makes Hannah smile. "Come on. Let's go and see if they're all done. Did you eat something yet today? It'll help calm your nerves."

"Yes, Grams made me," her sister says with another smile and then a grimace.

"Good. It's the one time I would have to agree with Grams force feeding someone," Reagan tells her as they walk slowly toward the kitchen.

Kelly is sitting at the island with Grams, and he has cleaned up and showered. He immediately comes to Hannah and hugs her openly in front of everyone. He inspects her bandages carefully and grimaces at the marks and bruises on her gentle face. They go off to the music room together and nobody questions it.

"Where's everyone else?" Reagan asks Sue who is holding Jacob. She takes her inherited child from her sister and rests him on her hip.

"Derek's upstairs getting cleaned up. The boys are downstairs doing the same, and John's finishing up in the horse barn. That stupid gelding finally came home today along with the horse Sam was riding, and John's getting the tack off of him to turn him out," Sue explains.

"Ok, thanks. I'll go out and help him," Reagan says and shakes her head as Sue reaches for Jacob again. "It's ok, Sue. I've got Jacob. He can go with me. Can't you, buddy?"

For some reason, Reagan is reluctant to let little Jacob go. There has just been so much death on the farm lately that it's nice to hold this innocent baby boy with his slobbery fists close to her, even though he smears her cheek with his wet hand. She grabs his tiny fleece jacket off of the hook near the back door and heads out to find John. The sun has nearly set, and a light on in the barn floods into the yard with a yellowy luminescence.

She needs to see John. He hadn't come to bed last night at all, and her concern for her family also extends to him. When she arrives at the horse barn, he's already removed the gelding's tack and is turning him out to pasture with the other horses. He pivots toward Reagan, after he fastens the lock on the gate, and stops in his tracks momentarily when he views her. Looking at John always stuns her to her core. She hasn't seen him at all today because the men have been so busy. John looks to the ground and then brushes past her and Jacob to go back into the barn, the very same barn where he'd taken her virginity and showed her that not all men, who have the ability, want to just hurt and brutalize women. She follows him inside and leans against a horse stall watching him. His clothes are filthy, understandably so. He's filthy, also understandable after the last few days they've just had.

He remarks quietly, "Think that gelding must have run through about every briar patch in the woods on the way home. This saddle's beat up and scratched. I'll work on it tomorrow and see what I can do. Plus, my weapon's gone."

He says these things without looking at her. Reagan walks over to him and puts her finger on his pistol.

"Your weapon's right here," she says teasingly.

"That's my sidearm. My weapon's gone. It must've been lost yesterday when I went down with the horse. And that stupid horse is lucky because I'd be tempted to shoot him with it," he says lightly.

At least she hopes he's kidding. The men do all seem to revere their Army M16's.

"Oh, you mean your rifle," she says.

"No, I mean my weapon," he corrects her.

Reagan frowns at him. "Why do you not just say rifle?"

"Because it's not a rifle. It's my weapon. It's one of the first things that gets drilled into your head when you join the Army. My weapon is for killing, and I've lost mine," he says as if he's lost an appendage.

Once he's taken the saddle and bridle to the tack room, he finally stands still in front of her, but he seems hesitant to meet her gaze. She doesn't point out the obvious that he's quite skilled with his pistol or a knife, too. Reagan's not sure John even needs a gun.

"You can just get another rifle out of the arsenal. Grandpa has a couple AR's in there. A few..." she tries to offer.

"It's cool," John interrupts. "I'll figure something out."

His hands are covered in dirt, his gray shirt is covered in grime and probably other things she doesn't want to consider. It doesn't matter to Reagan. A truckload of dirt couldn't make him any less handsome. He's remarkably calm and relaxed for killing people yesterday and burying them all day and last night. They'd also towed the non-functioning RV all the way out to the main road and left it near an abandoned home. Derek had told her that they'd searched it again and found a stash of pot and two small baggies of crack cocaine.

"Everything ok?" Reagan asks him and steps closer.

"Yeah, you?" he asks.

He finally looks directly at her with that dark blue gaze. John steps closer, and Reagan feels the same familiar butterflies in her stomach that she has always felt around him. She'd misread those feelings for fear for so long and what they really ended up being was simple, physical attraction. Everything about John is sexy and sensual. Even a macabre few days like they've just been through can't squelch the fact that she is intensely and highly attracted to, drawn to John.

"Yes," she answers and steps toward him. Jacob instantly starts squirming, wanting John to pick him up. Reagan bounces him on her hip to quiet him and it works. She's learned this trick by watching John with him. "Thanks to you."

"Almost got us both killed. I wouldn't say thanks to me if I was you," he says testily.

It dawns on Reagan why he is so standoffish. He's blaming himself for the attack on her, probably Hannah, hell, the whole farm.

"If it wasn't for you, all of you guys, we'd have been dead a long time ago, John," she says and steps closer to link her free arm around his waist and rest her head against his chest where she fits just perfectly under his chin. After a moment, his arms encircle and squeeze her. They stand like this for some time until Jacob's squeal breaks them apart. John still seems hesitant to believe her, though.

"I'm sorry I had to kill those people in front of you. That's why I didn't want you to…" he starts.

"I'm not," Reagan corrects him. "John, I don't give two shits about those pricks. They were the sludge of society. They were fully prepared to kill all of us to stay on here. And the sickening thing is that they wouldn't have had a clue how to manage this place anyways. And you know what the plan was for us women. You did the right thing," she says with a shiver and lays a hand against his chest as his arm still rests behind her lower back.

"I killed your great-uncle, though," he says and frowns.

"So? I told you to do it. I wasn't fooling around when I said to kill him. You know that. You know me. My moral compass doesn't allow for rapists, thieves and murderers to live on our farm," Reagan discloses which is hard for her to do. She's not crazy about the idea of John knowing her so well, but he does and he especially knows more about her than any man has ever known.

"Yeah, but I don't want you to look at me... I don't know-differently because I did that stuff. I don't want you to be disgusted by me," he explains.

He looks so worried over it that Reagan actually drums up the courage to pull John's head down for a brief, forgiving kiss.

"I don't look at you differently and I'm sure as hell not disgusted by you. You do what has to be done, whether that means farm work or killing someone to keep us safe. If anything, I have more respect for you. You killed that piece of shit Bobby for what he's done to Sam and for what he tried to do to me, and not very many people could have done that. I mean he was just a teenager for shit's sake. We live in a time now when you can't hesitate, where you have to kill or be killed. You had the balls to do what needed done and I respect that about you. You'll always take care of Jacob... and me I guess," Reagan says and rolls her eyes at him. He just smiles down at her. She doesn't actually relish in having to say the last part out loud. At hearing his name, Jacob reaches up and smacks at Reagan's cheek, but John captures the baby's tiny hand.

"I will. I promise I'll always take care of you. And I promise I'll always take care of Jake and your family, our family," he swears.

His declaration makes Reagan pull back with discomfort at the serious direction of the conversation.

To make it worse, he adds, "I love you, Reagan."

She doesn't answer, but he doesn't look disappointed in her lack of a response which is a good thing because she's never going to say that. This love talk is annoying, but if he feels like saying it, then that is fine with her. Out of everything else that's happened the last couple of days, this is almost the scariest. She nods awkwardly, and John captures her mouth with his in a searing, meaningful kiss. However, their kiss is brief because she has a cut on her lower lip from that dick, Bobby. She flinches away.

"Sorry, honey. Are you ok?" John asks as he pulls back while still holding her closely.

Jacob reaches up and grabs John's ear, and he chuckles down at the baby.

"Yeah, I'm fine."

"Did he hit you?" John inquires after Bobby.

When she nods twice, the look on John's face is so violent and malevolent. He mumbles something unintelligible under his breath.

"I'm ok, though. I'm not nearly as banged up as Hannah," she tells him, trying to lessen his anxiety.

"I know. I saw her briefly this morning and spoke to Kelly last night when we were burying them. What's wrong with people that they would hurt someone like Hannah? She's not a threat to anyone. She's completely defenseless," John tells her. "Bastards!"

His hoarsely whispered expletive is worse than any she's ever heard before. His fierce passion for the protection and safety of her family gives her hope for their future.

"It's over now. Let's just try to forget about it," Reagan says and kisses Jacob on the cheek as he snuggles into her neck with his soft face.

"No, we can't forget about it. We're having a meeting tonight after the kids have gone to bed. This can't ever happen again, Reagan."

"Who's having a meeting?" she asks as she allows him to lead her out of the barn and toward the house again in the dark. The air is cool, the sky warns of an impending storm. There are no stars visible, and the leaves turn over on the old maple in the back yard from sharp wind gusts.

"Your grandfather and us adults. And probably Simon and Cory. Sam maybe. I'd like to get some more information from her, but I doubt she'll talk. It might take her awhile before she's ready," John tells her.

Reagan knows the feeling well. It's been almost seven months since her attack at the university, but she is far from being ready to talk about it.

"Dadda," Jacob blurts.

The baby reaches for John again. It stops them both simultaneously in surprise. Neither of them knows what to say, how to feel about this. Perhaps Jacob is just babbling. He does that a lot. John takes him from Reagan and kisses his forehead, breathing deeply for a moment. There's a softening in John's hard eyes that stirs unfamiliar feelings in Reagan that she immediately suppresses. The way he is with Jacob is so endearing, even though he's not really his son.

336

"Let's go in," John recommends.

He wraps his arm around Reagan's shoulder while also carrying Jacob high on his wide chest with the other. It's only now that she notices that he's still limping, badly.

"I still need to examine you. That was a really bad fall you took yesterday, probably the worst I've ever seen, and I've seen a lot of horseback riding train wrecks, John," she says as she slips her arm around his waist for support.

"I need to examine you, too," he says in a strange way.

Why would he examine her? He isn't a doctor.

"I'm fine. Grandpa already checked me out, but I could've told him it was a waste of time," Reagan answers.

"That's one of the things I like most about you. Did you know that?"

"What are you talking about?"

"You never get my sexual innuendos, boss," he teases.

John squeezes her shoulder as he presses a kiss to her hair. Neither of them has showered or cleaned up yet today, and they both desperately need to.

She has to tell herself more than once that she's holding his waist to help him, but she knows the picture they must present as they walk up to the back porch. Grandpa and Sue are sitting in the dark on the porch swing with just the lights from the kitchen coming through the windows, and Kelly leans against the banister smoking a cigarette. None of them say anything, but she can only imagine what they must be thinking. John shifts his weight to his good leg.

"Ready?" John asks Kelly.

"Sure, right after you shower," Kelly jokes with a grimace.

It's nice to hear after a day of so much of the heavy stuff. Sue chuckles, and Grandpa agrees heartily.

Kelly takes a puff and continues, "Like I was saying, we escorted them about fifteen miles north of here before we came back. I don't think we'll ever see them again."

Kelly is obviously talking about the visitors, or what was left of them.

"I'm helping John because he's pretty hurt," Reagan blurts. Everyone looks at her strangely.

"Ok, nobody said anything," Sue says and shakes her head.

Reagan would like to club her sister.

"That's quite the limp you've still got there, John," Grandpa notices. "Reagan, you'd better take a look at that. This will be your first introduction into injury medicine without the aid of x-ray and CAT scan equipment. Let me know if you need help," Grandpa offers kindly.

He is smoking his pipe which is probably why he's on the porch.

"Where's Grandma?" she asks.

"She went inside to put the littler ones to bed, and then she's turning in, too. It's been a rough few days for her," Grandpa explains to which everyone grimaces. "I didn't tell her. It was hard enough for her."

Reagan nods, and they all do the same or look away because they know he's talking about Grandma's brother.

"I'm sorry, sir," John says.

He shifts his weight to his bad leg and swiftly back again. Reagan is worried that John is hurt more seriously than he's letting on. This worry is like a deep pang in her gut that won't go away.

"Don't be, John," Grandpa allays John's stress. "You did the right thing. I always knew he was a shit, but I didn't know how big of one he truly was. Take an hour, you two, to get ready, and we'll convene in the dining room."

John nods with a frown. "Yes, sir," he answers her grandfather.

They go up to their third floor space, and Reagan starts Jacob in his nightly routine of being put to sleep which usually involves rocking him in the rocking chair that John brought up a few weeks ago. She told him it was a stupid idea to start bad habits like that, but he'd insisted on it. He leaves to get his shower, which she'd forced him to take before her, and she holds Jacob in her arms and then against her chest. She feeds him his bottle of goat milk, which he doesn't finish. He falls quickly to sleep sucking his tiny thumb, turning the skin to a prune-like texture. Reagan assumes that John has started this habit of rocking him because there's just something about holding Jacob close, hearing his baby puffs of breath in her ear, feeling his warm little body and knowing he's safe and that they're the ones who are keeping him that way. If it is comforting to Jacob, it's a thousand times more so to her and John. Stroking his downy head,

338

Reagan rocks and rocks and just about falls asleep, too, when John's footsteps startle her. He kisses her forehead and takes the baby from her.

After her shower, she goes back upstairs to retrieve John and finds him sitting in the same rocker near her bed watching Jacob sleep on it. He rubs at his chin, deep in though. He's quiet and reflective for a long moment while she busies herself around the room getting dressed and picking up dirty clothes.

"He's so innocent," John finally says with a touch of sadness and an angry scowl.

Reagan tries to walk past him to pull a blanket over the baby, but John pulls her onto his lap instead, pressing her back against his hard, muscular front.

"I wish his life wasn't going to have the kind of violence like we've seen, but I'm afraid it'll be more of the same... or worse," John ponders.

"He'll be fine. He'll be tough like you," she reassures him as he rocks them both.

"Tough like you, maybe," he says with a smile and kisses her neck.

She's glad she took the time to use the blow dryer on her hair and then braid it, even if her scars show more prominently. Reagan doesn't always feel quite so self-conscious of the scar on her face anymore or the ones on her body. However, she'd also not let John look at her with the lights on or in the daylight and insisted that they have sex without any lighting at all.

"Yeah, I'm really tough! I couldn't even get away from a damn teenager," she argues softly and leans her head back against his shoulder.

Reagan brings her knees up and plants her feet in between his legs on the seat of the rocker. Her feet are bare and cold even with wearing sweatpants that drag on the ground, of course.

"In your defense, he was a lot bigger than you," he says.

Reagan can tell that he's smirking like a damn smartass. His hand runs up her navel to cup her breast through her long sleeved, black tee with the saying on the front: *The Difference Between Genius and Stupidity is; Genius Has Its Limits- Albert Einstein.*" It seems a suitable saying with which to end the day. John's touch isn't sexual but comforting, perhaps comforting to him, as well.

"Yeah, I guess I should take on people more like Justin's size," she says, referring to their seven year old nephew. John chuckles and kisses her shoulder.

"Maybe you should just leave the taking on of anyone to me. 'Kay, boss?" he says against her shoulder blade where there is a scar, one of so many.

"Fine, but we can teach Jacob how to play the piano *and* shoot assholes just like you do so well. Can't we?" she asks cheerily, and he squeezes a giggle out of her. "How's your leg? Am I too heavy?"

"It's fine, boss. I think I'm gonna live," he tells her.

She runs a hand behind her and up through his damp hair that desperately needs cut. It curls on the ends and is coarse, yet still soft.

He adds with a smile against her shoulder blade, "And no, you aren't too heavy. Your clothes are kind of heavy. Can you take them off?"

"No!" she admonishes but leans back for another neck kiss. "I'll check out your leg after our meeting which we're going to be late for," she tells him in her best authoritative tone. His fingers lightly stroke her cheek and her arm. His touch always sends pin pricks down her spine.

"Yeah, I guess we'd better get going. Just let me prop him with some extra pillows, then we'll head down," John says.

He snags two more pillows from his ridiculously small bed. His concern for the baby never fails to touch a strange part of her that she's shut off to the world, a part of her that she doesn't necessarily want to re-open. When he turns back to her, he smiles, breaking her trance.

"Nice shirt."

Reagan looks down and says, "Thanks. Thought it kind of said it all."

John smirks, nods and kisses her quick on the side of her mouth so as not to hurt her before they go to the meeting in the dining room.

Most everyone is waiting as Sue comes in last. Even Hannie is present, but Grams has opted out to catch up on sleep. Sam is also

340

absent. Seeing Hannah sitting there with white bandages on her forehead and hand sends a sickening flutter of butterflies to Reagan's stomach. Kelly looks like he agrees with her sentiment of Hannah's plight. The younger kids have been put to bed, but Cory and Simon are present. For some odd reason that she can't quite put her finger on, Reagan's glad that the teen boys are here for this.

"Sam go to bed, too?" Reagan asks of Sue before the rest begin talking.

"Yeah, she was beat, understandably so. I talked to her for a while out on the back porch earlier today- just the two of us. I think she'll be ok, eventually. It's just going to take her some time," Sue explains and puts her hand over Reagan's.

For the first time in a very long time, since before John came to the farm, Reagan allows her sister's hand to rest there a few moments before pulling it back out from underneath. Sue tilts her head to the side and gives Reagan a smile that has a whole lot more written behind it than Sue could ever verbalize. Her sister's touch isn't revolting, but it does not offer the same comforting result of John's.

"She's not the only one who's going to be ok, sis," Sue tells her.

Reagan nods but is not at all sure that her sister is right.

"All right, it's late so let's get started," Derek says, taking charge for which nobody argues.

Grandpa leads off with the question they probably all want to know, "Where did you bury the bodies?"

"Not anywhere close, sir. Unmarked graves way out in the woods, not near anything," Derek answers and Grandpa nods solemnly.

"Good, I don't want them anywhere near our home. This is our home, and we need to keep it as such," Grandpa says keenly.

"We have talked, Herb, and there has to be some changes made around here," Derek states.

By 'we' Reagan knows he means the military men and maybe the two young men, as well. This discussion probably took place while they all buried the dead or during night watches last night that Reagan believes they'd all stayed up for.

341

"Yeah, we obviously need to invest in a bull-dozer," Reagan says sarcastically, referring to the body burying.

John, Kelly and Derek laugh loudly. Even Sue and Grandpa chuckle. Hannie doesn't, but it's because she's too sympathetic, too soft and kind and everything that Reagan isn't and it's ok.

Sue shakes her head and scolds, "Reagan."

There is hardly any real judgment behind it. The joke was morbid, admittedly, but the laughter from the exhausted, apprehensive men made it worth the criticism.

"Uh… ok, anyways what I was going to say is that we need to make security changes, *Reagan*," Derek says.

He is still smiling and she returns a smaller one. He is cool like that. They used to stay up late and play board games and poker together with Grandpa and Sue on the rare occasion when Derek would make it to the farm. And Derek never treated her like a nerd genius. He's always been like a big brother to her.

"Right, we'd like to talk about blowing an abattis on our road, not the driveway, but the road that brings people here, that could bring more people here," John explains and Reagan interjects.

"Abattis, French for… tree barrier?" she asks, gaining a bewildered look from John. Then he points to the word "Einstein" on her shirt and smiles. She sends him a grin of her own. She sure as hell isn't anywhere near the level of Einstein's genius, but Reagan can't help but blush under the praise of John.

"Yeah, boss, French for tree barrier. How do you know that?"

"Um, not sure. Think I read it studying French military history when I was in grade school. I mean I didn't take it in school as a subject. I just read a book on it from the library. It was about the French military and their wars, so it was a short study," she says, gaining laughter from the men again at the friendly poking fun of the French and their poor warring track record. "And I speak French, duh."

"Can you explain this abattis?" Grandpa asks patiently.

"See, what we'd do is fell two trees at the same time at an angle so that they face toward oncoming traffic," Kelly says. "Then we'll take down two to four more. The limbs and branches will become a tangled mess. They won't be pushed around when we're done. Someone would have to literally chop a hole through them to

342

get down our road with a vehicle," Kelly explains as he demonstrates while intertwining his fingers. "They'll form kind of an interlocking "V" and they aren't movable- well, not without a tractor or some kind of equipment like that. Or a chainsaw, which most people won't have with them."

"Right, it keeps people out," Derek says. "No more anybody driving down the driveway- ever. Anyone that wants to get here has to walk in. It would protect us, the Reynolds and the Johnson farm, not that their farm matters anymore since they left it."

"I think that's a very good idea, Derek," Grandpa says.

Hannah agrees with him out loud. Nobody questions why sweet Hannah would feel this way. Kelly squeezes her hand gently on the table and then releases it.

"And we blow the bridge from your town- not Clarksville, the new city from hell, but where you had your practice, Doc, in Pleasant View," John says. "It would block that county road that leads out of town. I remember we crossed that small bridge coming here. It's not exactly like you couldn't still get out here from town, but you'd have to know all the back roads. I mean we're only about eight clicks from town, but it would certainly discourage anyone who even wanted to head west of that town for any reason. They could take other roads if they knew them, but once you get out onto some of the back roads in this county you can get lost pretty easily," John finishes and Grandpa nods slowly.

"Yeah, and anytime we want to go back to your town, we'd just go in from one of the longer, more roundabout ways," Derek adds sensibly.

Sue smiles at her husband from across the table. Grandpa strokes the gray whiskers on his chin which he hasn't shaved today. Cory and Simon sit quietly, absorbing this new information.

"And what about our neighbors, the Reynolds?" Grandpa asks thoughtfully.

"We can go over and tell them our plan, but it's in their best interest anyways," Derek says. "They are so close to the road that this will help with their security. And once Cory and Simon fix the other radio that got busted up yesterday, we'll give it to the Reynolds so that if they're ever attacked again, we can get over there more quickly."

Reagan wonders why he is making the boys fix the radio. It's not like they broke it up. John's horse did. Perhaps it is a rite of passage kind of thing or something. Neither of them looks surprised at hearing this, though, so they must've already been aware of the assignment. She's going to have to remember to ask John about it later.

"I was planning on taking the three hogs over there next week to butcher and to smoke the meat with Wayne, so that would be a good time to meet with them. And I want to share the meat, as well. They've always been good, God-fearing people, and I think we should help them as much as we can," Grandpa says. "Reagan you can ride along and help if you'd like. You can check Chet's shotgun injury."

"Reagan is better off here, sir. Chet Reynolds should fear *me* and forget about God if he keeps stalking Reagan the way he does. The leech," John verbalizes with instant antagonism and crosses his arms across his chest, his biceps bulging.

Kelly barks a loud laugh, Derek chuckles and shakes his head and Grandpa gives John an appraising look. Reagan's face flames three shades of red, her eyes grow huge. She literally lowers her head, shielding her gaze from everyone like she's staring at a ghost in her lap.

"Shut up!" she hisses and punches his sore leg. John is way too vocal about his claim on her. Next he'll be lifting his leg to mark her, the bastard.

Grandpa, not one to miss a beat, simply says, "Ohhhkay."

"Moving on," Derek says on a grin and keeps things flowing right along. "We can also hunt deer soon, and I'd be happy to bag a buck or two for them, as well, Herb."

"That's very thoughtful, Derek," Grandpa says.

"And we can butcher that cow you wanted done, Doc," Kelly volunteers. "I don't know how to unless they're like guttin' a deer, but I'd be happy to learn and so would Cory and Simon. Right, guys?"

"Yes, sir," the boys answer in unison.

They are coming to realize what their roles on this farm will be. It will take every person on the farm working together for their continued survival.

"If they haven't finished their solar panels, I'd like to see if we can't help the Reynolds family to build them. I'd like for them to have electricity again. Having them for neighbors could prove to be an asset in the future. I want to keep them as our friends," Grandpa remarks.

He looks pointedly at John who stares right back. Shit, he sure as hell doesn't back down from her grandfather.

"John!" Derek says firmly.

This causes John to tear his gaze from her grandfather's. Most men don't challenge Grandpa, not that John was necessarily challenging him. But he sure is driving his point home about the Reynolds.

Derek continues, "That's fine with us, Herb. We'll help them all that we can. Eventually our country will have to be completely rebuilt, so this can be the first step that our family takes toward that."

"Fine, we'll help them," John says with finality that still holds underlying antagonism toward Chet Reynolds.

Reagan's seen more times than she'd like what happens when he loses his temper; people usually end up dead. Plus, he'd punched Bobby just for talking down to Sam. And he'd eventually killed that dumb kid. When she'd spied him hit Bobby on the front lawn, though, her respect for John had soared. Obviously he doesn't like women to be mistreated, even the ones he has no claim on or isn't related to.

"Let's all turn in and get some rest," Grandpa says, ending the meeting.

"Agreed. Herb and I will take first watch, and Kelly and Cory will take second and John and Simon will take third," Derek says. "John, Simon's going to need taught quite a lot, but I know if anyone can help him, you can. And in a few weeks we'll start both guys on weapons training, basic training, hand to hand combat, demos and everything we know," Derek announces.

Reagan watches both teens perk up. Oh brother, why do men love blowing shit up so much?

"Yeah, and by the time you're both twenty you'll be a couple of bad-asses," Kelly says.

Everyone laughs. That is everyone but Grandpa who looks troubled by this. These boys have lost their youth, and it's not something to be regained. But Sam has lost just as much, if not more than the two boys. Having a couple more bad-asses around the farm isn't such a terrible idea in Reagan's opinion. They sure as hell make her feel remarkably safer on their farm. John especially makes her feel safer.

Everyone rises, but Reagan looks at John with admiration only to have it replaced by worry when she notices the swelling on his eyebrow and cheek. He'd taken some pretty hard punches yesterday.

"Before we go upstairs, I'm going to grab some ice cubes. Your face is still swelled in a couple of spots," she remarks and touches his cheek and eyebrow gently.

"Yeah, didn't you know you're supposed to duck when someone takes a swing at you?" Kelly asks jokingly to which Derek laughs heartily.

"Yeah, yeah. You two are a couple of comedians. I kind of had an animal the size of a one ton truck stuck on my leg!" John argues with mock irritation toward the other two men.

"Whiner," Derek jokes.

He and Kelly bump fists before they depart.

As Reagan collects the ice in the kitchen, she overhears John and Kelly talking after everyone else has gone their own ways.

"You want me to take your watch tonight, bro?" Kelly asks with sincere sympathy.

"Nah, I'm good. Thanks, though," John tells him.

Their level of commitment to each other is deeper than most marriages Reagan has ever known, and she can tell that Kelly is genuinely concerned about John's injuries. Kelly, naturally, doesn't have a scratch on him.

Once they are upstairs, John goes to their closet and starts taking measurements with a tape measure which Reagan hadn't even seen him pocket. He never rests, though he needs to, especially after the week they've had. She joins him in there, and her cold, bare feet are glad to be on carpeting finally.

"What are you doing?" she asks as he stretches the metal tape out from side to side in the closet. He hobbles over and looks around in the back of the room.

"Taking measurements. I'm thinking that we could get Jake's crib in here when we get one. Then we'd have more privacy," he tells

346

her like he's just giving her a grocery list to run errands and not talking about the obvious reason for their need for privacy. "Oh yeah, there's plenty of room."

"I didn't say I wanted to do that. You can't just go and make this decision without asking me. This is my bedroom," Reagan complains at him.

"It's my room, too, now, so I get a fifty percent say, boss. And I'd like to not sleep in a bed that my feet hang off the end. I'd also like to be able to make love to you whenever I want," John answers so matter of fact.

He just keeps taking his ridiculous measurements as if nothing is unusual with this conversation.

"Hey! You don't get sex from me whenever you want. I have a say in *that*, too!" she says as her voice is starting to rise in pitch. John stalks right up to her with his limp and kisses her dismissively on her forehead.

"I think it works out in your favor when I want it, so you shouldn't complain," he turns away.

Reagan huffs and clenches her fists in frustration. He's such a chauvinist sometimes.

He replies without turning back to her, "And I told you it's not sex so stop calling it that."

"Whatever. Do what you want. Here, you need to put this ice on your face," she tells him and grabs his forearm to get him to hold still. "I should've looked at your leg last night."

"I don't need that," John says and dodges her hand. "I could show you some other uses for it, though, if you're interested."

"What do you mean? Like what?" Reagan asks confusedly. John raises one eyebrow at her and then chuckles as she still continues to look at him with confusion. "Here, put this on!"

"No, I'm not a child. I'm fine. Just got banged up," he argues.

John drops to his knees where he pulls out, from the bottom of his closet space, the rucksack that they'd taken to the city.

"What are you doing now? Would you quit moving, so I can look at your leg and ice your face, damn it?"

"No, I'm busy," he replies assertively.

He dodges her hand and pulls out the boxes of rubber bands they'd taken from the hobby store.

"Hey, I meant to ask, why do you guys want the boys to fix the radio?" she inquires as she kneels beside him.

"Because they have to learn to work together and not rely on us for everything. We're not gonna' be around forever to take care of them," John says.

Reagan's stomach does a sickening flip. John simply continues on like he hasn't said something devastating and horrible.

"I couldn't find these. I thought they were in the other bag, but nope," he says about his rubber bands and stashes them back away again.

"Lie down on your back so I can look at your leg," Reagan demands, wanting to put his morbid comment about croaking someday behind her. Surprisingly, John actually lies down, shocking her to the core. "Oh, good," she says uncertainly. Reagan has him raise and bend and flex his leg and then works his hip, feeling for anything out of place. He winces twice and then scowls at her.

"See? I'm fine, hon'," he says so easily.

Reagan hates it when he calls her this, or any endearment for that matter. She frowns at him, still kneeling on both knees near his hip.

"I don't think anything is dislocated or broken, but you're going to be sore as hell for a few days. You may have ruptured a few tendons or ligaments. Maybe just take it easy for about a week," she orders and meets his gaze.

"Only if you are gonna stay in that bed with me for the next week. If not, then I've got projects to work on, babe," he tells her.

His wicked grin ignites a flame within her.

Reagan clears her voice and looks back at his leg again. "What the heck are the rubber bands for? You never did tell me," she asks as she feels along his tendons and his inner thigh.

"Napalm," he answers simply.

His blue eyes bore into hers with an intensity that she's beginning to recognize as desire.

"Like the napalm that the military used during the Vietnam War?" Reagan asks and pushes in on his hip and rotates it back out.

"Of course you know that. Yeah, like in that war. We'll mix some gas and these rubber bands and make some tweaks, show the boys how to do it. They can be very effective incendiary devices," he says with a smile.

348

John presses the back of his hand against the side of her cheek. The one with the scar

"Sounds violent," she says and then smiles. "I like it."

John laughs and pulls her down on top of him.

"Remember when you wanted to be the boss so bad? This might be your chance, kid," he quips.

He flips her quickly until she's straddling him on the carpeted floor of her closet.

Reagan places her hands on either side of his head and presses herself down against his erection.

"Now where's that bag of ice?" he jokes.

John kisses her mouth and then many other parts of her, leaving them both breathless and exhausted and her without any more questions about the use of ice. And later as Reagan is falling asleep on his chest, he stands and hoists her in one fell swoop into his arms and carries her with his limp to her bed. John places her gently down beside Jacob. Reagan falls asleep thinking of John and the protection he so selflessly offers to her and her family.

Chapter Twenty-four
Kelly

"Are you sure, Cory?" Kelly asks his brother for the third time. Weeks have sped by since the departure of the visitors, and the entire family has been working on refortification projects, harvesting the last of the summer's crops and butchering livestock. The men are slated to go in a few days to pick up the processed and smoked pork products from the Reynolds family in exchange for two pigs for breeding.

"Yeah, man. I told you already. It's cool, Kelly. I'm actually glad," Cory says as they join the family for dinner.

John is holding Jacob who is already clanging a spoon loudly against Reagan's plate. Reagan simply confiscates the spoon and gives him what looks to Kelly like a dog's rubber chew toy. Apparently kids like them, too. Reagan takes Jacob and sets him in his new-used high-chair behind them where the baby proceeds to bang his chewy thing on the plastic tray in front of him. They seem to have adapted well to parenthood for two people so young and unmarried and un... everything.

Kelly takes his seat next to Hannah who has healed almost completely from her attack and who keeps pressuring Kelly to sleep with her again. Out of respect for her grandfather, the respect that he should've maintained before, he hasn't been with Hannah since their discussion in his office.

Somehow his Hannah is not mentally traumatized from her episode with Crazy Willy, thank God. The other day he spoke with her about it after she insisted on being kissed first, to which he'd complied but had only done so hesitantly. As they sat for a spell under a brilliantly-colored maple tree on the hill at the top of the cattle pasture, the one that overlooks the entire farm, she opened up and talked to Kelly about her attack and how she felt about it. She even told Kelly that she forgave Willy for doing it. She has a bigger heart than him because if he could, Kelly would like to have gone back and killed that bastard more slowly, more painfully, show him what it was like during an interrogation of Syrian terrorists done by men who had the government's full authority to do whatever was necessary to prevent another D.C. attack. If anything, she's been trying to be in closer proximity to Kelly than usual. He's left to believe that she has some residual insecurity about being out of his perimeter, and that's fine with him because he prefers to keep her within his direct line of sight for many reasons, some just for the pleasant view she affords.

"Hello, Kelly," Hannah says in her heavenly, lilting voice. "Have you had a good day?"

"Uh, yeah sure," he answers with hesitancy.

Sometimes when Hannah talks, it's like there isn't anything going on in the rest of the world like World War Three, tsunami and nuclear apocalypses, mass spread disease, devastation and sickness and basically the end of the world, and it never fails to shock him. With Hannah, it's more like the right here, the right now and that's it. It keeps Kelly grounded, and he likes just being near her. Plus, she always has a very soothing effect on the kids, as well, when they could all so easily sink into depression and despair. Just being near her optimism and high spirits makes everyone feel a tiny bit better.

"What did you do today?" she asks.

She turns toward him with her sightless, mismatched, beautiful eyes that are more expressive than a person who has their vision.

"We finished the oats and got 'em sacked up. Then John and I repaired the roof on the hog barn 'cuz it had a leak. You know, the usual," he tells her with a grin. "What did you do today, Miss Hannah?"

She gives him one of her light-filled smiles and says, "Mostly I was wondering why I wasn't with you."

"Is that so?" he asks her in a playful manner and glances nervously around to make sure nobody else has heard her. But not everyone is in the dining room yet, which Hannah probably already knows.

"You're always so busy that I hardly see you anymore," she says.

Her comment holds a touch of pouty sadness that makes Kelly long to kiss her… and then maybe just ravish her a little, too.

"I sat with you yesterday during Sunday service," he reminds her, and she nods with a half frown.

"Yes, but you wouldn't hold my hand. I miss you, Kelly. I miss *all* of you," she sensually adds.

Kelly squirms uncomfortably in his chair and clears his throat loudly. When his Hannah talks like this, it always knocks him off guard. He just never expects anything naughty to come from her innocent lips. He's made the mistake of underestimating her since the moment he met her, and it is probably the reason he can't do anything but think about her most every hour of the damn day.

They are interrupted from further conversation because the family is gathering in a noisy hoard to the table, the teenage boys being the most excited. If they take in any more teenagers, Kelly thinks they should definitely add on an additional dining room with sound-proof walls and a steel door. They are both excited about a flock of turkeys they saw this morning and plan to take shotguns out tomorrow to shoot a few. Cory has taken to sitting next to Sam, though the girl does not talk to him. Sometimes she'll scoot to the far edge of her chair so that she doesn't have to be too close to him. Most of the time she looks scared of his brother, but it's understandable. He's a big kid, getting bigger every day it seems. He has to be about six-two or three now, and Sam is only about Hannah's height at around five-four.

Kelly talked to Cory about Sam last week because he doesn't want his brother to get any ideas where she is concerned. But Cory had confided that he just felt protective of her because of what she'd been through, that he didn't look at her "that" way. Kelly had given him a stern lecture about her, though, just in case. Sam is only fifteen. Simon is a year older and Cory will be eighteen next month. Simon will turn seventeen the month after in December, the same month as Kelly's birthday. But Sam has only just turned fifteen this summer. Kelly can't imagine going through what she's been through at such a young age. When he was fifteen, all he worried about was playing football, basketball and chasing girls. This girl has lost her family in one day, her whole way of life and had likely been repeatedly raped, though nobody has confirmed this. The teens on the farm don't need to be making the same mistakes that he and Hannah have made. However, the way that Sam looks at Cory, Kelly's fairly certain that won't happen any time in the foreseeable future. She'll hang out with the boys, but only for a short period of time. She sticks by Sue or Reagan most days and avoids overly long contact with Cory. She is most trusting of Simon. She carries a sketch pad with her almost everywhere she goes, and Sue said that the girl is a very talented artist. They like drawing and painting together.

It probably doesn't help Sam feel comfortable around Cory since he has the same dark looks as Bobby. His brother has a ruggedness about him, though, whereas Bobby could've been a teen model if it hadn't been for the coldness in his black eyes. Simon is simply tall, lanky and a bit geeky. They've put both of the young men on firewood chopping duties, and they are already bulking up, even Simon who had come to the farm as skinny as a rail. Firewood is a bitch of a chore, and he'd been glad to put the boys on that particular job. His dad would be so proud.

Doc leads the family with a prayer, and the chaos begins and eventually ends with apple pies for desert made from freshly-picked apples from the orchard. The women, even Reagan, have picked the last of the season's apples and have turned them into applesauce, apple pie fillings and put crates of them in cold storage in the old part of the basement where they will stay good most of the winter. Each of the kids, the teens included, had been taught to make the apple-sauce, as well. It is a good idea to teach them as much as possible for survival. The future is so uncertain, and they may not all live long enough to take care of and raise these kids.

The men have worked on deepening their security efforts after their guests left, including going to town and blowing that bridge which Reagan had tagged along for because she needed to see how it would work. What a nerd. She'd even laughed loudly as it went down, something Kelly's never heard from her before. If a woman could have a rotten, bawdy laugh, then that's how he'd describe that little nut job's laugh. They'd cut the tree barriers at either end of their road with Cory and Simon. In addition, they snagged two additional security cameras from one of the mansions in the burbs that they'd immediately tied into their own. These cameras will cover the end of the driveway and the road. For as long as the solar power will last, the McClane spread should be covered for security purposes. John and Derek have started both of the teens on basic training, minus all of the drill sergeant screaming in your face stuff. But they do have them on long runs, weapons training, hand to hand combat and a whole lot more than those kids probably ever would've thought a year ago that they'd need to learn. Simon had found John's missing weapon out on a patrol one morning with Cory, and Kelly thought his friend was gonna cry like a girl over it which he'd kindly pointed out, earning him a punch to the shoulder. It was like a fly landing there, also something he'd pointed out. And they've been asses and elbows deep in farm work and getting everything finished before hunting season starts in the middle of November, in the middle of the deer rut, which is in three weeks. It is amazing to Kelly, but there is always something that needs done around the farm, and he really can't imagine how Doc and the girls would've managed if they hadn't made it home to this farm.

As the meal concludes and people begin to rise from their chairs, Kelly stops them with an announcement. "Hey, everyone, if I could just take a minute of your time," he says and stands and then takes Hannah's hand in his, pulling her to her feet.

"Oh, where are we going?" she asks musically.

She acts as if he's tugging her along to hop a plane and go on some exotic vacation. She never fails to surprise him with her cheerfulness and absolute trust. Hannah allows him to lead her to the opening of the dining room doorway. He takes both of her frail hands into his mammoth ones.

"Hannah, I wanted to do this in front of your family and my family and our new family," he says directing his gaze toward Sam, Huntley and Simon. Simon and Cory smile knowingly.

"What did you want to do, Kelly?" she asks with a smile.

Her brightness gives him the courage to continue.

"I love you, Hannah McClane. And it's screwed up to even say this but I'm glad for what happened in the world because I might not have ever met you or come to this farm. I would have never had you in my life, and before I met you I didn't even know what I had been missing. You never try to change me or make me any different

354

than what I am: a rusty, old, ragbag of a soldier, I guess. When you were attacked, I was so scared I'd lost you for good when I couldn't find you. I don't ever want to feel that way again. You've never asked me to be something I'm not. And you're so good and pure and hopeful, Hannah, that you make me feel hopeful for the first time in a long time. I want that long time to be forever. I want to be with you forever, here on this farm with our families. I'll defend this farm to my dying breath, and I'll defend you against anything that comes our way. I promise I'll protect you and love you forever. Will you marry me, Hannah?"

Kelly goes down on one knee and presses a ring from his pocket into her palm so that she can feel it because he knows she certainly can't see it, which is probably a good thing because it's small, salvaged from the floor of a raided Sam's Club in the city that John had snaked per his request. Hannah doesn't answer but starts crying in earnest and hugging Kelly's head to her stomach. When he lifts his gaze to meet hers, she is nodding and weeping at the same time.

"Yes, Kelly, I will marry you," she finally says.

Everyone in the room starts clapping. He slips the ring onto her slim finger and it's just a tad loose but not so much that it will twirl around. He's vaguely aware that there are other people in the room, but all he can see is his Hannah. She's lovely and crying and smiling as she places her hands on his face.

John calls out, "It's about time!"

The guys shake his hand and so does Herb which means more than he can say seeing as how disapproving he'd been of Kelly's earlier inappropriate behavior with Hannah. Grams squeezes him tight and also has tears in her blue eyes.

"Well, give her a kiss, Kelly!" Sue shouts above the melee.

Derek is trying to explain to the children what's going on and why their Aunt Hannah is crying. Kelly gives her a quick peck on the cheek because he doesn't want to blow his nanosecond run of approval from her grandfather.

Little Arianna shouts, "I thought they already were married!"

The entire family laughs uproariously.

"How will this work? How can they marry?" Derek asks.

"Herb will just have to do it according to the Good Book, and we'll all bear as witnesses. There's nothing else that can be done," Grams says so simply.

The actual ceremony isn't something Kelly had thought of when he'd decided to throw in all his chips and ask her to marry him. The most important thing to Kelly had been getting his siblings approval which he had. A few days ago he'd sat down with Em and had a long talk to her and was surprised when she'd so wholeheartedly gone along with it. She told him that she loved Hannah like a big sister and that she never wanted to leave the farm, ever or to be more exact: ever, ever ever, never. And yesterday he'd given Cory the option to give his opinion on the matter and his brother had said the same. To be sure, he'd asked him again before dinner had commenced.

"Yes, I suppose you're right, Maryanne," Doc says. "But I'll draw up legal and binding paperwork, as well, by copying our own marriage certificate. We'll sign it. Someday if there's ever a courthouse for which to file the proper documents, we'll have them ready. But I doubt that it's going to happen anytime soon. So as far as I'm concerned if it's good enough for Kelly and Hannah, then it's good enough for me," he declares.

With that being said, they all retire to the music room. Sue leads Hannah by the arm as they laugh and cry and talk in hushed tones. The kids bound ahead, high on sugar and the rare, upbeat mood of the family.

Kelly is stopped in the hall by Reagan, and John stands behind her holding Jacob. She looks like she has something to say, but she's mostly staring at his chest. If this goes too badly with her, then he'll tell Grams on her that she's still wearing her dirty Converse in the house. Reagan isn't afraid of much, but everyone fears Grams.

"You're still an asshole," she says.

"Nice, Reagan," John scolds her with a frown as he bounces Jacob on his hip.

"I know, little Doc. But I did tell you that I loved her," he confesses and snatches Reagan into a monster bear hug. She doesn't kick him in the balls, but she also doesn't return the hug. She's come a long way in the five months since they've come to live here. She pulls free after about three seconds.

356

"If it had to be somebody, then I'm glad it was you, Kelly," she says and storms off before anyone can comment.

He looks at John who raises his eyebrows, mirroring Kelly's shock.

"Wow, that was almost… friendly," Kelly remarks with a smirk.

"We've been working on that," John jokes good-humoredly.

"Mm hm, sure you have. I notice you said that *after* she walked away," Kelly observes with a laugh that John echoes so readily.

"I never said I was stupid," John says on a grin. "But I am happy for you, though, brother. I think you guys will be good together. And you can quit sneaking around at night," John says.

Kelly's mouth drops.

"What? How did…"

"You aren't as stealthy as you might think, dude. Besides, the one night I was on watch and was in the pantry looking for Reagan's hidden candy stash when I saw Hannah go by. Don't worry, though. I never told anyone. I'm the only one who knew," John says with a confident wink.

Yeah, well John apparently didn't have to tell anyone. And he only thinks he's the only one who knew. Shit, who all does know? Is there anyone in the house who doesn't know might be a better question?

His friend shakes his hand and gives him a one-armed hug that Kelly returns.

"Thanks, man. I'm crazy about her and for some reason she likes me, so I figured I'd better snatch her up before she comes to her senses," Kelly laughs.

"No kidding," John tells him as they walk together.

Jacob stretches for Kelly who takes him from John. The kid is growing like a weed. Having food and milk readily available on the farm instead of whatever his mother had been able to scavenge has obviously helped with his growth. He giggles and gurgles, and Kelly smiles down at him before he presses a kiss to his nearly bald head.

When they get to the music room, there is a lot of planning going on in the women's corner, and Grams is suggesting that the Reynolds come over. Sue proposes that they should hold the wedding on Saturday which is five days from now. Talk about a rushed ceremony. No going back now.

"I think that would be just fine, Maryanne," Doc offers. "It will be a relief to finally celebrate something instead of mourning and death and the vast negativity that our world's come to. And I think the Reynolds kids could use a break from it, too. We'll radio them to let them know."

"It *will* be so nice to celebrate something!" Grams announces happily to which everyone heartily agrees.

Kelly takes a seat next to his Hannah on the floral print sofa. He reaches for her already outstretched hand, taking it into his own. It's so nice to be able to finally hold her hand. He'll save the kissing and the rest for after the ceremony. He doesn't want Doc to shoot him just yet.

Chapter Twenty-five
Hannah

The next four days fly by in a blur of planning, decorating, cooking and preparing for her wedding, but all Hannah can think about is Kelly. Yesterday morning he'd stolen her away for a walk through the woods. She'd worn her baggy blue-jeans and a sweater to guard against the cool autumn air. After a short distance, Kelly had hefted her onto his back and just piggy-backed her the rest of the way. She hadn't minded in the least. She also hadn't minded the kiss he'd given her before leaving her in the kitchen and going out to work on welding a headstall in the cow barn.

"This is almost done, Hannie," Sue announces.

Hannah snaps out of her trance about Kelly's fine kisses. Sue chuckles quietly.

"Your veil, sort of. It's almost done. This ring of flowers will look just lovely on you, Hannah."

"Thanks, Sue," she offers. "You guys have done so much for this. We really didn't need to go to such fuss. Kelly and I don't need anything fancy."

Reagan scoffs unladylike. "Duh, you're only gonna do this once. Besides, Grams wouldn't have allowed us to half-ass it anyways."

"Reagan," Hannah scolds. Grams is in the kitchen with Em, luckily for her potty mouth sister.

"What?" Reagan asks, incredulous of the swear.

Knowing Reagan like she does, her sister probably doesn't even realize she's done it again.

Without missing a beat, her sister just continues on, "Grandpa talked to Wayne's family yesterday and they're coming, too. He also said that Bertie actually smiled for the first time he's seen since it happened."

The 'it' Reagan refers to is the murder of three of Bertie's in-laws. She'd been deeply depressed about her miscarriage, as well. So many people in their country are probably dealing with such similar, devastating events.

"Might get to spend some time with Chet, Reagan," Sue hints.

There is a smile, probably an ornery one, in her older sister's voice.

"Yeah, I want to talk to him about breeding the goats again in the spring," Reagan says with absolutely no clue.

"Reagan, don't just throw them in a ball. Fold them like Grams showed you," Sue corrects her crazy, brainiac, clueless sister who has been given the duty of folding the linen napkins that they'll use tomorrow at the wedding dinner.

Reagan snorts. She is probably wishing she was studying one of her books instead of folding antique linens.

"If we're just gonna wipe our mouths on them, then what the hell's the point?"

Sue groans in reply. "The point is you are going to earn Grams's wrath. Is that what you want?"

Reagan must not because she doesn't respond. Hannah smiles at her sisters' interaction. It feels so normal, so nostalgic and she's just happy to have any time with them when the children, other family members, chores, or life-threatening turmoil aren't interrupting their time together. They just don't get much of it anymore, and Hannah realizes just how much she's missed it. It used to just be the three of them all the time, but not after Sue got married and moved away. And also not after Reagan went away to college which had left Hannah extremely depressed for a while. She'd never told anyone about it, especially not Reagan because she would've quit school and come home to her. Reagan would never have allowed her to feel that way. Sometimes her sister is so protective of her that it almost frightens Hannah. And now the house is always full of a ton of people and children, not that it is such a bad thing. But it is hard to find sister time.

"Besides, it's going to be lovely when we're all done with everything," Sue tells them both.

Hannah is busy braiding ribbons together that they'll run down the middle of the long tables which will be placed outdoors for the dinner tomorrow. It seems to be one of the few things that she can help with in all of the preparations.

Sue says on a raucous laugh, "Anyways, I wasn't talking about Chet to bring up goat breeding, you doofus."

Reagan replies with confusion written into her voice. "Then what did you mean?"

"Well, I just thought you might be happy to see him for other reasons," Sue clarifies but doesn't receive an answer. "Reagan, I mean like you might be *into* him."

"What?" Reagan asks in a high-pitched voice. "Get real. He's basically a dullard. I just need his goat. I'm not 'into' him. I never was. Why are you even insinuating that? You know I wasn't ever interested in him or any of the other boys around here."

"Or anyone else, ever!" Hannah verbally jabs at her high-spirited sister who snorts in return.

Sue gives a short laugh. "Hm, maybe you're into someone else," her sly sister suggests. "Seems like you and John have been spending a lot of time together."

"No way," Reagan mumbles.

"You're blushing!" Sue exclaims.

"Shut up. I am not," Reagan retorts angrily.

This is getting interesting. Yep, just like old days.

Reagan defends herself quickly enough, "I'm not blushing, Hannie."

"You are. You're blushing, Reagan McClane," Sue says again, antagonizing their feisty sister. "What the heck happened in the city, little sister? We haven't really had much time to talk to you since you guys got back- what with those people being here and all. Is there anything you want to tell us?"

"No," comes the abbreviated, annoyed response.

Hannah chuckles.

"Come on, Reagan," Hannah prods. "You know everything about me and Kelly. It wasn't like I had a choice, either."

She's referring to the bladder infection, of course, but Hannah also hopes that Sue doesn't question this. Nobody but Reagan knows of her and Kelly being promiscuous before their wedding.

"Nothing happened. Well, not much happened," Reagan says slyly.

Hannah can tell that her sister is frowning. It's one of her signature expressions.

"What do you mean?" Hannah pushes.

"I don't know really. I just saw a lot of stuff about John that made me look at him differently," Reagan acknowledges.

"Like what, Reagan?" Sue asks more seriously.

They are sitting in their grandparent's bedroom suite working on decorations and wedding items. They are using supplies from a large box of silk flowers and ribbons that Sue found in storage. The children are outside playing and enjoying the last vestiges of daylight while the men work on evening chores. The babies are being watched by Grams. Grandpa has been holed up in his study a lot lately, and Hannah isn't sure if it is because he is working on the wedding ceremony or something else. He's been in there more than the usual amount of time even back before the visitors came or Kelly had proposed. The house is unnaturally quiet and still. Hannah and Reagan are seated on the floor while Sue sits at their grandmother's writing desk.

"For one, he saved my ass like a dozen times," Reagan tells them.

"Yeah? Well, he is a Ranger. That's kind of what they do," Sue says with a laugh.

"Yeah, I guess," Reagan says unsurely.

"Were you scared spending the night with him?" Hannah inquires.

"No," Reagan answers too quickly.

"I would've been. It's not like we go around sleeping with strange men all the time. That would've been awkward," Hannah says honestly.

"Not really. That wasn't too bad. It was just a lot of other things I didn't like," Reagan says.

She's opening up but only a smidge.

"What do you mean?" Hannah asks her.

362

"He's just different than I originally thought. He has such a strong moral conscience it's unbelievable. I mean, he didn't have to take in Jacob like he did. But it was so surreal. He didn't even bat an eye. He just grabbed him up and assumed a hundred percent instant responsibility for him," her sister explains.

She is talking as if her mind is side-tracked by memories. It doesn't sound to Hannah like her sister dislikes these things about John at all.

"I think he feels the same about you, Reagan. Feels that same sense of responsibility," Sue tells her.

Hannah couldn't agree more. Reagan puffs air through her nose.

"I don't need him to. I'm doing fine taking care of myself," Reagan argues.

"Doesn't matter. He still feels it. I can see it in John," Sue elucidates.

"He also loses his shit and kills people pretty easily, too. It's like he has a switch he can just flick on and off and do whatever it takes to stay alive…"

"Or keep *you* alive," Sue corrects.

"Yeah, I guess," Reagan states, although her voice is heavy with the burden of this knowledge. "It's just weird. I've never been around someone like him before."

"Or someone with such nice muscles or cheekbones?" Sue hints with a rotten laugh.

"Sue!" Hannah shouts with a laugh of her own.

"I don't look at his… muscles. I don't even know if he has any," Reagan lies so badly.

They both laugh *at* her this time.

"Yeah, right!" Sue cries with another laugh.

From what Hannah can tell just from hugging John, he is just as muscular as Derek and Kelly. Her sister is obviously fibbing to cover her own embarrassment. John is also very kind and very much in love with Reagan. Hannah doesn't need vision to figure that one out.

"Shut up," Reagan mumbles.

Her sister moves around the room. She can pace around all she wants, there's no way out of the room before she finishes her assignment.

She grinds out, "Next subject. Seriously."

"Alright, alright, Reagan. Sorry," Sue apologizes. "Hannah, I have white shoes that will go perfect with your dress if you'd like to borrow them. I think we're the same size, right?"

"I think so," Hannah agrees. "That would be great. Oh, unless they have a high heel, then forget it."

Sue chuckles. "No, sweetie. No heels. They're totally flat, like a ballet flat. Don't want you to bust your butt."

"No shit. Then Kelly's gonna beat me up because I'll be laughing at you," Reagan chides.

"Good grief, Reagan," Sue scolds. "She won't trip. She's going to be so beautiful."

"You don't need fancy shoes or some ridiculous, frumpy costume to look beautiful, Hannie," Reagan offers.

"Thanks, Reagan," Hannah replies on a sardonic frown. Her sister does not have a way with flattery or prose.

"Are you nervous?" Sue asks.

Hannah just smiles demurely to herself. "No, not at all. I love Kelly very much. We were meant to be together. I'm glad that we're getting married. And I'm really glad that my family will be there with us tomorrow."

Reagan stands beside her and places a slim hand on Hannah's shoulder. "I feel bad that Kelly's parents won't be there to see it. I'm sure they would've loved you, Hannie. Hell, everybody does."

"I wish they were going to be there, too," Hannah tells them. "We talked about it. Kelly's sad, too, but he's glad that his brother and sister will be there. They're all he has left now."

"No, not all. He has you now. And you'll make a good aunt slash mom to Em, Hannah. You're really good with her for not ever having any kids of your own," Reagan says before walking away again.

"They're so great. It's not like it's hard to help Kelly with them. Mostly they are just going to need someone to talk to now and then. They've both been through so much," Hannah corrects them.

"No kidding. Seems to be the theme of the day," Reagan replies with sarcasm.

Then she sprints around in her normal flurry of movement.

She blurts quickly, "Hey, I forgot to tell you. I got you a few things the other day when I went with John to the condo community."

"What'd you get, Reagan?" Sue asks first.

Reagan plops down beside Hannah on the floor and there is a rustling, clanking of items.

"It's a bag of goodies, Hannie," Reagan explains.

She's always been good at explaining things for Hannah's clarification. Reagan even takes her hand and runs it over a cotton or canvas sack and gives it a jingle-jangle.

"Oh? What do you have there?" Hannah asks with piqued curiosity.

"I had him take me through a few houses near the condos and we found some useful crap. It was mostly boring stuff like sugar, gas, lighter fluid. Boring. But then we went into Pleasant View and we raided a few stores and some of the buildings. There was a surprising amount of junk still there. Grandpa's practice is trashed all to hell, but some of the other buildings aren't too bad. The pharmacy's screwed, nothing left there at all. Anyways, who cares about that? I found this little brooch of two blue birds on the floor of Bernson's Jewelry store in town. That place had already been hit hard, but I found the brooch. I don't know if it's real diamonds or sapphires or what it's made out of, but it's sparkly. Jewelry has never exactly been my thing. It can be your 'something blue.' Well, only if you want it to be. You don't have to feel obligated," her sister offers.

It's highly unusual for Reagan to be sentimental about anything, so it leaves Hannah smiling.

"That would be wonderful, Reagan," she tells her as Reagan presses the brooch into her palm. Hannah can feel the jagged edges of rhinestones or crystals. Sue comes closer to Hannah, standing at her shoulder.

"That's great, Reagan. It's quite lovely, Hannah. Here, we can pin it to her dress," Sue considers as she gently extracts it from Hannah's hand. "Wow, it's stamped 14k on the back. I'd bet these are real gemstones. They don't usually set fake gemstones in real gold. I think it'll be just lovely on your dress, Hannie. We could pin it to the top, near the lace at your collar. It will be so pretty, and it matches your eyes."

"Ok, that'll be fine," Hannah accommodates them both.

"Gold is Au on the periodic table of elements. That always bothered me. Why not just make it a big G? Everyone would've known it meant gold, duh," Reagan babbles.

Her sister just yammers about sciency stuff while Sue continues on without missing a beat.

"And we can set your hair in soft rollers tonight," Sue says when she comes back from the closet where Hannah's dress is hung. "It'll fall in loose waves tomorrow if we set it. It always looks so pretty that way. We could pull half up and leave half down or whatever way you want it."

"Ok," Hannah says again. She's not concerned about her hair or a brooch. She just wants to be married to Kelly. All of the pomp and circumstance involved in planning and executing the actual process aren't so much of an interest for Hannah. She can't see any of it anyways.

"Hannah, you could pass that brooch on to your daughter someday. If it is real, then it's probably worth money. Well, it used to be worth money," Reagan snorts.

Hannah smiles. She's still stuck on the brooch.

Reagan adds, "Maybe you might want to invest in underwear and socks instead to pass down to your daughter. Not like any of those are gonna get manufactured anymore."

"Reagan, it might not always be like this. As a matter of fact, I feel quite certain that things will get better," Hannah tries to put on a positive spin.

"Don't get your hopes up too high, Hannie," Reagan says harshly. "As long as men still run the world, it'll stay fucked up for a long time."

"Reagan!" Sue berates. "Besides, nobody's really running anything. It's not the worst thing ever, either. It'll be a fresh start, a do-over for everyone in the world."

"Yeah, but eventually men will take over everything again and then they'll just…"

"I do believe, genius, that the only woman President this country has ever had is the one who made the Syrian mess that involved our military. And that royal screw-up was still going on

366

before this started. Remember, smarty pants? Let's not argue. People will always try to destroy each other and take what doesn't belong to them. I'm a mom! Trust me on this one. My own kids fight over toys on a daily basis. They're just smaller versions of adults," Sue says with a laugh that Hannah and even Reagan echo. "Hey, this is Hannah's night anyways. We aren't going to be negative today."

"Ok, whatever," Reagan finally says in a huff.

"It's ok, Reagan," Hannah lets her off the hook. "I have enough hope for the both of us."

She takes Reagan's slim hand in her own, and her sister actually lets her hold it for a minute before pulling away. Hannah instead presses her palm to Reagan's cool cheek. Hannah feels the long, thin scar there and some deep, primitively protective instinct within her surfaces as it always does. Either of her sisters in pain is not something she likes to think about, ever. However, her sister pulls away more quickly this time. The bag jingles again, the sounds of metal, perhaps wood and other things bumping against each other.

"I also got something else at the jewelry store. It can count as your 'something new.' It'll count as something new for all of us actually," Reagan says and presses something into Hannah's hand again.

"What do you mean?" Sue asks.

"I found these gold bracelets under a desk in the back room. There was a scattering of jewelry and coins on the floor like the owner had been packing things away when he was come upon or… something. Let's not speculate on that," Reagan insists.

None of them wants to. It is likely a macabre tale.

"Oh, they're pretty, too, Reagan. This is definitely real gold," Sue exclaims.

"Here, Sue, I got this one for you; and one for you, Hannie; and one for Em and Sam, too, since they're kind of our adopted little sisters. And one for me, of course," Reagan explains.

Hannah allows her fingertips to glide over the smooth, polished metal of the bracelet. In the exact center of the flat, intertwining link of the chain is a cross that is connected on either side with some sort of filigree or design. She frowns.

"What is it, Reagan?" she inquires.

"It's a Celtic symbol on either side of the cross, Hannie," Reagan replies quietly. She is still kneeling beside Hannah. "Here, let me work the clasp for you."

"What does the symbol mean do you think?" Sue asks.

Reagan chuffs again. "Don't be silly. I know exactly what it means or I wouldn't have taken them. It's a triple spiral. Feel, Hannie. Feel the circles? They don't close all the way. It's usually an interpretation of women according to the Celtic world of symbolism. The three sides represent the three life stages of a woman from young to old and usually mean power, change and strength, blah, blah, blah."

"It's really beautiful, Reagan," Sue says after a moment's pause to think about the bracelet and what it represents.

"I just thought they were cool. You know, kind of badass like us. We're powerful women. And this links us together forever no matter where we end up, or if God forbid we'd ever be separated," Reagan says.

She knows her sister is trying her hardest to seem nonchalant about such a poignant gift. Before Reagan can rise and leave her again, Hannah reaches out and pulls her sister close for a long hug. This time Reagan doesn't swiftly draw back but actually returns it. Sue joins them, and soon she and her oldest sister end up with tears streaming down their cheeks. Reagan does not return this expression of feeling, though. That would be too much for her.

"Good grief!" her feisty sister finally says and pulls away. "This is not the powerful badass stuff I was talking about!"

Sue laughs aloud, not caring what Reagan thinks. Hannah smiles.

"I can't wait to show Em," Hannah expresses on a sniffle. "She'll think it's so great being a part of this. It's so hard for her having lost her mother. If she feels a connection to the three of us, I think it will help her."

"Oh, I agree, Hannah," Sue says with a smile in her voice. "She's so sweet and good. She'll feel like she's a part of some inner circle when she gets this. I know I sure do."

"Me, too. And someday you can pass yours on to Ari," Hannah agrees.

No matter how much she loves and cherishes Kelly and will until the day she dies, there is something about being bonded to her sisters that is unexplainable. There will always be aspects of her life, aspects of her as a woman that he will never fully understand. There will always be things that she will only share with her sisters. And there will always be a love so powerful that has bound her to them and them to her for the rest of their lives. Perhaps it was because they'd all lost their mother of whom they'd loved so deeply. Perhaps it is simply the way things are with all sisters. It doesn't matter to Hannah. She'll always be a part of them, and they'll always know that they are a part of her.

Sue hands her a handkerchief, probably Grandpa's. "I pinned the lace from Grams's wedding dress to the inside hem of your dress, Hannah. Even though we may be living in a modern apocalypse there's no reason not to do this right. You now have all four elements of the 'something' tradition. We've got old, new, borrowed and blue. The end times have got nothing on us."

"Yep, we're a regular, freaging bunch of party planners around here," Reagan sarcastically remarks.

Sue scolds Reagan again, but it isn't heartfelt and lacks any real scrutiny. A short while later, they finish the decorations and her crown of flowers. And Sue finishes Reagan's linens. Hannah's quite sure her that her wily sister has complained ceaselessly about it just to get out of doing it. After all, she is a genius.

They make their way to the kitchen together just as the men are coming in from doing whatever outdoor chores they've been working on. The kids follow noisily behind them as Grams joins the melee. Sue and Derek depart, taking their children with them. Kelly sends Cory upstairs for cleaning up and Em downstairs for the same where he follows her. One by one the family disperses, leaving Hannah and her grandmother alone in their special room of the house.

"How are you feeling, love?" Grams asks of her.

Hannah takes a seat at the island while Grams stands on the other side.

"Ok, I suppose. Tired," Hannah grants.

"You need to get some rest, honey," Grams advises. "Big day tomorrow."

Hannah grins. "You need rest, too. You've been working so hard around here all week," she says as she slides her hand across the island and finds her grandmother's.

"I wasn't about to allow my granddaughter to have a shabby wedding. Not on my watch, young lady. You deserve the best. I just wish this all hadn't happened so that we could've thrown you a proper ceremony," Grams divulges.

Hannah can tell that she is scowling.

"I don't need any of that. Sue was worried about the same thing," Hannah dispels her grandmother's fears. "I'm just happy to be marrying Kelly. I'm happy that my family will be here and that we're all ok. That's all I need, Grams."

"You were always so easy to please, Hannah dear. So eager to please, so easy to please. That's the way you've always been, my darling. It's not easy to find happiness in this world. But you've always managed to find happiness in any circumstance. It's probably why he loves you so much, you know."

Her grandmother's words bring tears to Hannah's eyes. "I don't really know why he loves me. I'm just glad that he does."

"Oh, I know why. It's your spirit, Hannah. You've given Kelly more than he ever thought he'd find in this life. He'll be a good husband to you. He'll always feel like you're more than he deserves. And he'll take good care of you, sweetie. He's a lot like your grandfather if you ask me."

Hannah smiles gently and nods. "I think so, too. I can't put my finger on it, but he is like Grandpa."

"It's not such a bad thing," Grams jokes with a similar smile in her voice.

"I suppose I could do worse," Hannah quips and Grams chuckles at her.

"I'm just glad that he wants to stay on the farm and not move away somewhere with you. I don't think I could've borne that," Grams admits with a heavy heart.

"Me either. I don't know if I could've left," Hannah allows. She's always been completely honest with her grandparents. She's never known another way to be with them. They are her everything, especially Grams.

"You always stick by your sisters. Stay on the farm. Stay close to Sue. She'll always be able to give you advice and help you with

Kelly or your kids someday. She's very wise for being so young herself."

"I'll always have you for advice, Grams," Hannah corrects with a frown.

"Your grandfather and I won't be around forever, Hannah."

"Don't talk like that, Grams," Hannah says with an uneasy smile. She doesn't like it when her grandmother says such things. It always sets off a flurry of nervous butterflies in her stomach.

"Just stay here on this farm. Stay with your sisters. They'll always take care of you along with Kelly," Grams repeats.

Hannah wishes she would stop talking like this.

"Now, enough of that. Do you have anything that you want to talk to me about before tomorrow?"

Hannah shakes her head, still thinking about the depressing comments her grandmother has made.

"All right then. I'm off to bed, sweetie. Sue said she's coming back up to set your hair on rollers, so I'll just take myself to bed," Grams says.

Her loving grandmother presses a kiss to Hannah's forehead. Hannah breathes deeply of her grandmother's scent. She always smells just a little like talcum powder and lilacs.

"Good-night, Grams," Hannah says with a smile. Her grandmother pulls her close for a strong embrace. Physical affection isn't something she does often and it takes Hannah by surprise.

"I'll always love you, Hannah. I love your sisters, too. Don't get me wrong. But they both left at such young ages. And then it was just the two of us because your grandfather worked so much. You've always been like a daughter to me, like the daughter I could've never had. I never dreamed the death of your wonderful mother would've given me such a gift. I'm honored that I could stand in for her and be there for you. I just hope she's smiling down on the banged up job I've done of it. I love you, honey."

Grams pulls away and leaves before Hannah can even reply. Fresh tears stream down her cheeks, but she feels no shame over them. Her Grams left before Hannah could tell her that she's sure her mother would be proud of the job that Maryanne McClane has done with her and her sisters. Hannah can remember small tidbits of her mother and the memories she has of her are always met with joy and love. She has the same feelings toward Grams, perhaps even deeper ones since her grandmother is the only mother Hannah's known for so long. Yes, her mother is absolutely smiling down upon Grams.

Chapter Twenty-six
Kelly

On an unseasonably warm Indian summer day at the end of October, the year of our Lord 2031, Kelly Ryan Alexander marries the love of his life, Hannah Elizabeth McClane, in an intimate ceremony outdoors under the rose arbor near the greenhouse and gardens. Somehow the women have even managed to do some decorating with flimsy white material, live and silk flowers, and dark green ferns from the forest floor. The entire family is amassed along with their three surviving neighbors. John plays the guitar for Hannah to come down the makeshift aisle, and Kelly is blown away by her beauty, as usual. She's wearing one of her white dresses, this one more formal, something she must've worn to church. The sleeves are long and billowy and sheer. Pearls are about her neck and in her ears, and a ring of tiny pink flowers surrounds her head like a halo. Long, thin ribbons trail down her back. Her pale, shimmery hair is loose and flowing about her in soft waves, and there's a touch of pink to her soft cheeks.

He and John raided the burbs over in fancyville three days ago with Cory and Simon, going house to house until he finally found a dress shirt and black pants that would actually fit. They'd also found some nicer clothing for the men on the farm. Even the teen boys have been forced to dress up in duds that they've also found for themselves in a mansion that once housed four boys ranging in age from pre-teen to a collage-aged boy. They'd also taken a full pick-up truck load of provisions from the raid on the empty homes. It is strange to see everyone not in work clothes and covered in dirt. The neighbors have worn their best clothes, as well, which was probably a whole lot easier for them since they hadn't left everything they owned on an Army base six states away.

During the ceremony, Kelly holds both of Hannah's hands, his thumb rubbing over her engagement ring while her grandfather reads from the Bible. But Kelly has trouble focusing on what he's saying because he is too enthralled by Doc's granddaughter and her brilliant, different-colored eyes that shine from time to time with tears of happiness. When she does allow them to escape, Kelly wipes them away for her. How the hell can this woman be so happy to be hooking herself to him for the rest of their lives? He'll probably never know or figure it out, but he's sure as hell not letting her back out.

Reagan stands beside Hannah as her maid of honor and John beside him as his best man and nobody even considers that this isn't a legitimate wedding of two people in love. Doc even drafted up that marriage certificate in his scrolling, cursive handwriting, and Hannah and he had both signed it. He repeats the vows after Doc as does Hannah. Finally it comes to a close with a kiss that Kelly keeps crowd appropriate so as not to anger her grandfather again. Kelly is just grateful to be able to kiss her in front of people at all.

When the ceremony is over, Sue takes a picture of them, though they have no way of ever developing it. She says she'll use the image to paint their portrait by downloading it onto her computer's screen. Even though Kelly knows without a doubt that he'll never forget the way Hannah looks today, he also knows that she'll want something to show their children and grandchildren someday. He's not sure that they'll ever be able to have a photograph taken again once the battery life of their cameras and computers permanently die.

Wayne Reynolds and John have brought out an antique-looking barbeque from the back of the horse barn per Doc's request. It's about four feet in length, and the men fill the bottom of it with wood. Then Doc and Wayne commence with making steaks for everyone, except the children who nag for hotdogs. Luckily for them, they have some sausage that they'll disguise for the kids as hotdogs from the recent hog butchering at the Reynolds' place. Kelly and the other men, including the teen boys, now know how to properly butcher a hog and a cow for future use which he's sure they will need to know. Last month they'd all worked alongside Doc on butchering the meat chickens, two roosters and seven hens that are no longer laying eggs. It was grisly work, but having two freezers full of meat will help them all sleep a little easier this winter.

Long tables, which were most likely handmade by Doc, were dug out of a barn yesterday, cleaned and set up for everyone to sit together on bench seating. Grams covered them with her antique, "good" linens, whatever that means. There are long, tapered candles in silver candle holders running down the center of the table. The children are reluctant to sit just yet and instead run and frolic in the yard and on the swing-set in their clean clothes. The adults are socializing, relaxing on lawn furniture or bustling about helping with the meal.

"Need some help?" Kelly asks of John who is carrying a load of firewood to the round pit where he's been told the family used to enjoy the occasional bonfire.

"Nah, I got it. Just hang out with Hannah, dude," John offers.

"She's kind of occupied," Kelly quips and indicates to his bride who is surrounded by women. John laughs once and nods.

"Sure, man," John agrees amiably, the only way his friend knows. "I'm just haulin' wood over to the pit. Doc said it might be nice to have a bonfire tonight."

"Ok, cool. I can help with that," Kelly says and joins John for the next half an hour hauling armloads of firewood to the pit surrounded by small sandstones. They fall into easy conversation like always.

"Feel different? I mean, being married and all," John asks as they walk back to the wood pile near the hog barn again.

"Nah, not really. Kinda' relieved, though. Won't have to sneak around like I'm hunting a terrorist in the desert anymore. We can just be ourselves," Kelly explains.

"Yeah, that's cool," John confirms.

"You might wanna' try it," Kelly jokes. John just laughs and shakes his head.

"Don't think that's gonna happen any time soon, bro," John informs him.

"We can always tie her down and force her," Kelly says with a laugh. John chuckles this time.

"I'm not doing it, so unless you're volunteering for the job then forget it. That she-devil will scratch out your eyes," his friend says with a smile.

"Think I'm gonna have to pass on that job. Guess you're on your own," Kelly says as they both grab more pine for the fire. The hardwoods will be reserved for use in the big house this winter. "I've seen your buddy talking an awful lot to her."

"Yeah, I know. Trust me, I know," John says with a frown.

Chet Reynolds is always a thorn in John's side. Kelly would like to tell his friend that he has no worries there, but it is likely that he won't believe him. John is pretty blinded by his own fascination with Reagan to see clearly sometimes.

"He's ok, man," Kelly tries. "They've been through a lot with both parents being killed and losing their kid brother. Maybe we should give him a break. He's probably just lonely or something."

"Mm hm," John murmurs tightly.

"To hear Sue tell it, a lot of the guys around town had it bad for Reagan. She just never cared, or the more likely scenario noticed any of them. But she only came home from college on breaks, so she didn't exactly have time to start a relationship. That and she's completely clueless where men are concerned," Kelly explains patiently.

"No kidding."

"I think Chet's harmless, John. Besides, it's not like it matters really. She'd never leave her family to go over there or get married to him and live over there. She's not leaving this place ever again. She said that to me once when we were talking about where I could go if I left. She had some suggestions for me on where I could go. Mostly they were crude," Kelly says on a chuckle.

"I'd be more surprised if they weren't," John jokes.

"Don't worry, bro. Little Doc's not attracted to him. She's just in her own world. Hell, she probably doesn't even know he's interested in her," Kelly laughs.

"Yeah, probably not," John says with a shake of his head.

They dump the loads of firewood near the pit and rejoin the groups of people that have broken into clusters talking about different things. Kelly decides to join Hannah and Sue, who is speaking quietly with Samantha.

"...you're so lovely in that dress, Sam," Sue offers kindly.

She places her hand on the shy girl's shoulder. Sam is wearing a long, navy blue dress that hangs like a sack on her. It's not at all flattering, but Kelly knows that Sue is trying to be kind to the girl. It's at least one size too big, and Kelly suspects that it doesn't even belong to her even though she'd brought all of the clothing she owned from her former home. She seems to wear frumpy, unattractive clothing a lot.

Sam mumbles a quick thank-you. "You look so pretty, Miss Hannah," she redirects the attention away from herself.

Whatever has happened to Sam while she was with the visitors has damaged this young girl. Kelly only wishes that they'd kept a few of them alive to be kept tied up in the back of the cattle barn for some interrogation. He and John used to be rather skilled with that sort of thing.

"I'm sure you do, too, Samantha," Hannah says lightly and takes the girl's hand into her own. "Someday I'll be a guest at your wedding."

"Um, I'm just going to go in and help Grams and Miss Reagan," Sam replies and hurries away.

Hannah frowns, but Sue nods with understanding.

"It's just going to take her some time, Hannie," Sue explains.

"I know," Hannah answers sagely.

For not being able to see, Hannah is an expert at reading people. Sue hugs her sister tightly and also leaves to help with the meal that the women are working on in the kitchen.

"She'll be ok, Hannah," Kelly says, trying to convince her. He's also trying to convince himself. He's not at all sure Sam will be alright someday. She's very messed up from whatever has happened to her. Her darkness reminds him of Reagan, but whereas Reagan is outspoken and downright hateful, Sam is withdrawn and morose.

"She will. I know," Hannah nods and repeats.

He leads her to the front porch for a few minutes of alone time before the dinner commences. There he kisses her as they sit together on the swing. Unfortunately it doesn't take long before the kids find them and Ari wants attention while she cartwheels around the yard. Soon everyone is called for dinner.

The women have made delicious food to go with the steak feast including mashed potatoes enough for an army, corn bread, stewed green beans with ham bits, baked squash with crunchy walnuts that the children collected from the ground around the trees near the apple orchard, crisp vegetables from the greenhouse, rolls with fresh-churned butter, and Grams and Em have worked since yesterday on making Hannah a proper wedding cake for which she smiles gratefully. The candles down the center of the table have been lit and the outdoor lights on the back porch are left on. The sun is setting as they eat, and the atmosphere is romantic and subtle as the sky lights up with bright pinks and fiery reds. The meal is great, but all Kelly can think about is the delicate, feminine woman beside him.

She also seems distracted, which isn't difficult since everyone wants to talk to her. But she does occasionally reach under the table to hold his hand. She sips at her sweet tea, which has been placed in tall glass pitchers around the tables. And every once in a while Hannah leans over and kisses his cheek. All Kelly can do is smile down at her.

The Reynolds family seems surprised at the quality of the meal, and Grams and Sue talk to Bertie about helping her out with learning some of their techniques on making food items go farther and how to do canning of which she is not yet familiar. They make plans to go over in a few days to their farm to show her how to can the remainder of her garden.

"Wayne and Chet have been going out the back of our property to Glen Road- you know the one that leads to town?" Bertie explains.

Kelly isn't sure it's a good idea to go to town. Sue nods to Bertie and encourages her to continue. The men have stopped eating and talking and are all listening to her, as well.

"They go on short trips for supplies and food items that we don't have. They go to Pleasant View and once all the way to Clarksville. But I worry that what they're doing is too dangerous."

"It can be," Derek says to Wayne who nods.

"We take our shotguns and I've got my dad's old pistol, too," her husband Wayne explains. "Plus, we've got those guns you guys took from those... men. Thanks for leaving those with us. We've run into some trouble from time to time, but we try to just avoid people if we can."

"Yeah, that's best," John agrees.

His friend sends a look to Chet.

"Maybe if you radio us the next time you guys go, one of us can tag along. It's safer to move around together," Derek offers.

John and Kelly both nod. Kelly notices that Doc does not.

"And Bertie should probably come over here while you're gone. It's not a good idea for her to be there by herself in case anyone comes in on foot," Grams adds.

The men all nod at this offer. Bertie doesn't seem like the kind of person who could shoot anyone even if she had to.

"Ok, we'll gladly take the help, Derek," Wayne acknowledges with a nod.

The conversation ebbs and flows again while everyone praises the food and especially the steaks. John, Derek and Wayne all eat two each. Even the littler kids seem happy to sit a while longer at the table while the adults continue to converse.

"It sure is nice to have electricity again, Doc," Chet offers up.

Wayne and Bertie heartily agree. Kelly feels bad that they hadn't been able to go over sooner to help with their power source.

"Haven't had a hot shower since this all happened," Wayne discloses.

"Or hot water for sanitizing the milkin' equipment," Chet tells them.

"Or for washing our dishes or for anything really unless we boiled it on the stove," Bertie says.

They will obviously need to work with this family throughout the winter to help them survive because they do seem like good people as Doc had assessed. Even if John keeps sending dagger glares down the table toward Chet, who stares like a love-sick puppy at Reagan.

"We're all glad to help, Wayne," Derek tells the other man who nods with appreciation.

These two have become fast friends. Perhaps it is because they are both the oldest in their respective families and feel that added sense of responsibility.

"We're going to go back to the condo community we've been establishing and help them, as well," John tells them in between bites. "There's another new family now living there. The more we can help others with simple things like getting electricity going again, the better."

"You guys are welcome to come and help," Derek says.

"Yeah, sure, Derek," Wayne says. "I mean you guys helped us. Now it's time to help others. Only seems right to me. Right, Chet?"

Chet nods in agreement before pushing his long hair away from his face. It doesn't seem to be an accident that he is sitting right next to Reagan. John is sitting on the opposite side of the table, two seats down from Kelly. His friend seems more and more frustrated as the day goes by. Reagan is completely unaware of Chet and is mostly talking with Sam on her other side. Kelly's afraid John may jump across the table soon.

As the evening progresses and the sun sets completely, the men build a large bonfire between the house and barns in the yard area, and everyone gathers around on outdoor lawn furniture. The kids chase fireflies, each other, the puppies and cook marshmallows on shaved wooden sticks. Sue and Grams bring out blankets for those who want one while John and Reagan put both of the babies to bed. Kelly wraps Hannah in a plaid wool blanket as the air grows chillier, and they snuggle closely on a two person glider rocker. They are completely oblivious to the rest of the family, the world. Kelly cannot imagine a more perfect wedding day than this has been or one more intimate. Having their family, extended new family and friends present has made it seem more personal than some of the ostentatious wedding events he'd gone to in the past held at country clubs with five hundred guests, six course meals and champagne.

Their fingers play and intertwine, and it's such a relief to be able to finally touch her in front of other people and not feel like he is on a covert mission just to steal a secretive kiss from his woman. The ladies have clustered and are discussing whatever women talk about as the men do the same. Even Bertie, who has been through so much and had not taken it well at all, seems to laugh and smile a few times. It's obvious that nobody wants this day of good cheer and good feelings to end. It's just been too damn long since anyone's had one.

"I hate it when you leave the farm, Kelly," Hannah says out of the blue. "I wish you wouldn't go on so many trips. I don't like that you're also going to go on runs with the Reynolds now, too."

"I'm fine, Hannah," he tells her, squeezing her shoulders gently. "I won't take any risks, but we have to help people. Those people out there could've been me and my brother and sister if we hadn't made it to this farm. It's the right thing to do, baby."

"I just don't like it. I don't ever want to lose you, Kelly," she states with a soft frown.

"You won't. I'm hard to kill, remember?" he jokes lightly. She nods as Kelly presses a kiss to the side of her mouth, effectively making her frown disappear.

"Now what do we have here? Your fingernails are pink," he tells Hannah quietly as they press their foreheads together and he holds up her hand with the long, thin, graceful fingers to look more closely using the light of the campfire.

"Are they? Sue wanted to do everyone's nails last night. Did you see Em's?" she asks.

She strokes her finger over the simple gold band on his left hand ring finger. Another Sam's Club discount. It doesn't surprise Kelly that she questions him about Em. She never thinks of herself, and Hannah would want him to notice his little sister's nails before her own.

"Yeah, I saw them. There were little white flowers painted on hers. Sue's really artistic and apparently so is Sam. Em was excited and came to my room before bedtime to show me," he says with a smile. "It's exactly what she needs, being with you girls. I can't imagine raising her with just me and Cory."

"Well, now you don't have to," she tells him and kisses his bearded cheek.

"Right, now I don't have to. You're the most giving person I've ever known. I love you, Hannah."

"I know, my love. Besides, you two would be showing her how to shoot the guns and beat people up all the time if she didn't have us women to look out for her," she teases and kisses his fingers.

Kelly chuckles.

"You're probably right about that. Although I'm glad I've got you for a few other reasons, too," he teases back with a smile. She's told him before how she can tell when people are smiling by the sound of their voice. Kelly feels like smiling every time he's around her, and he knows it will always be like this for him.

"Oh?" she asks knowingly.

Hannah smiles brilliantly at him, lit only by the campfire's warm glow. Sometimes her beauty takes the wind out of him.

"Yep, and I'll tell you about those later," he promises as he presses a kiss to her fingertips.

"I think I'm going to hold you to that, Sergeant," she teases right back.

Hannah is sometimes surprising in her ability to be naughty when she wants to be.

"Oh, you won't need to. Wild horses couldn't drag me away," Kelly says as he presses a light kiss this time to her mouth. Her fingers tighten their grip on his, even at this brief interaction. She's the most passionate woman he's ever known.

"I love you, Kelly," she tells him when they break apart.

"I meant what I said, Hannah. I'll take care of you," he tells her reverently and presses a kiss to her forehead.

"I'll take care of you, too, Kelly."

Hannah tells him this so stoically that he believes her.

Chapter Twenty-Seven
John

When John comes back with an armload of firewood, he notices that Reagan is missing and so is Chet Reynolds, which instantly makes the hair on his neck stand up straight. Derek, Doc and Wayne are discussing the abatisses and the increased security on their road. He goes straight for Sue who is roasting a marshmallow for Justin. The women made homemade marshmallows yesterday in the hopes of being able to do the bonfire tonight. John has never even heard of making them from scratch, but they smelled up the kitchen really nice when they were done and he's pretty sure he saw his woman sneaking a few when nobody was looking, the sugar freak.

"Have you seen Reagan, Sue?" he asks as she tries to untangle the stringy, gooey mess from her stick.

"Um, yeah, John. I think she took Chet to the hog barn to check out the new baby goats. They should be back soon, though. Did you need her?" Sue asks.

Does he need her? He needs her to stay away from Chet, but that isn't something he wants to blurt in front of everyone.

"Ok, thanks," he tells her.

"Uncle John, sing us another song!" Ari says excitedly.

She tugs on his pant leg and jumps up and down.

"In a minute ok, kiddo?" he says and walks away before she can answer and, more importantly, before she can use her wily charms and persuade him to stay. He hears Sue telling the kids to get ready for bed as he gets further from the campfire, so he's hoping he's off the hook for the song. He's not too great at telling any of the kids on the farm no. None of the adults are. The kids have all been through enough.

He makes it to the hog barn without breaking his neck and uses the man door since it's already illuminated by a reddish orange glow coming from the interior. There are other lights on deeper inside of the barn which flow into the center aisle where he sneaks. Voices filter from the rear of the barn where the goats are being kept until the babies are big enough to be turned out to pasture. They've already shot three coyotes and found wild dog tracks in the forest in the last few weeks. Unless they want to feed the wildlife around the farm, they need to increase the security of their livestock.

He moves stealthily toward the end of the aisle. John pauses behind a stack of baled straw to listen before he retrieves Reagan back to the campfire where she belongs. Back by his side where she belongs.

"...we're glad to help, Reagan. Just bring 'em around again in the spring so that we can breed both again," Chet says.

John sincerely hopes that his competition is referring to goats. He risks a peek and sees Reagan sitting on a double stack of straw that the kids climb upon to look in the goat pen. Chet is standing close to her, too close, near her leg.

"Cool. We probably will. How's your hip? I meant to ask earlier and forgot. I... couldn't come over earlier this week to check on you. I was... busy," she lies.

John had basically forbid her from going; that's why she was busy. He threatened to tie her to a chair and instead took her out to work on napalm demos which she thought was "awesome." She can be a little on the warped side sometimes. Burning people alive with homemade napalm incendiary devices isn't exactly what he'd call awesome.

"That's no problem. I'm healed up just great thanks to you," Chet replies. "You're a real good doctor, Reagan. You should be proud of yourself. I mean we all heard you were going to college when you were what, fifteen or something? We thought that was just crazy," he compliments so smoothly. "And here you are a doctor. Herb said you would've been one of the country's best doctors someday."

"Yeah, and who cares? It's not like I'm ever going to do what I wanted with it anyways. All I do is sew people up and treat wounds

384

and shit. It's not like I'm ever gonna be a surgeon because we don't have that capability anymore," she swears angrily.

John smiles in the dark.

"Um... oh. You're a special girl. Did you know that?"

"Special, huh? You have no idea," she jokes.

John notices that Chet either doesn't understand her sarcastic wit or doesn't think she's funny because he just blathers on.

"You're really pretty, too," he praises.

Reagan must roll her eyes at him because Chet hastily continues.

"No, really you are. You always were. Even with the scar on your cheek there, you're still a good-looking woman, Reagan. I mean I always thought so. Guess I shoulda' said something a long time ago, but you've been gone away at school forever. I just hoped you weren't hitched or anything when you finally came home," he says.

This almost makes John laugh. If he'd been interested in Reagan before this all started, he would've went after her, not waited for her to come back. He also doesn't like where this sounds like it's going, but he decides to back off for the time being and give the guy some credit.

"Oh ok," Reagan says with her usual disinterest that she shows everyone.

She probably isn't even listing to poor Chet or even looking at him but is likely thinking about his wound and what she could've done differently or better. Or her mind is out in the med shed where she and the doc were spending a lot of time studying infectious diseases so as to be better prepared for any sicknesses that make it to the farm like the pneumonic plague had. John hears movement, a shuffling of feet against the wood floor. Is he moving closer to Reagan? Does she want him to?

"Are you with any of those guys out there?" Chet asks her to reveal her relationship status.

"No, duh, I'm here with you," she answers rudely.

Her curt reply doesn't put her off admirer, though.

"I guess what I mean is: are you *with* any of them?" he repeats.

Reagan doesn't answer him, but he knows her well enough to know that she's probably giving him a cantankerous look filled with misunderstanding and impatience.

"Do you want me to take a look at your hip?" she asks.

John can tell that her patience is waning even thinner as she changes the subject which was probably irritating her anyways. She prefers directness, not coy questions.

"I mean is one of them on your list of marriageable guys, Reagan? As in, are you the girlfriend of any of them?" he asks.

This should be interesting.

"What the fuck? No!" she answers hostilely.

Good, let Chet get a taste of her temper. That ought to run him off. Her answer doesn't please John, however. He would've liked it much better if she'd admitted to being with him at least for the sake of being left alone by Chet.

"Oh, ok good. Maybe we could go riding some time together. Do you still like riding? You used to have a really good seat," Chet says with a lot of implication that Reagan won't get.

Chet with his long ponytail of flaxen blonde and the light blue eyes and farmer's tan is going a bit too far for John's taste.

"Why?"

"Why what?" he asks stupidly.

"Why would I go riding with you?" Reagan asks him point blank. "I always ride with John."

Well, that is at least something. John shakes his head.

"I don't know. So maybe we could be alone," Chet adds suggestively.

John's wondering if she's getting it yet. John sure as heck is, and this guy won't let up. Chet is certainly tenacious. Of course, there aren't a lot of choices for a possible mate anywhere anymore, and Reagan is the most desirable prospect around in John's opinion. The most desirable prospect he's ever seen or known despite her sassy mouth and her mean attitude.

"Why would I want to do that? We're alone right now," she says.

Nope, not getting it.

"So I can do this," Chet says.

"Whoa, what…" Reagan exclaims with shock as her words are cut off.

386

John has had enough. When he rounds the corner, Chet is kissing her, and he has her by the shoulders and then by her small waist. He's handsy, way too handsy for his own good.

He wastes no time yanking the guy back from her and cold clocking him in the jaw, taking him by surprise. John holds onto Chet's shirt so that he doesn't go down. Then he pulls him eye level with him.

"I told you once before not to touch her, dude. Reagan's with me. We're together. She's never going to be with you so don't ever try that again," he tells Chet in a deadly calm voice while the guy gathers his wits and stands upright again. John releases his shirt and steps back in case the guy wants to continue the fight. He doesn't appear to want to do so as he holds his hand against his jaw. "Now, Doc wants our families to get along, so I don't want any hard feelings over this, ok?"

"Uh...," is his only response.

Maybe it's all he's capable of.

"Apologize to Reagan and go on your way. I think your family is leaving anyways," John tells him. Chet blinks hard twice. Geez, he'd hardly hit him.

"Uh, sorry, Reagan. Sorry, man. I didn't know you two were together," he manages before he makes haste from the barn.

When John finally looks at Reagan, she's still sitting on the bales of straw in her short, emerald green dress that she'd borrowed from Sam's home. The men had buried Sam's family for her near their horse barn that had once housed Sam's prized show horses, where her parents, older brother and twin baby siblings had been executed. Doc had held a small ceremony for her there to get some modicum of closure. A few of the family members had gone to be with her, to support her, while some had stayed at the farm to keep it safe. They'd allowed her to pack whatever she wanted from her house, namely her bedroom, and John had taken a crib and a highchair and the rest of the baby clothes as well as the clothing from her brother's room for the two teen boys they have on the farm. Sue had talked with Sam about it first to make sure that she felt ok with the McClanes looting her home, and she'd said that she was glad that the items would go to the McClane family and the new babies Isaac and

Jacob. The visitors had only raided Sam's house for food and drugs and, unfortunately, her.

And here was Reagan wearing one of the dresses borrowed from Sam's mother's closet which had also been cleaned out. She looks completely cute, albeit a little angry, but still cute. It hits just above her knees and is form fitting, something John hadn't been too crazy about especially with Chet coming over. He'd not been involved in the choosing of the dress, but Sue had helped her- and just look how that had ended. He hopes Sue never helps her again. John would much rather she traipse around in her Converse, dirty jeans and shirts covered in horse sweat and grime when she is going to be around men who would be attracted to her, which just so happens to probably be most men.

"Do you want to explain that?" John asks about her encounter with Chet.

"I don't know what happened. He wanted to see the kids, so I brought him out here to show them to him and we were talking..." she starts explaining.

John cuts her off, "Was that some new form of sign language? I'm not familiar with the tongue down the other person's throat kind," he accuses with hostility and crosses his arms over his chest. Reagan looks up at him from her straw bale, frowns and tries to get down, but John places his hands at either side of her waist to stay her. She huffs.

"Hey! What are you talking about?" she vents.

"Well it didn't look to me like you were trying too hard to get away from him," John bites out, maintaining his stance.

"How do you know what I was doing? I was trying to think of one of your idiotic moves you showed me to get free of him. But then I thought it might hurt him, so I was having a mental conundrum," she explains, her hands motioning while she speaks.

She does this a lot, probably from sugar overload.

John's eyebrows rise of their own volition as his eyes widen with surprise and a touch of anger. "You didn't want to hurt him?"

"No, he's our neighbor!" Reagan says.

She mimics his crossed-arms move. It only pushes her breasts higher out of the low cut of her dress and sidetracks him. His eyes fall there, and he has a torturously hard time dragging them away. If she was any other woman, John would think she is doing it on purpose to distract him.

"So? Are you going to let all the neighbors kiss you?" John says a bit louder and plunks his hands on his hips.

"What if I am? What are you going to do about it? Punch all of them in the face? It's none of your business, John!" Reagan says louder than him.

She always has to get louder than him, but little does she know he could bring down the barn if he wanted to. However, he always tries to converse in a reasonable, calm manner with her because of her traumatic past. He has never wanted to add to her fear of men, specifically, him.

"Yeah, I will punch all of them! And it is my business. You're my business…"

"No, I'm not. You don't own me just because we had sex. That's not how this works!" she hisses and tries to get down from the straw again.

John pushes her down more forcefully onto her bottom this time and insinuates himself between her legs so she can't attempt to flee again. A few of her spirals come loose of her updo which exposes her elegant neck and collar bone and chest.

"It *is* how this works for your information. You're with me now. And Chet Reynolds and any other men around here need to understand that…"

She cuts him off again, further pissing him off.

"I'm not *with* you! It's just sex, John!"

He can't take another second of her denial and yanks her to him where his mouth takes over silencing her irrational ranting. It isn't just sex, at least not for him, and he's sure that she feels something for him, too, though she won't admit it. His kiss is punishing, demanding, and she finally yields to him, softens, and sinks her hands into the hair at his nape pulling him closer. He slides his hands under her skirt and pulls her tighter to him as her head lolls back. John lavishes her neck and collar bone with kisses.

"Just sex?" he whispers hoarsely. "Is that all I am to you?"

She doesn't answer but pulls him closer, pressing her breasts against his chest. John slides his hand up higher under her dress, touching her most sensitive core and leaving her breathing heavily.

"Is it?" he repeats, the rancor still in his voice. Unlike Reagan, he has some modicum of control over his body when he's around her. Not much, but some. He likes that he can make her lose her faculties with just the smallest caress or kiss, but he wants more from her.

"Yes," she whispers hoarsely.

John can feel through her panties that's she's ready for him, but he's not sure if she's answering his question or begging him to take her on this bale of straw. Her constant readiness, her need for him never fails to surprise John.

"Yes, I am just sex to you or yes, don't stop what you're doing?" he asks with a salacious grin against her mouth.

"What?" she asks with genuine confusion.

John revels in her shortness of breath. She's clearly getting too far gone to answer that question, so he decides to pose another that's nagging at him.

"Did you want Chet to kiss you?" Maybe he can use her desire against her to get the answers he seeks.

"No, don't be ridiculous. I wanted him to go away," she complains.

Reagan presses firmly against him. Her hand slides down the front of him until she reaches his crotch where she squeezes hard, almost too hard. Sometimes her sexual aggression is almost painful. Sometimes she leaves claw marks. Sometimes he doesn't care.

"Does he kiss as well as I do?" he asks jokingly but also with a slight touch of serious insecurity. Her hand squeezes around him through his dark trousers that are considerably thinner than his jeans or fatigues. John sucks in a sharp breath.

"No, not even close. He's lucky I didn't throw up wedding cake on him," she says.

John laughs against her mouth. It dawns on him that they have exceedingly strange conversations before and during sex, and he's never laughed during or before sex with anyone, either. Of course, he's also never had a real relationship with a woman before. Although he highly doubts that there is anything normal about their relationship.

"Do you think he does this as well?" he asks and strokes her through her flimsy, lacy panties. These must be new because

390

everything else she wears is practical cotton. She cries out into his neck and shakes her head distractedly.

"I don't... I don't care what he does or how he does it. He's just the neighbor. Why are we even talking about him right now? Just do it. Just do it now, John," she begs.

"No, Reagan, there are a lot of people out there, not to mention your grandparents," he says raggedly as her hand strokes his length and her other grabs at his shirt.

"I don't care. My grandparents probably went to bed anyways," she says rationalizing.

And it's all the encouragement John needs to pick her up, wrap her legs about his middle and take her to a dark corner of the barn where he does not put her to her feet.

"Reagan," he says as he frees himself, pushes her panties to the side and plunges into her with a ferocity that leaves them both hungry and insatiable for the other. And when they are spent and breathing heavily John whispers to her as he always does, "I love you."

She says nothing as he sets her gently to her feet which are not covered in dirty boots or old Converse for a change, but beige, feminine flats. Something doesn't sit right with John that he can't quite put his finger on. His mind isn't clear, but he feels like something is wrong between them. She has a staggering way of making him fuzzy-headed.

"You looked so beautiful today," he tells her and presses a kiss to her forehead as he re-tucks his shirt.

"Get real. You don't have to say that, duh. Obviously you didn't need to flatter me to get me to have sex with you," she replies as she pulls her dress back into some semblance of order.

John freezes until she realizes that he's not talking or moving. He's learned that this is one way to get her to stop, to slow down and interact with the rest of the humans.

She blurts, "What?"

"I said you look beautiful today, Reagan," he repeats. "I've never seen you... clean before or wearing shoes that don't have horse dung on them."

"Uh, oh... thanks," she mumbles uncomfortably. "You look nice, too. Or at least you did look nice until you came out here."

She picks a few errant pieces of straw out of his hair and re-buttons his shirt for him. The lightness of her fingertips brushing against his skin is heavenly. One of the buttons of his shirt, however, is gone. He'd like to tell her that she'd ripped too roughly at his shirt earlier, causing it to pop off, but he thinks better of it. Sex is still so new to her and maybe this is just how she has to deal with it for now. He'll just have to remove his own clothing more quickly from now on.

"Thank you very much, ma'am," he tells her and pulls her in for a kiss, finishing it with a rub of her top lip. Her fingers, the nails painted black or dark blue or something completely *not* feminine, cover his and Reagan presses them harder against her mouth. "No more kissing the neighbors, ok?"

She smiles slyly up at him and says, "If this is how you'll punish me, then I'm going to find a neighbor every day to kiss."

John turns her swiftly and spanks her bottom.

"Ouch! Jerk," she grinds out in instant anger.

She is so easy to antagonize and so fast to get feisty.

"Oh, it can get much worse if you go trolling for neighbors," he warns.

He rests his mouth on the back of her neck and then presses her against the barn wall again. His hands roam over her as he pulls her back against his front. She grinds her behind against him and, whether she knows it or not, he's ready to go again. Unfortunately, Reagan also has this effect on him. He can't ever seem to get enough of her. His passion for her is completely unappeasable which she seems to return. But he turns her back around and kisses her swiftly.

He suggest, "Let's go back. People will wonder where we went to."

"Who gives a shit?" she says and tries to pull him back.

"Language," he admonishes, wags a finger at her and tugs her along after him as she pouts prettily.

As they exit the barn, the night air blasts him, and he is reminded once again that it's almost November in Tennessee. "Are you cold?"

"A little," she says.

John wraps an arm around her shoulder. However, as soon as they come into the vicinity of where the remaining family sits at the dying fire, she jerks free before they can see. Only Derek, Sue and the three teenagers are still near the fire pit. Her pulling away from him bothers John more than he cares to admit, but at least he understands why they need to be discreet around the family for the time being.

"Where have you two been?" Sue asks suspiciously.

Sometimes John would like to strangle his sister-in-law if only he didn't love her so much.

"Uh, checking the goats," Reagan lies awkwardly.

She snatches up a blanket and won't sit on the glider rocker with John but on a single seat two chairs away.

"Oh? Wasn't Chet out there with you earlier?" Sue asks with mischief.

"Yeah, what was up with Chet, John? He looked sort of... different when he left with his family," Derek points out.

His brother is even more mischievous than his meddling wife. Surely the punch hadn't bruised the neighbor that fast. Apparently his brother had noticed anyway.

"Must've tripped," John mutters to his brother who nods knowingly.

"Gonna be an easy hunting season, it looks like," Derek comments, purposely changing topic.

"Yeah, Simon and I saw a huge heard of deer up in the top pasture the other morning," Cory says excitedly.

"It'll be like shootin' fish in a barrel," Derek comments with a laugh. "Maybe not next year once more people have to start hunting for food, too. I think we'll always be ok here, though."

"We could always catch some and build higher fences and just raise our own," Simon offers, and the men nod and agree reflectively. "My mom grew up on a small farm up in Northern California, and her parents had deer. They'd sell venison to people in the area and to expensive restaurants."

"Had you heard from them after California got hit?" Sue asks, but Simon shakes his head with a frown. "Do you have any other family, Simon?"

"I have a sister. She's two years older, though, and was in college, Georgia Tech. That's kind of why I went with my aunt. I thought maybe if I got close enough, I'd just take off and try to find her on my own. The last email I was able to get through to her I told her that I was going with Aunt Amber, and we were coming to this area to find your farm. Your Uncle Peter told us the name of this farm and your town, so I emailed it to her, but she'll probably never find her way here I guess. I don't even know if the email got through. I was gonna try and get to her, but once we lost cell service and internet capabilities there was no way of contacting her. So now I don't know where she is."

"I'm sorry, Simon," Sam offers quietly, and he nods at her with a grimace.

"What is your sister's name?" Cory asks kindly, though they all know she is likely dead.

"Her name's Paige and she has long, dark red hair. She's kind of tall just in case she ever comes down the drive, so try not to shoot her," he says with a faint chuckle.

"Sure thing, man," John agrees, and they all nod solemnly because the likelihood of Simon's sister ever making it to their farm is about a million to one odds. Everyone at the campfire, including Simon, knows it.

After a few more minutes of conversation about hunting again, Reagan excuses herself and tells everyone she's turning in. Not caring what anyone thinks, John follows her a few moments later.

They lie in the dark, in their respective beds because Reagan hasn't invited him to actually sleep with her even though Jacob is in his crib in the closet. She fully expects him to go back to his tiny twin bed when the sex is over.

"That was a great day today, don't you think?" he asks her, trying to pry information from that brain of hers.

"Sure, I suppose so. At least we didn't have to shoot anyone today. That's good."

"Hannah seems really happy," John says pointedly. He doesn't point out that the shooting could've been Chet's fate if he'd kept up his behavior with his woman.

"Hm. Well, that's Hannah for you," Reagan answers noncommittally.

"Yeah, but I mean she's happy because they're married now," he tells her with heightening irritation.

"If that's what she wanted, then I'm glad for her," Reagan answers.

"The wedding ceremony was really sweet. They seem like they're both going to be able to relax now," John hints.

"Unnecessary if you ask me but nice enough," she replies and turns toward him in her bed.

"What do you mean it was unnecessary? The wedding?"

"Yeah, the wedding. I think marriage is stupid, but if that's what Hannah wants, then so be it," she replies with certainty.

"I don't think marriage is stupid at all. And they won't have to sneak around and hide their feelings for each other anymore. If you love someone, you should marry them. That's kind of how it works, little Einstein," he teases.

"Well, there you go. There's the flaw in your theory," she tells him.

She says this like he knows what the heck she's talking about. Most of the time he has no idea what the heck she is talking about. Sometimes he wishes that Reagan had come with an instruction manual.

"Where's the flaw?"

"Love. It's a scientifically proven fact that love is just endorphins being fed to the brain that emit feel-good feelings, and that's why people think they're in love," she explains so efficiently, yet so irritatingly.

John springs out of his bed and goes to her, kneeling beside Reagan's bed. He'd like to shake some sense into her but figures that .45 is under her pillow.

"Look at me," he orders her and grasps her chin in his hand. "Endorphins or not, I *do* love you. I'm not just saying that because it makes me have feel-good feelings or whatever science nonsense you just spouted. I've been with women- you know that- and I've never had this feeling with any of them, Reagan. I know what I feel is real. I do love you."

She doesn't say anything but stares hard at him. She is lit only by the moonlight coming through the windows and French doors, but there's still enough light that John can see that she clearly doesn't believe him. Figuring it's best not to press this further tonight, John places a tender kiss to her mouth and returns to his own bed. She needs time to get this all worked out in her science brain and he'll give her some but not forever.

Chapter Twenty-eight
Reagan

Two months have passed without incident or attack or any more death, and the family has settled into familiar winter time routines that involve animal care, schooling the children, hunting and occasionally trading with the neighbors. The men go out each morning and work for long hours on the construction of the first cabin that will belong to Sue and Derek and their kids. It's actually coming along better than Reagan would've thought given their limited resources, but the ingenuity of the men on the farm seems to know no bounds. They've made short runs to surrounding neighborhoods for building supplies that include: hot water tanks, plumbing and electrical supplies, and doors and cabinets for Sue's kitchen. Derek is predicting that by late spring the new cabin will be ready for them to move into.

They've only lost power twice so far at the farm and had to heat the massive house with the wood-burning stoves in the basement, but it had only lasted for one day each time. Thanksgiving and Christmas and birthdays have passed, usually without much more than a simple birthday cake and maybe something small that she and John had confiscated from the city trip. But nobody seemed to care. They are together, safe, have a roof over their heads, protection thanks to the men, and food in their stomachs. These seem to be the only things that matter anymore. Even the younger kids didn't notice that for Christmas they didn't get the latest video games, electronic gadgets and plastic packages from China filled with toys that would likely break by the end of the day. Grandpa, Cory and Kelly built doll furniture and a doll house for Em and Arianna to share and a wooden train set for Huntley, Justin, and eventually Isaac and Jacob. The children were ecstatic over these simple gifts.

Cory and Simon have become very familiar with chopping and splitting firewood and on most days do so without dragging their feet too slowly out the back door. It's hard, back breaking work, and Reagan doesn't envy them, nor does she volunteer to take either of their places. But whenever firewood is used to heat the house it has to be replaced in case the winter season is long and hard.

Most of Reagan's days are kept busy watching Jacob while John is out with the men either on patrols or working on the cabin. She's also overseeing teaching Sam, Simon and Cory high school level sciences. Cory and Sam don't have much of an interest, but Simon shows a lot of promise and he's a smart kid, catches on quickly. Cory would much rather be tearing something apart, putting it back together and improving it like Grandpa does. Most of the time he dashes right after lessons and goes out to the cabin to help on the build. And Sam is all about drawing, music and horses. She frequently rides and is learning piano from Hannah. She even brought her own riding boots and apparel from her old house. She's fitting in well with the family and opens up a little at a time, mostly to Sue who has this influence on people. Sam had shown Reagan and Sue a photo album of her family and talked about each member while crying. Reagan has her doubts that Sam will be alright someday. Hell, Reagan is having her doubts that she will ever even get over her own traumatic ordeal.

Today the younger kids are watching the new peeps out in the barn where they will be kept away from the adult chickens until they are able to better fend for themselves, and the teens are out on a patrol ride which Reagan doesn't envy because it looks cold enough to snow.

"Whatcha' doing, sis?" Hannah asks from behind her.

As usual, she is startled by her sneaky sister. Reagan is holding Jacob on her hip, staring out the kitchen window and wondering why John and Kelly are getting into the pick-up truck and leaving. The truck has a load of firewood in the back which is strange.

"Where are Kelly and John going?" she asks because John has been withdrawn and strange with her the last week or so and won't even have sex.

He is moody and distant, and Reagan wonders if he just doesn't have the winter blues. But she figures Hannah would probably know where her husband is going because she seems to never be out of his sight for long. They are everything one would expect from a couple of honeymooners and it gets old. They kissed, laughed, hugged, and kissed more. Kelly had moved into Hannah's bedroom suite with the attached bath which allowed the kids to have the basement rooms to themselves. Sam has even moved into Kelly's old room, leaving the younger kids to themselves again. But she is still more than helpful with them and doesn't seem to mind when they tag along everywhere she goes. Being around them probably reminds Sam of her own deceased siblings and perhaps helps to fill a small part of the gap in her broken heart.

"Oh, I think they were going to the Reynolds to help them with some things and then on to the Johnson farm," Hannah says and places her hand on Reagan's arm.

"Why do they need to go to the Johnson's? It's abandoned," Reagan asks as her sister feels along the counter top.

"I'm not sure. Kelly said that John wanted to go," Hannah tells her.

Hannie returns to the island where she is dicing chunks of beef for a stew they'll enjoy for dinner later. Reagan joins her there and sets Jacob on his butt on the long island. He immediately grabs for everything, so Reagan hands him a wooden spoon that he happily bangs on the counter top. Then she picks up a knife and starts dicing vegetables for her sister. Strange how she should be using scalpels doing surgery on a patient at Nashville General and here she is cutting up vegetables at the farm and hanging out in the kitchen with her sister. She'd initially been devastated not being able to live out her dream of being a surgeon and then taking over her grandfather's practice, but she has finally resigned herself that it just wasn't in the cards for her. There will be times, though, that she'll put her medical experience to use and eventually perhaps things will go back to normal. And if not she can always teach the kids about medicine so that they can at least keep each other healthy.

"So, how do you like being Mrs. Hulk?" she asks her sister teasingly.

"Oh, it's wonderful, Reagan. He's wonderful, too. And it's nice not to have to hide our feelings for each other and be able to kiss him whenever I want," Hannah says so cheerily.

"Hm," Reagan says noncommittally.

"He's so tender and loving. You'd never know Kelly was capable of being like that, but when we're together he's so different," Hannah drones gaily.

Her lovable sister goes on for a while about how great it is to be married and how much she loves Kelly and the kids and mostly just life itself. Reagan is genuinely happy for Hannah and glad that Kelly will always be around to take care of her sister, but it doesn't change how she feels about marriage and monogamy and tying oneself to another forever.

They simply work on preparing the evening meal for over an hour of uninterrupted talk without the noisy kids in the house or the intrusion of a million things like visitors, bandits, farming, fortification and everything else that usually goes on. It reminds Reagan of the old times with her sister, which is nostalgic and comforting.

"How are things going with John?" Hannah suddenly asks out of the blue, not missing a beat as usual.

Reagan doesn't like the direction of this conversation. They had been discussing Sam's drawings which are fantastic and beautiful.

"What do you mean? Things aren't going anywhere. I'm sure he's fine…"

"Reagan," Hannah says as if she is talking to Ari or Justin. "You can be honest with me. If you want to play it like that with everyone else, then that's fine with me, but you know that I know you better than anyone else, dear."

"What? There's nothing going on. He's just… my roommate," she lies and hopes Hannah will just drop it, which of course she doesn't. Reagan goes to the fridge and pours a full bottle of goat's milk for Jacob that she'll take upstairs with her for his nap in a few minutes.

"I don't think John sees you as just his roommate, Reagan. And you're raising Jacob together. Perhaps you two should marry, too, especially since you have Jacob to consider now. That could be confusing for him someday," her sister says.

Hannah scrapes the vegetables into a simmering pot on the stove. Next, she uncaps and pours in a quart of canned tomatoes to join the vegetables and beef tips.

"We're not raising Jacob together, like a couple together. We're just his... guardians."

"He calls John "daddy," Reagan. And he'll soon be calling you his mommy so you need to consider this. Besides, John loves you. It's plain as day how he feels about you. I think the question is, do you even know how you feel about him?" Hannah asks with her damned irritating intuition.

"I... I need to put Jacob down for his nap, Hannah. We can talk later," Reagan tells her and flees from the room with the baby before Hannah can nail her down to a time or stop her from leaving.

Once she's in her bedroom, Reagan rocks Jacob while he drinks his bottle and stares up at her with his big, trusting eyes. The sounds he makes around the bottle's nipple like tiny coos and gurgles are so adorable that she can't help but smile down at him. After he's out, she puts him down for a nap in his crib at the back of her closet because he's overdue and can get cranky if he gets put down too late in the day. He immediately rolls to his side, snuggles his blanket, sticks the thumb in the mouth and closes his eyes again. Her closet actually makes the perfect baby room because it's the quietest place in the house and is always a tad on the dark side, having no windows. Sue always says what an easy baby Jacob is, but Reagan has no experience with the day to day care of an infant and he seems difficult and needy to her. John is much better with him, more patient, affectionate and doesn't seem to care that he wants twenty-four hour a day attention.

She closes the closet door and plans to stay in the attic to study until it is time for chores. When she goes back into her room, though, Em and Arianna are waiting for her there.

"What's up, monkeys?" she asks playfully.

"Will you sing us a song, Aunt Reagan?" Ari begs with her pleading, soulful eyes that nobody can resist. "Please, please, please?"

"Uh... sure. Why not?" Reagan says and retrieves her guitar from the corner. It's so much easier to just agree to the song than to argue with the kids.

400

They all three plop down on Reagan's bed which is made sharply enough to put the best five star hotel to shame. John makes both of their beds every morning, though she told him how pointless this task was since they were just going to mess them up again the next night. The only time she ever made her bed was when Grams had forced her to. He'd only laughed at her and said that some habits from the military were hard to break.

"Watcha' guys want to hear?" Reagan asks as she tunes her beat up, old guitar.

"Sing a song by Tina B. Sing it, sing it!" Ari's begs.

"Tina B? Your mom lets you listen to that crap?" Reagan asks with distaste. Apparently she needs to have a talk with Sue. Tina B was the latest pop tart teen singer who barely clothed herself on stage and only made so many number one hits because she freely made use of auto-correction dubbing equipment in the recording studios. Of course, she likely lived in California as did most of the celebrities in the U.S., so she is probably dead.

"Yeah, Tina B!" Ari yells with delight.

"Why don't I sing a song from another female singer, ok? She was one of the first female rock stars and was really cool. She could actually sing, and she kept her clothes on," Reagan mumbles the last sentence under her breath.

She strums a few chords and starts singing. The song is more up-tempo than she is singing and playing it, but sometimes she likes to break down music to its bare bones and slow the pace. When she finishes, Em claps and Ari complains.

"That wasn't Tina B! That sucked!" the ruffian declares.

Reagan laughs loudly, heartily at her niece's childlike honesty.

"Oh, Ari. Don't ever change, kid," she says approvingly, though she knows her parents would have a fit for her talking like that.

"I liked it. That was really pretty, Miss Reagan," Em praises openly.

"Thanks, Em. Guess the critic here wasn't a fan," she says with another laugh pointed toward Ari, who scowls.

"Let's go play in the barn, Em," Ari says.

Reagan can tell that Em would rather not, but she follows her annoying shadow anyways.

"Oh, hi, Uncle John!" Ari says.

Reagan's eyes dart to the door. He ruffles the hair on top of Ari's head as he comes into the room. When the girls are gone, John crosses the room to her.

"That was amazing, Reagan. I didn't know you could sing like that. That song sounded familiar, but I don't think I know it," he praises.

Reagan would like to die on the spot of mortification. She sure as hell wouldn't have sung for the girls if she'd known he was hanging in the stairwell listening. She's positive that she's blushing ten shades of pink.

"Oh, um... it was a Pat Benatar song called "Promises in the Dark." She was a big singer in the 1980's. I was gonna sing her other song, "Hell is for Children" but I didn't think it would be good if Ari went around here mimicking the lyrics. Well, at least not around Grams," she explains as she sets her guitar aside. John chuckles.

"It sounded great," he says.

This only further embarrasses the crap out of her, so she tucks her guitar away in the corner again.

"You're a good singer, boss. You should sing when we have music nights."

"No way," she tells him bluntly, and he laughs softly, knowingly.

"Sometimes I feel like I don't know you at all," John says.

Reagan crosses the room to her desk where she won't have to look at him.

He says, "You're like a flower."

This draws her attention, and she laughs bawdily.

"Yeah, right. Me a flower?" she jests. He comes up behind her and presses a kiss to the top of her head, something that would've freaked her out so many short months ago.

"Yeah, like a flower. Every petal I peel back reveals more and more of you that I didn't know about. You're like this strange anomaly, a real mystery," he says.

He praises with way too much admiration that makes Reagan squirm uncomfortably.

"Whatever you say," Reagan returns with disbelief. John kneels beside her on one knee.

"And it all just makes me love you more, Reagan," he remarks softly.

"I need to do some research work on something, John," she lies to him so unconvincingly and when she looks directly at him finally meeting his gaze, Reagan sees his scowl. He nods reluctantly and rises again.

"Ok, I'm going to hit the shower," he says.

John leaves her sitting there without so much as a kiss good-bye which he always gives her.

Men! They are so damn confusing! She decides to check on Jacob and goes into the darkened closet space where she finds him fast asleep. As she's leaving the closet again, her foot hooks on the strap to John's bag, causing her to trip.

"Damn it!" she whispers and stoops to unhook her snared foot from the satchel but notices that some of the contents have strewn about on the floor.

Reagan kneels to gather the items to put back into his bag which are mostly more demo making equipment, his military headset, spare socks and a small white pouch that jingles when she picks it up. Thinking its contents are simply more things to make demos, Reagan opens the drawstring and empties the bag onto the carpet. What she sees is not at all what she had expected to see. Before her are John's service medals and a green beret. There seems to be quite a few medals. She's not entirely sure what they're all for, but one of them is a Silver Cross. When she flips it over, she finds an inscription: "*For Gallantry in Action.*" There are also three Purple Hearts and she knows that those are for being wounded in battle. There are other medals and ribbons with which she's unfamiliar. And at the bottom of the pile is a gold, star-shaped medal hanging from a blue ribbon. Inscribed on the front is: "*VALOR*" and on the back: "*The Congress To John James Harrison.*" Reagan knows that this is a Medal of Honor, the highest medal that the United Sates government ever issued to a serviceman because her father was an officer, and she'd overheard many conversations about such medals and how rare it was for a soldier to receive one. Her father always wanted his medals displayed in glass cases for all to see. He'd never been awarded anything even close to this level of merit. John's medals are stored away in a duffle bag, tossed to the back of a closet. She seriously doubts that he'd even want everyone to know about them. He doesn't seem to want recognition for the heroic acts he's done while living on her farm, being in the Army, protecting her in the city. None of it.

Something unfamiliar and strange tightens in her stomach, and her eyes well with tears. Many men are awarded the Medal of Honor posthumously, but John had done something so remarkable and saved many men's lives to deserve this and had lived to receive his award. He'd put himself in danger, in harm's way without thinking of his own safety to deserve this. From what she's come to know about John, it seems fitting, but she'd had no idea what kind of military hero he had been.

"What are you doing?" he barks from the entranceway of the closet.

Reagan nearly jumps out of her skin.

"What? I'm... I tripped," she says like a moron, and John scowls deeply at her before dropping to his knees in front of her.

"Why are you going through my stuff?" he accuses angrily.

"I'm sorry. I really didn't mean to. I tripped and then..." This doesn't even sound believable to her.

"Tripped and my medal bag fell out and all this junk fell out of it?" he scoffs and starts jamming the medals back into the small sack.

"John, these are hardly junk. You should be proud of them. This isn't something that just anybody gets. I know you have to be recommended by your commanding officer and some of the guys in your unit or something, right? You received the Medal of..."

"Yeah and what did my friends get? Some of them got nice, shiny caskets to come home in. Stay out of my stuff, Reagan" he grinds out.

Why is he being so angry, so distant lately? Do men get PMS? She is going to devote some study time to men's hormones later and find out.

"We could make a display case for them and put it in the music room if you'd like," Reagan offers and touches his hand. He blows through his nose and shakes his head. And he won't look at her.

"No," he says decidedly.

John yanks his hand back, tosses the bag back into the closet and starts rummaging for clean clothing.

404

"But those are something…"

"I said no, Reagan. Just leave them be," he snaps.

He shrugs into a flannel shirt as he'd been wrapped in a towel and nothing else.

"O… ok, fine. Sorry," she stammers out an apology and steps closer to him. Keeping her voice soft and friendly, Reagan asks, "Need help?"

"No, just privacy," he answers curtly.

Is he serious?

"What… what's wrong? Is it because I got into your stuff? I said I'm sorry," she says pathetically and hates the sound of her own debility.

"No, it's cool. I'm not mad about that. I just need to get dressed so I can go out and do some reloading before dinner," he says on a sigh.

She knows he is referring to bullet reloading as he grabs clean jeans and underwear from a rack beside her.

"Why did you go to the Johnson farm?" she asks curiously.

"Checking it out. That's why," he replies brusquely without giving her a firm answer.

"Why did you take firewood with you?" she prods. "Did you drop it off at the Reynolds's place?"

"No, I left it at the Johnson's," he tells her.

This only serves to confuse her further.

Reagan grabs his forearm gently and tries to gain his attention, but he shirks her off. "Why did you take firewood over there?"

"I don't want to get into this right now with you, Reagan," John says testily.

"Um, ok, then let me make it up to you for getting into your things," Reagan says and leans into him again, placing her hand on John's bare chest because he has not buttoned the shirt yet. She hopes he doesn't button the stupid thing at all. She secretly wishes that he'd take it back off.

"Reagan, I'm busy," he argues.

However busy he is, his muscle still jerks under her palm.

"Too busy for me?" she leans up on tiptoe and presses a kiss to his closed mouth. It's been too long since they've had sex, and she's about ready to throw him on the closet floor. "I... I want you."

Things like this aren't easy for her to say, to even express. She usually allows John to initiate sex with her, not the other way around. Most nights he would come to her in her bed and return to his own afterward. She revels in his slightest touches, the barest whisper of his knuckles against her sensitive skin, the way he uses his mouth, his tongue, his hands and... the rest of him in the most torturous, sensual manner that she's never even dreamed possible. And her damn, responsive body is learning to crave his touch and being near him. At least he is discreet around their families and keeps his hands to himself unless he was helping her down from a horse or if she was climbing a ladder or for any other reason that he could put his hands on her that didn't seem to have insidious purposes. But lately he has been unresponsive, sometimes even cold with her. Or he just doesn't touch her at all.

"I want you, too, Reagan. I always do," he responds in a serious tone.

His hands slide into her hair right before he caresses her mouth with his own. When he finally pulls back, she's clinging to him like a wanton, wild woman as usual. Why is it that he can so easily do this to her? Why hadn't her reaction to Chet's kiss in the fall been the same? Why had she not been attracted to anyone before John? She'd certainly been around enough men in college and been asked out by them, but she never felt even the slight attraction to any of them. She'd never met a man like John before, though. He is the sexiest, most fearless, and selfless man she's ever known.

"I love you," he whispers against her mouth.

And there it is again. Why does he have to talk like that? He knows damn well that she's never going to return his false feelings of love.

"Ok," she says because it's all she's capable of. A dark storm cloud comes across his features as his eyes harden into sapphire glints that pierce into hers.

"Ok? Is that all you're going to say? I tell you that I love you and you say 'ok'?"

John pushes away gently and then releases her from his hold.

"What do you want from me?" she asks brokenly and hates the cool rush of air between them.

"Nothing," John clarifies.

He turns his back to her as he throws on his damn ridiculous clothing in lightning speed.

"I don't want anything from you, Reagan."

And with that, he leaves to do his irritating reloading.

At dinner that evening, he's quiet still and basically ignores her during the entire meal, though she goes out of her way to engage him in conversation. He's frustrating the hell out of her and even Kelly and Derek are behaving strangely. They both glance her way a few times during the meal as if they are expecting something.

So instead of joining the rest of the family in the music room as they all do most nights after dinner, Reagan takes Jacob and goes to her bedroom. Two hours later after she's already put Jacob to bed for the night, she hears him in the hall one floor below talking to his brother for a minute before he comes up to their room. She's sitting at her desk studying herbal treatments for healing the sick from a book they found during their city raid. John crosses the room and removes his clothing down to his boxer briefs, then shrugs into a black t-shirt which fits snugly across his chest. Since he's obviously still ignoring her, Reagan turns off her desk lamp and crosses to her bed where she crawls under the awaiting, thick comforter. Next week it will be January and the old farmhouse sometimes gets drafty. With the men using wood as an alternative backup in case the gas fails, they'll be warm all winter and more importantly the pipes won't freeze and burst.

Reagan reaches for the wall sconce but stops as John swings his legs back out of his bed and stalks purposefully toward her.

"Leave it on," he orders.

John pulls back her comforter, pushes her over and comes down onto her. His mouth fiercely crushes onto hers as his hands move over every square inch of her body, turning her mad with lust as they trail along. His attack is relentless, and Reagan can barely catch her breath as he nearly rips her clothing from her and then his own where they end in a disorganized heap on the floor beside her bed.

"Let me… let me just turn…" she says as she stretches under him for the light switch.

"I said leave it on," John states.

His tone and attitude are overbearing, as if he is somewhat annoyed. His tone surprises her. John has been true to his word when he'd told her that he'd be the one in charge in the bedroom with her, but this is downright tyrannical. He grasps her wrist in his palm almost painfully. His other hand guides him into her body with a single, deep plunge as he hoarsely, savagely breathes against her mouth. Reagan moans against him while John kisses her neck, her mouth. It's always this way with him when they have sex. He demands and demands from her until she can't control herself anymore, until she forgets to care about control at all.

"Is this what you want? Is this what you've been trying to get from me?" he whispers into her ear. "Is it?"

Reagan has lost her ability to speak and instead nods as he builds them both toward that familiar peak where she crests so easily up and over, whimpering, moaning and breathless. John spills himself onto her flat stomach, something he's never done. Her chances of ever conceiving a child are very slim at best. He uses his discarded shirt to wipe her stomach which is embarrassing as hell because she knows that he can clearly see her scars and her entire naked body. She pushes at his hands.

"Reagan, stop. Hold still and let me get this," he tells her and claims her hands with one of his.

Reagan stops fighting him but is no less humiliated. She's humiliated because he saw her scars, and she's humiliated because it seems cool and indifferent to have sex this way.

When he's done, though, he pulls her against his front and snuggles with her. This is the point where he normally goes back to his bed, but Reagan doesn't mind it tonight. Perhaps he'll stay all night, though he usually leaves. She's wanted to ask him to stay with her through the whole night many times but has never found the courage to say it aloud.

"You didn't have to do that. I told you before that I can't get pregnant," she says with a great deal of mortification.

"I didn't want to take any chances," he says quietly.

"Well…"

408

"I love you. You know that, right?" he interrupts her and asks.

Reagan is confused by his statement and question. She squirms and this time the embarrassment is for another reason.

"Um...," is all she can manage. John rolls her to her back and holds her chin with his hand so that she cannot look away from him.

"I love you, and I'll always love you, Reagan. There won't ever be anyone else for me," he says so gravely.

Reagan frowns slightly at him with confusion.

He finishes with, "But I can't do this anymore."

"What..."

John kisses her on the mouth but only briefly before he climbs over her, retrieves his discarded boxers, turns off her light and goes to his own bed. Reagan is stupefied. She has no idea what the hell that was supposed to mean, and for the next hour she stays awake trying to figure it out. Why had he said it like that? What did that mean that he can't do this anymore? Did he mean sex? She sure as hell hopes that isn't what he meant. Reagan has never felt anything in her life like when she's with John. He's awakened a side of her that she didn't even know she had, and she's not ready to give that up yet. He is so sensual, so sexual. But the love talk and feelings and mushy, sensitive stuff is just too much for her. Her mind cannot wrap around it, and it sure as hell can't embrace it. Like she normally does, Reagan pushes these thoughts down into that black well where she likes to store things that are too difficult for her to deal with. She'd like to talk to him about it, but talking about feelings isn't exactly her forte. And when she can't stay awake a moment longer, she allows her body to succumb to sleep.

Chapter Twenty-nine
Sue

After the morning meal, all hell breaks loose on the McClane farm. And it had been going so smoothly. The kids have done the clean-up and are now out in the barns playing. Hannah and Grams are in the kitchen planning meals for the rest of the week while watching Jacob, and Sue is nursing Isaac at the island. Kelly has moved the pick-up truck from the equipment shed to the front of the house for some reason. John enters the kitchen from the upstairs and is carrying two bags. One is a diaper bag and one his military rucksack which both appear full. Kelly comes in through the front entrance of the house, which doesn't get used very often.

"Ready?" he asks John who nods.

"Ready for what?" Reagan noisily butts in as she enters the kitchen from the back porch.

She's wearing a short winter jacket and her long riding boots and jeans. Her messy curls stick out beneath a knitted, wool toboggan cap of many colors. The first snowfall came last night, blanketing the farm with a light dusting of fine white powder. However, the temperature is steadily rising which should hold off any more snow for the day. John says nothing but frowns as he wordlessly takes Jacob from Grams.

Sue has a bad feeling about this. Grandpa and Derek have also come to stand in the entranceway joining the long, main hallway and the kitchen. They both look expectant as if they know what is coming.

"What's going on?" Sue asks as Grandpa and Derek look at each other knowingly. "Hey, guys, you wanna' let us in on this? What's going on?"

"John has decided to leave, Sue," Grandpa declares with solemnity and looks immediately to Reagan.

"Leave where? What are you talking about?" Reagan asks.

Her sister has not removed any of her outerwear. She has not used the side entrance where the mudroom is located and is now dripping wet snow off of her boots onto the hardwood floor.

"Are you going on a run for supplies or something? I'll go, too," Reagan further questions.

"I'm going to the Johnson's farm. I'll be staying there from now on," John says coldly and turns to leave.

"John!" Sue gasps. "You can't go over there."

"Sorry, Sue," her beloved brother-in-law replies.

"What?" Reagan says unfathomably. "Wait a minute. What are you talking about?"

"It's for the best," John states simply.

"What's that supposed to mean? Best for whom?" Reagan demands.

John doesn't stop but keeps going until he's all the way out the front door. The entire family assembles on the grand front porch as John walks determinedly toward the truck where he fastens Jacob into a car seat and shuts the door. Sue notices the small animal cage in the bed of the truck. One of the nanny goats is inside of it. He then tosses the two bags in the back all the while Reagan is getting louder and louder and more demanding in his ear while he mostly ignores her or answers too quietly to be heard by the rest of the family.

"Why are you going? I don't understand. Are you just going over there for the day or the night? Are you working on something over there? I can go and help," she asks again.

Her sister's scratchy voice is etched with apprehension.

She's pretty sure her young sister is the only one who doesn't understand because Sue sure as hell does. John finally turns to Reagan, mostly because she is yanking at his jacket and arm or anything she can to gain his attention.

"I'm leaving, Reagan. I'm going to live over there. I'm not coming back. I can't live here another day," he tells her with slightly more force this time. "I can't do this anymore!"

"Do what? Don't leave. Stop! Just stop, John! You can't take Jacob from me! We're supposed to be raising him together, remember?" her sister pleads.

Sue is fairly certain that it's sinking in for Reagan now. She, too, is starting to realize that this isn't just a trip. She has ahold of John's arm again, and he yanks it forcefully from her, although she tries to cling on. Reagan stumbles back a step.

"Reagan, stop!" John says more loudly. "Don't try to hold onto me. I don't want to hurt you."

"Then stop!"

"No, I'm done. This is done. I just can't do it anymore."

"What are you talking about? I don't understand. Can't do what anymore?"

"Do this!" John shouts and points between them and back again. "I can't do this! It's not fair to me. And it's not fair to Jacob, either. He needs to be raised by someone who loves him and can show him how to love in return, Reagan!"

Sue is momentarily afraid for Reagan. John is furious and frustrated which can be dangerous in some men. Also, she's never heard John raise his voice, ever. All the times those two have gone at it around the farm it was mostly Reagan raising her voice while John remained passive, subdued and in control at all times. He is clearly losing his calm demeanor.

"I do care about Jacob. You can't just take him, damn it!" Reagan shouts as her wrath builds.

John paces back and forth a few steps and pulls at his hair in frustration. He growls loudly then holds his hands at either side of Reagan's head without touching her anywhere else as if he's afraid he'll hurt her. John releases her just as abruptly.

"You don't care about anything or anyone! You've got a great big hole in the middle of your heart, Reagan! It's the place where most people have love and compassion. But you've got nothing there. You've got nothing to give someone, and I can't take it anymore. I've been patient. God knows I've been patient. I thought you'd come around, but I see now that you aren't going to. You know I love you! God, I've told you a hundred times, but I'm not just going to be sex for you. I want more! Jesus! This is so messed up," John says with exasperation and snatches back his arm that Reagan keeps tugging at.

412

Sue is worried how their grandparents will take the news that Reagan and John have been sexually active because she knows how against premarital sex they both are. Unfortunately, she's too engrossed to turn away for even a second to gauge their reactions. She certainly hadn't known of their apparent sex life. Of course, they sleep on the third floor of the house and when they were together around the rest of the family there hadn't been any clues that anything was going on. Sue can't imagine that Reagan is ok with him touching her long enough to have sex, but, then again, she seems very different around John than she is with the rest of them.

"What are you talking about? What do you want from me? I'm sleeping with you for God's sake!" Reagan retorts angrily.

"I want the one thing you won't give me, Reagan. Good grief. This is what women say to men who use them for sex. It's not supposed to be the other way around!" John expounds.

Sue frowns sadly as John laughs aloud. It is humorless and acidic as he jams his large fists onto his hips. She's never heard him like this before. His normal, happy-go-lucky personality is gone.

Reagan tries a different approach, "You can't go there! It's not safe, John. It's not safe for Jacob, either. You have to stay here…"

"We'll be fine. Jacob deserves more. Someday he's going to realize that you aren't able to give him the love he needs. Reagan, I deserve more, too. I'm not going to stop you from seeing him. You can come and see him anytime you want. The road's safe now. We knocked down the barriers. You know that. But I can't keep living here hoping that you'll change, that you'll somehow miraculously grow a heart. I can't take it because I love you too much, and it's killing me."

Grams stirs beside Sue. Her hands fret.

"Herb, do something!" her grandmother cries out in a panic.

Grandpa simply lays a hand to her shoulder to calm her. Sue wishes that he'd do something, too. But she knows this isn't their affair to stick their noses into. It's bad enough that they are all eavesdropping the whole intensely personal scene.

"Easy, Maryanne. We can't get involved in this," he says softly.

"But he's going to leave if we don't do something," Grams says with frustration.

"Let them be, Mary," Grandpa argues. "If he feels like he has to leave, then there's nothing we can do. This is between the two of them."

Everyone's attention is drawn back to the fighting couple as Reagan is becoming more desperate.

"Don't go, please. Don't go," Reagan nearly begs.

Her sister presses her hands to the front of John's coat. He snatches them and they do an awkward tug of war until he finally grabs her by the face and plants a terribly rough, seductive kiss on her mouth nearly bending her over backwards. It goes on for an uncomfortable amount of time.

"Good-bye," he says when he lifts his head.

This must piss Reagan off because she smacks John across his cheek. Hard. In the quiet valley of the farm, the crack is loud and clear, but John does and says nothing about it. However, Sue does notice his jaw flex in anger. She also hears Grams's sharp intake of breath. Finally, he raises his eyes to Reagan's again and nods with finality.

"Fine, go!" she screams. "I hate you! I fucking hate you! I hope you *never* come back!"

John ignores her, so she kicks the driver's side door after he shuts it. John salutes the men on the porch with a sad grimace and a half wave and turns the truck around. He pulls away but not before Reagan picks up a small stone and throws it at the truck, hitting the tailgate.

When her sister turns, she stops, stunned that everyone has overheard their whole interaction. Reagan was apparently not aware that everyone had followed and basically spied on them. She is not crying, though. Her face is furious, not sad. Sue's crying. So is Hannie and Grams. But Reagan is so hard that she can't cry over the fact that the man she loves, who loves her in return has just left her. She merely fast walks and then sprints for the barn area.

"Oh, what do we do?" Hannie asks with anxiety. "He has to come back, Kelly. He just has to. What do we do?"

"There's nothing we can do, my love. Come on, Hannah. Let me take you inside. It's too cold out here for you, baby," Kelly proclaims.

414

The huge man ushers her delicate sister gently inside where she will be warmer. They'd all been taught not to coddle and baby Hannah growing up, even though it was hard not to. But someone needs to give Kelly the same lecture. She seriously doubts he'd listen. His love for her sister is so powerful, so all-consuming, and Hannah just takes it in stride like Kelly was brought to this farm just for her and she's never once questioned it. And if he'd been protective of her before the attack from the visitors, then he is about a thousand times more so now. His young brother is becoming increasingly protective of the farm and everyone on it, as well. Cory will be a force to reckon with some day, and he watches over Sam and Em like it's his sole responsibility on this earth to keep them safe and secure.

"Will he come back?" Sue asks Derek, who looks like he knew this was coming.

"No, he's not comin' back," he tells her and wraps an arm around her shoulders.

"Did you know about this, Herb?" Grams says with a touch of accusation.

She loves John. Heck, everybody loves John. John is just that kind of person. It is impossible not to like him. Everybody, that is, except for the one person he wishes most to be loved by.

"He talked with us a few days ago," Grandpa answers her.

Her grandfather looks toward the drive like he wishes he could bring John back. Finally, he takes Grams by the hand and leads her inside, as well.

"Why didn't you tell me?" Sue asks Derek when they are alone.

"He made us promise not to tell any of the women. He wanted her to stop him and I thought she would, but John said she wouldn't. He was quite sure she wouldn't. That's the problem, Sue. She's so cold inside. He wasn't going to put up with it forever. He's been patient with her, Sue. He was becoming miserable just being around her. Guess he knows her better than I do," Derek says with a hint of anger.

She knows her husband's anger is aimed at Reagan for running his brother off. But as much as Sue knows this, she also knows that Derek won't hold it against Reagan. She's a mess and none of them know how to help her.

"The Johnson's is completely abandoned. There's no heat, no water..."

"He and Kelly have been going over there a little each day for the past couple of weeks. It's ready. He's got food and heat and water. He said he'll come back every two weeks for provisions and to help out around here. But he just couldn't be around her anymore. It's just too hard on him, Sue," Derek explains patiently.

Sue feels fresh tears forming. Her husband hugs her close for which Sue is glad for the offered support.

Derek adds, "Come on. There's nothing we can do. Let's go inside, honey."

They break apart, but not far apart and go inside with the remaining members of the family minus Reagan who has gone off, probably on horseback. Her sister has gone off to be alone because being around the family won't heal her heart, nor, unfortunately, will it open her heart to love.

And true to his word, John returns two weeks later, but Reagan goes to the barn and won't even look at him or Jacob. Her sister's already hardened heart has turned to solid granite against John. She doesn't speak of him, nor does she like it if anyone else does and usually leaves the room if John or Jacob is brought up in conversation. The family dynamic has also changed but not for the better. The mood is usually heavier, less fun and lighthearted as when John is around. He is the biggest cut-up of the group and was always cracking a joke, being silly, engaging the kids in mischief and all in all just lightening the negativity. Grandpa has been spending even longer amounts of time in his office by himself, and Reagan is usually nowhere to be found most days until the evening meal where she speaks to nobody. Whether she knows it or not, her sister is suffering from severe depression.

As John leaves with Jacob and their box of provisions, Sue looks out the front window and watches with great sadness as her brother-in-law departs their farm again. He'd only stayed for a one hour visit. Hannah had tried to convince him to stay longer to which he'd inquired as to the whereabouts of Reagan. Nobody could bring themselves to answer him. He'd hung his head with disappointment, and the hardness had returned to his eyes almost instantly. Then he'd gone back to making brief small-talk before departing.

416

"... I'm telling you that I'm sick!" Reagan's muffled voice comes from Grandpa's study.

She's back to being bitter, angry, resentful and doesn't like anyone to touch her overly long again. Yesterday, Cory said that he saw her sitting in the loft of the hog barn staring at that damn black Volkswagen for a long period of time.

"Darling, I've checked you again and again..." Grandpa says, trying to appease her.

"But I've got chest pains. I can't breathe. My stomach is sick all the time. I can't eat. I'm not sleeping. Am I having panic attacks? I've read that some of these symptoms are inclusive of post traumatic..."

"Reagan, enough! Honey, you could probably diagnose and cure most any sickness or disease this world has to throw at us, but this is the one thing that medical science doesn't have the answer for," Grandpa tries to tell her as patiently as possible.

"What are you talking about? If you think it's a disease, then tell me so that I can research it and treat it," she argues.

Sue can hear her pacing back and forth in their grandfather's study. Her nervous energy has been at an all-time high lately.

Their grandfather tries to explain, "It's not a disease. It's not a known or proven illness. There's no cure and no scientific evidence of one or that it even exists..."

"What the hell is it? Could it be a new..."

"Heartbreak, honey. You have a broken heart, Reagan," he tells her simply.

Reagan makes a gagging, retching and generally obnoxious sound.

"Don't be ridiculous!" she comments with fury.

"Look, you and I are different, have always been different than most people."

"Of course I know that! I've kind of been a misfit my whole life, Grandpa," she says with unconcealed disgust.

"I know you know. We've both always known, but I never knew how to help you with it because I never knew how to help myself, either. We just don't process experiences the same as other people. We don't deal with things the same way. We don't think about situations like most people do. Our minds are scientific, and we see things in what we can and cannot fix. We research. We study. We read and what we don't do is interact well with others. I see so much of myself in you sometimes that it scares me. And I almost lost your grandmother for the same reasons that you're about to lose John. You just love him, honey, and there's nothing wrong with that."

"Damn it, Grandpa! I'd expect this kind of bullshit from Hannie… or Grams even but not you," Reagan spouts off nastily.

Sue would like to pummel her for being crass with their grandfather. Her grandfather, however, has learned not to take a whole lot of Reagan's shit over the years and comes right back on her.

"Well, you can think it's bullshit all you want, young lady. But I'm not the one who feels sick, am I? Think about when your symptoms started. I'd just bet they started about two weeks ago? I'd say that John was a whole lot more patient than anyone could expect, Reagan. And he loves you and that's not something that is going to be easy to find anymore. Just think about that. Now, get out of my office because I have something I need to actually devote my time to and not your silly, made up sickness that you can't fix," Grandpa says harshly.

Reagan comes out, slamming his door. She catches Sue in the hall and gives her one of her signature mean looks and stomps off in an unresolved, angry sulk. Sue wishes she could go to Reagan and talk with her, but she knows for certain that she'll be shut down, shut out.

Instead of dealing with her sister, Sue decides to join her children for some outdoor play and to check on the winter lettuces in the greenhouse. The atmosphere of the house has become downright depressing since John left, and she feels that being around her kids and getting some fresh air might help lift her spirits. Anything would be better than what it's been like. She hasn't even had the nerve to tell everyone that she's pregnant again because the mood has been so morose lately. Only she and Derek know, and her husband is over the moon and planning on adding another room to their cabin that isn't even finished yet. He'd just laughed and kissed her and told her that everything would be just fine and, of course, she'd believed him because when she is in his arms everything always is.

Chapter Thirty
John

"Hold on, Jake. It's coming, bud," John says as he stokes the fire in the wood-burning stove in the small sitting area off of the kitchen. This is also where he does the majority of their cooking since this place doesn't have electricity anymore which voids the use of the electric stove.

Jacob's squawking and wanting his morning bottle, but John is working on heating the house first before he can heat the baby's milk. There is an older model refrigerator on the back porch where he keeps things cold since it's the middle of winter. He's definitely got to get the electricity back up and running before the weather turns too warm to use the non-working outdoor fridge. The kitchen has cold tile flooring which is not exactly easy on the feet first thing in the morning. But usually within an hour he can get the whole house heated to a toasty warm.

"Dadda, up" Jake spouts.

He pries at the leg of John's jeans. It makes him chuckle.

"Ok, buddy. You want up? Come on up. You can watch daddy get our breakfast, ok?" John says and picks up the little tyke. Jacob clings onto him like a baby chimpanzee. Luckily, John is getting fairly adept at doing things one-handed because Jake likes being "up" all the time. It seems to be his new favorite word.

Although he never really gave any thought to being someone's dad someday, John finds the role comforting and even grounding in a way. Having another human being on this earth relying solely on just him for their survival is a burden like he's never felt before, not even in all of his years in the Army. But it's also the most rewarding role he's ever filled in his life. He had just been hoping to share in that role with Reagan.

They've adjusted pretty well to their new living arrangements on the Johnson farm, and he and Jake share a bed upstairs in the master bedroom which is sparsely appointed to say the least. He's planning on retrieving the crib from Reagan's bedroom on his next visit so that he can avoid the squirming elbows and knees of his constant companion, at least while he sleeps. This house is nothing like living at the McClane spread, but at least he doesn't have to see her anymore.

They use oil lamps at night to see their way around, but it's usually fine because it's just him and Jake. He plays the guitar for the baby before bed or reads books to him. Kelly and Hannah came three days ago to visit, but being around her had just reminded John of Reagan and how different they are. Being around their newfound marital bliss was also like taking a bullet.

One major inconvenience is not having hot water or even running water. He has to go down the short hill behind the farmhouse to the Johnson's spring-house to collect buckets of cold water in the damp, stone basement of the building. Then he heats water in metal buckets on the stove-top that he pours into the first floor bathroom's claw-foot tub for himself and Jacob. It's time consuming, but it works just the same. In the spring John plans to add the solar paneling to the roof so that they can have hot running water and electricity and minor conveniences. He's even been chopping firewood outside when Jake goes down for his naps. Sometimes if the weather isn't too bad, like today, he bundles him and lets him sit on the porch with some toys while he splits the firewood in the yard close to the house.

He stays busy. Mostly he just tries to stay busy. Because when he's busy he doesn't have to think about her or think about the heady, sweet scent of her or her curly hair or her curves or her rare smiles or the way she feels under his hands. And he definitely doesn't have to dwell on the soft, delicate sounds and whispers and moans that she elicited when he made love to her. Or the sassy sway of her slim hips when she walked. Or how easily he had picked her up and made love to her against the wall of the barn on the night of Hannah and Kelly's wedding. Or the inexperienced and sometimes too rough way that she caressed him. To say her passion was most times unbridled was the understatement of the century. He'd never been with a woman as passionate as Reagan.

After a breakfast of fresh eggs and sausage thanks to the kindness of Grams who'd sent the new supplies with Hannah and Kelly, John bundles Jacob in his winter clothing and takes him to the front porch where he spreads out his toys on a thick blanket. Tennessee winters sure as heck are a lot milder than anything he'd ever experienced growing up in Colorado. Then again, Doc said that he thinks it's unseasonably milder this year because of the environmental changes in the atmosphere from the global nuclear warfare, earthquakes and tsunamis. He said that the weather patterns could change substantially in the next few years, but Doc's hoping against it because it could upset their crop seasons. John had concurred. They are all surviving this so far and the last thing they need is to lose crops.

The thermometer points to fifty-four degrees, perfect weather for chopping wood. The sun is warm and it feels like it's going to warm up even further as the day goes on. John leaves his coat on the porch with Jacob and just wears his thermal undershirt with a flannel shirt over top, along with his tattered, faded jeans. After a half an hour, of splitting wood, John ditches even the flannel shirt and goes with just the cream-colored thermal that he pushes up to his elbows. They could easily have three to four months of cold weather still to go, and he and Jake might need this wood for their survival. He can't just drive over to the McClane farm to bum firewood. The family may also need everything that the men had spent last summer chopping.

The low purr of an engine alerts John, and he momentarily stops to stick the ax into the massive, thick log on which he's using to chop the smaller logs. His M16 is only a foot away, leaning against the railing of the stairs going up to the porch.

A minute later, Doc McClane's SUV pulls slowly down his drive and comes to a stop. He can't see the driver because of the glare on the windshield, but when the door opens, it's her. She's thinner than normal which isn't good. Reagan isn't the kind of person who can afford to miss a few calories or any. She approaches him slowly, and John has that same punch to the gut he experiences every time he sees her, every time he's seen her since that first time. She's wearing dirty jeans, her ugly, stupid Converse- the red ones from the city- and a black hoodie. Upon closer inspection, John notices that it's his hoodie that she wears, the one he'd loaned her on their return trip from the city. He had wondered where it had disappeared to but just figured that it got lost in the laundry shuffle at the farm. The bright yellow ARMY letters had never looked half as good stretched across his chest as they do on hers. Her hair is a wreck and there are dark circles under her eyes. She stops when she's about fifteen or so feet from him. She looks completely harried, worried and anxiety-ridden.

"What's wrong? Is everyone ok?" John asks her, and she doesn't immediately respond but frowns hard and looks away, looks at the house, at Jacob, at him briefly. She shakes her head and sniffs. "Reagan? Is everyone ok? Has something happened?" Now she's scaring John as he steps tentatively closer.

Reagan shakes her head, looking at her feet.

"What are you doing here? Is everything at the farm…"

"It hurts," she says finally.

Her voice croaks and sounds raw. John steps closer again.

"You're hurt? Where? What happened?" John asks with worry. Reagan shakes her head again as she looks up at him. She puts her hand on her chest and nods.

"It hurts here. I thought I was sick," Reagan says.

John feels instantly nauseous. Is she sick with that pneumonic plague crap? He knew she shouldn't have been allowed to take care of those sick people!

"Did your grandfather look at you? Is it…" he asks with genuine concern and steps closer until he's within a few feet of her. Her eyes are also bloodshot. She's very pale. She does look sick.

"No, you don't understand," she says with exasperation as if he's being stupid. "It hurts because you left. You left and you took Jacob with you."

Realization is finally setting in and when he looks closer, there are tears streaming down her soft cheeks. He hangs his head, feeling like a piece of dirt. It takes a moment, but he looks up at her again.

"I'm sorry if this arrangement hurts you. That wasn't my intention, Reagan," he explains on a frown and places one hand on his hip. It's better than reaching for her, which he'd like most to do.

"I want you to come back…" she demands almost petulantly.

422

He shakes his head and frowns harder, "I'm sorry, but that isn't going to happen. I can't keep doing things like we were." If she says it again so pathetically and pleadingly, then John's afraid he will buckle and pack up for the farm in a heartbeat. He can't stand this situation, either.

"I don't want us to," she says.

Johns head snaps up quizzically.

"I... I don't... shit, this is hard. This is so hard for me. You don't understand. You're asking me to believe in something I didn't think was real, like the damn tooth fairy or something."

"I don't want you to change for me, Reagan. That wouldn't be..."

"Shh! Just shut up and let me talk," she says with an impatient sniff.

John almost laughs but decides not to so that she doesn't stop talking.

"Look, I've never really fit in with other people or the way people thought. My brain just doesn't work like that. I like doing stuff that's... different like dissections, surgeries and yes, studying my gross books- as you like to call them. I didn't have friends growing up, only one in college who was murdered and no, I never had a boyfriend. And after... after...," she takes a deep breath. Her fingers go to her throat which she clears loudly. "After that night at my school, I didn't think I could ever stand anyone to touch me again or even be close to me. I'm so fucked up and broken. I know this. I know that nobody thinks I know this about myself, but I do. How can I not? I'm a freagin' doctor. Of course I know!"

Her face is tormented and beautiful, and John has to resist the urge to drag her into his arms and kiss her and make everything right in her world again. But, from experience, he knows that doesn't work with Reagan. He'd tried. He'd already tried this approach, and it had failed miserably.

"You're not screwed up. Don't say that..." John tries to appease her, but she cuts him off.

"Yes, I am. And when you first started touching me, it freaked me out... a lot. And then you'd touch me again and then again and each time you did it, it didn't seem as bad as the last. I didn't realize you were even serious when you were flirting with me.

I'm so stupid. I just don't get people most of the time. And then you kissed me and I realized that I felt desire for you and not fear anymore. I miss you touching me, John."

He was afraid this is where the conversation was going to end up. She just wants sex again. She came here hoping for a sex visit. Reagan steps closer to him and he backs up, taking her by surprise. She only nods and swallows hard on a frown.

"Ok. It's ok, I understand how you feel. I get it. I didn't before, but I do now. I thought I was just sick so I kept running my symptoms over and over and I couldn't figure it out, and you know how it is for me when I can't figure something out. And then it got worse and I kept crying and couldn't eat, and then I couldn't breathe. I've been so miserable. The only thing that made me feel any better was when I thought about you. And that's when I figured it out," she says quietly and steps forcefully closer to him.

The proximity of her being so near is killing John.

"What did you figure out?" John asks her hesitantly as she toys with the tie strings of her stolen hoodie.

"I miss you and it hurts me to be away from you. And… I don't… I don't want you to be away from me anymore. I didn't know how I felt about you, and I'm sorry. I've just never had those feelings before, so I just didn't understand them. I was so scared of feeling like that. I like having sex with you. Sorry. I mean making love with you. But it's obviously not the only thing I like about you because I've been thinking about all of this a lot the last few weeks."

John has no doubts that her big brain has been puzzling and working through it. She rubs her forehead as if her nerd brain actually hurts. She's probably overtaxed it. Maybe he should talk to her grandfather about it. However, he's not going to interrupt her at this point because she's finally talking to him for the first time about her feelings, about anything really that has to do with her feelings.

"I like it when you and I just talk sometimes. And that's really strange because I don't usually like to waste time just talking with most people when I could be studying something. I know you aren't as book smart as I am. Obviously. Most people aren't so don't feel bad."

She says this in such an unembroidered way that John has to suppress a smile.

"I don't know anybody smarter than you, Reagan," he agrees, and she shakes her head at him.

"But you're really smart, too. Just in a different way. I mean, hell, you know how to make shit blow up. How cool is that, right? You're better with people than me. That was kind of obvious. Sorry."

Reagan pauses to kick a pebble away angrily. When she continues again, she looks directly up at John.

"And the way that you protected me in the city and then again at the farm from those dicks? That was amazing, John. I would be dead many times over if it wasn't for you. When that stupid horse fell on you and I thought you might be killed, it bothered me so much, but I just refused to think about it. Sometimes, though, when I did let myself remember it, I felt like I couldn't breathe and my chest felt tight. But I just figured it was a minor asthma attack or a slight palpitation or ataxia or... whatever, sorry. I didn't put it together that it was anxiety because I was worried about you. And the way you are with Jacob? It's crazy because he isn't even really your son, but you honored your promise to that woman. You really love Jake. I've seen how you look at him because it's how you look at me. And I didn't like it when you looked at me like that. That's why I would look away from you all the time. It just made me too uncomfortable. I couldn't take it. It scared me, you know? But when you left, that's when it finally dawned on me. I love you," she explains thoroughly and won't look up at him.

John can't believe his ears. He's waited so long to hear those words from her that he's praying she really did just mumble them uncomfortably while still not meeting his eyes. When she finally raises her head, there are tears streaming down her lovely face again and she is half smiling, half frowning up at him.

"You do?" he asks like the idiot she's always accusing him of being.

Reagan nods, and it's all the encouragement John needs to walk the last five feet and crush her to him, bringing his mouth down onto hers in a powerful, searing kiss that tastes of her salty tears. Her arms extend up around his neck, and John grasps under her bottom. He lifts her until she wraps her legs around his waist. She has lost weight, which she didn't need to do, and it troubles him that she's been so upset over him leaving. When he pulls back, Reagan is smiling shyly at him.

"Say it again?" John asks, wanting to hear it once more and up close.

"I love you... and I love Jacob, too. I want us to raise him like real parents," she says but won't meet his eyes.

It's fine with John because it's a start. This is hard for her and he's not going to push her more than what she can take. At least not by making her say the words that make her so uncomfortable. She has finally admitted it, and they can be together.

She exclaims, "I have something for you."

"You do?" John asks with a smile of pure joy as he sets her to her feet again. She fishes in her jeans pocket and pulls something out.

"Hold out your hand," she tells him.

When he does, Reagan places something in it and closes his fingers around it. John is seriously hoping that it's not something disgusting like a frog leg or some other dissected animal part.

"Look."

John unfolds his fist and finds a tiny red Skittle in his palm. When he looks at her, she shrugs and smiles. He throws back his head and laughs and then eats the candy. It's more than a start. It's the perfect beginning.

"Where have you been keeping that stashed 'cuz I know you ate that whole bag of these?" John teases her through another kiss.

"I hid it in my shoe at the back of my closet," she confesses. "And I didn't eat the whole bag. I shared some with the kids when we got back from the city."

"You just let me eat a piece of six month old candy that you had hidden in one of your disgusting, dirty shoes?" he asks with slightly feigned outrage, and she giggles and shrugs. The fact that she had it hidden away, had given it thought all the way back then and was thinking about it all this time gives John hope. They both laugh and then kiss again as he picks her up.

When they finally break apart, though, he doesn't put her down as Reagan says, "Our kid's chewing on a stick."

John looks over his shoulder and sure enough Jacob has found a small stick on the porch floor and is indeed chewing on it. John sets her to her feet again.

426

"Oh, yeah. He's not chewing on it, though. He's fetching it. It's just this trick we've been workin' on," John jokes, and Reagan laughs and pulls his hair.

"He's not a damn dog," she growls feistily and pulls him close for another quick kiss.

John retrieves Jacob from the porch floor. Reagan immediately takes him, kissing his chubby cheeks, his bald head and his tiny fingers.

She speaks quietly to Jacob, softly cooing, whispering gently. "I missed you so much."

"It's a good thing you came back to us when you did. I was gonna teach him to roll over next," John jokes. He places both of his hands on either side of her lovely face, pulling her close so he can talk more seriously again. "I love you. I'm sorry that I caused you pain, Reagan. And it hurt me to be away from you, too. I don't ever want that again, ok?"

John digs in his own pocket for something he's also been hiding and goes down on his right knee. He holds up the small ring in front of her. She's still cuddling Jacob who seems delighted to have her back, as well. His chubby little fists are already tugging at her messy curls.

"I don't care how weird you are or how many gross things you want to dissect or how screwed up you think you are. I just love you, Reagan. I think I loved you since that first day when you wanted to blow out my brains and then you saved Derek. I even still loved you after the black socks and the white dress fashion tragedy. You were so… different than anyone I'd ever known before. You were way different than any women I'd known before. And you're way smarter than anyone I've *ever* known. But you are also so innocent and naïve. It's almost comical sometimes. I don't want you to change, sweetie. I just want you to let me in and Jacob, too. I want to marry you. I love you. I'll always love you. I'm loyal to a fault, and I'll never stray or leave you or the farm. If you want to stay there, then that's where we'll live. If you want to dissect stuff, I'll go hunt it down and you can cut it up. And you don't have to rush healing yourself. I think you're fine just the way you are. We'll work all of that out together, babe. You don't ever have to deal with it on your own again. Will you marry me, Reagan?" John asks. He realizes that it is probably the strangest marriage proposal in the history of marriage proposals but so is their relationship. Reagan frowns. It's not the expected reaction.

"Really?" she asks with a pissy attitude and a huge grimace. She even wrinkles her nose as she bounces Jacob on her hip.

"Yep," he gives it right back. "It's all or nothing, boss. I want to be with you, and I can't be with you at the farm the way we were. It's wrong, and I know your grandparents wouldn't approve."

"Yeah, but I don't know about marriage. Jesus, John. I just gave you the Skittle," Reagan complains and rolls her beautiful green eyes.

"That was… something," John says sarcastically as she screws up her face at him. "You gave me an old piece of candy, and I still want to marry you. I'd say you better jump at the chance, woman."

"Damn it!" she curses and then reluctantly holds out her hand. "Oh, all right."

"Wow, such flattery, such prose. It's a good thing you went into medicine and not poetry writing," he teases and slides the diamond ring onto her finger. Instead of rising, John snatches her and Jacob down onto his lap where she straddles over him. "I love you."

"I… love you, too," Reagan says and stares at his chest before she leans up hesitantly for a kiss. "Don't leave me again."

This is not a request, and she isn't asking kindly. Plus, she has a handful of his hair in her right hand.

"I won't. I promise," John swears with a grin, and she smiles and comes in for another kiss.

"Oh crap!" she says.

She breaks away, hands him the baby and sprints toward the truck.

"I have to radio Grandpa to let him know I got here ok."

He just comes to his feet and chuckles. She's definitely right about one thing. Her brain doesn't work like anybody else's, and he's glad for it. Because with her innumerable strange quirks, her bad temper and her feisty attitude John can easily say that she'll be the only woman that he ever truly loves. Lord help him.

After she has made contact with her family, she comes back to John and together they collect Jacob's toys and go inside where they make lunch and talk about what's been going on at the farm.

428

They take Jacob for a long walk at sunset and then make dinner, and John is glad to see her eat. Another week of separation and she may have emaciated away to nothing. That night after they put Jacob to bed in the room next to the master bedroom, John makes love to her, and it is more poignant and life affirming than anything he's ever experienced before. And later while they lay in each other's arms, John tells her what he did to earn his Medal of Honor.

"We were pinned down tight in this small village in Syria. We were way outnumbered and outgunned," his throat constricts because he's never discussed this with anyone outside of the military, and it's more painful saying it out loud. "Our intel had been wrong on this mission. The enemy was anticipating us, and they'd called in enough of their own men to get the job done. Kelly and his team were trapped on the other side of this crappy town we were in, and some of my men were stuck between their Hummer which was blown to crap and an abandoned car. I went out and started dragging some of the wounded back to my position with the rest of my men. We had better cover behind a building. I couldn't call in an airstrike on the enemy because my guys would've been hit, too. I knew we were screwed. I didn't want to get anyone else killed."

The oil lamp on the old pine dresser in the corner of the room flickers, bouncing eerie shadows onto the pale blue walls. Normally John would've extinguished it, but tonight he'd wanted to look at Reagan. He hadn't realized how much he'd missed looking at her.

He swallows hard before continuing, "So, one by one, I dragged or carried four guys back where they'd be safer. They were pretty beat up. One was…"

This is simply too hard to finish. His friend had taken mortar fire and been killed by the blast.

"Then I heard Kelly in my earpiece. He was knee deep in it, too. I told my men to stay put, use short bursts to keep the enemy back, and I took off for the other part of the town which was two streets over. I didn't tell Kelly my plan because he would've tried to come out of his secure location. I knew he'd be killed, and I couldn't let that happen. I came around behind the enemy there and took them out. When I ran out of ammo, I went hand to hand and used my knife. Kelly called the airstrike. It was finished pretty quickly after

429

that. I'd been shot twice, but I didn't even know it till Kelly came for me. My men told me that I had been shot the first time while carrying one of them out on my side of town. They said they tried to tell me, but I don't remember that part. That's the scar down low on my stomach that I showed you. The other one is up here on my left shoulder. I don't remember getting shot at all. That's the weird thing. I guess the adrenaline didn't allow me to register it, which was probably good. You were right. My commanding officer at the time and Kelly and the men in my unit put in for me to get that medal. I didn't want it, though. I didn't feel right about it 'cuz six of my men were killed despite me making it out. They told me that I saved twenty-nine lives that day, but all I remember are the guys I lost."

"John, you're so brave. I've never heard of anyone as brave as you. Or as selfless," she says on a sniff because she's been weeping at his tragic tale.

For John, it's not a story of bravery or heroism. It's sad and depressing, and he doesn't like remembering it or the friends he'd lost that day. Her praise humbles him more than he can say.

She sniffs again and asks, "Were you a Green Beret, too? I saw the beret when it fell out of your bag. I don't understand. I thought you were a Ranger."

"I was. We were Rangers. Kelly and I also went through Green Beret training. We call ourselves Rangers. It's just easier that way. Helps us fit in with whatever unit we get posted to," he tells her.

"What do you mean?"

"We're a part of a different group, Reagan," he explains as his fingers stroke along her spine and into the curve of her hip. "We're actually a part of Delta Force. We were recruited into it. Everybody's kind of under the umbrella of Special Forces, but we had a little more authority to do… stuff. The higher ups can send us in wherever they need us. We used to do snatch and grabs, interrogations, whatever they wanted. But then we'd also go on missions with other groups like Rangers or Seals and we just called ourselves Rangers or Seals. Whoever we were working with at the time is what name we adapted. When I won the Medal of Honor, I was with a Ranger battalion. It just helped make things more cohesive. Made us stand out less."

"Wow. I didn't know that Delta Force was real. I thought that was something made up for movies. I've never studied it," she says, frowning against his chest. "Kinda' cool actually."

430

"It's why neither of us have any tattoos. Not allowed in case we get made. Makes you too identifiable. It doesn't really matter anymore," he says lightly.

"If the shit ever gets back to normal will you go back? Will you re-up?" she asks in the dark.

"Nah, getting too old. Besides, Kelly and I are farmers now. Now my mission is just to take care of you."

"Yeah, well you kind of do that pretty well. Kind of a full-time job. Saved my ass a lot. I don't know from what place in a person that you'd have to dig that deep for bravery. Guess I owe you. You're kind of a badass, John Harrison," she says.

John can feel her grin against him this time.

"Reagan, you're also brave, love," John tells her because he doesn't want to think any more on his medal or the reasons he received it. They lay for a short while in quiet solitude while she is contemplative. "It might make you feel better to unload it on me, honey. I can take it. I'll always be able to bear your burdens, as well as my own."

"What do you know?" she inquires knowingly.

"Not much. But I did see the car," he confesses, and she grimaces, turning away from him and rolling onto her side. John just follows and holds her pressed tightly to his front.

When she finally feels comfortable, sometime in the middle of the night, Reagan tells him about the attack at the college in all its horrific, gory detail. She trembles and shudders and cries and her breathing becomes rushed and then tight as she recalls the two men who tried to rape and kill her. She remembers them in graphic detail down to the color of their eyes and what clothing they wore. But John does his best to soothe and reassure her that they're gone and that nobody will ever touch her like that again.

"All I kept thinking is that I had to make it home to the farm. It's the only thing that kept me going. I just knew if I made it out of there and got home that everything would be ok and that I'd be safe. There were times when I stopped to change my bandages and I saw that they were soaked through again that I didn't think I was going to live long enough to get home. I've never been a faithful person like Grams and Hannah, but I believe that the only reason I lived through that night was because of God. And now that I have you and Jacob I

431

have to believe that He had a bigger plan for me than dying at that damned college," she says reverently.

John rolls her to her back and kisses her softly on her full mouth. His fingers stroke her damp cheeks. And when he pulls back, Reagan lets loose and cries. She cries harder than he'd ever thought one person could. And when she's done John just holds her and promises that nothing like that will ever happen to her again, not on his watch.

"I'm sorry if I hurt you, John. I never thought that I'd feel like this about someone. I never thought you *could* feel like this about someone," she tells him after some time.

"Reagan, you're the best thing that's ever happened to me. You never have to be sorry. I don't want us to start our lives together with regrets. I just want to take care of you and Jacob. I'll always take care of you," he answers honestly.

She tells him with hesitancy again that she loves him, and he reassures her that each time it'll get a little easier. Reagan falls asleep in his arms, leaving John to reflect on the day and on her and their relationship. He'd meant what he said to her. He'd lay down his life for her or Jacob if it ever came to it. And it is his job to make sure it never does. John believes that with time they will heal each other from the nightmares of their pasts. She'll come to learn about him that keeping them safe is the one job John can and will excel at.

She doesn't get chased in her sleep by demons with cold, blue eyes or overly enlarged pupils but sleeps heavily, dreamlessly, and John likes to think that it's because she finally feels truly safe because of him.

Epilogue
Herb McClane

It's March again on the farm, one year after Reagan made her harrowing return home to the family. The end of March is usually cooler than this, but that was before everything was changed. Even their planting season will be bumped back if this mild weather continues. Sue works tirelessly in the greenhouse with the children, teaching them about seeds and planting and natural composting. The newest addition to her family will be born in September, and he prays every day that the birth will be as successful as the last. The men are almost finished with the cabin and are working on building solar panels, tilling fields, mending fences and about a dozen other projects each week on the farm

Herb makes the final entry on the ledger that he's created to keep track of names, birthdates, marriages, births, and other important information about each of the people living on his farm. It is the only documentation any of them have now, and it's important to leave a written legacy of them all.

As he sits on the back porch of the old farmhouse, he can hear Hannah and Samantha in the music room playing the piano. She is fast becoming an accomplished musician, and they've learned that she used to play the violin, as well. The music in the house was usually their only source of entertainment this last winter.

Samantha's riding skills are unmatched by anyone on the farm, with the exception of Reagan, because the young waif used to show jump before the world fell apart. She enjoys hitting the trails every morning with Reagan and John or with the other teen boys and is very helpful with the care of the horses. She'd even brought tack and horse pharmaceuticals from her former home. Although she has not completely adjusted to her new life, Herb believes that she'll eventually come to like it here. He also fervently hopes beyond all hope that she will eventually be able to overcome the horrors of her past while the visitors had kept her captive.

Reagan and Simon are in the med shed working on a dissection, and Herb believes that he'll make a good doctor someday. Though not gifted like Reagan, he's a bright kid and has a love of learning like her. Then again, she is certainly an exception to the norm on the spectrum of the learning scale. Whereas Reagan was always a traditionalist when it came to medicine, Simon especially enjoys learning about plants and herbs and their potential medicinal uses. This kind of knowledge will prove priceless as someday their supply of medicines will be depleted and maybe even completely obliterated.

Laughter near the chicken coop draws his attention, and he watches Arianna, Justin, Em and Huntley play a game of tag. These children will hopefully prove too young to be traumatized by the bleakness of what's happened to the world and will only know love and kindness in this valley. Huntley has adjusted quite well and seems to enjoy the companionship of the other children. Having been a twin, the other half of a single pregnancy and bonded so uniquely to one other person on earth, Herb does worry about how Huntley will grow up and what losing his brother will do to him. But with the love and support of the family and always keeping his brother's memories alive, Herb can only hope for his mental health and that he can come to trust and love again in return.

Cory works most days, the same as this day, with Derek on equipment or building the cabin and seems to be the most mechanically inclined person on the farm and for that reason, among many others, Herb is glad to have him. He just prays fervently that he will not become hard and calloused or have to kill again because this young man has seen too much death already. He already has such a hard edge about him that Herb doesn't want him to grow up to be like John.

Kelly walks purposefully toward the back porch, tips an invisible hat to Herb, and continues on into the house. He only seems to be able to be away from Hannah for a few hours at a time. Newlyweds! Kelly is a good man and has earned Herb's respect many

434

times over since he's come to the farm. Kelly will also make an excellent father because of how he already is with his much younger siblings. But he can understand why Kelly needs to be around her so much. Hannah's just like that, and Kelly needs her lightness and cheer as much as she needs his shelter and protection. Herb hears her exclamation of pure joy that her husband has come in for an afternoon visit. It makes him smile. For anyone to find joy in this world now, it will be a rare thing indeed.

The screen door slams and Maryanne walks out with Isaac and Jacob in her arms. Herb quickly takes Jacob from her, and they sit together and swing and talk about their girls and all of the children. They both consider Jacob just as much one of their great-grandchildren as any of their biological ones. He's a real cutie, and John and Reagan are doing great with him for having no child rearing experience before this. It's not surprising, though, because John is a very patient man which was a good thing for his granddaughter and her fiery temper. Herb had seen the small changes taking place within Reagan since John had come to be at the farm, which was the only reason he'd allowed him to move into his granddaughter's bedroom. He'd also seen a darkness in John that he buried quite well. Herb had speculated that he might possibly be the one person in this cruel world who could help her move on. It also doesn't hurt that John's darkness will be what will keep his granddaughter alive in dangerous situations. Every member of their family had tried to help Reagan to deal with or recover in any small way from her ordeal, but John was the first one who'd been able to make a dent in progress with her. He'd seen the way the man had looked at Reagan even back in those first days when he'd come to the farm. Mostly he'd ogled his granddaughter with lust in his blue eyes, but sometimes he'd caught looks of such amazement and puzzlement that Herb knew that he'd been bitten by the charms that most people didn't see in Reagan. The love John feels for his granddaughter is so strong, so unbridled, and yet he is the one man Herb knows who can keep her in check which she needs from time to time. Reagan had come to him and told him about John's service medals, but he'd already known about some of them from Derek who had told him about four years ago during a visit to the farm. He can understand why John would not want these medals displayed. He doesn't feel he deserved them because the men who deserved to receive them right alongside of him were all dead. Yet through it all, he'd come out of it without being damaged by it and that was the only reason he'd been so good with Reagan, so able to help her. For this reason alone, Herb will always be indebted to John Harrison.

He and his brother are walking in from the hog barn where they've made some minor changes to the inside and built better, stronger stalls for the animals. Out of the corner of his eye a flash of movement catches his attention and Herb looks in time to see Reagan running full tilt toward John who catches her in mid-air with one arm while still holding a tool box. It's a fortunate thing the young man is strong and, more importantly, that Reagan is so petite. He's going to need a good, strong back.

"What is that smell, boss? Ugh!" John groans as he continues walking while holding her.

"Dissected deer liver," his granddaughter answers as if that's just a normal thing.

She's wearing those ratty-looking gym shoes she always wears, the same ones she'd worn on their wedding day in January when she'd begrudgingly married John, though everyone could see how much she'd come to love him.

"Ugh, gross. You know girls aren't exactly supposed to smell like dissected animal parts, babe," John tells her as Reagan pulls his hair and then kisses him.

Herb figures that she's forgiven him easily enough because they forget that they are standing in the middle of the yard in front of half of the family kissing like two teenagers. John's life will never be boring with Reagan. Herb can attest to that one.

"Everything has worked out for the best," Maryanne says with the slightest trace of sadness in her voice.

"Yes, it has, Mary," Herb answers gravely.

He knows the reason for her unhappiness. He knows because he's a doctor, and he's been working tirelessly in his office for months on the real reason for her melancholy. His Maryanne is sick. She has sworn him to secrecy so as not to upset the family. They'll eventually figure it out as she continues to lose weight and become sicker with time. He'd like nothing better than to consult with Reagan about it, but he knows there will be no cure for this. Life sometimes

436

throws these obstacles at a person, and he will treasure and cherish whatever time he gets with his beloved.

"Are you ever going to tell me what the "B" on those jars stood for?" he asks his wife who is kissing Isaac's fair neck, making him giggle.

"Oh, that. Well, those peaches and green beans were from last year, and the jars didn't seal right. So I marked them with a "B" because they could have botulism. I figured that we could set them out for the coyotes and raccoons that had been getting into our chicken coop," his dear wife explains so calmly.

"Botulism would kill those people, Maryanne," he says with surprise.

"Yes, it would, Herb. But the way I figured it is that there's no way that none of them didn't know about how abusive Frank was with his twins. And they had to know that the woman, your patient who died, was a prisoner of my brother and most importantly that Samantha was being abused or raped. They got what they deserved for that alone."

Maryanne says this as if she's just rattling off the nightly news report to him. He's grossly underestimated his wife's ability to do something so cold and calculated against another human being. But he supposes when children were involved, his Maryanne could be a mother lion. She is right about one thing, though. They had indeed given the spoiled canned goods to coyotes and predators.

"I'll not tell the children this, as well, love," he tells her, and she smiles gently at him before going back to blowing raspberries on her great-grandson's neck.

He watches Derek disappear into the greenhouse and a minute later, Sue's squeal of surprise follows. These men have kept him and the family that he so greatly cherishes safe and given them a sense of security they might not have ever known in these strange new times in which they all live.

Maryanne lightly grasps his hand while she sits beside him and they hold the newest, precious babies in the family. Herb smiles gently at her. Perhaps God has seen fit to forgive some of his past sins and grant him and Maryanne with the children they'd wanted after all. And then again, perhaps he is an old fool who wants to believe in forgiveness and absolution because he isn't getting any younger.

For now their farm is safe. For now they have a roof over their heads, food to eat, medicine for the sick, the protection of the men and all of their grandchildren and great-grandchildren with them. Herb knows it may not always be this way. But for now they have each other, simple small blessings and the love and comfort of holding their family together, and in the end that's all that matters anyway.

The McClane family will return in 2015.

Please visit Ranger Up.com or their blog site, The Rhino Den.com. It's a great organization founded by either current or former active duty soldiers. There are comprehensive articles there about the dangers of PTSD, soldier suicides and true stories to inspire. You can also make a difference by donating to their causes, all of which benefit soldiers or their families. Please encourage friends and family to check out this great organization, too. Twenty-two veteran suicides a day need to stop. We can make a difference. It's our duty to help in any small way that we can. After all, they ensure our freedoms that we hold so dear as Americans.

Ranger-Up.com, Rhino Den.com

Made in the USA
San Bernardino, CA
23 October 2014